AUTOPSY

AUTOPSY

A SCARPETTA NOVEL

PATRICIA CORNWELL

wm

WILLIAM MORROW

An Imprint of HarperCollinsPublishers

HarperCollins books may be purchased for educational, business, or sales promotional use. For information, please email the Special Markets Department at SPsales@harpercollins.com.

FIRST EDITION

Title page art by @Daniel Thornberg/stock.adobe.com
Endpaper art by @Mitchell/stock.adobe.com

Library of Congress Cataloging-in-Publication Data

Names: Cornwell, Patricia Daniels, author.
Title: Autopsy : a Scarpetta novel / Patricia Cornwell.
Description: First edition. | New York : William Morrow, [2021] | Series: Scarpetta series ; volume 25
Identifiers: LCCN 2021033438 (print) | LCCN 2021033439 (ebook) | ISBN 9780063112193 (hardcover) | ISBN 9780063112209 (trade paperback) | ISBN 9780063112216 | ISBN 9780063112247 | ISBN 9780063112223 (ebook)
Subjects: GSAFD: Suspense fiction.
Classification: LCC PS3553.O692 A95 2021 (print) | LCC PS3553.O692 (ebook) | DDC 813/.54—dc23
LC record available at https://lccn.loc.gov/2021033438
LC ebook record available at https://lccn.loc.gov/2021033439

ISBN 978-0-06-311219-3
ISBN 978-0-06-311223-0 (international edition)

21 22 23 24 25 LSC 10 9 8 7 6 5 4 3 2 1

To Staci, you make it possible
&
To Mom, who couldn't read my scary stuff

"THE WORLD IS FULL OF OBVIOUS THINGS WHICH NOBODY BY ANY CHANCE EVER OBSERVES."

—SHERLOCK HOLMES

From the Greek *autopsia*: to see for oneself.

AUTOPSY

CHAPTER 1

A FIERY SUNSET BURNS OUT along the darkening horizon in Old Town Alexandria at not quite five P.M. the Monday after Thanksgiving.

The wind is kicking up and fitful, the moon shrouded by fog rolling in from the Potomac River. Trees and shrubbery shake and thrash, dead leaves swirling and skittering over the tarmac. Ominous clouds advance like an enemy army, the flags flapping wildly in front of my Northern Virginia headquarters.

I crouch down by the fireproof file cabinet, entering the combination on the fail-safe push-button lock. Opening the bottom drawer, I lift out the thick accordion folder I've been hauling around for many months. I smell the musty oldness of declassified government documents going back to the late 1940s, many heavily redacted and almost illegible.

I've got much to review before the next meeting of the National Emergency Contingency Coalition, better known as the

Doomsday Commission, this time at the Pentagon. My White House–appointed responsibilities aren't for the faint of heart. But they're not nearly as pressing as what's right in front of me, and I can't stop thinking about the murdered woman downstairs in my cooler.

I envision the slashes to her neck, the bloody stumps left when her hands were severed, and I don't know who she is. I know virtually nothing about her beyond what her dead body has to say, dumped like trash by railroad tracks on Daingerfield Island, several miles north of here. After spending the entire weekend on her, I'm no further along.

Not even a month on the job, and it's been one ugly conundrum after another, accompanied by plenty of obstructions and hostility. It's an understatement that my presence isn't appreciated and I've been handed quite the mess. Taking off my lab coat, draping it over my office chair, I cover my microscope for the night as distant thunder cracks and reverberates, lightning shimmering.

From my second-story corner suite, I have quite the ringside seat for weather-related drama. The parking lot we share with the forensic labs has emptied quickly, streetlights blinking on blearily. Dozens of scientists, doctors and other staff hurry to their cars as rain spatters my windows.

I don't know most people yet, and just as many don't remember me from what seems another life ago. Millennials in particular weren't around when I was the first woman chief medical examiner of Virginia. I ran the statewide system more than a decade before moving on. I assumed I'd left for good, never imagining I'd be back, and I hope I haven't made the biggest mistake of my life.

On wall-mounted flat screens I can monitor live images of my building inside and out, and the night-shift security guard is walking through the cavernous vehicle bay this moment. I feel like a ghost or a spy as he yawns and scratches, unmindful of the closed-circuit TV cameras overhead. In his sixties, his first name is Wyatt but I don't know his last.

He looks like a sheriff in his khaki uniform with brown pocket flaps, walking up the concrete ramp leading inside the morgue, pressing a button on the cinder block wall. The massive door begins rolling down in the swirling exhaust of the hearse driving out, probably the suicide from Fairfax County, based on bodies scheduled for release.

"Dr. Scarpetta?" My officious British secretary interrupts my ruminations, opening the door between her office and mine. "So sorry to disturb you." She's not sorry in the least, rarely bothering to knock.

"I'm about to head out, and you should do the same." I move window to window, closing the blinds.

"I just spoke to August Ryan," she announces. "He wanted you to know that a situation has come up requiring your assistance."

"Is this about the woman downstairs?" I presume, and the U.S. Park Police investigator and I haven't talked since Friday night.

I'm hoping he finally has new information. The case is getting traction in the media, and rumors and theories are on the Internet. It's almost impossible to solve a violent crime when you don't know the victim's identity.

"He needs you to meet him somewhere." My secretary acts as if I answer to her instead of the other way around.

Dressed in her typical couture of a tweedy skirt suit and loafers, her steely gray hair styled like the 1950s, Maggie Cutbush eyes me disapprovingly over the wire-rim glasses perched on the tip of her sharp nose.

"He needs to meet me for what reason—" I start to say.

"He'll explain," she interrupts.

"Why didn't you just put him on the phone with me? He could have called directly for that matter. I gave him my cell number at the scene Friday night."

"August and I have worked together for years. He was polite enough to check with me first, and will call you when he's in his car," she says in her lovely London accent, having zero respect for a woman in charge.

Certainly not a second-generation Italian who grew up poor in Miami. I collect my coat from the coatrack. I'm eager to get out of here, and not because of present company and the weather. Today is my niece's birthday, a difficult one with all that's gone on, and I've planned a quiet celebration at home, just family.

"One of Doctor Reddy's strengths is he knows how to delegate." Maggie hasn't finished lecturing. "He didn't hand out his personal contact information like Halloween candy," as if I do. "He made it clear he wasn't at the beck and call of the police. It's a lesson you'd be well served to learn."

At every opportunity, she can't resist mentioning her former boss, the chief I replaced under somewhat false pretenses as it turns out. Or bait and switch might better summarize what happened once I'd moved here from Massachusetts. Everything changed in the blink of an eye.

It was too late by the time I discovered that Elvin Reddy wasn't leaving state government for the private sector as I was promised by him and others high up the chain. Instead, he was appointed the new health commissioner of Virginia, overseeing all departments responsible for the well-being and safety of the public.

That includes the statewide Office of the Chief Medical Examiner (OCME). Meaning I answer to him when push comes to shove, a slick political trick if ever I heard one.

"As you're seeing, it doesn't take long for people to get entitled," Maggie says ironically. "I'd suggest you take an investigator with you. Fabian's on call tonight. He was at his desk when I walked past a few minutes ago."

"IT DEPENDS ON WHAT we're dealing with," I reply. "It probably won't be necessary. I believe I can manage."

Looking around for the spray bottle of filtered water, I spot it on a shelf near the conference table.

"It's unwise for the chief to show up at all, much less alone, and it's not a good precedent for you to start," Maggie says as if I just fell off the turnip truck.

"Look, I'm sure you have my best interests in mind." I'm not rude about it, not even snide.

"I believe that goes without saying." She dominates our shared doorway as I step around boxes of books and other personal belongings I've yet to unpack.

"I realize my style isn't your cup of tea, Maggie." I begin spritzing my fiddle-leaf fig tree and potted orchids. "But I'm not the sort to stand on ceremony. If I can't be bothered then why should anyone else?"

It's all I can do not to admit the major reason I was asked to become chief again. The number of cases that have been neglected and mishandled for years is stunning. Especially here in Northern Virginia, which has its own special problems because of our location.

My office is but five miles from the Pentagon, and I stipulated that if I took this job, I had to work out of the headquarters here in Alexandria. Considering the various national obligations my husband and I have, it's important we're in close proximity to Washington, D.C.

"If the police want my help, that's why I'm here." I tell Maggie what I have before. "They don't need to go through you."

"I suppose we should postpone Lucy's birthday gathering." She curtly changes the subject. "Benton, Pete Marino, your sister, anybody else? I'll let them know."

"Nobody else, and I agree that's probably wise." I'll never

stop feeling awful about disappointing everyone on a regular basis.

But violence and senseless tragedy don't care who you are or the occasion, and someone has to respond. Returning to my desk, I vow to make it up to Lucy, as I've vowed so many times before.

"I can't imagine how difficult it must be." Maggie grimly shakes her head with phony sympathy. "Losing her partner and adopted son," she says, and I don't intend to discuss my niece and why she's living at home. "Not that I really understand that lifestyle. But this time of year, everything's harder for people who are unhappy."

"No reason to wait." I tell her it's fine to leave, and to drive carefully in the wind and rain, as I ignore how offensive she can be. "I'll see what's going on with August Ryan."

Hopefully, he has something helpful about the murdered woman in my cooler. One doesn't need to be a forensic pathologist to determine that she died of exsanguination after her carotid arteries were transected by a sharp blade. I don't know how old she is, possibly in her late twenties or early thirties when someone fractured her skull from behind, cutting her throat down to the spine.

Last Friday night was stormy as I worked the scene in a remote wooded area of Daingerfield Island. I can almost smell the creosote-treated wood, raindrops smacking on railroad ties as I went over every inch of the body with a hand magnifier. The beams of tactical flashlights slashed through the blackness like a laser show as cops searched the area.

Nothing turned up except a flattened penny, possibly run over by the seven P.M. commuter train as the engineer spotted what he thought was a naked mannequin sprawled by the rails.

"I hate to screw up your evening," August Ryan drawls right off when I answer my phone. "Because I'm pretty sure I'm about to, and I can tell you already that it's not pleasant driving out here. But as I explained to Maggie a little while ago, I wouldn't ask if it wasn't important."

"What can I do for you?" I write down the time and date in a pocket-size Moleskine notebook.

"We've got a missing person, and it's not looking good." The park police investigator wastes no time getting to the point.

"I'm sorry, is this about Friday night's case?" I puzzle. "Are you thinking this missing person might be the murdered woman in my cooler?"

"It's sounding like it could be. Alexandria P.D. called me after one of their officers did a wellness check on someone who's vanished. I'm on my way to your neck of the woods, Colonial Landing on the waterfront," he startles me by adding.

I know the new residential development all too well. Pete Marino and my sister Dorothy have a place there, the luxury townhomes an easy walk from the historic district where Benton and I bought an old estate that needs some fixing up. Lucy lives with us in the guesthouse, everybody safely close by for once. Or so I thought, not that any location is immune from violence.

But it's rare in Old Town. Homicide is an anomaly, on

average one a year, typically a robbery, a domestic fight that takes a fatal turn, based on the statistics I've studied. Rapes and assaults are uncommon, and mostly what the locals worry about is burglary and car break-ins.

"Gwen Hainey." August tells me the name of the missing woman. "A thirty-three-year-old biomedical engineer at Thor Laboratories. About twenty miles from you in Vienna, one of those big tech companies off I-95."

"I'm familiar with Thor, at least by reputation. What exactly does she do there?" I'm writing down the details.

"The person I talked to is the lab director, and he wouldn't say. Only that she's a scientist working on special projects, and as you may or may not know, a lot of what goes on is classified stuff for the government."

"Among other things they're pioneers in 3-D printing human skin, organs, blood vessels, and other body parts including ears." I give him the upshot.

"For real?"

"As science fiction as it might sound, it's already happening."

"Just one more thing to make life more confusing and our jobs harder" is what he has to say about it, and I don't know him well.

Friday night was the only time I've been around him so far, and he's what I'd call a cool customer, a smooth operator. Understated. Hard to read. Recently divorced, he has no kids, and I get the impression he's too busy for much of a social life.

"How do you get a DNA profile from artificial skin? What about fingerprints?" August's voice over speakerphone.

"We'll worry about that another day," I reply. "When's the last time anybody at Thor had contact with Gwen?"

"Apparently, not since Thanksgiving. She wasn't at work today, wasn't answering her phone, which hasn't turned up so far."

He goes on to explain that her lab director was concerned enough to call 911. The uniformed officer making the wellness check found Gwen's front door locked, no sign of anyone.

"Officer Fruge." August wonders if I might know her.

Fruge as in *frugal,* and I have a feeling the unusual name is one from my past. I wonder out loud if the officer he's talking about is related to the controversial toxicologist I once worked with in Richmond.

"Yep, that's the one," he says. "Blaise Fruge is her daughter, and she was at the scene briefly Friday night, was the first responder."

He says that the Alexandria police officer was on routine patrol when the body was discovered. She heard the radio call, and likely was gone by the time I showed up. But I wouldn't have a clue who was there, the park crawling with police while I dealt with the body.

"A wannabe plus full of herself, and they're the worst kind," August adds as my fitness tracker bracelet vibrates, messages and e-mails landing. "You've got to watch her, and she thinks she's the next Sherlock, but trust me, she's not."

"Let me make sure I understand," I reply. "Officer Fruge responded to the body found on Daingerfield Island. And now she's responded to a missing person report that may be connected. It would seem she gets around."

"I don't think she's got a life, you want my opinion."

"What happened when she arrived at Colonial Landing?"

"She had to get the manager to let her into Gwen Hainey's townhome, and it's clear that something violent went on." August's voice sounds over speakerphone as I glance at the text Benton just sent.

He's heard from Maggie, and is on his way home, running late, and that's strange. I didn't know he was going anywhere today, thought he was working remotely. Texting him a quick reply, I ask if everything's okay, while August continues to explain what Officer Fruge discovered inside the townhome.

CHAPTER 2

Her backpack is on the kitchen table, wallet and keys inside, doesn't seem to be anything rifled through. But like I mentioned, no sign of her phone," August says as I get up from my desk. "We'll request records from the carrier to see when she last made or answered any calls, and with whom."

"What about her car?" I walk into my office bathroom where I keep changes of clothing.

"From what I understand, she worked from home several days a week." His voice follows me as I move around. "The rest of the time she catches rides with colleagues or takes lift services. There's no vehicle registered to her."

"That seems a bit unusual," I reply as Benton texts me: Driving back from an unexpected meeting.

"What else do we know about Gwen?" I'm taking off my shoes and pants.

"That's another thing that's unusual," August says. "If you Google her, there's nothing. It's like she doesn't exist."

"Including on social media?" I hang up my suit.

"Nope. Not even Twitter. No news stories, either. Nothing."

"What about photographs inside her condo, maybe framed ones placed about? A scrapbook? Any pictures that might be her?" Sitting down on the toilet lid, I pull on a pair of warm socks. "Do we know what Gwen looks like?"

I envision the murder victim's face, her long brown hair and athletic build, and I suspect she was attractive. But it's hard to tell.

"I asked Fruge the same thing, and no pictures so far. Her lab director describes her as around five-foot-five," August says as I work my legs into a pair of black cargo pants. "Maybe a hundred-and-twenty-five pounds, brown eyes and shoulder-length brown hair."

"Sounds about right but that could be a lot of people," I reply, caught in my usual predicament.

I want the victim identified. But I wouldn't wish what happened to her on Gwen Hainey or anyone.

"I've got an electronic copy of her driver's license," August says. "It's an old picture, her hair really short and blond. D.O.B. is June fifth, nineteen eighty-eight. She's five-foot-four, which is almost right. But thirty pounds heavier, and I can't swear it's the same person. Apparently, the town house she's in is a short-term rental, and there are very few personal belongings."

"Does she have a tattoo?" I'm putting on my boots.

"Her lab director wasn't aware of any visible ones, and I didn't volunteer what we know about the tattoo the murdered woman has."

"And do we know why Gwen temporarily relocated to Old Town?" I'm tying my laces in double bows.

"From what I've been told, she was starting her new job at Thor. She didn't want to make any long-term commitments until she was sure it would work out. It would seem it was urgent for her to get into the townhome right away."

"Relocated from where?" I put on a long-sleeved black tactical shirt with the OCME crest on it, a caduceus and the scales of justice embroidered in blue, gold and red.

"Boston," August says as I walk out of the bathroom, buttoning up. "I texted you a picture, what Fruge sent me. A ten-pound kettlebell weight that's in the townhome's entryway. A weird place for it unless it was being used as a doorstop, right?"

"I'm opening the photo now," I tell him as I do it.

The kettlebell is round, flat-bottomed, bright blue with a shiny stainless-steel looped handle. It's lying on its side to the left of the front door on the hardwood floor, and August wonders if an attacker might have used it to hit Gwen in the back of the head.

"Assuming she and the murdered woman from Friday night are one and the same," he adds.

"Are we sure Officer Fruge didn't move anything?" I enlarge the photo on my phone.

"She says she didn't except for looking inside the knapsack. When she did her walk-through, she had on a mask and gloves, was being careful. That's what she says."

"And then what?"

"And then she waited until the crime scene unit got there. They've done their overall, taken video and photos. But they won't come in and process anything until you and I take a look."

"Except we don't know if it's really a crime scene, do we?" I ask the most glaring question.

I imagine the missing biomedical engineer returning home and finding cops inside her place, turning it upside down. Even worse if the medical examiner is there, and I don't need that my first month on the job. I have enough trouble.

"Do you feel you have probable cause for a search warrant?" I ask August.

"We'll have the warrant within the hour."

"What makes you think something violent happened?" Opening a cabinet, I pull out the big black Pelican case I take to scenes. "What signs of a struggle are we talking about?"

"Apparently there's blood inside the garage, and the furniture is disarranged in the living room. I think you'd better come," he says, and we end the call.

Putting on my coat, I lock up for the night, following the windowless corridor of shut office doors, the walls and floor pale gray, the lighting low. Wyatt the security guard is walking off the elevator, headed toward me, carrying what I suspect is his bagged supper.

"Have a good night," I say to him. "Hopefully, a quiet one."

"It's always quiet around here, ma'am. Too quiet." He hangs

a left into the breakroom where the on-call forensic investigator is making a pot of French press coffee.

Fabian is dressed in the same uniform of tactical field clothes that I have on, and my preference would have been not to run into him right now. It's obvious that I'm headed to a scene, my big Pelican case in hand, and I don't want him riding shotgun or even thinking about it.

"You shouldn't show up by yourself," he says, and obviously my secretary got to him. "I saw Maggie when she was leaving a few minutes ago, and she felt it was better if I went with you to the townhome. I'm ready and waiting, and the coffees can be to-go. Would you like one?"

"No, thank you."

Clearly August shared the details with her, and he shouldn't have. I imagine Maggie then passing them along to Fabian, giving directives as if she runs the place, and that shouldn't have happened, either.

"YOU SURE YOU DON'T want me to drive?" He flashes a smile, and he can turn up the charm when he wants, I'll give him that.

A physician's assistant in Louisiana before working here, he's in his late twenties and could pass for a goth model with his silver jewelry, tattoos, fine features and Cher-like long black hair. By far he's the best investigator of the three I've got, one of them about to retire, the other nothing to brag about.

"I'll let you know if I need you," I tell Fabian. "But I don't think so."

"I haven't heard about any deliveries," Wyatt is quick to pipe up over the noise of the microwave oven, looking at me suspiciously. "There's nothing expected, isn't that right?"

"Not so far, and we'll hope it stays that way," I reply.

"It sounds like where you're headed might be related to the murdered lady from the railroad tracks." Fabian pours a cup of his strong coffee, a smoky chicory blend that his mother ships to him from Baton Rouge.

"Possibly," I reply, wondering why everybody thinks it's okay to crash my boundaries and interrogate me.

"I mean, if it's important enough to ask you to look?" He stirs in his preferred sweetener of agave nectar. "You sure you don't want some help? It's not like I'm unfamiliar with the case."

He worked with me at last Friday night's scene, but that doesn't mean I need his assistance now. It's but another example of what happens when the person in charge is shuttered away, not paying attention. Elvin Reddy has managed to foster a pervasive spirit of entitlement.

Telling Fabian and Wyatt good night, I walk off. I'm avoiding elevators whenever possible since the coronavirus. My boots echo dully inside the concrete stairwell, and on the lower level I open the windowless fire-escape door. I step into another corridor, this one hospital-white with bright lights, and there's no sign of anyone. No one alive that is.

The CT scanning room is locked up, the light green outside the door, the technician gone for the day. The autopsy suite is empty, its stainless-steel tables, carts and countertops shiny-clean, awaiting new cases. There always will be more. The next accident or homicide. Another person ends it all or drops dead unexpectedly, those left behind irreparably altered.

As I near the anthropology lab, I hear the quiet clatter of bones defleshing in bleach-infused water that will simmer for days. Through observation windows lining both sides of the corridor, I can see the five-gallon stockpot steaming on the portable cooktop, the decomposing skeletal remains discovered last week by a hunter.

Through another window I see his rotting boots, clothing, a pack of Marlboros, a pint of Fireball whisky, a wallet and its contents spread out on a paper-covered table inside the evidence room. The cause and manner of death are still undetermined. I suspect he died a year ago based on what the police discovered when going through the retired mechanic's house near Fort Belvoir.

Inside the intake area, the cloying odor of industrial deodorizer is strong as I set my scene case, my briefcase down on top of a cart in front of the walk-in cooler and freezer. Their digital displays show the temperatures and other information that I can monitor on an app. Everything's in the green, and I put on exam gloves and a surgical mask.

Finding a six-inch plastic ruler, I tuck my phone inside an antimicrobial protective sleeve so I can take additional photographs if needed. Opening the cooler's stainless-steel door, I walk inside, the loud blowing air frigid and foul. Her black pouch is on a gurney in a back corner, and there's nothing on the toe tag except the date *11/30* and a location of *Daingerfield Island RR tracks* scrawled in smeared ink.

I partially unzip the heavy vinyl, and the murdered woman's face looks worse than when I autopsied her a few days ago. Abrasions and contusions are an angrier red in contrast to her pale, bloodless body. The vital tissue response to her injuries indicates she survived long enough for her killer to finish what he'd started.

There's no obvious indication of sexual assault, but that doesn't necessarily mean very much. No question this is a sexually motivated homicide, all about overpowering, and I suspect she didn't know her assailant but may have trusted him at first. Otherwise, I don't understand how he gained access to her home or wherever it was that he confronted her.

After she was dead, he lewdly displayed her nude body along railroad tracks to shock those aboard the next train going by. That's if you ask my forensic psychologist husband with his internal database of nightmares, and he's probably right. Benton usually is. There's no question that her body was deliberately displayed, and I take a picture of her face.

The pupils of her cloudy eyes are fixed and dilated, her lips a purplish-blue and crusty. The gaping wound to her neck is dark red and dry, and I smell the stale stench of refrigerated decomposition as I manipulate her head, turning it to one side. She hadn't been dead very long when I examined her at the scene, her extremities beginning to stiffen.

Since then, rigor mortis has come and gone, her muscles unclenching as if unable to resist the inevitable any longer.

The shaved back of her head is cold and boggy through my nitrile gloves as I palpate the depressed skull fracture, feeling the edges of bone punched in by a single crushing blow. Possibly by the kettlebell in question, and I'll know better when I can take a closer look at the scene.

The contused and lacerated area of her scalp is approximately four inches in diameter, the round shape of it consistent with the possible weapon. Whatever was used, the blow to her head would have been immediately incapacitating.

She wasn't walking around or talking afterward. It's not the cause of death although it might have been eventually. Surviving long enough for swelling and internal bleeding, she died after her throat was sliced ear to ear with some type of nonserrated cutting instrument.

After death, her hands were cut off, and that means no fingerprints. Maybe that was the reason. But there are other ways to identify someone, and we're not having any success so far. She's not in the FBI's Combined DNA Identification System database better known as CODIS. Maybe we'll get lucky with a genealogical profile.

We might learn something important from other evidence I began collecting at the scene, mostly microscopic particles of rust, wood, and various minerals consistent with the rocky railroad bed. But I also found fibers all over her body including in her hair, and suspect the source of them might be whatever the killer wrapped around her during transport.

Something like a multicolored blanket made of a synthetic

fabric, and I suspect she was first attacked indoors. I envision her panicking, trying to get away from her assailant, bumping into things as he grabs at her before knocking her unconscious.

Then transporting her somewhere, he finished her off, possibly near the railroad tracks where he left her. We found no evidence of such a thing when we searched the area Friday night. But it was raining hard enough that any blood would have washed away or been next to impossible to find as big and densely wooded as the park is.

Taking several more photographs, I zip up the body bag, pulling off my gloves. I step around gurneys bearing other patients in this sad clinic. Outside the cooler, I remove my personal protective equipment (PPE). Into the red biohazard trash bag everything goes, and I help myself to a big dollop of hand sanitizer before collecting my belongings.

I walk past the security office, and there's no sign of Wyatt behind the bulletproof glass window. No doubt he's holed up in the breakroom, monitoring the security cameras on the flat screen in there. He doesn't like the morgue, especially after hours. A lot of people don't, and it's always struck me as silly, because it's not the dead who will hurt you.

I exit the building through the vehicle bay where bodies are delivered and driven away. The size of a small hangar, it's empty now, just our mobile emergency response truck. Near it is a zodiac boat and pallets of heavy-duty water-recovery body bags, disposable sheets, gallons of disinfectant and other necessities.

The beige epoxy-painted floor is still wet from being hosed down, my boots making a quiet sticky sound. Zipping up my coat and pulling up my hood, I open the pedestrian door leading outside, startled by the guttural rumble of a turbo-charged engine idling in the volatile dark.

CHAPTER 3

PETE MARINO CREEPS UP in his blacked-out Ford Raptor pickup truck as I wait in the downpour next to the morgue's shut bay door. His headlights illuminate my take-home Subaru in its parking spot reserved for the chief M.E., perhaps the only perk of the job as it's turning out.

"Get in, Doc. No way you're driving yourself anywhere right now," he booms through his rolling-down window, and it's been a while since I've seen him this keyed up, maybe not since his wedding day.

A knit cap covers his bald head, and he has on a ballistic vest under his camouflage hunting jacket, his demeanor as serious as a heart attack, to borrow one of his expressions. Obviously, Maggie must have gotten hold of him, passing along that I've been detained and need to postpone Lucy's birthday celebration.

But that doesn't explain why he's picking me up unannounced while commandeering and ordering me about. I know that look on his sun-weathered face. Something has pushed his panic button, and I set my scene case on the floor in back near his Heckler & Koch MP5 and an Army surplus ammo box.

"What's happened?" The rain is blowing like mad, soaking my cargo pants and streaming into my eyes as I climb up into the passenger seat.

"This couldn't be much worse, Doc." He hands me a dingy microfiber towel to dry off. "Best I can do, sorry. But better than nothing. I thought I had a roll of paper towels in here, dammit! I can't believe it!"

"Am I in some sort of danger that no one's told me about?" I wipe myself down, getting a whiff of Armor All. "Is my sister all right? Is Lucy okay? What's got you in such an uproar?"

"I can't believe this is happening." He's not talking about the storm or my dripping all over his immaculate cockpit that still smells new.

I place my briefcase in my lap, mindful of the 10mm pistol on the console, his matte-gray Guncrafter Industries 1911 built from billet with Trijicon optic sights and custom grips. Cocked and locked with the thumb safety on, it's loaded with two-hundred-grain Buffalo Bore rounds that could take out a grizzly, I have a feeling.

If that's not enough firepower, he has his submachine gun and plenty of highly destructive ammunition within reach on the backseat. I suppose if we end up in a shootout I could pitch in with the Sig Sauer P226 in my briefcase, I think sardonically, halfway wondering if he's losing his marbles.

"Are you expecting a gunfight, a riot, an insurrection?" I put on my shoulder harness, and I'm not being funny. "What's got you in such a state? You're scaring me." I keep thinking of the victim in my cooler, and his missing neighbor, Gwen Hainey.

"I'm pretty sure I know who the murdered lady is from Friday night. Someone Lucy and me tried to help, someone Dorothy was friendly with. Our damn neighbor." He's out with the name, my stress spiking.

"You and Lucy tried to help her?" I don't understand.

"We gave her security advice once. Obviously, she didn't listen. And whoever did this? He has to be familiar with the area right here where we live. You, me, all of us. He had to be watching Gwen and no telling who else."

Like Hannibal Lecter says, it all starts with what you see. Marino repeats one of his favorite lines, pointing two fingers at his eyes. Rain hammers the roof as we drive through my parking lot, passing the OCME's small fleet of windowless vans, shiny black like limousines, the crest of Virginia in gray on the doors.

"Point being, it might not be a domestic homicide," he adds.

"I'm not aware that anyone's thinking the homicide from Friday night is domestic," I reply, baffled. "And where did you hear about—"

"I dropped off Dorothy at your house." Interrupting, he's barely listening. "We were out running an errand when I heard the call over the scanner. A wellness check at an address two houses down from ours. I didn't want Dorothy staying alone at our place right now. She's with Lucy."

He says he has information about his missing neighbor but it's not a subject I can discuss easily. Marino isn't a police officer anymore. He has no official capacity, and Lucy doesn't either, their new investigative company private. Truth be told, I shouldn't be comfortably ensconced inside his truck right now, everything black leather and carbon fiber.

His new ride is but one of my sister's many grand gestures since the two of them got married last year during the worst of the pandemic. He also has a sport boat docked behind their waterfront townhome, a tricked-out Harley-Davidson touring motorcycle in the garage, and an unlimited budget for his growing arsenal.

My sister does well as a graphic novelist, and I'm still getting used to Marino's newly acquired affluence and management. Hardest for me is not confiding in him like I used to, going back to our earliest years working together. It's not really possible to ring him up or have a drink, to brainstorm about murder, mayhem or anything much. I wouldn't dream of discussing cases or anything private, not with my only sibling hovering.

"I think we know what's happened to the woman whose place you're headed to." He slows to a stop at a red light, a lot of churches and funeral homes within a stone's throw of my headquarters.

"How did you hear about where I'm headed?" I hope it wasn't over his portable scanner charging on the console, the volume turned down to a faint chatter.

"Maggie called to postpone dinner tonight, saying August Ryan needed you to meet him, and I put two and two together," Marino says as I glance at more messages landing on my phone, one of them from Lucy:

You with Marino yet? she texts.

In his truck, I answer, and obviously they've been in touch and are coconspirators.

Assuming she knows where I'm going and why, there's no question my niece realizes someone she and Marino gave advice to briefly and informally likely has been murdered.

"Thankfully, Gwen Hainey's name hasn't been mentioned over the air, just the address," Marino is saying as Lucy and I continue texting.

I let her know I'm thinking about her. I'll see her later. We'll toast her birthday with something special I've been saving since my last trip to France, I promise.

"Do you know Gwen Hainey personally? More than just neighbors and someone you tried to help?" I ask Marino.

"Lucy and I both were around her only once." He adjusts the defrost while inching along, an accident up ahead. "This wasn't long after Gwen moved in, we were with her maybe an hour and a half max trying to help out."

"How did you get involved with her in the first place?

Because you both live in the same development?" I'm thinking of my sister, having an idea I know the answer.

"DOROTHY MET HER FIRST," he confirms my suspicions.

Apparently, Gwen told her that the reason she moved to Old Town was to get away from an ex-boyfriend who's been stalking her. She gave that as the reason for taking the job at Thor Laboratories.

"In a lot of ways her ex, Jinx Slater, fits the bill of someone who could be violent. But what's happened might not have anything to do with him," Marino says.

"Where was Gwen before moving here?" I'm wondering what she told Marino and Lucy compared to what I know from August Ryan.

"Boston, where her ex still lives." Marino offers me a pack of gum, and I shake my head no thanks. "After MIT, she went to work in that huge lab up there, Red Feather Biomedical." He crams two sticks of gum into his mouth because he's desperate to smoke.

"Like Thor they're in the business of artificial human organs, skin, brain machine interfacing, that sort of thing." I give him the upshot, blue lights flashing ahead, traffic cops detouring drivers around a crashed black SUV.

For a moment my heart stops. Benton drives a black SUV, but this one is a BMW. It's not him.

"What can you tell me about the dead lady from Friday night, Doc?" Marino begins his inevitable probing.

"That she's a homicide, a sexually violent one," I reply.

"Yeah, I think the whole world knows that much," he says, and I don't respond.

He and Lucy would be aware of what's been in the media, which is very little, I've made sure. They've not seen the body from Friday night, and prior to this I've not mentioned the case to them. It's none of their concern, neither of them officially involved. Except now they could be.

"Some job we did." He tightly grips the steering wheel, the veins roping in his thick wrists, and he was formidable enough before dating my sister.

But now he's quite the land mass, spending hours daily on cardio and lifting weights, and I have to say he's never looked fitter.

"What a way to start a business, right?" He blows out an exasperated clove-scented breath.

"You need to calm down, and let's not overrun our headlights. Maybe quit tailgating so we don't rear-end someone," I continue backseat driving.

This stretch of King Street is heavily wooded and residential, and gracious homes on generous lots are decorated for the season. Lampposts and columns are wrapped in blue and white lights that flicker in the soupy overcast. Christmas trees glitter through windows, candles glowing cozily.

"I'm pissed at myself for not paying enough attention. Now I sure wish I had," Marino says. "But I couldn't have seen this coming. If Jinx Slater did it, how'd he find her? She'd gone to a lot of trouble making sure nobody knows where she is."

"Or that's what she told you," I reply. "But assuming she's telling the truth, he might have tracked her down, that wouldn't surprise me. It's getting harder to hide in this high-tech world with cameras watching from everywhere including outer space."

"But I don't know why she'd turn off the alarm and open the door, assuming that's what she did," he says.

As afraid of him as she claimed to be, she would have freaked out if he showed up at the guard gate, much less on her doorstep. She would have called 911, Marino supposes.

"Or she could have called me for that matter," he adds, his four-wheeler growling over pavement, the oversize tires splashing through puddles. "She had my number, and Dorothy and I were home last Friday night. I would have been there in two minutes."

"So far, Gwen's phone hasn't shown up." I tell him that much while scrolling through messages I'll deal with later. "It sounds like she has an alarm system, and that's important. What about cameras around the townhome's perimeter or at least covering the entrance?"

"We recommended it but she was worried about hacking. She said she keeps the alarm on all the time while she's home."

"Did she have the security system installed herself?"

"It was already there."

"I wonder who else has the code."

"I asked her that. She said only the landlord in case of emergencies. But who knows who that person might have given it to," Marino says.

"Exactly. And you have to tell August Ryan what you're telling me," I reply.

"And he needs to listen and not be a jerk. I'm not sure that's possible, it almost never is when you deal with the Feds."

"Have you two met?"

"Not yet but he could use my assistance," Marino replies. "I'm familiar with Gwen's townhome unless she's changed it since Lucy and I did a security evaluation of it. I know exactly what was in there as of pretty recently."

"Including your DNA," I remind him, as if the situation isn't tricky enough.

"I'll be up front about it when you and me get there," Marino says. "It shouldn't stop me from looking around, hopefully before a herd of cops go tromping through."

"I'm not sure how I'm going to explain showing up with a private investigator in tow. Or even worse, having one chauffeuring me."

"I'm not chauffeuring. Right now, I'm your friggin' protection detail," he retorts, and it isn't only *right now*.

He's acted like this for as long as we've known each other. My personal well-being and business somehow end up in his self-determined jurisdiction.

"It's not that I don't appreciate you looking after me," I reply as diplomatically as I can. "But my first month on the job, I'm having a hard enough time with people around here, and this isn't going to help."

Flipping on his strobe lights as if he's a cop again, he guns around the Mini Cooper in front of us.

"Well, I don't give a crap what August Ryan thinks about my showing up, let's start with that," Marino says aggressively. "What counts is someone's been murdered. Probably my neighbor, and out of self-protection if nothing else I've got a right to know what's going on."

"Legally, you don't." I inform him of how things work because he seems to have forgotten.

"You gonna tell me the details so I know what we're dealing with?"

"You know I can't."

"You can do what you want, Doc."

"Not without consequences."

"You're the chief medical examiner of the entire Commonwealth," he says. "Just like the old days. It's up to you."

He's right but not without a few rules and conditions. I let him know how this would have to be engineered. He's worked for me in the past, and as scary as it may sound to both of us, he needs to work for me again. It's that simple if he's to legitimize driving me around.

"Or showing up at the morgue. Or the labs. Or court," I'm saying. "Anywhere except the privacy of our homes and family gatherings."

This is nothing new but it's been years since we've been professionally connected. For sure it will complicate our lives now more than ever with my sister in the mix.

"I'm not talking about a position that requires you to have an office in my building or spend much time there," I continue. "I don't want either one of us feeling controlled or crowded." I don't need that again.

"Except what if I want an office? You know, so I have a quiet workspace when I'm helping out, and people can't hear every word I say over the phone," Marino says, his eyes scanning the mirrors.

CHAPTER 4

I DON'T HAVE TO BE a mind reader to realize what Marino is angling for, a private space, a slice of his old life back. Maybe a place of his own where he can get away from his wife now and then.

"And you need someone around who's got your back," he adds, and he's not wrong.

"We can hire you as a private contractor, a forensic operations specialist." I make up the title as I'm sitting in my heated leather seat. "You can help give oversight to the investigators. But you answer to me, working as needed and paid accordingly."

"How much?"

"As little as possible. Pro bono is much appreciated."

"Sure." He shrugs, the rain billowing in sheets, and we have a deal.

Effective immediately, he has an official role that's reasonable and defensible. I begin sharing what I know about Friday night's homicide, finding the video clip the commuter train's engineer gave me. The brief seconds of footage were recorded by the outward-facing camera as the two-hundred-ton locomotive sped through the dark wooded park on Daingerfield Island.

Shoulder to shoulder, Marino and I look at my phone's display as we wait at a red light behind an endless line of traffic. I detect the citrusy scent of his Acqua di Parma cologne as we watch the train's headlamp illuminate the tracks around a bend . . . barreling down at more than a hundred miles an hour . . . suddenly braking to the deafening noise of screeching steel and compressed air . . .

As a flash of the body goes past, naked and exposed, sprawled on the rocky ballast next to the tracks, arms and legs spread like a snow angel . . . Then nothing but the black hulking shapes of trees, of distant lights blurring past as the train comes to a hissing, clanking stop like a petulant dragon.

"I can't tell if that's her but it looks like she has a tattoo on her belly?" Marino creeps ahead in his truck as the light turns green. "I can't make it out but that's not good. Gwen's got a tattoo. She and her ex got the same one together."

"A tattoo of what?" I ask, the wipers thump-thumping, thunder percussing.

Looming over us in the roiling mist is the George Washington Masonic National Memorial, its soaring tower up-lit red and green, and barely visible.

"A jellyfish," Marino says.

"I'm going to show you a few pictures I took with my phone right before you picked me up."

Skimming through the photographs I took inside the cooler, I find a close-up of the dead woman's tattoo. The jellyfish is multicolored with cartoon eyes, its long tentacles salaciously trailing down her belly. I was careful not to cut through them when making a small incision in her upper abdomen.

No matter what new technologies come down the pike, I'm still going to insert a thermometer into the liver. It's the most reliable way to get a core body temperature at the scene.

"Crap." Marino glances at the photograph, scowling as he drives. "I mean, it's not like there are many people around here with something like that."

Then I show him a close-up of her dead face.

"I think so," he says. "I'm pretty sure."

"No releasing anything until we confirm identity with dental records or DNA," I remind him. "And of course, her next of kin will have to be notified. But it's likely that your neighbor Gwen Hainey is the woman who was murdered last Friday night."

"This is bad," is all he says.

Looking out at the stormy darkness, I halfway listen to the quiet chatter on the scanner, catching codes and phone numbers. I've been around long enough to know when the police are more guarded than usual about who might be eavesdropping. But anybody paying close attention can glean that something serious has happened.

"How long do you think she'd been dead by the time you got there?" Marino asks.

"Unclothed, slender with very little body fat, and she'd lost most of her blood," I reply.

Flipping back pages in my notebook, I illuminate my small snarly writing with the flashlight app on my phone.

"She was going to cool more quickly anyway, especially in conditions similar to refrigeration," I begin to explain.

For the most part, postmortem changes would have been slowed by the cold. It was forty-eight degrees when I examined the body at the scene, and rigor and livor mortis were in the early stages. As I fill in the details, I'm texting August Ryan that I'm caught in terrible traffic. Creeping along in Marino's strobing war wagon with its oversize tires and multiple fog lamps, we might look formidable but we're not getting anywhere any faster than anyone else.

"She'd been dead several hours," I estimate. "But I don't think she was outside all of that time or even most of it."

I look out at scenery strange and familiar, nothing seeming the same because of what I know. Wrought-iron gas lamps flicker in the overcast, dully shining on wet brick pavers littered with dead leaves and broken branches. Nobody is out walking their dogs or jogging.

Buildings are pristinely preserved, many of them historically registered, and George Washington really did sleep in

a number of places. Wooded properties are tastefully decorated, not a single inflatable Santa or reindeer. There's nothing worthy of a tacky tour, much to Marino's disappointment
when he was informed of residential covenants.

Old Town is perfectly appointed and cared for, no improve-
ments or ornamentations allowed that aren't deemed appropriate. I've learned the hard way that you can't repaint your
shutters, replace the roof or install a backup generator without
permission. The list of restrictions has been the only liability
in what otherwise are ideal living conditions. Or that's how I
felt until now.

Surroundings I've found charming and a comfort in the
past suddenly seem ominous. Tall evergreens and winter-
bare trees rock violently on the roadside, the Baptist church
shrouded in veils of fog. Its steeple light eerily turns off and
on as the recording of the tolling bell plays nonstop, caught in
some kind of computer glitch.

FLASHES OF LIGHTNING ILLUMINATE huge trees that have
blown over in Ivy Hill Cemetery, where the father of the U.S.
space program Wernher von Braun is buried, among other
notables. I catch a glimpse of muddy exposed roots and up-
ended centuries-old monuments as more alert tones sound on
the scanner and our phones.

Ten out, I text August to the *kerblam* of thunder.

In the manager's office, he writes back, and I continue to fret.

Perception is a problem but a much bigger one is August

and Marino getting along. None of this is helped by the fact that my new forensic operations specialist also happens to be my brother-in-law.

"Jinx manages a restaurant in Boston's North End, picks up extra money bartending when he can." Marino tells me what Gwen said about her ex. "He's mostly been unemployed these past two years, and started drinking more, doing drugs, getting increasingly unstable."

"Are we certain about any of this?"

"Nope." Opening the ashtray, he grabs the pack of gum again. "But I should have looked into it, Doc."

"We're looking into it now," I reply. "Boston's a long way from here, and it shouldn't be hard to find out if Jinx Slater made a recent trip to this area. Does he have a history of violence?"

"After she told him she didn't want to see him anymore, he started acting out in ways that were disturbing. Like you said, *supposedly*."

"Such as?"

"Constant phone calls. Leaving a strangled teddy bear by her front door. Dead roses in her mailbox. Following her slowly in his car when she was out jogging."

"Did she report any of this to the police?"

"She didn't, and I was pretty sure she was lying like a dog."

"You and I both know that not all victims are honest or innocent." Resting my pen on my notebook, I look over at him.

"No kidding, and I have a feeling she's one of them."

"People who have terrible things happen to them can be

terrible people themselves. And some might think they got what's coming." I offer an ugly truth I wouldn't say in public.

"Gwen wasn't all that nice, seemed pretty stuck on herself, like she's smarter than everybody else," Marino says. "But you know how it goes. Dorothy asked if Lucy and I would help, and we tried."

Knowing Dorothy, she stopped by with a housewarming gift accompanied by her snooping around and gathering information. Boundary crashing under the guise of southern hospitality, she volunteered Marino and Lucy's services. It would be just like Dorothy to play the hero.

"Did Gwen ever take out a restraining order against her ex?" I text Benton again, wondering if he's home yet. "Not that they solve the problem most of the time."

"She didn't."

"Is there any evidence to support her accusations, is what I'm wondering."

"She said the only way to be safe from him was to go far away to someplace where he can't find her," Marino says. "So she took the job with Thor and moved here. That's her story. Some of it might be true, a lot of it probably isn't. Lucy and I didn't check it out. We didn't get further involved because Gwen didn't want us to, wasn't interested."

"Then why go along with it to begin with?"

"Dorothy's not good at taking no for an answer," he says. "Besides, it would have made Gwen look suspicious if she's so worried but doesn't want help."

"It's all looking suspicious," I reply, and we've reached Alexandria's old brick train station.

Crossing Callahan Drive, we bump over the same railroad tracks the murdered woman was found along just north of here. Gwen Hainey, I have no doubt, envisioning the copper coin on a rail, deformed and flattened as thin as paper. It bothered me when August found it, and bothered Benton even more when we talked about it later.

"What if I told you there was a penny on the tracks at the scene?" I say to Marino. "And likely it was run over by the seven P.M. commuter train that stopped when the body was spotted."

"I don't like the sound of that," he says, and we're in the heart of the historic district, shops and restaurants cheek to jowl, mostly empty in this weather.

"It was on top of a rail, close to the body."

"How close?"

"Barely six feet away." I envision August taking photographs and measuring the distance.

"It sounds like it was just placed there," Marino says. "When I was growing up, I used to put pennies on the rails at the railroad crossing near my house, a lot of us kids did. It was a thing in New Jersey because of Hookerman."

It's not the first time I've heard him tell his spooky tale about a railway worker losing an arm in the past century. His lantern-toting ghost is spotted along the tracks on dark nights, first appearing like a floating lighted orb from afar.

Approaching slowly, the levitating light gets bigger and brighter before suddenly vanishing.

"What's known as ball lighting." I remind Marino of the scientific explanation. "Granite, quartz, the steel rails, they're great conductors of electricity."

"Whatever." He's not interested in what the geophysicists have to say. "But going out after dark looking for ghosts along the railroad tracks was really stupid. A good way to get killed, and we never found most of the pennies."

"I don't think the one from Friday night had been out there long," I reply. "It wouldn't make sense that it's been run over repeatedly, and somehow was still there. Not to mention, it's conveniently near a murder victim's body? That's too many coincidences."

"Was it tarnished?"

"No. And you're wondering the same thing I am. If the killer put it there."

"Yeah, I'm wondering that. Who else knows besides him, and where's the penny now?"

"August Ryan found it, as I've mentioned, and it's in the labs," I reply. "This morning we took a look with scanning electron microscopy and X-ray diffraction."

"August was there for that?"

"He wasn't, and what we've discovered so far isn't very helpful. The penny's composition is copper and zinc, the date two thousand twenty."

"You can forget DNA and fingerprints if it was run over by

a train." Marino bypasses traffic, cutting through another side street, bumping us over pavers.

"Benton feels it's probably not random, and likely is symbolic," I add.

"The penny doesn't fit with a violent ex-boyfriend," Marino decides as I look out at my favorite French bakery, dark and closed. "I sure hope August keeps his mouth shut about that and everything else."

"He's in charge of the homicide investigation. You'd best get along with him somehow. There's but so much I can do if he decides to make a big fuss about you."

The murder is federal jurisdiction because the body was found inside a national park, I spell out. The U.S. Park Police is running the show whether Marino likes it or not.

"And if the victim is Gwen Hainey as we suspect, nothing will change. August is still running the show," I add, and up ahead blue and red emergency lights are a throbbing nimbus over Colonial Landing, where Marino lives with my sister.

The sliding metal front gate is wide open, the management office to the left lit up. August Ryan's Dodge Charger is parked in a visitor's spot next to a Prius that I've noticed before. The pricey residential community is directly on the Potomac River, and surrounded by a high wall on three sides, with tall wrought-iron fencing in back.

The waterfront townhomes are on half-acre lots, their slate rooftops and chimneys all that's visible from outside the compound. It can't be accessed without physically entering codes on squawk boxes at egresses, each covered by closed-circuit TV cameras. They're monitored remotely by the resident manager, who I met briefly many months ago.

I'm the one who encouraged Marino and my sister to move here. Finding the listing, I even previewed it for them during one of many trips to Alexandria while discussing my new job situation. It's very likely that Lucy would have settled into this same development had there been anything else available at the time. Thank God there wasn't.

CHAPTER 5

WE STOP AT THE entrance, the gate locked in the open position, enabling the police and other responders like me to come and go freely. That also could include the media or anyone else who shouldn't be allowed inside an enclave that prides itself on security and privacy.

"Sit tight for a second." Marino opens his door.

He climbs out of his truck, the rain slashing through his headlights shining on the open gate. He directs his flashlight at the hardwired security camera mounted on a pole above the squawk box. Walking around to the exit gate, he checks that camera next.

"They look okay as best I can tell," he reports when back inside the truck, his face wet, tucking the flashlight into a pocket. "There's nothing obvious, like they've been damaged, the wires cut or whatever."

"It sounds too good to be true that we might have video." I hand him the same towel he let me use earlier as we drive through the open gate. "Also, an assailant would have needed a code to enter. How did he manage that?"

"Good question," Marino says.

Each townhome we pass is redbrick with generous windows, and columned patios and porches. They have big kitchens, attached garages and boat slips, the backyards spacious enough for small swimming pools and gardens. I'll never forget Marino's excitement when they bought their place, three bedrooms, a man cave, and a dead-on view of the river.

All his years of living on a cop's wages, and it's as if he won the lottery. That's what he says, and I can see the smudged lights of Christmas trees, the shadows of people moving around behind drawn curtains. A man has stepped out on his porch, staring in the direction of the pulsing police lights as he talks on his phone.

He waves at Marino while the elderly woman next door emerges from her front door, staring at the big strobing truck. Frantically motioning to us, she hurries down her sidewalk, unmindful of the rain and that she's in slippers and a bathrobe.

"I'm so upset! This is dreadful! Do you know what's happening?" she calls out to Marino as he lowers his window. "Has there been a burglary?"

"We don't know what we're dealing with yet," he says to her sweetly. "But don't you worry, we're going to make sure everybody's safe."

"It's that woman jogger who moved here not so long ago. Not at all friendly, that one. The police are at her place so something must be horribly wrong." Marino's neighbor is visibly unnerved, her glasses speckled with rain. "I've never talked to her but she runs past my house every morning."

"When's the last time you saw her?" he asks.

"Several days ago. I'm not sure exactly. She runs up and down the street a few times, then heads out the gate. Usually at the crack of dawn, and is back an hour or two later."

"You need to get back inside and out of the rain. I don't want you getting sick," Marino says kindly but with authority, and you might think he's the mayor. "You got my number. I'm just a phone call away."

Thanking him, she hurries back to her house, and he waits until she's inside before driving on. He takes in every detail, looking for anything else that might indicate a monster has accessed his cloistered neighborhood.

"Maybe we turn off the strobes." Finding the switch, I do it for him.

I don't want it looking like we're making a grand entrance, and in his badass pickup truck we're more than a little conspicuous no matter what.

"I'll get out while you stay put, giving me a chance to explain that you're with me," I add. "I'm leaving my scene case, and will ask you to bring it if need be. Hopefully they've got PPE."

We pass the townhome where he lives with Dorothy, and the porch light is on, an American flag over the entrance snapping in the wind. Strands of white and blue LEDs are wound around shrubbery and columns. There are electric candles in the windows, a fresh wreath with a big red bow on the door, everything tastefully complying with residential code.

Two properties down from them is where Gwen Hainey had been living for the past six weeks, and it's undecorated, not so much as a hint of the holidays. The last townhome in the row of them, it's on a cul-de-sac, a wall in front, another one on the right side, and the tall wrought-iron fencing in back along the water.

There are no eyes or ears except for the neighbor on the left, some CEO who spends the winters in Florida, Marino says. Gwen's place is the most remote one, and that was helpful to whoever targeted her.

"It makes me wonder if the location is a factor," I comment as we park behind Alexandria P.D. cruisers and a crime scene van, their light bars going full tilt. "It's pretty desolate back here in this corner."

"Even more so this past Friday night," Marino says. "A lot of people were gone for Thanksgiving."

"I guess I'd better leave this here." I take off my coat.

There will be no good place to put it or my briefcase once I'm at the scene, and I place them on the seat. I climb out of Marino's truck, the rain steady but not nearly as hard.

I notice the TV news truck ahead, and that's just my luck. Shutting the door, already I'm getting wet, the rain cold on top of my bare head. I can feel the eyes of the cops inside their cruisers, their engines rumbling as I trot past coatless and in a chilly hurry.

Bright yellow crime scene tape flutters in the wind, and I

recognize the local TV news crew up ahead, the same one I was confronted by three nights ago. Their camera lights flare on at my approach.

"This is Dana Diletti, live from Colonial Landing on Old Town's waterfront," she says into her microphone.

Great Dana, as she's been nicknamed, is six feet tall, a former college basketball player, and now a celebrity news anchor who has her own show. Dressed in rain gear, she's appropriately somber as her crew holds up umbrellas, tending to her every need, the cameras running constantly and with no regard for decorum.

". . . We're here live at the scene where a woman recently employed by Thor Laboratories has gone missing," she says to my dismay, and so much for verifying the victim's identity. "Approaching now is the chief medical examiner . . . ," she adds.

It's the same thing I put up with Friday night when they showed up at the train tracks on Daingerfield Island. I didn't want to be on TV then, and don't want to be on it now. Walking with purpose, I avert my rain-slick face from them.

"DOCTOR SCARPETTA, CAN YOU tell us why you've been called to this townhome in the heart of Old Town's waterfront?" Dana says into her microphone.

She and her umbrella-holding crew are in pursuit.

"Is it connected to the murder from Friday night? Is the victim Gwen Hainey? The thirty-three-year-old scientist who recently moved here from Boston . . . ?"

My answer is to duck under the yellow-tape perimeter, disgusted by what just happened on live television. I hope that Gwen's family, friends, her allegedly abusive ex don't find out in such a callous fashion. But there's nothing I can do, and I follow the walkway past police in rain gear setting up a pup tent.

"Hey, stop right there!" an officer shouts, and then he's next to me, an Alexandria crime scene investigator probably half my age. "Who are you?"

I pull out my badge-wallet, showing him my credentials. He looks embarrassed, apologizing, all of it caught on camera.

"Investigator Ryan asked that I come." I explain why I'm here.

"I believe he's in the manager's office right now. They're reviewing security videos."

"Are we good for me to go inside?" I inquire.

"Everything's been photographed. We're just waiting for you guys to do your thing," the officer says as I head to the door.

It's slightly ajar, a female officer standing guard on the other side. The name on her uniform is B. FRUGE, and she directs me to step onto the white sticky mats covering most of the entryway, and that was smart. The police are making sure nothing is tracked inside.

In addition, any trace evidence already on the floor such as hairs or fibers will stick to the adhesive. All will go to the labs, and hopefully nothing will be lost.

"Kay Scarpetta, the new chief M.E.," I introduce myself.

Showing her my creds, I push my rain-dampened hair out

of my face, no doubt looking like something the cat dragged in. At least there's plenty of PPE, and a 3-D scanner has been set up on a tripod, a box of evidence markers and scene cases nearby.

"I know who you are." Officer Fruge shuts the front door.

Every sound is amplified by the emptiness, and from where I stand I don't see a stick of furniture. There are no rugs or wall-to-wall carpet, nothing to absorb noise except for velvet draperies that likely were here when Gwen moved in.

"I for one am glad you're back," Officer Fruge adds, as if there are plenty of people who aren't.

"Thank you, and I may have worked with your mother years ago. Greta Fruge?" My wet boots leave dirty tread-prints on the mats as I walk back and forth.

"Yep, I heard about it enough when I was coming along, that's for sure. You two worked that big case on Tangier Island, the crazy scientist who tried to poison everyone with free samples they got in the mail."

"I remember your mother very well." The last thing I'm interested in at the moment is strolling down her morbid memory lane.

"I'm Blaise, but if you call me that nobody will know who you're talking about," she says, and I'm guessing she's Lucy's age, short and strongly built, with spiky hair and plenty of attitude. "Everybody just calls me Fruge."

She goes on to inform me that her mother is retired from the state. She now works in the private industry, and Fruge tells me the name of the biotech company in Richmond.

"It's perfect because she can do a lot of the work in her lab at home." She continues filling me in about someone I've had my share of problems with in the past. "Which gives her more time for her horses, all her crazy hobbies. I don't know if you heard that she moved to an old farm in Goochland County."

"Sounds like a good place to be during a pandemic. Please give her my best," I reply from a sticky mat, looking around, getting my bearings.

"Funny what happens in life." Fruge's dark eyes are riveted to me. "Mom worked with you when you were the brand-new chief. Now here you are back in Virginia and starting all over again, only with me this time. Talk about going full circle."

"The media knows that the missing person is Gwen Hainey." I stay focused on the grim business before us. "Dana Diletti just announced it on the air."

"I was waiting for that. I'm willing to bet she got it from the manager. The guy who unlocked the door for me is a real chatterbox and way too curious," she says as if she's not. "First name is Cliff, last name Sallow. I had to tell him to stay clear of this place."

"When he unlocked the door for you, did he come inside?" I'm making notes.

"He wanted to badly enough, had his phone out ready to take pictures if you can believe that. No way I was letting him," she says. "He drives a red Prius, so be on high alert if you see it because he wants to know what's going on some-thing awful. And I can sure as heck see why."

What's happened on Cliff Sallow's watch won't be good for his career, Fruge predicts. He could end up fired.

"When's the last time he saw Gwen or heard from her? Did he say?" I ask from my sticky mat.

"The day after Thanksgiving. He told me he saw her jogging early Friday morning, that she usually was out the door at sunrise. Apparently, she was a big runner, and would pick up the Mount Vernon Trail and go for miles."

"How might he have known her running habits?"

"I guess she must have mentioned it to him. And he usually knew when she was back because she'd enter her code at the gate." Fruge says the same thing Marino's upset neighbor did. "The media must have gotten their information from him. How else could it have happened when her name isn't connected to this property?"

Apparently, if you look up Gwen's townhome, it's in the name of the owner who lives in New York, Fruge says.

On another sticky mat is the field case of PPE. Squatting by it, she begins picking out what she decides I need, looking me up and down, checking on sizes.

"What about the cameras at the security gate?" I ask. "I'm wondering what they might have picked up the Friday afternoon or evening of the murder."

"You and me both. I'm dying to know," she says.

Handing me size small Tyvek coveralls and other protective gear, she tells me to suit up as if she's in charge.

"To give you a quick road map, there's very little in the way of furniture and stuff as you're probably already noticing," she says. "Nothing on the second floor at all. You can go up there if you want but it's just a big empty bonus room with piles of construction crap covered by plastic tarps. The door is shut, the heat turned down low."

She explains that Cliff Sallow, the manager, said the unit was being renovated when Gwen asked about a short-term rental. She was in a desperate hurry, her needs simple. She wanted a place that was private and safe. She wanted it instantly. The rental couldn't be in her name, and no one else was allowed access under any circumstances unless it was a life-and-death emergency. Gwen took the townhome as is, and Fruge is an impressive information gatherer.

"I guess she must make a really good living because she didn't seem concerned about money," she says. "Or the fact there's almost nothing inside, not even a bed. She has one of those inflatable ones. You'll see it when you get there."

"How much is her rent?" I pull on a pair of nitrile exam gloves.

"I should have asked that," Fruge says with a flash of impatience. "But I'll find out."

"And did she give a reason for the urgency beyond the new job she was starting?"

"Not that I was told," she replies as the front door opens wide, wind and rain gusting in.

CHAPTER 6

I'M GLAD YOU MADE it," August Ryan says to me, and he's short and slight, with braces on his teeth, his hair curly and gray.

He doesn't come across as intimidating in the least, and that works well for him, I have no doubt. People tend to underestimate him, to let their guards down, assuming he's sensitive, even gentle. It's rather much the antithesis of how they react when Marino shows up.

"Just so you're aware, Doctor Scarpetta, nobody's been in here besides Fruge, me, and the crime scene guys who did the walk-through," August says.

He steps on a sticky mat, suited up in white Tyvek from head to toe. I figure this is as good a time as any to mention my new forensic operations specialist.

"Pete Marino is with me and waiting in the truck," I let them know, as if it's a given. "He's former Richmond P.D., and also worked with numerous other law enforcement agencies and my various offices over the years. Now he's a private consultant who's assisting my office, and I've asked him to take a look."

"The fewer people in here the better," August says, and what he really means is, hell no, he doesn't want Marino around.

"He lives two doors down and has been inside this townhome before." I cover my phone with a protective film. "I'll let him elaborate on what he knows about problems Gwen Hainey allegedly was having with a former boyfriend before she moved here from Boston last month."

"Well, that sounds important," August replies, his interest kicking up.

"What kind of problems?" Fruge wants to know. "Because an estranged boyfriend might make sense. Obviously, she turned off the alarm and opened the door to whoever it was. It was locked when I got here, the alarm off. Everything was locked except for the door near the kitchen that leads into the garage."

"I'm waiting for a callback from the alarm company," August adds. "To get the history, see when she turned it on and off last."

"Marino has information I think you'll find helpful, and he can fill you in himself." I won't take no for an answer.

"If that's what you want, Chief." August isn't happy about it. "We've set up a pup tent, and he can suit up like the rest of us. But I want you to walk through first, see what you notice."

"I gotta call the manager back and find out how much she was paying in rent." Fruge steps outside, shutting the door behind her.

"What about the security gate's video recordings?" I ask August.

"That's a good question." He gets quieter, more serious.

"I assume you've reviewed them?"

"We got an unusual situation here," he says. "There's an hour of Friday night's video that has no images, only audio. In other words, the cameras were covered for an interval."

The microphones picked up the sound although it's muted, and August describes seeing something being slipped over one camera, then the other.

"As the video is blacked out, you can hear a quiet crinkly noise, maybe some type of plastic bag," he explains.

This occurred at 5:13 P.M. Two minutes later the code 1988 was entered to open the entrance gate. The year Gwen Hainey was born, and a stupid code for her to pick, August says.

"I've got to admit I'm wondering if it's possible she orchestrated all this herself." He grabs a pair of gloves out of a box as we continue suiting up inside the townhome's entryway.

"Gwen covered the cameras, then open and shut the gates? How would that make any sense?" White Tyvek makes a rustling sound as I pull the hooded jumpsuit over my boots and clothing.

"It wouldn't unless she's staged something elaborate because she wanted to disappear," he suggests. "And she's trying to make it look like something happened to her."

"There's nothing staged about the dead woman inside my cooler," I remind him.

"If it's her."

"It's certainly looking like it so far. Did the cameras continue recording audio after they were covered?"

"Yes. But all you hear is the gates opening, and this creepy music, like someone was playing it inside the car really loud."

"But you don't hear the sound of an engine?" I double up on face masks, and a plastic shield goes over them, the visor flipped up for now. "Because that's rather odd."

"Well, the mics were covered, and maybe the engine's a quiet one," he says as I wonder what kind of car Gwen's ex, Jinx Slater, drives. "Maybe the labs will pick up something when the recordings are enhanced."

"The loud music you mentioned. Did you recognize it?" I ask.

Already I'm starting to sweat in my protective clothing as we stand on our sticky mats.

"I don't think so, you hear it for only a few seconds," August says. "But it sounded like something out of an old Boris Karloff movie. Then the same thing at six-oh-seven P.M., the exit gate opens, the spooky music playing loud. Four minutes after that, the crackly sound again when the cameras are uncovered. I'll e-mail the clip and you'll see what I mean."

During the hour the cameras were covered, August says he didn't hear anyone coming in or out of Colonial Landing. The gates weren't opened or closed again, no other codes entered, and I'm not surprised. The weather was bad that night, and a lot of people were out of town. Others were staying home, not working the day after Thanksgiving.

"We don't know if the person might have been on foot.

Maybe his car was parked somewhere else," August says as Gwen's front door opens, wind gusting into the entryway. "And he walked through the gates playing the spooky music on his phone."

"Possibly," I reply as Fruge steps inside. "But he had to have a vehicle to transport the body out of here, and to the railroad tracks on Daingerfield Island."

"I just got off the phone with the manager." Fruge starts collecting PPE, getting ready to suit up. "The rent is seven grand monthly, and she paid three months up front."

"She paid twenty-one thousand dollars?" August asks. "Holy smoke."

"CASH, AS IN COLD and hard. As in the owner of this place was happy to take it under the table and maybe not declare it on his income tax." Fruge pulls on coveralls.

She tells August what she told me, that the townhome is off the market for renovation, and Gwen apparently didn't mind what she paid or what shape the place was in as long as she could get in right away.

"She wanted to be back here behind a big wall with a gate," Fruge adds. "And that would fit with her being afraid."

"Certainly, it fits with someone who's very private," I reply, and I ask about the kettlebell. "Was it just like this when you first walked in?"

Without touching it, I look closely at the ten-pound weight near the door on an area of flooring not covered by mats. I don't see any blood but I also wouldn't expect it on whatever Gwen was struck with because she was hit only once. The blow was severe enough to punch out bone, causing subarachnoid hemorrhaging and traumatic brain injury.

Assuming the kettlebell was the weapon, then it likely wouldn't have gotten bloody unless she was struck again after her scalp was bleeding. I notice there's a shallow dent on the floor that may have been caused by the weight falling or being dropped, and I suspect Gwen was knocked unconscious as she attempted to escape out the front door.

When the crime scene unit is let loose in here, they'll 3-D scan the scene, placing evidence flags, taking more photographs, packaging everything for the labs. But at this point, nothing should have been disturbed in any form or fashion. What I'm seeing should be exactly as it was left, and I question Fruge about it.

"Like I've been telling August, I haven't touched anything except for digging inside her backpack on the kitchen table."

She pulls on a pair of gloves, letting me know she's done everything by the book.

"The matching kettlebell's inside the sunporch off the living room, and you have to wonder why this one's here," she's saying. "Unless maybe he was chasing her through the house, and whacked her good. Maybe as she was trying to get out the door?"

That's a lot of *maybes,* and what I need is to be alone with my own thoughts and observations. I suggest to August that he find Marino. He should be sitting in his pickup truck waiting for my call. The two of them can confer, giving me a chance to make a high recon.

I want to observe and digest without prompting from anyone, and that won't be easy with Fruge shadowing me. She watches in the doorway as I walk into the guest bedroom off the foyer directly to my left. There's no furniture or overhead lighting, and I turn on my small flashlight, shining it around.

Picture hooks are still in the walls from artwork taken down. Wires dangle from the ceiling where light fixtures or fans once hung, and exposed jack wall plates and cable connectors are from missing phones and a television. I paint my light over the bare maple floor, the pale-yellow-painted walls.

The gold damask drapes are drawn, and I see nothing that might make me think a struggle went on. My booties make a slippery sound as I return to the sticky mats, making sure I don't track anything from one room to the next. I head to the master suite on the other side of the entryway, making swishing sounds as I walk.

"I didn't see anything in there, either," Fruge informs me as she tags along. "The crime scene guys will do their thing once they're let loose in here, and they'll leave no stone unturned. But it appears to me the confrontation, the struggle went on between here and the sunporch. And then most importantly there's the blood inside the garage."

"I'll save that for last," I let her know as I walk into another dark bedroom.

There's no overhead lighting in here either, just a lamp that's not turned on. My flashlight finds more of the same bare flooring, pale-yellow-painted walls, exposed picture hooks and wall plates. The inflatable mattress Fruge mentioned could use some air, its sheets and two pillows slightly askew. I don't see a blanket or cover anywhere.

A TV has been set up on a card table, and there's a single folding chair with a warm-up suit draped over it, a pair of running shoes nearby. Opening the walk-in closet, I continue finding no sign that Gwen ever really moved into this place. It's as if she fled from Boston with little more than the clothes on her back.

"Nothing's making a lot of sense," Fruge says as I direct my light at two pairs of running shoes still in their boxes and ankle-high boots neatly lined up on the floor. "Are we sure she was living here all the time? It sure doesn't look like she planned to stay here long. Any possibility most of her stuff is somewhere else?"

"Your guess is as good as mine." I illuminate two jackets and four blouses on hangers.

The rest of Gwen's belongings are in four plastic storage containers despite plenty of built-ins for her few pairs of running tights, her T-shirts, hoodies, socks and undergarments. What I'm seeing isn't consistent with a short-term rental. It's more in keeping with someone on the lam who wanted to hide while staying light on her feet.

Had she decided to beat a hasty retreat, she could have packed up in no time and been gone. Or it's possible she wasn't staying here much, was back and forth to some unknown location. Living a secret life, in other words, and that's what I'm picking up about the missing biomedical engineer. She had something to hide.

Ducking into the bathroom next, I shine my light around. Confronted by my own reflection in the mirror over the sink, I take off my fogged-up face shield because wearing it isn't manageable. I feel overheated and clammy, and the reflection staring back at me looks like holy hell, my blue eyes slightly bloodshot above my double masks.

I open the medicine cabinet, empty except for a box of tampons, and I shut the mirrored door. The granite countertop around the sink is clean, nothing on it but a toothbrush, toothpaste, dental floss, facial soap, a hairbrush, a drinking glass. Some of it will be a good source of DNA. But the absence of other personal effects including cosmetics and jewelry is perplexing and disturbing.

"Something's very wrong with this picture." August's voice sounds behind me.

It's as if he's reading my mind, standing outside the bathroom doorway with Fruge. He's shining his light around, his eyes scanning behind clear plastic that's fogging up.

"Where's everything else?" he asks. "I've seen more crap than this in a flophouse hotel room that someone's hired by the hour."

"I agree it's peculiar." I hand him my face shield because I simply can't wear it.

"I'm having the same problem," he agrees, taking off his.

I open the shower door, the powerful beam of my tactical light flaring off the glass. Inside are shampoo, conditioner, a body cleanser, a razor, and that's it.

Next, I check the cabinet under the sink, finding rolls of toilet paper and a toilet brush. The white towels on the racks look used, and I suggest those should go to the lab on the off chance a killer cleaned up in here, although I see no sign of it.

Sweat is running coolly down my back and chest as I investigate the wastepaper basket that doesn't appear to have been emptied in a while. It's filled with multiple empty toilet paper rolls and wadded tissues, and on top of them is some type of wrapper.

"Strange." I shine my light on the cardboard backing and plastic. "From an ink pen."

But not a normal one. The writing on the packaging is in English and Japanese, the pen actually a fabric marker that uses purple water-soluble ink.

"I don't know if this is important but it might be," I explain to August and Fruge. "Pens with water-soluble ink aren't something your average person has unless they're writing on a whiteboard or doing magic tricks."

"Maybe it was something she uses at work," he suggests.

"Like on a whiteboard in a lab," Fruge adds.

"I rather much doubt it," I reply. "Also, there's no cover on the bed, and maybe there wasn't one. But I would expect a blanket, a duvet or something, and we'll want the linens checked for DNA in addition to fibers and other trace evidence."

CHAPTER 7

STEPPING OUT OF THE bathroom, I put on a new outer pair of gloves, stuffing the used ones in a pocket of my coveralls.

"If she were attacked, the assailant may have needed something to wrap her in after knocking her unconscious," I suggest.

I remind August that I collected a lot of synthetic fibers from the murder victim in my cooler. The source is something her body was in contact with, something like a blanket.

"What about her clothing?" Fruge asks. "Whatever she was wearing when she was attacked, where is it? I've not seen anything in the house that makes me think it might be what she had on. Nothing on the floor, nothing torn or bloody."

"If Gwen is the victim from Friday night, I have a feeling the killer stripped the body, did whatever else he was going to do once he got her out of here," August weighs in.

"Got her out of here how?" I bring them around to the question of the killer's mode of transportation.

"It was raining Friday night, and it appears to me that someone drove a vehicle in and out of the garage." Fruge adds a new detail. "You can see the dried tire tracks, and that's probably important since she doesn't have a car."

"Depends on how long the tire tracks have been there," August replies. "For all we know it's since before she moved in. As for the blood? We don't know how long that's been there, either."

"What I'm thinking is, after he knocked her unconscious, he might have driven his car inside and shut the door," Fruge continues, painting a scenario that may very well be what occurred. "Then he has time and privacy to get her body into the trunk or wherever he put it."

"I'll look at the garage last." I don't want to hear any further scripting or conjecturing. "It would be helpful if you could convince Dana Diletti to stop saying Gwen Hainey's name over the air." I direct this at August. "Or at least remind the public the identity hasn't been verified."

"She doesn't care what we say or how much damage she does," he replies as the front door opens again.

Marino appears swathed in white like an abominable snowman.

"What the hell?" he complains behind his fogged-up plastic face shield. "How am I supposed to see anything? Where are the defog wipes?"

"That we don't have." Fruge closes the door.

He takes off his disposable face shield, all of them deposited in the red biohazard trash bag, followed by our soiled gloves.

"That or baby shampoo like you use on dive masks," he says. "You should always have it on hand."

"Hey, PPE's not my department," Fruge replies. "You can complain to the crime scene guys."

"You good with your overview?" Marino says to August, walking back and forth across the mats in his Tyvek booties. "You gotten a bird's-eye view, taken photographs and all the rest?"

Otherwise, it really would be a bad idea for either one of us to be here right now.

"We're good. Maybe take a look in the master bedroom for me," August replies, and they seem to be getting along fine. "See if anything looks different from what you remember when you were here with Gwen last month."

Marino leaves us, and Fruge resumes her post by the door as August and I head to the living area. The furniture is disarrayed, the brown leather sofa and reclaimed-barn-door coffee table likely belonging to the owner. They're out of place as if someone bumped into them hard, and I envision the angry red bruises on the murdered woman's hips and lower legs.

On the floor is a plastic spoon and a broken Thor Laboratories pottery mug. Pieces of it are in a coagulated puddle of chicken noodle soup that's consistent with the murder victim's stomach contents. I suspect she'd begun eating when she was violently interrupted, and the stress of the attack would have shut down her digestion.

Set up in front of a shade-covered window overlooking the river is another card table, this one Gwen's workstation. On it are two laptop computers, a router and backup drive, the folding chair in front of them on its side. But what grabs my attention are the purple fabric markers, the water-soluble pads of white notepaper.

"I can't come up with a logical reason for needing water-soluble ink and paper," I say to August and Fruge. "Unless you're playing party tricks or games with disappearing writing. Or maybe quilting or embroidering patterns on a backing that vanishes in the wash after you're finished."

I see no evidence that Gwen was into arts and crafts, I add. It's crossing my mind she might have been passing along information that can be destroyed completely and without a trace. In other words, spying.

"Everything about this just gets crazier," Fruge replies. "So, you could flush a note down the toilet and bye-bye it's gone forever?"

"Easier than that, you could drop it in a glass of water and drink it," I reply as Marino emerges from the master bedroom.

"What gets crazier?" he says. "What now?"

"How did things look in there?" August answers him with a question.

"The same as when I was here last month. She definitely had a blanket on the bed. A kid's blanket with a Star Wars theme. Darth Vader and a flametrooper."

"Do you recall the colors?" I envision the magnified images of multicolored fibers I recovered from the body.

"Black and orange. And white. Also, some yellow and red," Marino says.

"Possibly consistent with the fibers I collected," I reply. "Under the microscope, you can see red, yellow, black and orange pigments on cross section, a polyester blend."

Obviously, we're not in possession of whatever she might have been wrapped in, I explain. I wish we were but had it been on the bed, there should be fibers transferred to the linens.

"We'll see if they match the ones I collected from the body," I add.

"HITTING HER IN THE head with something at the scene?" August tries to work out what might have gone on. "Using some type of cover he took off her bed if that's what he did? Doesn't sound like he showed up with a murder kit."

"Most violent psychopaths don't show up with freakin' murder kits." Marino isn't very diplomatic about it. "I've seen victims stabbed with screwdrivers, scissors, beaten to death with a clothes iron, a teapot, a laptop computer, a stick or a rock. Whatever's in reach. They show up with their bare hands and sicko fantasies. It's part of the thrill."

"When you did your walk-through with Gwen last month," I say to him, "did she mention anything about paper and ink that can be dissolved in water like a magic trick? Did you notice anything like that anywhere inside the townhome when you did your security check?"

I can tell by the blank look on Marino's face that he has no idea what I'm talking about. I show him the fabric markers, the pads of white notepaper on the card table.

"Nope, there was nothing like that here when I walked through." He leaves out that Lucy was with him. "Nothing I saw, anyway."

"I'll bet Gwen Hainey didn't say a word, making sure certain items were tucked out of sight," Fruge replies, and I suspect she's right.

"I'm glad you noticed because I'm not sure I would have," August says to me, going out of his way to ignore Fruge. "I've never heard of dissolving paper."

"I'm worried we may be dealing with more than one crime." I state the obvious. "Espionage could be a possible explanation for what we're discovering so far. Industrial spying if nothing else. But it could be much more dangerous than that since the companies she's been involved with do a lot of highly sensitive work for various governments including ours."

"That's what I'm thinking," Marino agrees. "It might be the real explanation for her sudden change of jobs and living like a fugitive. And believe me, if I'd known any of this when I met her, my antenna would have gone up, all right."

August is looking at the laptops, his gloved fingers tapping keys.

"Password protected, of course," he says, and I leave them so I can finish my walk-through.

Fruge bird-dogs me as I reach a door that opens onto the patio. It's off the dining area, another barren space with more empty picture hooks and wires dangling from an electrical box in the ceiling where a light fixture once hung.

"This door is locked, and was when I got here," she says. "I walked around outside earlier and didn't notice anything unusual. Just some furniture, a barbecue, the bird feeders. And the crime scene guys looked around, too."

"But this is another possible egress, another way to access the house," I reply. "There's the front door. The back door off the sunporch. And this one, each with an alarm keypad."

"Also, the garage. Except it would be trickier leaving that way," Fruge says. "You can't close the garage door from the outside. Not unless you have a remote."

"Have you seen one anywhere?"

"Actually, now that you mention it, I haven't." Surprise glints in her eyes, followed by a spark of irritation. "*That's two strikes, Fruge,*" she chastises herself, her voice dropping an octave. "*First you forget to ask about the rent. Then you don't notice there's no garage opener.* But Gwen doesn't have a car." Talking to me again, her voice back to normal. "Not even a bicycle that I've seen."

Outside the kitchen is a granite countertop, and on it a small unopened FedEx package with the return address of an electronics company. The receipt shows the delivery was this past Friday morning.

"I find it interesting she didn't get around to opening whatever she'd ordered," I say to Fruge as I walk into the kitchen.

"Sometimes I leave mail and stuff lying around unopened for days," she feels compelled to share.

On the windowsill over the empty sink is a terra-cotta bonsai pot of parched cacti, zebra plants, aloe variegata, and African violets. The dish garden is the very sort of thoughtful gift Dorothy would present to a stranger she's descended upon with friendly suggestions in addition to helpful guidance and histories about the area.

The succulents are dried up, the violets a withered blackish-purple. They've not been watered in recent memory, maybe ever, and how disgraceful. Like the absence of so much as a single holiday candle. Like everything I'm seeing.

"Was the kitchen light on when you got here?" I ask. "In fact, were any lights on?"

"Yes, the ones that are now. Here, the living room, master bedroom, and entryway. And the garage, everything is exactly like it was when the manager let me in. I didn't touch a thing except for going through the knapsack on the table." She heads that way to show me.

"I'll get there eventually. One thing at a time," I let her know, because I won't be hurried or directed.

I imagine Dorothy appearing at Gwen's door, welcoming her to the neighborhood with a dish garden. Likely it was my sister who set it on the windowsill with its northern exposure, and it catches my attention that the faux wooden blinds are open. The kitchen lights shine through the glass, dimly illuminating the patio.

I can see the cover on the grill twitching in the wind, the empty bird feeders and suet basket hanging from wrought-iron shepherd hooks, the table and chairs. If a stalker, a killer had gotten into the patio area when she was fixing soup with the blinds open, she would have been visible through the window over the sink.

"Especially after dark." I point this out to Fruge. "I'm curious why the blinds are open, and find it odd. The drapes are drawn everywhere else I've looked so far. Yet she was inside the kitchen late afternoon, early evening, and didn't close the blinds?"

"Why are you making a big deal out of a dead plant?" She watches curiously as I use my phone to take pictures of the dish garden. "What's so important about it?"

"I'm making sure we have a record of what it looked like before it was moved." I pick it up. "And tampered with." I dribble in tap water from the sink.

About a fourth of a cup should be enough, and I set the ceramic pot in the dish rack to drain, feeling increasingly uncharitable about the person to blame.

"How hard is it to take care of something that needs minimal sunlight and watering only once a week?" I can't help but remark.

"By all appearances, Gwen Hainey didn't seem to have much respect for anything," Fruge agrees. "Probably selfish as heck, like a lot of these people who grew up on social media."

"Except from what I've been told she has no presence on it," I reply. "It would seem she was skilled at staying off the radar."

My next stop is the kitchen table, what's actually a butcher block that no doubt belongs to the house. On top of it is a green leather knapsack, a wallet. Gwen's driver's license is near a set of keys simply labeled *#14,* an abbreviation for the address of the rented townhome.

"When I first got here there was nothing else on the table except the knapsack I went through," Fruge says. "I was look-ing for a picture ID and for her phone, which still hasn't turned up. I don't think it's here anywhere, and I'm thinking the killer took it."

The wallet and knapsack are an expensive designer brand. There's a large amount of cash inside, and I run my thumb through the crisp hundred-dollar bills. What must be thou-sands of dollars, and it's consistent with the story of Gwen's paying three months' rent in cash.

"Where's she getting all her money?" Fruge wants to know. "I didn't count what's in there when I looked for her license but obviously it's a lot. Who walks around with that much cash? What does she make as a scientist? Because my mom's sure not gotten rich from being one."

"We don't know what Gwen was earning," I reply. "I doubt it's a fortune, and paying cash for most things certainly raises questions."

"Well, it looks like she was getting mail-order food, and you can't pay cash when you're ordering off the Internet."

"She doesn't have much in the way of credit cards." I return the wallet to the table. "Amex, a debit card, assuming noth-ing's missing. She might have resorted to an online payment service if the point was to stay below the radar. Like PayPal, Google Pay, there's a number of them."

"It's obvious that she's involved in some sort of dirty business. Maybe spying like you said."

"What's apparent is robbery wasn't a motive for whoever targeted her," I reply. "Her money, her laptops weren't taken. It would seem they were of no interest."

CHAPTER 8

HER DRIVER'S LICENSE WAS renewed four years ago, apparently while she was living in Boston, based on the address. In the photo, she's heavier, her short hair dyed platinum blond, exactly as August described when he called me earlier.

At a glance she's not recognizable as the murdered woman. Although on closer inspection there are similarities in bone structure, the shapes of the ears, the slope of the nose. Their heights aren't the same, the Department of Motor Vehicles listing Gwen Hainey as five-foot-five.

I happen to know from measuring the body that she was an inch shorter than that, assuming the victim in my cooler is who I believe she is. The inconsistencies don't necessarily mean much. I'm used to lies about personal details such as dental work, plastic surgery, health habits, various implants, and all sorts of secret vices.

The truth comes out if your last visit to the doctor is with a medical examiner, and I ask Fruge if it's all right to check what's inside the kitchen cupboards.

"Help yourself."

Shelves are bare except for two Thor Laboratory coffee mugs like the broken one in the living room, and a box of surgical masks. Unopened, they're the same brand we use at home, and Dorothy enters my thoughts again. Since the pandemic, she hands out masks to anybody who thinks it's fine not to wear one under any circumstances.

I check the pantry next, and there are plenty of paper plates, napkins, aluminum foil, paper towels, baggies, plastic silverware. Gwen was well stocked with cans of soup, energy bars, and there are bottles of water in the refrigerator, and protein smoothies. Also, ketchup, mustard, and what looks like chicken noodle soup in a lid-covered pot.

Inside the dishwasher, I find the spoon used to stir it, and she must have poured what she wanted into the mug now shattered inside the living room. The rest of the soup she placed inside the refrigerator, not bothering to transfer it into a proper container.

Sliding the trash out from under the sink, I find it full of paper napkins and plates, soup cans, prepared food wrappers. There are plastic water and protein smoothie bottles that should be recycled, I add to the list of infractions.

"The garbage hasn't been emptied in several days at least." I'm reminded of the wastepaper basket spilling over in the master bathroom. "The freezer is full of prepared foods one can order off the Internet. Fried chicken tenders, pizza, burgers."

"Sounds like she should have been getting a fair number of packages on a regular basis," Fruge decides. "In other words, she's been living the way a lot of people are ever since the start of the pandemic. I still avoid going to the store, and get a lot of stuff shipped to me."

"I don't think the way she's been living is because of the pandemic," I reply. "And I assume whatever she's been ordering has been delivered directly to the manager's office."

"He sure has his nose in everything around here. I'd be looking into him pretty carefully if it was up to me," Fruge says. "Maybe it's just a coincidence but he's been in Old Town not even a year. And not long after he moved into the management office, that woman jogger turned up dead on Daingerfield Island."

"I don't know what case you're talking about," I reply with dismay. "The first I've heard of another death on Daingerfield Island."

What else has my predecessor screwed up? What else am I about to find out?

"The night of last April tenth. Cammie Ramada," Fruge informs me.

For some reason, the manner of death was ruled accidental, she says. How did that supposedly happen? The victim had some kind of health problem and took a stumble while running along the Mount Vernon Trail?

"Which isn't all that close to the water, by the way," she continues filling me in. "Yet somehow, she ends up on the shore with her face in the river?"

"Was there any evidence of violence?" I ask.

"One of her running shoes was maybe twenty feet from the body. And she looked pretty banged up. But your office decided it was an accident without a doubt, and without testing evidence, I might add."

"It wasn't my office then." I'm quick to remind her I hadn't moved here yet. "Obviously, you were at the scene."

"I was on evening shift, and heard the call around nine-fifteen P.M. A not-so-nice night to be out for a jog, it was chilly, raining on and off," Fruge recalls, and it's uncanny how she gets around. "To be honest, it creeped me out when I pulled up before other cops got there."

It was very dark, and a train was going by at the back of the park, the couple who found the body totally freaked out, she describes. Approximately half an hour after she arrived, U.S. Park Police Investigator August Ryan showed up.

"He didn't mention the case when I was with him Friday night," I reply. "That surprises me a little."

"Not me. Nobody cared," Fruge says. "And the less attention drawn to the situation, the better. It was the beginning of tourist season, need I say more?"

"I hope that's not what was going on."

"Alexandria has almost a thousand acres of public parks. Tourism's big here. And this close to D.C.? Let's just put it this way. About the same time the park police's ace investigator August Ryan got there, so did Doctor Reddy," she adds to my surprise and growing unsettledness.

For my predecessor to show up is completely out of character, and I keep thinking about my earlier phone call with August. I recall the hours we were together Friday night, and it seems there's important information he's not sharing.

"Had you ever known Elvin Reddy to show up at a scene before?" I ask.

"Are you kidding? Not even once," Fruge says as I detect the papery sound of approaching Tyvek. "The unspoken rule has always been that you don't contact him directly, and he's not to be bothered after hours. Rumor has it that he likes his martinis."

"I'm going to be a while, Doc." Marino walks into the kitchen, his face flushed and sweaty. "Sorry about that but I doubt you'll want to hang around."

"I'm almost finished up." I remind him I need my belongings out of his truck.

DIGGING IN A POCKET of his coveralls, Marino tosses his key to Fruge.

"Don't forget to give it back to me before you leave," he says sternly to her, and never mind how I might get home.

My car is at the office. I didn't bank on Marino's uninvited ride being one-way but he and August are going to be a while turning the place inside out. That's what my new forensic operations specialist says, and it would seem he and the Feds are hitting it off.

"I may have to call someone for a ride," I let Fruge know as Marino returns to the work area in the living room where August is talking on his phone.

"My car's out front," she says as we resume my tour. "I've got you covered."

Beyond the kitchen is the laundry room, the light on. I look inside the washer and dryer, both of them empty, and in a basket are running socks and tights that I assume are dirty. Next is the door leading into the empty garage, and I'm mindful of the tire tracks and dried blackish drops of what looks like blood some ten feet from the doorway.

I know by the roundish shape of the drops that they fell almost perpendicular to the ground, and I envision the lacerations to the back of the murdered woman's head.

"The kettlebell or whatever she was hit with split her scalp," I say to Fruge, imagining the victim wrapped up in a blanket and carried into the garage. "She would have bled heavily assuming she was still alive at the time, that she still had a blood pressure, in other words."

"The killer must be pretty strong if he carried her."

"So far, I'm not seeing any sign that she was dragged," I reply.

"The blood is where the trunk might be if the vehicle was backed in."

"And this is what it was like when you first got here?" I ask. "The light was on?"

"It was."

"And the door you just opened was shut and locked?"

"It was shut but unlocked."

"The garage door was down?" Using my phone, I take pictures of the tire tracks, the bloodlike drops in a gory blackish-red constellation on the concrete.

"Yes, and I don't know how he did that from here unless he had a garage opener," she says. "You can't push the button on the wall and run through while it's shutting. The safety mechanism won't allow that."

"What would you have done?" I always like to ask what others might come up with to solve a problem.

No need to be criminal, just human. Because at the end of the day, our nature is what it is, and we don't have to be a monster to imagine one.

"I would have put the body in the trunk, and driven the car out," Fruge says as we stand inside the lighted garage, looking around.

"Gwen doesn't have a car. And if her killer stalked her, he would have known that."

"If it was me, I'd have some type of vehicle parked off the property but close by." Fruge plays it out.

She'd tuck it inside the garage, closing the door behind her. After she loaded the body inside the trunk, she'd drive out.

"Then I'd shut the garage door from inside," she says. "And I'd exit through the house."

"How would you do that?"

"Probably through the same door I'd used earlier when I first got there," she says.

I strongly suspect it was the one off the dining room that leads to the patio, I tell her. It might explain why the blinds over the sink were open while the kitchen light was on after dark.

"She might have looked out to see who was on her patio, possibly knocking on the door," I add as we return to the kitchen.

"And it seems she let the person in. What does that tell you?"

"That she wasn't afraid at first," I reply. "Possibly, they were familiar with each other."

We walk back through the living room, and there's no sign of Marino, August or anyone else. Taking off our PPE, we leave the townhome, walking past the pup tent and police cars. The storm has retreated, soon to be followed by another one, and wet dead leaves litter pavement and bricks like soggy bits of cardboard.

"I'm always running out of everything important." Fruge insists on carrying my scene case, deciding she should keep something similar in her police car. "I'm constantly going through stuff like Purell, Lysol. Not to mention Narcan."

Referring to the nasal spray naloxone hydrochloride that reverses the effects of opioids, she says that the last drug overdose she worked was in an alleyway this past Friday. She went through the Narcan she had in the trunk.

"Both victims had gotten hooked on pain meds, and now are hard-core heroin addicts who've had to be revived several times before," she explains. "Whatever they got hold of was really bad stuff. You've got to be desperate to trust what you buy off the street, and they'll O.D. again if something else doesn't get them first."

"I'm happy to share," I reply.

I let her know that I insist my medical examiners and investigators are well stocked in Narcan, also EpiPens. You never know when you might be able to save someone, including saving yourself.

"Nice ride." Reaching Marino's stealthy Raptor truck, Fruge gives it a once-over. "Your sister must do pretty well with her books. It must be kind of weird though, him being married to her."

I wonder what else she knows about my life as we walk off in the drizzly fog. Crime scene investigators suited up in protective garb are carrying equipment and forensic supplies through the front door, and another television news truck is pulling up. At least Dana Diletti and her crew have left, and uniformed officers are guarding the perimeter.

Marino and August are ghostly figures in white Tyvek probing the patio with flashlights. Fruge walks swiftly toward them, returning Marino's key while neighbors walk their dogs around the cul-de-sac, staring at what's going on. I text Benton that I'm headed home, informing him that an officer is driving me.

Getting out the Scotch, he answers.

I text for him to make it a double as I watch Marino disappear with August around back toward the wrought-iron fencing and boat slips. Fruge trots back to me, ready to take me home.

"What would be most helpful is if you drop me at my office," I suggest as she unlocks her Ford Explorer Interceptor parked at the curb. "That's where my car is. There shouldn't be much traffic at this hour, and I'd very much appreciate it."

"No can do, Chief." She opens a back door of the SUV. "My orders are to take you directly home, to get you there safe and sound," she adds to the thudding of our doors shutting, and I don't ask whose orders.

I have no doubt they're Marino's, and once again I've been hijacked, left horseless, and I ponder how I'll get to work tomorrow. If I'm called to another scene after hours, it could present a problem. Fruge sets my Pelican case on the seat, and plastic clasps snap loudly as I open it.

"This should tide you over." Finding four doses of Narcan inside, I hand them to her.

"Thanks, but I don't want to take all you've got."

"I have more where these came from," I assure her.

She slides behind the wheel, her duty belt creaking, the keys on it jingling. Setting her portable radio on the charger, she arranges herself and all her bulky ballistic gear, a pistol on one hip, a stun gun on the other.

"I don't miss much around here. Not just because it's my job, but it's my personal responsibility to protect Old Town's assets," she finds it necessary to let me know. "Politicians, other important people like you and yours have a huge impact on what happens in the world."

CHAPTER 9

CRANKING THE ENGINE, SHE doesn't bother with her seatbelt, reminding me of Marino.

He incorrectly assumes his chances of survival are better when unrestrained. God forbid he has to bail in a hurry before getting shot, blown up, set on fire, dragged out and beaten by violent mobs.

"I make it my business to notice most of what goes on when I'm out on patrol." Fruge slows to a stop at Colonial Landing's exit gate. "Old Town is Mayberry, and it's not hard to know which residents are home, getting along, fighting, you name it."

She waits until the gate slides open before bringing up my niece, asking what it's like having her on the property.

"I heard what happened." Fruge fills the silence when I don't answer. "It must be really hard for her. I can't imagine it. Losing your partner and child at the same time."

"I wasn't aware that you and Lucy are acquainted," I finally reply.

"Only in passing. I've seen Marino and her cruising around on their Harleys now and then. The other week I noticed her coming out of the vet's office with her cat in the carrier."

I wonder how she knew it was a cat as opposed to some other small animal.

"And I'm pretty sure I saw her helicopter flying along the Potomac some months back," she says as I wonder how she knew it was Lucy's. "I've never been in one."

"Were you on duty last Friday night?" I get her off the subject of my life and those in it.

"Sure was. But like I said, I was tied up with those O.D.s where I used up all my Narcan."

"Then you wouldn't have noticed any strange vehicles around here during the interval when Gwen might have been attacked and abducted."

"About the time we're thinking that happened, I was several miles west near a methadone clinic, in the alley where the two victims had been shooting up," Fruge says. "I was there for hours, and that's too bad. Had I been on patrol as usual, maybe I would have seen something."

"I strongly suspect that whoever appeared at Gwen's townhome has spent time in this area. Driving or walking around, finding the best ways in and out, using side streets and alleyways the same way we are." I crack my window to get a little fresh air.

The worst of the weather has moved on, and people are venturing out. I notice a few customers picking up dinner at the Fish Market restaurant where Lucy is a fan of the clam chowder and lobster avocado toast. Bugsy's is up next for the best pizza and wings in town if you ask Dorothy, and several cars are parked in front.

I ask Fruge to tell me something about herself, figuring it will get her off subjects I prefer avoided, and she says she graduated from Virginia Commonwealth University (VCU) fifteen years ago. Since she was a kid, she's wanted to be a prosecutor, her dream to go to law school. But she never got as far as applying.

"I'd hear Mom talking about all these cool court cases she'd testified in," Fruge explains. "But as it's turned out, my being in front of a jury wasn't in the cards."

I sense the disappointment beneath her seeming indifference, her flippant way of expressing herself that can come across as aggressive and too big for her britches. But she's probably just persistent and eager to do well for herself, to be known for more than her very visible and successful mother.

"You'd already left Richmond, and probably didn't hear about my dad falling off a ladder while cleaning the gutters," Fruge says. "I'd just graduated from VCU, and stayed home to help take care of him."

"No, I didn't know about that," I reply. "I'm very sorry."

"Law school wasn't going to happen, and I decided to be a cop. But forget working around Richmond. No way I would, because of Mom."

"You didn't want to be in her jurisdiction much less her shadow," I reply, and I can understand that.

How awkward to testify in the same trial, and I've experienced similar conflicted situations most of my career. Not only with Marino and Benton but finding myself entangled in cases involving an only niece who may as well be my daughter.

"A lot of people in the Richmond area have heard of Tox Doc." Fruge dramatically drops her voice again the way she did earlier. "I mean, you know my mom. Let's be honest, she's never met a camera she doesn't like."

We slowly bump over wet pavers past the backyards of historically registered estates. Fruge has her window down, the hand-controlled spotlight's powerful beam painting over thick shrubbery, wooded lots and dormant gardens. Many properties like the one Benton and I found are older than America, our modest main house and two outbuildings built by a sea captain in 1770.

Fruge carefully probes any place where a killer might have tossed clothing, a blanket, a weapon or other evidence. I explain that I seriously doubt he did that around here. More likely, he got rid of anything incriminating in a less obvious location.

"Perhaps a landfill or dumpster between here and Daingerfield Island," I suggest as we weave through cobblestone alleys and side streets originally meant for horses and carriages.

We're taking a circuitous route like Marino did earlier. It's not possible to travel along the river point to point as the crow flies. There are too many gated apartment complexes and new ones under construction. Also, the public parks, beaches, hotels and boat clubs crowd the waterfront.

"Where do you live?" I can see my house lights and gas lamps glowing through trees. "I hope I've not taken you too far out of your way."

"Off Wilkes Street near Tannery House, not far from here."

"That's very close to where my secretary is."

"I see her out walking her Corgi," Fruge says, and of course Maggie has the same breed as the queen of England.

"If you'll push the intercom button," I suggest as we reach my gated driveway, "someone will let us in."

I'm not giving out the code, not even to the police, and she rolls down her window. A loud tone sounds, then the noise of the gate sliding open on its tracks. As we drive through, it's captured on the many cameras Lucy has installed on the property, and she's probably watching right now. Or maybe Benton is, and it's reassuring that I'm expected, cared for, and missed.

People who matter are waiting for me, and they're glad I'm alive and well, that I'm still around. It's become more of a comfort than I ever imagined, the pandemic giving as much as it's taken depending on one's perspective.

OLD TREES ARE WINTER-BARE, their branches rocking in the blustery night. Wavering gaslight barely pushes back the darkness as we follow the cobblestone driveway past Lucy's detached cottage.

Small but cozy, it's whitewashed brick with a slate roof, the same as the garage and house. When Benton and I found this property, it wasn't with the thought that my niece would be moving in, and the first thing she did was install blackout shades. Any interior lights, televisions or computer displays aren't visible from outside.

I can't tell if she's home right now, and it surprises me that she hasn't stepped outside to greet me. Fruge stops in front of the house, wireless candles glowing in the windows, the boxwoods glittering with white LEDs. The door opens, and Benton appears dressed in a suit and tie, casting a long shadow, his silver hair bright as he walks through the headlights.

"Cool." Fruge can't take her eyes off him. "I mean, he's a genuine legend. That's saying a lot coming from me because I don't like the Feds, especially the FBI."

"He's not been with the FBI for a long time." I open my door.

"But he started out with them, was their superstar profiler, and probably does the same sort of thing for the Secret Service." Fruge continues reciting our history, filling in the blanks as she sees fit.

"I'm Benton Wesley." He introduces himself to her as I climb out with my bulletproof briefcase. "I appreciate you getting her home safely. Thank you."

She introduces herself, making sure he knows she's heard of him, that her mother used to talk about *the psycho whisperer.*

"I don't need to tell you of all people to be careful around here." Fruge leans across the front seat, talking to him through the open passenger door. "Whoever murdered Gwen Hainey knew exactly what he was doing."

Benton grabs my scene case, and to look at him, you wouldn't think he knows anything about it. But I suspect the opposite is true, and I continue wondering where he's been today.

"Come on," he says to me. "Let's get you inside."

Thanking Fruge again, we watch her drive off in a huff. Or perhaps it's just my imagination.

"I think she was hoping you'd invite her in," Benton says as we follow the walkway. "She obviously enjoys your company."

"Well, I don't know what she enjoys but I was beginning to think she might ride around with me all night. Searching roadsides and alleyways with her spotlight, asking a lot of questions about us."

"I had a feeling something like that was going on."

"I think she's lonely, and I'm afraid I wasn't very sociable," I reply, feeling another twinge of guilt. "But my personality is used up for the day."

"Lucky me," he says.

The alarm system chirps as we walk into the house, the antique pumpkin pine floorboards creaking under the entry-way rug. I can hear the TV news in the living room, Christmas music playing though the intercom, and at the moment I could do without both.

"I talked to Marino a little while ago," Benton says. "When he told me who was driving you, I figured she was acting like old home week."

"You remember her mother from our Richmond days."

"Who could forget Tox Doc?" He's not a fan.

"Let's leave my scene case by the door, please." I take off my coat, feeling wilted. "I want to make sure I don't forget it in the morning, ending up with two at home and none at the office. And I need to replace the Narcan I took out of it."

"I'm glad to see you." He kisses me. "We've got a lot to talk about."

I can see the preoccupations in his hazel eyes as he sets the big Pelican case in the corner. I leave my briefcase on the entryway table, giving him a hug, and he's striking in pinstripes. His perfectly knotted blue silk tie is vibrant against his charcoal-gray shirt with monogrammed French cuffs.

As always, he smells good, his platinum hair brushed back from his chiseled face, and he gets more handsome with age. At least that's how it seems to me, and I apologize for my dishevelment.

"And for being late, and messing up our dinner plans." I open the entryway closet, asking where he's been. "I thought you were working remotely today. What's going on?"

"I had an urgent meeting at headquarters."

"About?" I hang up my coat.

"Gwen Hainey," he replies, to my surprise and confusion.

"How did you know about her before I did?" I don't understand. "You were already on the way home from your meeting when the police called me. Before anyone knew she was missing, in other words. Did the Secret Service have information before the rest of us? And if so, why?"

"Because of something else involving her." That's as much as he's going to say now that my sister Dorothy is walking in, jingling and strobing like a two-legged carnival.

Decked out in a Grinch onesie embroidered with tiny Santa sacks of purloined presents, she has on pointed-toe booties tipped with bells. The glow sticks wound around her arms and neck flash green and red, and it's enough to cause vertigo.

"Something else involving who?" She picks up on what she overheard. "My dead neighbor, no doubt," directing this at me. "It's simply dreadful! I've been glued to the news, which includes you ducking Dana Diletti outside Gwen Hainey's townhome."

"It's gone national," Benton lets me know.

"On Fox and CNN." Dorothy sounds impressed, her strobing accessories disconcerting, her hair below her shoulders and streaked with gray.

It's tied back with a sprig of mistletoe that combined with her glittery green swaths of eyeshadow make her appear somewhat extraterrestrial. Since various forms of remote communication became the norm, she's taken to wearing themed makeup and outlandish outfits.

I don't think a day goes by when my sister's not on camera for one reason or another, in addition to launching podcasts and selfies over social media. Tonight, her festive getup is unrelated to the actual occasion of her only child's birthday after the worst year imaginable. I would have bet money on Dorothy being thoughtless.

It would seem that a lack of remorse and empathy are deficits she comes by naturally. They're milled into her DNA. The older she gets the more she evolves into a carbon copy of our mother, who died last year in a Miami retirement home after suffering a stroke during the worst of the pandemic. Vivacious and charming, Dorothy "Doro" Scarpetta, for whom my sister is named, was a charismatic narcissist, and the coconut didn't fall far from the palm.

Not in my case either when it comes to our hard-working, laconic father. If you ask my sister, I'm the boringly responsible one, all business, no play or sense of fun. In other words, "dull with an air of the inevitable" as if I wear "a dream coat woven on the loom of tragedy," my sister's words not mine.

I'm not sure what she really remembers about our childhood except that I was named after our father, both of us Kay Scarpetta. His firstborn and namesake, I had special status, at least in my sister's mind, and his reliance on me made her only more resentful.

CHAPTER 10

IF YOU WOULDN'T MIND maybe switching off your jewelry," I say to Dorothy. "I've seen enough flashing lights for one night, please."

"Of course, but no fun." She does it with a long-suffering sigh. "There now, isn't that better? I've gone all dark just like you."

Eyeing me up and down, she makes sure I know what a wreck I am.

"You look like a wet dog and probably smell like one." Her teasing often has a sharp tip when aimed in my direction.

"More like Armor All, actually," I reply, and occasionally I still get a whiff of it. "Marino let me borrow a towel."

"I wouldn't know since he's not answering my calls or texts. Almost never does when he's busy playing cops and robbers with you."

"He's not with me, and hasn't been for hours. I expect him to be out with the investigator for a while." I ignore her slights.

"Details please," she demands as Benton looks on, and watching us spar isn't new or interesting, either one. "I want to know what we're up against, and if I could be at risk. How do we know who else this maniac has noticed nearby and might have on his radar?"

"I can't talk about it, Dorothy."

"That couldn't be more unfair! I have a right to know what's going on when someone's been abducted and murdered two houses down from us."

The weather was awful, she launches into her story, saying that she and Marino decided to stay in watching TV. They were drinking hot toddies, eating Thanksgiving leftovers, having no clue what was going on with their new neighbor.

"That's what I can't get over," she says, and there's no one more dramatic than my sister when weaving a tale. "If only we had, if only! We could have done something. Pete would have shown up with one of his big guns, and that would have been the end of it."

"Did you hear any cars driving past while you were watching TV?" Benton asks.

"No, but that doesn't mean much," she says.

The townhomes are solidly built, with double-glazed windows. The soundproofing in addition to the stormy weather, the television playing, and it's possible they might not have noticed a car going past. With the drapes drawn, they wouldn't have seen it, either. But they have cameras above each door leading outside, and I ask if Marino checked the recording.

"I'm wondering if they might have picked up anything, assuming the street's not out of range," I explain.

"Of course, he's checked," Dorothy says unhappily. "But you can't see anything. The cameras don't cover the street, and this is so upsetting. I was barely acquainted with Gwen but more than I wish, and right about now I'm feeling sorry I got involved."

"I would imagine the police will need your DNA for exclusionary purposes since you've been inside her townhome." Benton begins unbuttoning his shirt collar, loosening his tie. "How often? And how recently?"

"Just that one time I stopped by to welcome her to the neighborhood right after she moved here," she says, and I'm not going to mention the near-dead dish garden. "Then Pete and Lucy did their security walk-through with her a few weeks after that."

"By the way, where is she?" I ask.

When I got home, Lucy should have seen it in the gate cameras and others along the wooded perimeter. She monitors them on computer displays, also an app on her phone. I admit it hurts my feelings that she hasn't shown up yet, and I hope she's not annoyed with me for being late for her birthday.

"I have to say that Gwen was neither grateful nor friendly," Dorothy summarizes. "In retrospect, I'm deciding that she acted like someone with a lot to hide."

"Did you ever call her after the one time you dropped by?" Benton continues his questions.

"I don't have her number. I could tell she didn't want to give it out."

"What about Lucy and Marino?" I inquire. "How did they set up their walk-through?"

"When I was with Gwen, we picked a date for mid-October."

"This was how long after she moved in?" Benton wants to know.

"A couple of weeks," Dorothy says. "But when I met her, she'd just gotten there, and what a disaster. I don't know how she stood it."

The townhome was being renovated, and was not really habitable. She recalls the strong smell of paint, the noise of the construction crew clearing out their debris and trash.

"I remember hearing them stomping around, packing up their tools, covering stuff upstairs with plastic, and whatnot," she adds.

"How long were you with her?" I envision what I saw inside the townhome, the empty picture hooks, the dangling wires.

"Thirty, forty minutes tops," she replies. "And when she told me about her problems with her ex, I suggested the security check. She wasn't all that interested but I was insistent it was the smart thing to do. So we set it up, and just so we're clear, I wasn't present when Pete and Lucy were there."

"I'm afraid you may not hear the end of this for a while," Benton says.

"Well, I just hope it won't ruin where we live." Dorothy never fails to circle back to herself. "I'm not sure how safe I'll feel anymore. Not to mention privacy issues now that Colonial Landing is all over the news."

"You know you're always welcome to stay here." I remind her of what I honestly don't want to happen.

I can't imagine living under the same roof with my sister. Maybe it's not nice to say but I have my limits.

"I assume by now they've taken Gwen's ex into custody for questioning?" Dorothy asks. "I recall his name is Jinx, and that's who I'd be looking at based on what she said about him."

"I'm interested in everything she told you," Benton says. "You and I can talk while Kay goes upstairs and showers. I'll bring up a drink." This to me. "An aged single malt on the rocks, a double, just what the doctor ordered."

"That sounds wonderful but not until I know what's going on with Lucy," I reply, and by now it's apparent she doesn't intend to greet me. "I assume she's home but can't tell when her shades are down."

"WHO KNOWS WHAT SHE'S doing, recluse that she's become," Dorothy says. "Not that she won any awards for being sociable before all this. Despite my efforts to teach her a few manners, my constant reminders to focus on the positive."

"How has Lucy been?" I ask Benton. "What's her mood like today? Do we know if she talked to people on the phone? Did anyone reach out to her? Did she reconnect with anyone or even try? Has she done anything remotely fun?"

"Since she's been isolating, I'd say her mood's not been great." Her mother takes it upon herself to further assess.

"When's the last time you saw her?" I ask.

"Midday when the man came to finish painting the trellis while it wasn't raining. Lucy and I were outside for a few minutes," Dorothy says, "and I've not laid eyes on her since."

I have a pretty good idea what my niece has been up to since I saw her early this morning as the sun was coming up. On my way to work, I stopped by her cottage to wish her a happy birthday, and she was drinking coffee at her desk. I wanted to give her a little something I'd had made for her, a gift that's more symbolic than anything else.

The bracelet is titanium and rose gold, a simple flat cuff with fragments of dinosaur bone and a meteorite inlaid in the shape of the infinity symbol. Engraved inside is the date, and *To Lucy, Love Aunt Kay,* reminding her that who we are endures forever.

I knew she was in for a gloomy time on her birthday, and her remedy of late is the same. When she has spaces to fill and moods to chase away, she's on her computer, lost in the invisible world of open-source artificial intelligence (AI) coding. The machine-learning platforms she uses are available to anyone, and I suspect she's professionally networking in the anonymity of cyberspace.

Maybe she's personally connecting as well. That's dangerous when you can't be sure who or what's on the other end. Someone good or bad, and are we certain your new contact is even human? Maybe it's an Internet bot masquerading as a person.

Of more concern is what Lucy might be doing on her own, hour after hour, day in and day out. What occupies her attention when no one's looking, when she's not logged onto one of her preferred shared sites? I imagine her possessed, a magician conjuring up what she must have to give her meaning and a purpose, a reason for trying.

"I'm deciding she might be better off on her own again somewhere else." Dorothy aims another dart at me, always hurled with a smile.

Her Grinch booties jingle whenever she moves, constantly looking at her phone, typing with her thumbs.

"I would think that living with you simply serves as a reminder of what she needs to get over. It's time to move on and not look back," she says, as if it's that simple or even possible.

"I've not talked to her yet," Benton replies. "I haven't seen her since I got home a little while ago. Usually, she'll step outside to say hello as I'm putting my car inside the garage. But she didn't this time."

"I'm going to check on her, tell her to come over." I intend to do that before anything else. "Somehow we'll salvage what's left of her birthday."

"I think that's a good idea." He doesn't suggest accompanying me, and I know why.

Benton is in favor of my spending quality time with Lucy, just the two of us. Except for exercising, riding her motorcycle or running a few errands, she's been holed up inside our guest cottage since moving here in the early fall. There are days when I don't see her at all, only her cat wandering about, and it's not for a lack of trying on my part.

Maybe Lucy will show up for dinner, maybe she won't. She might call me or drop by for a chat. Then again, she might not, and that's not terribly unusual. But she became increasingly isolated during the worst of the pandemic after Janet and Desi were stranded in London, and she wasn't able to get to them.

Locked down in their flat, they couldn't have been more responsible and careful during the months following the last postholiday peak. This was before the vaccine was available, and mother and son managed to stay away from everyone until a leaky pipe required an emergency visit from a plumber.

Later it would turn out he was positive for a variant of the coronavirus, an asymptomatic spreader. While replacing a corroded pipe joint, he was inside the flat with the windows shut for almost two hours, at times pulling down his inadequate mask. Several days later, Janet lost her sense of smell. Desi developed a cough and a fever, and Lucy couldn't be there.

The fatality rate in the U.K. was so high at the time that funeral homes ran out of body bags. I remember hearing the dire anecdotes from colleagues about not being able to order them from anywhere. Hospitals were storing the dead in refrigerator trucks, and some cemeteries resorted to mass burials in trenches.

There were no viewings or funerals. No graveside services in a peaceful resting place, no flying the bodies home to loved ones. Most people dying from the virus were cremated, the remains sealed inside cheap boxes shipped by mail or UPS. Such a parcel was delivered to Lucy, and I can't think of anything colder or more callous.

She never got the chance to say good-bye, and I fear she won't accept that Janet and Desi are gone. In a way, they aren't if she didn't witness it. If she never saw the bodies, she has no evidence really. Leaving her in a state of limbo, her family neither here nor there, and technology has added to the problem while making it better.

"See you in a few," Benton says as I head to the door. "In the meantime, we'll start getting things ready," he adds, and I go on to give a few instructions.

Dorothy can set out the cheeses I'd planned for tonight. Sharp provolone, cheddar and fresh mozzarella. Also, the prosciutto, pickles, roasted red peppers and artichoke hearts.

"I'll throw together a nice antipasto, warm up some garlic bread, and pick out just the right bottle of wine," I promise before venturing out into the blustery dark.

Water *drip-drips* from trees that are a lush canopy over the driveway in warmer months when everything is green. A sharp wind gusts in fits and starts, leaves blowing everywhere. The temperature isn't cold enough for ice but I pay attention as I walk briskly, wishing I'd bothered with my coat.

Fortunately, I don't have far to go, the guest cottage tucked amid tall spreading firs, spruce pines and magnolias. It's on the other side of a garden that must have been ignored many decades as overgrown as it was when we moved here. You wouldn't know anything grand was ever there without re-viewing old records as I did.

Working like an archaeologist, I carefully cleared out a dense morass of thorny shrubs, grapevines and creepers chok-ing herb and flower beds. In the process I uncovered a marble griffin, a sundial pedestal and other treasures from the 1700s. There's no telling how long they'd been out of sight and mind. I have a feeling the eccentric former ambassador who lived here last was unaware of what was hidden under his backyard thicket.

It also doesn't sound like he did much to take care of the place, and I turn on my phone's flashlight, detecting the sharp odor of fresh paint. Checking out my new dark-green wooden trellis, I imagine roses climbing over it in the spring. The garden will flourish again, and I'm thinking of adding a wrought-iron table and chairs. How nice it will be to sit out here having coffee.

Returning to the driveway, I text Lucy that I'm headed in her direction, and she doesn't answer. But I've come to expect that when she sees me in the security cameras she monitors. Maybe she'll come out to greet me when I get close. Or she might be preoccupied, tied up as she watches my approach.

CHAPTER 11

Wet pavers are slippery beneath my booted feet, and puddles glower in the uneasy glow of gas lamps. I catch shadows moving in the corners of my eyes, the wind rushing and moaning. The hair pricks up on the back of my neck, and I have the feeling I'm being watched as I near Lucy's cottage.

Her blackout shades are doing their job, and I turn off my phone's flashlight, not wanting to make myself a bigger target. I sense eyes on me, something lurking in the dark foliage, but it's my imagination, I'm sure. My pulse picks up as I look and listen, reminding myself I have good reason to feel jumpy after a day like this one.

Taking the brick path that leads to Lucy's backdoor, I dig my keys out of a pocket. The boxwoods rustle nearby, the motion-sensor light blinking on as I step up on the wooden porch. I almost yell out loud when something brushes against the back of my legs, Merlin shadowing me again.

"You're going to be the death of me, sneaking up like that!" I whisper, my heart hammering. "Goodness!"

Lucy's Scottish fold cat stares up with full moon eyes, and he's wet and most unhappy, making his muttering meowing sounds as if trying to speak. I'm alarmed that he's outside with no collar, rubbing against me the way he does when he wants something. He's unsettled and twitchy as I continue looking around, beginning to shiver.

"Merlin, it's too cold and nasty to be out here. What's happened?"

I rap my knuckles on the backdoor with its built-in acrylic cat flap.

"And where on earth is your collar?"

I knock again anxiously, my attention darting around as if any moment something hideous will sneak up.

"Stay here with me and I'll get you inside."

He mutters, weaving between my legs, and Lucy wouldn't allow him to wander at will without his radio frequency identification (RFID) chipped collar that she 3-D prints for more than identification purposes. The radio signal is the cyber key that enables him to enter the cottage through the flap in the lower part of this door, and also the one leading into the basement of the main house.

Both high-tech portals are too small for a person to crawl through, while keeping out four-legged offenders like skunks, raccoons, opossums, and small deer and bears. Merlin can come and go autonomously. He can visit wherever he pleases without human intervention or a breach of security. But at the moment he's locked out.

It's not like Lucy to allow such a thing, and I've been concerned for a while about how distracted she's become. At times forgetful or simply bored, doesn't care, and I'm liking it less that she's been alone all day. I suspect I know what she's been doing, and birthdays and other special occasions will always be painful.

"Okay, let's hope for the best," I say to Merlin, and I'd never let myself into Lucy's place unannounced unless I thought something terrible had happened.

Fast reaching that point, I unlock the door.

"Anybody home?" I step inside, and the alarm is off. "Hello, Lucy? It's me!"

Merlin is on my heels, and I continue calling out but my niece isn't answering. Quietly, I close the door, on high alert, my heart thudding hard.

"Lucy?" I call out.

My briefcase is back at the house, my pistol inside it, I'm unpleasantly reminded. Inside the small kitchen, I detect the familiar odor of Hoppe's gun-cleaning oil as I look around for anything out of the ordinary.

"It's me!" I yell.

The soapstone countertops are tidy, and there's nothing in the cast-iron sink, only a plate and coffee cup in the drain rack. Nearby is Lucy's Kevlar briefcase similar to the one I carry. Her tactical pump-action 12-gauge shotgun is propped in its usual corner, and on top of the butcher block is a disassembled Heckler & Koch P30 pistol and a gun-cleaning kit.

As usual, my niece has quite the deadly collection, and opening the drawer under the toaster oven, I lift out the gun I know she keeps there. A .40 caliber Smith & Wesson, double-action with a double-stack capacity, and then I hear her voice inside the living room.

"Okay, okay, I'm listening," she's saying to someone. "I know everything's about attitude and perspective . . ."

It sounds like all is safe and sound on the western front, thank God. I return the gun to the drawer, grabbing a dish towel. I can hear only one side of the conversation, and I dry off Merlin while he nuzzles and purrs. I'm not sure who my niece is talking to but I have my suspicions.

"Now on top of everything else, someone we could have helped ends up with her throat cut," she says. "And I'll be honest, I wasn't paying close attention. When probably I would have in the past no matter what I thought of the person."

I open a closet, leaving the towel on top of the washing machine.

"Do you have any idea how hard I'm trying?" Lucy then says.

She's unaware of my entering her small living area of dark oak beams and redbrick walls that are original to the property.

"You'd feel the same way under the circumstances," she adds. "And you'd be talking to me right now just like I'm talking to you. Or at least I hope so."

Merlin silently slinks past, jumping up on his favorite leather ottoman. He stares at me, tail twitching, perched protectively near Lucy's desk facing the fireplace. Her back is to us, giving me but a glimpse of her striking profile as she gestures and talks.

Headphones on, she's surrounded by an array of big flatscreen displays. As I ease in closer, I see that Janet's lovely face fills one of them, and the sight runs through me like a blade. I can't hear what she's saying but have no doubt it's understanding, kind but firm and wise.

"I realize you're trying to make me feel better," Lucy says. "But there's no point in wasting your words."

Try as I might, I'm having a hard time getting used to this, and not sure I should, considering the risks.

"The fact is, if I'd been there things would be different." Lucy adds what she can't possibly know.

It's what she's decided, and maybe getting back to London in time would have changed the outcome. But I don't believe it, and I'm certain Janet would agree, her face on the display somberly empathetic.

"I wouldn't be screwing up every which way but loose," Lucy says. "And that's all I've been thinking about this birthday if you want the honest truth. I wasn't there with you. Now you aren't here with me. Nothing's turning out the way it should with anything I do, and maybe never will again."

I can't hear Janet's answer, and Merlin saunters over to the desk. He jumps on top of it, and Lucy turns her head enough to catch me behind her. She's neither surprised nor startled, her green eyes wide, almost trancelike as she talks to someone dead.

"HEY THERE, I SAW you coming." My niece takes off her headset. "And where's your coat? It's close to freezing out there."

"Tweaking software?" I ask gently and without judgment. "Or are you having another visit?"

It's the latter I've become most concerned about as I've witnessed her spending time with the love of her life, asking for guidance and advice. While perhaps convincing herself that the image on her screen is more than a computer-generated avatar. The animation before us is an interface, a language-generating AI persona modeled after Janet while she was alive.

Code name *Adam,* the project is one she and Lucy had been working on for years, both of them computer jocks who met during their early days at the FBI Academy. As I look at Janet's face on the display, I continue to fret about Lucy's obsessive development of what's turning into her partner's surrogate.

"I didn't mean to barge in, and wasn't trying to spy." I put my hand on my niece's shoulder, and her rose gold–streaked hair is the shortest since college. "Are you aware that Merlin has been roaming about with no collar?"

"What? News to me, and how weird. That's not good." She reaches for him, pulling him into her lap.

"I guess you didn't see him in the cameras?" I scan different murky live video feeds on one of the flat screens.

"When he sneaks around under the shrubbery, forget it. He must have gotten his collar snagged on something."

"You weren't answering texts or the door so I thought at the very least I should get him safely back inside."

"I figured he was at your place." She pets him. "Thanks for finding him. Wow, that's bad. I don't know how that happened. It never has before."

"Well, I didn't find him. He found me, and you know I'm not a fan of pet doors, lockable or otherwise." I repeat a lecture she's been hearing since moving in. "For so many reasons, and this is a perfect example. He got out but couldn't get back in. I assumed he was at your place, and you assumed he was at mine."

"Look, I don't like it any more than you do but he's an indoor-outdoor kind of guy, and that's never going to change. I should know, we've tried. What did you do out there, Merlin?" Talking to him as if he's a child. "What happened to your collar? Did it get caught on the bushes or something while chasing a squirrel?"

Merlin has no answer beyond purring like a buzz saw, and it would seem he's been largely unfazed by recent human tragedies and dramas. I suppose if a cat could make assumptions his would be that Janet and Desi are still in London. They're safely ensconced in a nineteenth-century building overlooking a park on the Victoria Embankment.

I've stayed in their flat many times. It's an easy walk to

New Scotland Yard, where Janet and Lucy had begun con-sulting before the pandemic. They'd been dividing their time between the U.K. and Boston, and when I began discussions about the position in Virginia, there was no thought of them relocating with us.

My niece wouldn't be here now were it not for a mutating virus that attacks some far more viciously than others. Espe-cially if they have an underlying autoimmune disorder such as asthma or Crohn's disease. In quarantine, she couldn't be with Janet and Desi when they got sick on the other side of the Atlantic Ocean.

Testing positive herself, Lucy wasn't allowed to fly any-where, certainly not to other countries. She sheltered in place, suffering only mild symptoms, and I'm not sure she'll forgive herself for surviving when they didn't.

"What are you two talking about?" I indicate Janet's avatar on the large screen display.

"Don't go acting like I'm doing something kooky," Lucy says, her sharp-featured face emotionally flat, her troubled eyes as vivid as emeralds.

"This hasn't been much of a birthday, and I'm very sorry." It pleases me that she's wearing the bracelet I gave her, clasped on her right wrist, the infinity symbol glinting in lamplight.

Lithe and strong in a black warm-up suit and ankle-high sneakers, she's in her usual super-buff shape, but there's a weariness about her. As if a circuit breaker has been thrown, the power out in certain rooms, and she's having a hard time turning it back on.

"You know how I feel about birthdays," she says. "I'd skip them if possible."

"Well, this one was supposed to be fun." I think back on how many times I've said that when plans are disrupted. "And of course, we get lousy weather and then I'm tied up, but it's never too late to celebrate. Has your day been reasonably okay? I can see you're spending some of it with Janet."

I'm talking about the one on the computer display, the result of billions of parameters used in neural network algorithms. The language structure they create seems human as it predicts behavior, events, and answers questions. The performance runs rings around conventional search engines, and it seemed like a spoof when I first witnessed the Adam project's capabilities.

Whether it's composing stories, songs, even computer code while conversing amicably, somberly, angrily, depending on the situation. Or playfully and flirtatiously, looking deep into your eyes, gesturing the way Janet did when she was alive. I would swear that's who I'm looking at, her dimples showing when she smiles, her blond hair short and mussy.

But she may as well be a hologram, a reconstituted version that can't feel what she emotes, can't touch or be touched. She'll never be flesh and blood but would continue to change as the real Janet does. At least, that was the plan when the work began, but such an evolution can't happen anymore.

Janet no longer receives or transmits in a way that's relatable since she's not physically present to add to the data. She'll have no new thoughts or experiences. There will be no new achievements or setbacks, no biological changes or calamities that require altering parameters.

Future edits will become increasingly unreliable as the ever-changing model includes the traits of her maker. In this instance Lucy, and all who influence her. As she continues to refine and perfect, to tinker and second-guess on her own, the more her creation becomes like herself. Warts and all. Biases and emotionality thrown in at no extra charge.

Open-source Generative Pre-trained Transformer level three (GPT-3) technology is as stunning as it's scary. This early on, and already AI is leaving human capabilities in the Stone Age dust. An avatar can look, sound, gesture, act and react like anybody the software engineers decide.

In most instances this is accomplished with video and audio recordings knitted together. Often the source of the modeling is the programmers themselves. But it also can be relatives, friends, spouses, and that's how it started with Lucy and Janet. Their generated avatar was never intended to be the spitting image of either of them.

It wasn't to take the place of a partner or a relationship, and I'm beyond the point of thinking it constructive to criticize. After all, who am I to say? I can't know what's best when technologies fantastically surpass anything humans have experienced in the past.

I came along in an era when what I'm looking at with my niece this minute was the stuff of science fiction, of *Star Trek* and *Star Wars*. I don't pretend to know the answers I once thought I did. Including to the most fundamental questions about life and death. Are they really what we think? What makes us so sure?

Because I'm beginning to doubt it as I'm faced with an avatar that I'd swear is someone I trust and love. If I'm feeling that way, what must it be like for Lucy? I don't want to imagine if Benton no longer were here, and I started spending my days talking to his cyber doppelgänger.

CHAPTER 12

"Were you on the computer all day?" I sit down on the ottoman.

"I've been working." Lucy pulls up a software menu, scrolling through it.

"Well, last I checked, your birthday's not over yet, and what does Janet have to say about it?"

"I'll let her tell you herself."

With the click of the mouse, Janet blinks and smiles.

"Hey, babe, I'm back with a question," Lucy says to the avatar. "Hope you weren't lonely."

"Yes, I was, Lucy Boo," Janet says, the nickname going back to my niece's childhood. "What's your question?"

"What did you say to me earlier about my effing birthday that I'd prefer to effing ignore?"

"Two bucks in the swear jar!" And that's classic Janet. "I said you should be happy about your birthday. Maybe people will take you seriously if you don't look nineteen anymore," she adds flirtatiously.

"Ha-ha, very funny. I spent this effing birthday working like any other day." Lucy talks to the avatar as if it's her partner. "Do you think that was a mistake?"

"You're up to three dollars already, and such a silly thing to ask." Janet laughs. "You always work. Birthday or not, life goes on. Things happen that have to be addressed. And besides, Lucy, you're happiest and most at peace when you tackle problems, right a wrong, accomplish something."

As the dialogue continues, I'm noticing that Janet's language, gestures, her blinking and other facial expressions are vaguely stiff, too uniform and repetitive. I find her quiet and reserved. Thoughtful, deliberate and patient, rarely interrupting, and that's who she was. Her new translation is a bit stilted, but if I didn't know what I'm looking at, it's likely I'd be fooled.

I might sense something's off but never guess I was communicating with a cyber being. A programmable entity. A space-age Siri- or Alexa-type device with a powerfully familiar voice and face, a personality so believable that I feel an ache in my chest every time I'm given the latest demonstration.

"Guess who I have with me?" Lucy continues talking to someone no longer present.

"Hi, Janet." I hide the grief I'm feeling. "It's always nice to see you."

"Hello." She cuts her keen blue eyes toward the sound of my voice, staring right at me.

"You remember Aunt Kay, and how cool that she's decided to show up for a birthday chat." Lucy makes what seems like a trivial statement.

But the Janet on the screen hasn't spoken to me before. I've been nothing more than an observer now and then, and haven't asked her a question directly. You could say we've not officially met beyond my looking over Lucy's shoulder or reviewing the video clips she sends.

"Of course, I remember," Janet answers, her radiant smile just like days of old. "We've spoken many times. It's always nice to see you too, Doctor Scarpetta," as she's always insisted on calling me.

"I bet you can figure out precisely how much time the two of you have spent together," Lucy replies. "Let's give Aunt Kay a taste of your medicine, go ahead and do the math."

"It will be my pleasure," she says brightly. "Doctor Scarpetta and I have been in each other's company one thousand two hundred and twenty-one times since our first encounter."

"And where was that?" Lucy's attention is locked on the image on her screen like Narcissus staring at his reflection in the pond.

"We first met at the FBI Academy in Quantico, Virginia, when you and I were new agents," Janet continues.

"And over the years, how often have you talked?"

"Doctor Scarpetta and I have spoken on the telephone twenty-two thousand, nine-hundred and six minutes and twenty-one seconds. Would you like to know how many e-mails and text messages we've exchanged?"

"Now you're just showing off." Lucy is pleased with what she's wrought, and my fitness tracker alerts me that August Ryan has sent an e-mail.

"This could be important." I open it. "The recording from the security gate, and we're going to want to listen."

"A recording of what?" Lucy asks.

"Not much as it turns out. The cameras at the entrance and exit of Colonial Landing were covered for an interval of almost an hour last Friday night." I go on to repeat what August told me.

I rationalize that if Marino is working for me again, there's no reason Lucy can't. They're investigative partners, and I could use any help I can get. I forward the file to her, and she opens it on a computer display, clicking on PLAY. All we see is darkness, the muddy image of the road leading to Colonial Landing's walled brick entrance.

At 5:13 P.M., something is pulled over one camera, then the other, making a quiet crinkly plastic sound exactly as August described. Two minutes later, Gwen Hainey's code, 1988, is entered, and the entrance gate slides open. There's no car engine, no sound of anything driving through.

Just the wind and rain, then the faint strains of organ music getting louder, crescendoing like *The Phantom of the Opera*. But what we're listening to isn't Andrew Lloyd Webber.

"Next you hear the entrance gate close, and then nothing," I say to Lucy. "Apparently, all was quiet until fifty-two minutes later."

I fast-forward the recording almost to the end. We listen to the noise of the metal exit gate opening. Then the same eerie musical theme is playing again, and it's enough to make one's hair stand on end.

"That's bizarre and rather terrifying. Have you ever heard this music before?" I ask.

"I might have. But horror themes all sound kind of similar to me." She replays it. "Let's ask Janet. Can you identify this music?"

"It's from a TV show called *Shock Theater*," she says without pause.

"Never heard of it," I confess.

"HORROR FLICKS LIKE *FRANKENSTEIN, Dracula, The Wolf Man,* going back to the late nineteen forties." Lucy looks at information on her phone that Janet data mines as fast as we can think.

The theme is on YouTube, and as we listen, I'm increasingly alarmed. Sensing the presence of a cunning intelligence, I envision the dead woman sprawled by the railroad tracks, her neck savagely slashed, her head barely attached, her hands gone.

I can see the coppery glint of the penny flattened on the rail as if I'm right there in the stormy dark while a cold rain falls intermittently. And I suggest to my niece that we head home and talk to Benton.

"Let's see what he has to say and drink a toast before it's not your birthday anymore." I check the time, and it's getting close to eleven. "Janet, thank you for your help," I say to her as she stares at us with a manufactured Mona Lisa smile, listening on command, blinking as programmed.

"You're welcome," she says warmly, her dimples showing again.

"I'll see you a little later," Lucy tells her, and I detect the emotion she feels for what isn't real.

"It appears she's becoming your personal Google." I'm somewhat dazed by what I just witnessed, my emotions powerfully impacted by what I know is artificial.

"Pretty soon, everybody's going to be doing this." Lucy clicks the mouse, the display blacking out.

"I hope I'm not turning into a Luddite but I find what you're saying deeply disturbing," I reply, imagining people downloading an app on their phone so they can commune with cyber ghosts.

I have no doubt the temptation will be overwhelming to conjure up family, friends, enemies, world leaders and celebrities alive and dead, including those you have no connection to, and possibly haven't met. What an embarrassment of riches for stalkers, for anyone obsessed.

"I don't know what's going to happen as technology makes us increasingly detached from others," I explain. "How dangerous if we can't tell what's real from what isn't. What do we trust?"

"Since social media and the pandemic we've already become like that," Lucy says. "And it depends on your definition of *real*. Because once you get used to a tool like this, it's as real as anything gets. But forget privacy anymore. There's so much out there, you don't need to hack. Although we can."

"We?" I ask pointedly, and I know she means Janet.

"This is the way everything is going." Lucy gets up from her desk. "There's no choice, and no going back."

It will become commonplace to continue relationships in cyberspace, she says, as if there can be no question. Life's disconnects and disappointments will be remedied in ways never believed possible, what's unbearable becoming a matter of perception and re-creations, the undoable undone.

There will be fixes and patches for ruptures of all descriptions including illness, divorce, disability, bad choices and behavior, ruined opportunities, and most of all death. As miraculous and marvelous as such a renaissance may seem, it's equally sinister if exploited by the human malware among us.

"Janet and I talk through all kinds of things," Lucy continues to explain as if it's normal. "She's told me plenty that I didn't know, coming up with things on her own. It's incredibly helpful, and I feel she's there, that's the truth. As crazy as it sounds, we're pretty much working together like we always did."

"There you go saying *we*," I reply, feeling that ache in my chest again. "You've been saying it a lot, Lucy. And things aren't the way they were no matter how much all of us might wish it. I'm hoping you understand that it's not actually Janet you're talking to, as much as I wish otherwise."

"Depending on your definition of existence, it might be her." Lucy puts on her leather bomber jacket, stepping away from her desk. "It really might be her energy I'm channeling electronically, we don't know that it's not. There's so much we don't know. But that doesn't mean I think she's going to walk into the room like she used to."

"I just want you to be careful, please," I remind her gently. "You're not really talking to Janet even if that's your perception." As much as it hurts, I won't stop saying it.

"Everything in the algorithms is based on direct input from her," Lucy counters. "Or recordings and writings that represent her. For example, when I ask what I should eat for dinner, the answer is what she would say under the circumstances."

The software factors into the equation Lucy's mood and behavior, her health, her location. Also, the time of day and other information, including if she's exercised or is alone.

"As long as you know the difference between an algorithm and someone no longer with us." I follow her to the kitchen, Merlin right behind us.

"Of course I know the difference. But as fast as we're reverse-engineering biology, I have to wonder about a lot of things. Like if we'll end up on a computer chip someday. Or maybe we're already on one, and that's the meaning of eternity."

"Speaking of chips. What about Merlin's collar?" I inquire.

"I'm one step ahead of you." Lucy opens the cabinet where she keeps pet supplies. "I made a few extras," she says, retrieving another one, buckling it on him.

Sporting his jaunty bright-red replacement RFID collar, Merlin saunters past the kitchen door as if he's quite the cat's whiskers. He gets close enough to the cat flap that it opens with a sharp click. He sits, cleaning his face as if pleased with himself.

"I don't like it that the other collar is at large," I say to Lucy. "That doesn't strike me as particularly safe since it includes Merlin's name, a phone number, and a chip that unlocks the cat doors."

"It's a burner phone, and there's no address associated." She opens the same kitchen drawer I did earlier, retrieving her pistol and a lightweight pocket holster.

"I'd prefer we find his missing collar." I watch Merlin slink past the cat door again, clicking open the lock again.

Back and forth, again and again, and I halfway wonder if he's trying to warn us about something.

"We'll keep an eye out, maybe look around a little as we walk to the house," I decide.

"I have an app that can track it so that shouldn't be a problem. But even if someone else found it, no big deal." Lucy tucks the holstered gun inside her waistband. "No one's fitting through a cat door, no one's breaking in that way. Plus, we'd see it on the cameras, and I've got Janet monitoring them now."

What she means is the AI software is checking real-time video feeds for irregularities, and once again it's all about the algorithms. Lucy is constantly tweaking the computer code, adjusting if-else statements and variables.

"If there's something out of the ordinary," she says, "I get an alert on my phone, my fitness tracker. It's the same advantage

Gwen Hainey would have had if she'd installed cameras like I suggested."

Retrieving a down vest from a hook by the back door, she hands it to me.

"I guess by now you know that Marino and I had our own unpleasant brush with her, having no idea things would turn out this way," Lucy says. "But in retrospect it's not all that surprising."

"Why do you say that?"

"What you sow is what you reap," she says as Merlin jumps up on a countertop. "No telling the lives she's ruined, and karma always comes back around. It's never nice when it does."

Putting on the vest she hands me, I catch a hint of her sultry cologne around the collar.

"A lot of people end up dying the way they lived." My niece repeats what I've been saying since the beginning of my career. "I didn't like Gwen the minute we met. She was all about herself, and arrogant. Not to mention deceptive, only it's looking like we didn't know the half of it."

Setting the alarm, Lucy opens the kitchen door.

"How about staying here inside your nice warm cottage like a good boy?" she asks Merlin, and I hope he won't follow us.

I walk out on the porch, wishing he was an indoor cat, but that's not how he's imprinted after starting out life abandoned as a kitten. He fended for himself before making a beeline to Janet and Desi in a parking lot, knowing a good thing when he saw it.

That was four years ago, and the owl-like spotted Scottish fold is a hardwired peripatetic, especially after dark. It's the call of the wild when he wants to venture out, and there's no choice but to let him. Otherwise he yowls as if caught in a bear trap while tearing up the drapes or wreaking other havoc.

"I'm afraid you're right," I say to Lucy as we walk away from the cottage. "When I was going through her townhome, I didn't get a good feeling about her."

I describe the water-soluble paper, the pens I noticed. I explain that what I observed made me wonder if the biomedical engineer might be involved in illegal activities. Possibly she'd shown up in Old Town to stay below the radar while living on the lam.

"And in the process, I suspect that most of all she wanted to be close to Thor Laboratories." I turn on my phone's flashlight, shining it on either side of the driveway in search of Merlin's missing collar.

CHAPTER 13

LUCY STOPS WALKING, STARING at her phone in the dark, her frustrated face dimly illuminated by the display.

"Unless something's wrong with the app," she informs me, "no joy so far."

She's not picking up the missing collar's signal, she says as my light probes the woods and shrubs. Tendrils of fog drift, water dripping like a scene out of the horror show we were talking about earlier.

"What the heck has Merlin been up to?" Lucy's breath looks like smoke.

She moves the phone closer so I can see the message, *Device Not Found*.

"For some reason, I'm only pinging on the new one, which has a different serial number." She shows me on the app. "If the missing collar is in the area, we should be able to locate it."

"It must be out of range," I suppose.

Her exotic-looking flat-eared cat is often sighted blocks away, usually near a neighbor's bird feeder.

"Maybe he lost his collar on someone else's property. It could be anywhere," I add.

"Or something's wrong with it, maybe it got damaged," Lucy says.

The wind is raw and biting as we near the garage, and I turn around often, having that same feeling of being watched.

"Whatever actually happened to her, she sure acted like someone was out to get her." Lucy continues telling me her impressions of Gwen. "When Marino and I were with her, it was maybe two weeks after she'd moved in. I assumed most of her belongings hadn't arrived yet."

"It would seem they still haven't based on what I saw inside the townhome a little while ago," I reply. "Her secrecy and paranoia certainly fit with her leading a double life, and I'm betting we'll discover she has another place somewhere."

"Exactly, because where's her stuff?" Lucy shines her light around, still no sign of the missing collar. "Not in Boston, and it's not here. There's nothing in storage anywhere, according to Jinx Slater, her ex. At least that he knows of, and according to him, she likes to spend money."

"You talked to him?" I ask.

"Benton did today around lunchtime."

"How is that possible? The police weren't called about Gwen's disappearance until hours after that. Unless I've missed something important," I add as we near the house.

"Benton will fill you in himself," Lucy says. "But it would seem that Jinx made it pretty clear that Gwen was passing along critically sensitive information while selling proprietary technologies. Spying, and no big surprise."

It's suspected this started about the time she left MIT, which also is about the time she paid off everything she owed including substantial school loans. For the most part she stopped using credit cards, and soon after met Jinx, managing to fool him for years, he confided in Benton.

"It sounds like she lived beyond her means, and nothing was enough," Lucy summarizes as we follow the walkway to the front porch. "Talented and smart, she was greedy, relentlessly ambitious and lacking in integrity, and that's a bad combo. Accumulating a lot of debt, she made herself vulnerable to selling her soul to the devil."

Since finishing MIT, Gwen changed her job situation on average every ten months, according to Jinx. She'd stay in a department or division long enough to learn the ropes.

"Then she'd move on to the next one, and he began suspecting she was secretly meeting with someone," Lucy continues, passing on what Benton learned.

"As in having an affair? Or did he suspect she was involved in illegal activities?" I scan open the front door.

"He was increasingly worried about both, and when he confronted her this past July, that's when she moved out and started spreading lies about him," Lucy says.

"Where was she from July until moving here?"

"A short-term rental in the Boston area. Then she came to Old Town."

The alarm is off when we walk in, Christmas music and the television still playing in the background, and I don't see anyone. Benton likely is upstairs changing his clothes. Either that or he and Dorothy are in the kitchen.

"She has no car. How's she been getting around? Who drove her here?" Taking Lucy's coat, I hang it and my borrowed vest in the entryway.

"Very good questions, and I have concerns about the former boyfriend," Lucy says as we walk through the living room. "It sounds like he's not over her based on what Benton told me."

"As in stalking her? Following her here to Old Town? Or driving her here himself? What has he been doing? What do we really know about how estranged they were?"

"I know he's continued to try to talk to her."

"Based on?"

"Phone records," she says, and I don't ask how she knows that.

Maybe she's hacking again. Maybe Janet is. Even if it's not all that necessary anymore with open-source data.

"He'd text or call, and she'd ghost him," Lucy says.

"It sounds like she didn't bother to change her phone number."

"Which makes no sense at all if he was such a problem," Lucy adds as I pause to catch the latest replay on TV.

It's painful watching myself dodge Dana Diletti and her

crew earlier, averting my face like someone on trial. I look
a bit like a horror show myself, coatless and with wet hair,
ducking under the yellow tape, striding with purpose toward
the entrance. Worse is the caption spelling out the identity of
the guilty party:

*Dr. Kay Scarpetta, chief medical examiner, avoiding
reporters at the scene . . .*

"Her murder is a sexy story, and it's only going to get
bigger," Lucy says.

She collects two glittery glass ball ornaments from the rug
near the floor-to-ceiling Christmas tree. An artificial one, it's
overdecorated with multicolored LEDs and elaborate baubles
and figurines that mean nothing to Benton or me. They don't
belong to us, aren't from our past or exactly our taste.

Not the rampant gold Baroque angel on top of the tree. Or
the perfectly wrapped gifts beneath it that are fake like everything else. Left to our own devices, we would have settled
for a small living fir or spruce pine that later can be replanted
outside.

But Marino and Dorothy would have none of it. Planning
to spend Christmas here with us, they've appointed themselves in charge of festivities and set design as Dorothy put it.
And I know when to pick my battles.

"I've caught Merlin in here showing way too much interest," I let Lucy know as she rehangs the ornaments on crowded
silver plastic branches. "Not that I'm pointing a finger," I add,

and truth be told, I've caught him in the act more than once, swatting at things, sending them flying.

INSIDE THE DINING ROOM, the alabaster chandelier and sconces glow warmly, the wavy glass windows shrouded by heavy drapes.

We follow the sound of a knife against a cutting board, entering the kitchen with its exposed brick walls, thick oak beams and fireplace. Benton is at the butcher block, arranging cheeses on a platter, no sign of my sister.

He's taken off his suit jacket, tie and cufflinks, his shirt-sleeves neatly folded up. Over his clothing is a black Tissage de L'Ouest apron I brought home from my recent trip to France. Wiping his hands on a matching dish towel, he opens a box of wheat crackers, arranging them in a basket that he's lined with a cloth napkin.

"Sorry we took so long." I'm mindful of what sad shape I'm in, eager to shower, to wash away the day as best I can. "Lucy's been filling me in, and it's frustrating that Gwen Hainey likely was selling us out to the Russians or God knows who and for how long."

"I hate to think of the damage she's done." Lucy helps herself to a cracker.

"People like her are one of the reasons we've had recent massive cyberattacks on government facilities," Benton says as he pops off the lid to a jar of cherry pepper rings. "All it takes is a few bad actors to bring down the house of cards."

"I was telling Aunt Kay about your conversation with Jinx Slater," Lucy says to Benton, trying the cheese next. "Too bad he didn't come forward about her months ago."

"When did he or Gwen come to the attention of the Secret Service?" I try the sharp provolone, realizing how hungry I am.

"The first time we heard of her was this morning, which is why I was called into headquarters," Benton says. "We were contacted by a senior scientist at Thor who's on loan from NASA. He's the lab director, and was supposed to be supervising her."

They were scheduled for an important meeting with the Department of Defense at nine A.M., and no one could get hold of her.

"She wasn't answering calls, and her mailbox was full." Benton arranges baby carrots on the platter.

"What was she working on at Thor?" I ask.

"A top secret project involving stem cells and the three-D printing of human organs," he says.

Since starting there six weeks ago, some of her coworkers had been finding her behavior disturbing, he says, rinsing his hands in the sink.

"On top of everything else, she's a no-show this morning, and her lab director reached out to us," Benton says. "That's who I was meeting with at headquarters earlier."

"And then what? Did Jinx Slater reach out to the Secret Service next?" I preheat the oven.

"No, I reached out to him."

"Benton knows about the walk-through Marino and I did," Lucy says. "I passed on what Gwen told us." She sits down on a barstool as I open the refrigerator. "Where's Mom?"

"I think she may have had a wardrobe failure," Benton says as I find the foil-wrapped garlic bread. "She's upstairs borrowing a sewing kit, and I suspect busy with her latest posts on social media. I'm sure she'll be down eventually."

"This goes in the oven but wait about fifteen minutes." I place the bread on the counter, heading out of the kitchen. "I'm going to clean up but not before picking out a perfect wine for the occasion. One that will need to breathe for a bit."

Determined to end the day on a more civilized note, I have just the thing in mind. Past the laundry room I open the door leading to the basement, flipping on the light, trailing my hand down the railing. My boots are loud on steep old wooden steps, the cool air damp and dusty.

The rough-hewn wooden ceilings and doorways are low, the walls exposed stone, and there's scarcely space to navigate. It's depressing when I'm reminded how many boxes we've yet to unpack, how many wooden crates to pry open. Also, furniture, tools, all sorts of odds and ends that we haven't sorted through or put into storage.

I turn on another light that barely pushes back the shadows. Walking past the door leading outside, I almost come out of my shoes as the cat flap clicks unlocked, popping open. Merlin in his Ferrari-red collar pushes his way through, and I knew it. The little devil followed us.

"Sneaking up again, you're going to take an inch off my life! How did you know I'd be here?" I bend down to pet him, and he starts purring to beat the band. "Well, at least you didn't lose your collar again, but I was hoping you'd stay put."

He follows me to the wine cellar such that it is, an old refrigerator I've repurposed by setting the temperature at fifty-five degrees. I lined glass shelves with foam to protect the bottles, each one having its own special story. Opening the door, I feel a waft of cold air, talking to Merlin as he rubs against my legs.

"Of course, you're more than welcome to join in the festivities for Lucy's birthday. We don't want her to feel sad, now do we?" I survey my small collection that's off-limits to everyone including Benton.

It's a house rule that you don't help yourself to special vintages that I've collected over the years, fifteen bottles left, most of them red. I pick out the 1996 premier grand cru Bordeaux I carried home from France last month. The secretary general of Interpol gave it to me, and I have no doubt it will be splendid.

Turning off lights as I walk through rooms, I'm touched by an arctic draft that I've felt in the past. It's as if I'm moving through a cloud of ice crystals, and Merlin darts ahead of me like he sometimes does. Shadows move, and I catch a shape in the corner of my eye as he growls. Jumping up, he claws the air when nothing is there, as if attacking something spectral, and I've witnessed this before.

Then he bounds up the stairs, beating me back into the

kitchen. By now Dorothy has reappeared in her Grinch onesie, explaining she'd lost a jingle bell. She hopes I didn't mind her rooting through my bathroom drawers for needle and thread. Also checking all the cabinets to no avail.

"I had half a mind to dig into one of your scene cases," she says as I carry the wine into the kitchen, and Benton takes an approving look at the label. "I figured I could use a suture if all else failed. Then I found what I needed, a little travel sewing kit in your makeup bag."

"I'm hoping you really wouldn't go into any of my scene cases." I peel off the wine bottle's heavy foil, pleased that the cork seems moist so far. "It would be most unfortunate if I didn't have what I need." What I'm saying nicely is I'd better never catch her doing something like that.

She and Lucy busy themselves finding cocktail napkins and filling small plates with antipasto. Benton carries over wineglasses while I open the bottle, the cork sliding out with a perfect pop. I hold it up to my nose, inhaling the Bordeaux's rich nuances.

"Fingers crossed it's as fantastic as I think it's going to be." I pour a sip. "Especially after it opens up. Would you like to do the honors?"

"You first," he says, and I hold up the glass.

Swirling the wine, I admire its deep ruby legs, getting another noseful.

"By the time I'm done showering, it will be perfect." I take a sip of Lucy's birthday treat.

Swishing it around my tongue like a sommelier, savoring

the full range of the sensuous terroir . . . detecting blackberries, crushed rocks and flowers as Benton looks on . . . And Lucy does . . . Then I'm seeing two of them . . .

"Whoa, what's going on . . . ?" The floor is moving. "I feel weird . . . Something wrong . . ." Clumsily setting down the glass, I almost knock it over. "The wine . . . !"

"Aunt Kay . . . ?" Lucy's voice is far away. "Are you all right . . . ?"

"KAY!" Benton shouts as I gasp for breath.

"My scene case . . . !" I struggle for air, my vision blurring.

CHAPTER 14

THUNDER CRACKS LIKE SHOTGUN blasts, and the moaning wind sounds wounded. Rain beats the roof like angry sticks, splashing and thrashing this place I'm in.

Faster . . . slower . . . harder . . . softer . . . The digital time flares a hellish red in the dark . . .

. . . 8:37 . . .

. . . 8:38 . . .

Minutes twitch past blearily. I don't know where I am. Is it spring or summer? Winter or fall?

Why do I feel half dead?

As if I've been struck by a truck. How can I see when my eyes are shut?

. . . 8:40 . . .

. . . 8:41 . . .

What have I done?

. . . 8:42 . . .

. . . 8:43 . . .

What's happened to me?

And the clock hovers eerily. Threateningly. Screaming like a Stryker saw grinding through a skull. Water drums into metal sinks, a stretcher dripping blood on tile. Hot bony dust is in the air, the stench of death everywhere. I taste it, smell it . . .

Then gone, not there . . . Just the din of pouring rain . . . The wind howling like a legion of unsettled haunts about to spirit me away . . . While it drifts through my thoughts with queasy disbelief . . . The 1996 Bordeaux. . . . Sniffing, sipping dizzily . . . It's coming back slowly, disjointedly . . .

You were careless! The voice in my thoughts won't stop.

I'm under the covers in the upstairs bedroom, my head throbbing. My joints ache like a mother, and I've got to get going, should have hours ago. Lightning stutters, illuminating the window shades in the warm humid dark, and I remember the storm as Marino was driving me away from my office in his big pickup truck.

It must be Tuesday morning, the last day of November . . . My car is stranded at my office . . . I've missed the staff meeting . . . Won't make the nine o'clock deposition . . . There's much to check on in the labs. . . . What about any cases that may have come in during the night . . . ? Does Maggie know where I am . . . ?

"How are we doing?" Benton appears like a spirit, sitting down on the bed, warm and reassuring.

He kisses me good morning, and I can tell he's in cargo pants, a sweater, wearing his fitness tracker. He has on a chronograph timepiece with luminous hands and a carbon-fiber strap, and has been up for a while.

"Better?" He rubs my back, and I smell his musky aftershave, the coffee on his breath.

"Better than I deserve." I prop myself up, grateful to be alive and at the same time furious that I would be so trusting.

You should have been more careful!

"What matters is that you're still here. All of us couldn't be more grateful. I am, most of all," Benton says. "Are you ready for coffee?"

I shake my head no, I couldn't possibly.

You could have killed everyone!

"But thanks, maybe a little later." My mouth is as dry as paper. "Water, please."

He reaches for the bottle on the bedside table, twisting off the cap, my memories of last night shattered and hazy. I feel shame, paranoia, anger simmering around my edges, and I remind myself it's the aftermath of the drug. My chemistry is shot to hell, and I feel horrible for causing such a problem.

"Well, thank God for your scene case, and that you had the presence of mind to think of it." Benton's features are shadowed, his teeth indistinctly white in the near dark.

It's fortuitous I mentioned the Narcan to him earlier, commenting that I needed to replace what had been in the scene case I carried home from work. He didn't have to spend precious minutes rooting around. He knew exactly where to look, he says, and it was stupid of me to give all of the doses to Officer Fruge. What if I'd had none at home?

"The stars were lined up just right." Benton strokes my arm. "And you're going to be fine, good as new."

"It doesn't feel like it." I chug more water.

"I don't know when I've ever felt so helpless," he admits. "If the Narcan hadn't worked . . . ? Well, there was nothing more we could have done."

"Is everyone else okay? Lucy, Dorothy?" For an instant I'm seized by searing panic, remembering their shocked faces.

"Everyone is safe and sound. I made sure no one else touched the wine," he says, and there wasn't enough of the antidote to go around.

I had only the two doses in my home scene case, and whatever I was exposed to was potent enough to require both. In fact, it was barely enough, and I have no recollection of Benton administering the nasal spray but know he did because that's what he's telling me. I also don't remember Marino bringing extra doses to the house, and Benton giving me another one later.

He checked my vital signs throughout the night, all per my instructions, and it's a blank in my memory. How unbearable to imagine what would have happened had I poured a taste of the poisoned wine for him, Lucy, Dorothy. When Marino finally showed up, he would have found all of us dead. Depending on what he did, he might have been next.

"I don't remember the last time I felt this bad." My head hurts like it's clamped in a vise.

My pulse races, moods in flux, and my thinking is stream

of consciousness at times. It's as if I'm tripping, my hands shaky, my stomach lurching like a boat on rough seas.

"How about some Advil? Do you think you could hold it down?" Benton helps arrange more pillows behind me.

"Not this minute." Massaging my temples, I take deep slow breaths, exhausted in a way that won't be cured by sleep.

"What if I bring you toast?" He holds my hand, and I force myself to sit up straighter.

"I CAN'T," I REPLY, not ready for food.

"A hot shower would be good. But one thing at a time," Benton says as scenes flash behind my eyes like a psychedelic movie.

I remember setting down the wineglass with a loud clack, almost knocking it over . . . suddenly unsteady on my feet . . . Saying I felt strange, there was something wrong with the wine . . . as the room began to spin . . . I told Benton to get my scene case from the closet . . . but it was Lucy who did . . .

While he lowered me to the floor . . . and everything went black . . . Then Marino was there taking charge, gloved and masked, collecting my glass, the wine and all that went with it. Talking in his big voice with his strong New Jersey accent. Getting on the phone, waking up Rex Bonetta, exclaiming that someone just tried to poison the chief medical examiner of Virginia.

Marino was barking orders, throwing around his new title

of forensic operations specialist. He paced the kitchen while I watched from where I sat on the floor, leaning against the wall, overhearing every word. He would stop by my chief toxicologist's house to drop off the evidence personally, and Marino warned not a peep about this to anyone.

What's happened is extremely confidential, and there will be an international investigation, he promised, rather much threatened. Gathering up his brown paper bags sealed with red evidence tape, he reprimanded me again for being foolish. Next, Dorothy jumped in, the two of them quite the interrogators.

Why would I accept a gift that's consumable and could be tampered with? How could I think for a moment it was okay in this day and age? It doesn't matter if the bottle was from the president or the pope, how could I be that naïve? As if it's my fault I was exposed to a deadly opioid likely intended for the secretary general of Interpol.

At least I'm assuming it was an opioid since the antidote was successful. Two hits, and the effects were reversed. But I don't know what we're dealing with yet, and most of all if it's an isolated incident.

"What if the bottle I was given isn't the only one?" I fight back another wave of nausea.

"You can rest assured it's being followed up on," Benton says.

I was in Lyon the end of October, and a month is a long time when there could be other deadly vintages waiting to be uncorked. There could be deaths we don't know about in other parts of the world.

"More important at the moment is getting you back up to speed," he replies kindly, gently. "You need to eat. That will be the best remedy. We're going to get to the bottom of who's responsible, I promise. Assuming anyone's to blame, that it was deliberate."

"What other explanation could there be?" I'm dismayed by another flare of impatient indignation.

"If it were an allergic response to something like tannins." He patiently offers a remote possibility. "Anaphylaxis, in other words."

"Hypothetically yes. But not in my case."

I explain that a severe allergic reaction to tannins or anything else would have closed my airway, requiring epinephrine. Not naloxone, and I have the unsettling sensation that we've been through this before.

"Had you tried an EpiPen, it wouldn't have worked," I add. "I knew I was reacting to a powerfully intoxicating drug that was depressing my breathing, causing me to lose consciousness."

"You don't remember saying all this last night when I put you to bed, do you?" he replies.

"Some things are coming back slowly," I answer with an edge, and I hate that I can't control myself better. "A lot is lost. I have big empty gaps and disconnections. Hopefully it's temporary. But I don't know. I'm sorry, Benton. So terribly sorry for bringing the wine home, for opening it, for being in a foul mood, for everything."

"There's nothing for you to apologize about, so please stop," he says. "The good news is you may have saved Gabriella Honoré's life. Probably the lives of those closest to her too."

"For which I'm very thankful, couldn't be more thankful." All the same, I was as careless as I've ever been.

"You can imagine the intense investigation already mounted," Benton says, informing me that he talked to the secretary general earlier this morning.

The Bordeaux was a gift from a police chief in Belgium whom she knows well and trusts. As I recall from my visits over the years, it's not unusual for distinguished guests to arrive with fine wines, liquors, cheeses, tins of caviar. It's France after all, I remember the secretary general saying while I was with her late fall.

"*Amusez-vous,* Kay. *Bonne santé*" were her exact words when she handed me the bottle wrapped in brown paper, still inside its elegant gift bag from a shop with a Brussels address.

We were having lunch inside her corner office with its sweeping views of red terra-cotta roofs, and the Pont Winston Churchill spanning the river Rhône. The autumn foliage blazed against a deep blue sky, Interpol's headquarters of metal and glass glittering like a space station across from Parc de la Tête d'Or.

"*De l'espace à la terre à six pieds sous.*" From space to ground to six feet under, Gabriella Honoré said during our discussion of emerging technologies and the risks they pose to humanity.

There was no lack of worst-case scenarios for us to offer and ponder. It's not hard to imagine what happens when psychopaths get hold of nuclear weapons. Just as dangerous is what doesn't necessarily meet the eye in the invisible world of poisons, viruses and cyberattacks on anything one can think of including orbiting satellites and habitats.

"Life and death, good deeds and bad will go where people go whether on Earth or above," the secretary general said dramatically, speaking on and off in English while opening a bottle of Chablis. "The moon, Mars and beyond, there's no limit to *les actes monstrueux* people are capable of."

Then she shifted her attention to the grand cru she was pouring. After all, one must remember what's important, she said with her charming smile, serving the wine in simple bistro tumblers. Crisp and clean with hints of citrus, it was in perfect harmony with an entrée of raw oysters.

Followed by the *quenelle de brochet* with prawns that Lyon is famous for, and we had quite the scientific discussion about the complexities of white Burgundies.

"But I admit being partial to a full-bodied red Bordeaux, a blend like a Pauillac or a Margaux," she let me know. "And I think you, Benton and Lucy will find that nineteen ninety-six was *une très bonne année.*"

She made no pretense about the provenance, that the bottle she'd given me may be a very good year but it was a regift. The head of the most powerful police organization in the world, and she wanted me to consider it a token of her friendship and appreciation. Solicitous about my niece and her recent losses,

Gabriella hoped that all of us would drink the fine French wine to our good health.

Such an irony, and I wouldn't want to be in the secretary general's shoes right now. She must feel even worse than I do about almost sending death to my door. The wine could have killed my entire family, and the biggest question is when the bottle was tampered with.

CHAPTER 15

HOW DID IT HAPPEN, and who was the intended victim?"
Benton says. "Likely it was Gabi," as he calls her, and he wasn't
in Lyon with me.

In the midst of foiling the latest terrorist plot to overthrow
our democracy, he couldn't represent the United States at our
first international symposium of the Doomsday Commission.
As disappointing as that was, it's nothing new, and I traveled
alone.

"The first woman secretary general, and she comes on like
gangbusters against human rights violations and hacking,"
Benton says. "In particular going after Putin, and poisonings
are the Russian's special sauce."

"Interpol's relationship with China hasn't been so great,
either." I remind him that the former president of the international police organization was Chinese. "He vanished from
France and since has been arrested, as I recall from what was
all over the news."

"I agree," Benton says as I lean against him, my head on his shoulder. "It's improbable that the wine was meant for you or anyone around you, including me."

Whoever tampered with it had no reason to think that the secretary general might turn around and give it to someone else, he adds. It's also hard to imagine the Brussels police chief would have anything to do with such a scheme. It would be far too easy to trace, in fact, ridiculously so.

"For sure he's going to be questioned, and might even be blamed." Benton sets another bottle of water on my bedside table. "Not to mention the possible damage to his reputation if this becomes public. No matter what, there will be those who think he's guilty or at least wonder about it."

"We don't know that he wasn't the intended victim," it occurs to me next. "Or possibly it was the owner of the Brussels wine shop."

"That's right, we don't know much at this point. Without evidence, we can't even say a crime's been committed."

"Clearly the person responsible doesn't give a damn about possible collateral damage no matter how random," I reply angrily. "Doesn't care who might be ruined or killed. Someone's husband, wife, child, could be absolutely anyone," and the thought is sickening.

"That much is indisputable."

Benton walks past the brick fireplace and antique furniture, headed to the windows overlooking the water. He begins opening the shades, letting in the morning gloom.

"Bottom line," he says, "we won't know who the intended

victim was until we figure out when and where the bottle was accessed. And how it was done."

"Yes, and with what," I agree. "I'll start checking with the labs as soon as I can think straight and don't feel queasy."

From my vantage point on the bed, I can see old trees stirring in the wind, the gray sky churning over the Potomac River. The last weather report I remember predicted showers on and off today with another front on the way. This one could include freezing rain that in Old Town usually means power outages.

During bad storms, people around here stay inside, their focus on old roofs leaking and trees coming down. Some roads and alleyways flood, and the police are tied up with accidents and other weather-related calls. Beat officers aren't as eager to patrol in a downpour, and conveniently for Gwen's killer, Fruge was tied up on drug overdoses last Friday night.

In bad weather, surveillance cameras are less effective on the ground. They're not helpful from above when there's a heavy overcast. All of these factors created the very conditions Gwen Hainey's killer may have found ideal. My thoughts slide back into that dark hole while Benton remains fixated on the wine that almost killed me and possibly everyone I love.

"We have to ask who had access," he says, standing in front of his dresser, and in the dim light of the blustery morning, I see what he has on.

A black turtleneck sweater, black cargo pants, tactical boots as if just coming in from a police detail, and he retrieves his 9mm pistol, a Sig Sauer like mine.

"Let's look at every link in the chain. Gabriella gave you the wine while you were with her at Interpol." He slides the gun into a pocket holster that he tucks inside his waistband. "From there you carried it directly back to your hotel room in Lyon, where it stayed for several days?"

As he says this, I envision the tile floors, carved wooden beam ceilings and colorful silk-covered walls. I remember the sensuous perfumes of the candles and soaps, and the *bouquet floral et fruité* of the house Beaujolais, crimson like blood.

"That's correct. As you know, I was in and out of meetings that included lunches and dinners," I reply, and several days went by with our barely talking on the phone, both of us too busy. "I wasn't in my room much, and the bottle remained wrapped in paper inside its bag on top of the closet safe."

"In other words, it was accessible."

"Unfortunately." I feel stupid again. "Then it was in my luggage for the flight from Paris to London, where I stopped off for a day of meetings."

It's unthinkable what might have happened had I regifted the regift, passing along the tainted bottle to someone else the same way the secretary general did with me. Dinner was with New Scotland Yard's commissioner, and I spent a hospitable evening at her home. What if I'd shown up with that 1996 Bordeaux?

"As you know," I remind Benton, "I was in London only one night, leaving the wine in my luggage. The next morning, it was on to Dulles."

"Adding even more opportunities, unfortunately," he says.

"Since then, it's been here in the basement until last night."

"The least likely site of the tampering is our house. But I'm not saying it didn't happen here. For sure, there were workmen in and out while we've been getting the place in shape."

But since returning from France with the wine there have been few people in and out. Mostly it's been the security system troubleshooters, the police who've continued showing up when there are false alarms and other malfunctions.

"GOOD GOD, BENTON." FRUSTRATED, I push back the covers. "I don't know how we're supposed to trust anything anymore. Whether we're talking about someone negative for a deadly virus or if something is safe to eat or drink. And who's okay to allow on your property. Not to mention, what's true or false."

"It wouldn't be your average bear who tampered with the wine," he says, and of course he's right. "This was meticulously premeditated by someone who knows what he's doing."

My head might split open, another wave of nausea, and I couldn't be more annoyed with myself.

You of all people know better!

I should have been warier, more on guard. But it's hard to live like that constantly, and I'd be the first to admit I was preoccupied with far more than the demands of my first Doomsday Commission international symposium. I was distracted by my grief-stricken niece who isn't at her best when dealing with her emotions.

There's nothing I wouldn't do to mend her broken heart, to fill the emptiness and stop the hurt. When the secretary general presented me with the Bordeaux, my first thought was Lucy's birthday coming up. I imagined surprising her with her favorite meal accompanied by an exceptional wine that I carried home from France.

Best of all was the thought of spending quality time in front of the fire. I'd make sure it was just the two of us. We'd talk about the good times from the past, and better days to come. Drinking a toast to them, I'd remind her of the infinite possibilities ahead.

Never eat or drink anything from a stranger!

Except Gabriella Honoré isn't one, and the voice in my head is Marino's, not mine. I've been hearing it nonstop, making me feel carped at the same way my mother did, reminding me of every mistake I've ever made including my profession. A doctor to the dead because I can't bother with the living, she'd tell anyone who'd listen.

"This would be a good day to stay in, maybe work in bed, review all those old dusty files you keep dragging around," Benton says. "I'll bring you breakfast, I know just the thing."

"Not yet. My stomach has to settle. As soon as possible, I need to get to the office to see what's going on with confirming Gwen Hainey's identification so the police can notify the family. Not that they don't already know from the news," I'm reminded unpleasantly.

"Her murder has gone viral on the Internet, all sorts of theories cropping up," Benton says.

Lowering my feet to the floor, I stand up unsteadily, and he's close by and at the ready.

"You're dressed as if you're going somewhere." I put my arm around his slender waist. "Either that or starring in an action movie. What's on your agenda today besides dropping me off to get my car?"

"I never really went to bed," he says as I try walking on my own. "I changed into something practical, that's all, and you're not driving anywhere for a while even if you think you're back to normal. How are you doing?"

"I'll be fine."

"That's not what I asked." He pulls me closer.

"I've been better but I'll be okay," I repeat. "What have you been up to all night?"

He answers vaguely that there's been much to keep everybody scurrying about. Lucy has been reviewing security videos, making sure no one has been on the property that we don't know about, he says.

"We're talking about hours and hours of footage to review, and I was with her in the cottage for a while," Benton explains.

I head toward the windows, barefoot, and in scrubs I don't remember putting on.

"We're checking the security recordings going back to before we moved in," he says. "For one thing, to make sure no one might have been casing the place prior to our getting here."

I walk past a mirror that murkily reflects the oil paintings on the opposite wall. It's too dim to make out the Miró farm scenes or other fine art that I can't afford on my government salary. Most of what's rare and expensive doesn't come from my side of the equation, the property we're living on a perfect example.

Also, the Stickley trestle coffee table, the brown leather sofa, the barristers bookcases filled with old leather-bound volumes. My husband's New England pedigree traces back to the Pilgrims, his father a wealthy art collector. I'm the product of first-generation Italians who settled in Miami after the Second World War.

My father owned a small grocery store in a neighborhood made up of Cubans and Italians. I have no ancestral heirlooms, no inherited antiques or art, and it's safe to say that Benton Wesley didn't marry me for money.

"When we started living on the property a month ago, I put the wine in the basement refrigerator." I'm trying to work out what could have happened. "Meaning the bottle from Interpol was here while the alarm people and possibly others including the police have been on our property."

"To leave no stone unturned, Marino and I went through the basement." Benton waits by the bed, his eyes on me. "We especially focused on the area where you store the wine. We made sure there wasn't anything that might make us think someone was in there who shouldn't have been."

"Except I'm not sure what you'd be looking for that we wouldn't have noticed long before now. Assuming it was something that would be noticed at all."

"What I can say is nothing jumped out at us but that doesn't mean much," he agrees. "Certainly, there's no evidence that anyone has tried to break into the basement."

"Like I said, I think we would know that by now," I reply, looking out a window at the Woodrow Wilson Memorial Bridge spanning a wide swath of the Potomac, connecting Virginia to Maryland.

CHAPTER 16

THE COLOR OF THE water this morning is the gray-green of old glass. Protruding from it is a stubble of dark wooden pilings left from the dock that was there centuries earlier. I imagine the sea captain who built our house watching his moored ship from this very spot.

"Are you okay to be on your own while I go downstairs?" Benton asks as I walk away from a view I've come to love. "Or do you want me to stay up here while you clean up? I don't want you alone if you're dizzy or even slightly unsteady on your feet."

"I'm feeling much better, will be down in a few." I hug and kiss him, grateful he takes such good care of me. "You could have married somebody easier, you know. I warned you often enough."

"How boring that would be," he says, walking off.

The old pumpkin pine flooring is smooth and cool beneath my feet as I head to the bathroom with its white subway-tile walls, the claw-foot tub and glass-enclosed shower. Flipping on the light, I squint at my pale reflection in the mirror over the marble washbasin.

"Goodness," I mutter under my breath.

I look like death on a cracker, to quote my sister, my hair sticking up, and I hear Benton's phone ring on the stairs. Then mine does, the area code in the display 202 for Washington, D.C., the exchange 538, and that can't be good.

"Dr. Scarpetta," I answer over speakerphone.

"It's Tron," the familiar voice says.

The U.S. Secret Service cyber investigator's actual name is Sierra Patron, and she's a member of the Doomsday Commission task force. She's not calling to check in or chat because that's not what she does, and I squeeze hot water from a washcloth, apologizing for the noise.

"Hold on a second." I turn off the water in the sink.

Closing the toilet lid, I sit down. Tilting my head back, I place the hot compress over my eyes, and I can't let on how bad I'm feeling and why.

"How are you, Tron? What's going on?" I can hear the vague murmur of Benton downstairs, possibly getting the same notification I am.

"You're needed at the White House complex ASAP," she says, and of all times to feel as hungover as I've ever been in my life.

"I'm assuming Benton is being told the same thing. I hear him downstairs, our phones rang simultaneously." I remove the washcloth, running more hot water over it.

"That's correct."

"Both of us are needed?" I want to make sure, and what he mentioned a few minutes ago is exactly right.

I shouldn't be driving anywhere for a while, and how embarrassing. Closing my eyes again, I drape the steaming cloth over them.

"That's correct." Tron confirms that Benton will be accompanying me, thank goodness. "We've got a situation and need you here as fast as you can manage." She hopes that won't be a problem.

The way she says it makes me suspect she somehow knows I'm under the weather, and if I felt ashamed before, now I'm mortified. I hate to think what she would say about my carelessness, both of us in Lyon at the same Doomsday symposium.

I seriously doubt she carried gifts of food or drink home from France to share with family and friends. Wouldn't matter who gave it to her, and I'll never make that mistake again.

"I'm getting ready now," I let her know with enthusiasm I don't feel, back on my feet, opening the medicine cabinet. "Are there special considerations or instructions? Other details I should be aware of?"

She doesn't answer my question. The Secret Service cyber investigator isn't going to tell me anything else, my paranoia spiking.

She knows the stupid thing I've done.

I continue reminding myself that I'm probably not entirely logical at the moment. Why would Tron know about what happened last night? I'm not sure anyone does beyond my immediate circle, and of course Rex Bonetta, the toxicologist Marino woke up at oh-dark-hundred. No one called 911.

There's no police report, nothing to be leaked to the media, and what a field day the likes of Dana Diletti would have with the latest. Just the idea makes me inwardly cringe as I remember dodging her, watching footage of it on national TV.

Shaking four Advil into my palm, I swallow them without water, glancing in the mirror. I'm not sure it's possible to make myself presentable, and Tron goes on to inform me that Benton and I will be on a list at each checkpoint and guard shack.

"Stay safe, and I'll be waiting for you at the entrance of the West Executive Gate." Tron ends the call without further explanation, and I hear Benton on his phone, his voice drifting up the staircase.

I can't make out what he's saying but the fact that he's still talking tells me plenty. Information is being shared and discussed with him and him alone. Then the sound fades until I can't hear him anymore as he likely heads to the kitchen. Peeling off my scrubs, I drop them inside the hamper.

I inhale clouds of steam, tears flooding my eyes, everything catching up with me as I shower. Overwhelmed by misgivings about returning to Virginia, I'm gripped by the fear that I've been unrealistic and selfish. In the process I've dragged everyone here with me, and not because I asked them to move or even consider it. Because I didn't. I wouldn't.

They showed up anyway, and what was I thinking? Maybe I don't want to face that each day the road behind me gets longer than the one ahead, and there's no reversing the trajectory. Possibly when I was first approached about becoming the chief again, I deluded myself into believing we can go back to what we left.

Or more likely I was running away from what I didn't want to face after losing Janet and Desi. Worst of all is knowing what it's done to my niece. Death is the one thing I can't defeat no matter how much I wish otherwise, and it would seem I've done nobody any favors by returning to where I got started.

On the job a little more than three short weeks, and things aren't going very well. There's no one to blame but myself. It's time I do something about it besides just standing here and taking what comes while fretting constantly about offending someone.

You're too nice.

How many times has Lucy said that when she hears what's going on at work.

You can't be afraid to show them who's boss, Aunt Kay.

NOTHING WILL CHANGE IF all I do is worry about displeasing this one or another, and I feel the slow burn of an angry stubbornness setting in. I step out of the shower, drying off, and there's no better cure for discouragement than getting back into the saddle.

Putting on my bathrobe, I call the DNA lab, unfamiliar with the clerk who cheerfully answers, "This is Candi," as if she works in a nail salon. I announce myself, and when she doesn't respond beyond a grunted "uh-huh," I add, "Good morning."

"Oh hi, good morning. Um, who are you looking for?" is her distracted reply, and technically she doesn't answer to me.

But the lab director, her boss, does. I can get her in plenty of trouble if I'm sufficiently motivated.

"I realize we haven't met. I'm the new chief medical examiner," I add in case she hasn't connected the dots.

"I know. I've seen you on the news when Dana Diletti's tried to interview you. What's she like in person?"

"I need Doctor Givens, please," I reply, and Candi the clerk doesn't see him at the moment, doesn't know where he is.

"He's probably tied up," she figures as I imagine her yawning, looking bored. "Maybe you could try back later?"

"Candi?" I say her name in a way that gets her attention. "I don't care what he's in the middle of, I want him on the phone right now."

"Oh. Yes, ma'am. Okay . . . Um, h-hold on," she stammers, and in no time, molecular biologist Clark Givens is on the line.

"How's it going?" I don't have to tell him why I'm calling.

"We should have the answer within the hour," he informs me as I stand in front of the sink, tearing off a piece of dental floss.

I tell him to text me when Gwen Hainey's identification is confirmed, and make sure he notifies August Ryan at the same time so he can deal with the next of kin.

"Sadly, her family, those who knew her probably already heard what's all over the news, and that should never happen." I towel my hair some more.

"August has called here several times already. And the media's out of control, hounding everyone from what I understand," Clark lets me know. "When I got here a few hours ago, there was a TV truck on the street filming employees getting out of their cars, heading into the building."

"Let me guess." I open a drawer under the sink, finding the styling gel. "Dana Diletti again."

"Her producer is one of the people who keeps calling." Clark's voice over speakerphone inside the master bathroom. "Apparently, she's doing some big piece on the Railway Slayer, as she's dubbed Gwen Hainey's killer. And that's sure to scare the bejesus out of everyone."

"Making everything that much harder for those of us trying to work the case," I reply, and I bring up the disturbing death that Officer Fruge told me about.

Cammie Ramada, her body found on the shore of the Potomac River inside the same park where Gwen was found on Daingerfield Island, I explain to Clark.

"Apparently, this was in early April, and ruled a drowning, the manner of death accidental." I run a comb through my damp hair, working a dab of gel through it. "But a police officer I was with last night insists Cammie Ramada was murdered. There seem to be a lot of unanswered questions about the case."

"Which police officer?" Clark asks, and I can tell he's guarded.

"Blaise Fruge." I open a cabinet, and nothing is where it's supposed to be thanks to Dorothy rummaging through my belongings. "She and I spent a lot of time together going through Gwen Hainey's townhome."

"What is it I can help you with, exactly?"

"I'm interested in what you have to say since you were working here when Cammie Ramada mysteriously drowned." I remind him I hadn't moved from Massachusetts yet.

I also don't think the death made the news in a big way or I would have heard about it. I go on to say that Park Police Investigator Ryan hasn't mentioned the case to me, and one can only hope there's no conspiracy of silence going on.

"Because of tourism, local business, politics or anything else," I'm saying to Clark. "We need to make sure her death isn't connected to Gwen Hainey's," I add, and he responds with a startled pause.

"Just so we're clear," he finally says, "I was on vacation with my family in the Outer Banks when Cammie Ramada's body was found."

At the end of the day, his lab isn't responsible for the DNA analysis such as it was, he adds. There's not much to tell except what he knows from talking to the police, reviewing their reports, he says.

"The FBI decided to move samples to their Quantico labs and do the analysis there," Clark explains, and they'll try the same thing with me, I have no doubt.

But it's not going to happen. I've yet to let them take Gwen's evidence out from under us. The body and everything relating to it is the medical examiner's jurisdiction. Naturally, I extend that to include the flattened penny, and anything else I collected, the analysis in my labs already under way.

"Our hands were tied as you likely know if you've reviewed the records," Clark says over speakerphone. "Once the FBI took over, that was that."

"The problem is I've not looked at the records yet," I reply, fussing with my hair in the mirror. "I'd never heard of Cammie Ramada before last night but intend to get up to speed before the day is out."

"After the FBI took what they wanted, nothing happened. The case was closed."

He explains that the scene wasn't managed the way it should have been, too many cooks in the kitchen. There were problems with contamination.

"I'm not sure how well acquainted you might be with the former chief," Clark says, and he doesn't know the half of it. "But it's likely he hasn't worked many scenes in recent memory."

"I'd say that's accurate." I refrain from adding the rest of it.

Elvin Reddy is more of a politician than a medical examiner, having no passion or respect for the work itself and even less for patients living or dead. He'd far rather appear on the news or mingle with the prominent and powerful than talk to the family of a loved one who's died suddenly, tragically.

I knew what he was early on when he'd have his morbid fun with those he could bully. Nothing like asking the wrong person to open a body bag crawling with maggots. Or making lewd observations about a dead woman's "sizeable attributes, what a waste." I'd overhear his salacious cracks.

He was the sort to keep trophies such as artificial joints and breast implants until I caught wind of it. Suffice it to say, we did nothing but clash during my Richmond days when he was one of my forensic pathology fellows, the worst I ever mentored.

CHAPTER 17

"MIND YOU, THIS IS hearsay because I wasn't there." Clark continues to tell me what he knows about last April's case. "Doctor Reddy appearing at the scene only added to the confusion, and the cops were afraid to stand up to him if he did something they didn't agree with."

"Such as?"

"Not having appropriate PPE," he says. "Just a mask, gloves, and he had to be told to put them on."

Clark says he's seen the photographs of the former chief shining his light on the body, and he's not exactly a poster child for proper forensic procedures. Such trifling details are for everyone else to worry about, is the way he looks at it.

"Not to mention," he adds, "there's the obvious complications since we're talking about a national park. The Feds, in other words, and technically the jurisdiction of the park police."

But Daingerfield Island is located in the city of Alexandria, and of interest to their law enforcement. Also, the FBI could stake claims on the investigation. To confuse things further, Cammie Ramada's body was partially on Virginia soil, and partially in water located in the District of Columbia. What Marino would call a cluster-eff on flipping steroids.

"Talk about a mess." Clark's voice sounds from my phone on the edge of the sink as I do what I can to patch myself together. "Try dealing with a case involving the park police, the locals and the FBI. And meanwhile, the chief medical examiner of Virginia and those answering to him don't feel a crime was committed."

"I'm curious why Elvin Reddy showed up to begin with." Unzipping my makeup bag, I certainly can see that Dorothy rummaged through it for a sewing kit.

"I don't have a clue. All I can tell you is we picked up Doctor Reddy's DNA and excluded him. That's the contamination I'm talking about."

The investigation never went anywhere after it was determined by my predecessor that the death wasn't due to violence.

"Samples were never tested or entered into a database," Clark says, and now I'm really appalled.

"Are you suggesting that the FBI never ran the DNA through CODIS?" I'm hoping I didn't hear him right.

"It's my understanding that no profiles from the Cammie Ramada case were uploaded into CODIS," he repeats.

"Why not?" I ask, and just when I think Elvin couldn't be more negligent or incompetent.

"A submission can't be a fishing expedition." Clark recites the usual CODIS protocols that I know so well.

The DNA profile must be from the suspected perpetrator, and there isn't one if no crime was committed. Contaminated samples aren't allowed, and he knows as well as I do that bureaucratic obstructions can be gotten around if one is motivated by justice instead of self-interest or laziness.

"A murder doesn't go away because someone decides it." Staring in the mirror I go easy with the eyeshadow, just a touch of brown. "If Doctor Reddy had left the case pending because he wasn't sure what happened to her? The evidence would have been tested, and we likely wouldn't be having this conversation, Clark."

"I don't disagree."

"So, here's what I'd like you to do." I pick up the eyeliner pencil. "I want you to treat Cammie Ramada as the coldest of cold cases, and start over."

"What do you mean, start over? The case is closed."

"I've just reopened it. Let's see what's left of the evidence collected from the scene, the autopsy." I brush my hair back from my face, looking at my reflection, and it could be worse. "Anything that might be a source of DNA with the thought in mind that her death might not have been accidental."

I tell him to pay special attention to swabs taken from the body, from skin surfaces, inside orifices, and under the fingernails.

"And whatever Cammie was wearing when her body was found," I add while texting Lucy, asking her to see what she can find out about the victim.

"She was clothed when she was found, it didn't look like a sexual assault," Clark says as I text Marino next.

I let him know that I'm going to need his help later in the day. He's to stand by and I'll get back to him. In the meantime, I need him to find out what he can about Cammie Ramada's death this past April.

"Running tights, shoes, a long-sleeved jacket." Clark recalls what she had on when she died. "Again, you'll see from the scene photographs."

Lucy answers me with a "copy that" thumbs-up. She'll see what she can find out. She and Janet both will, I guess.

"We still have swatches we removed from her clothing but never analyzed," Clark says.

"How much of this is at the FBI labs?"

"They took the samples they wanted. But most of the evidence is still here."

"I want your lab to get started right way with rapid DNA testing," I tell him. "Any unknown profile or partial one we'll also want submitted to CODIS, and if we come back empty-handed we try forensic genealogical testing next."

"You do realize these samples still aren't going to meet the CODIS standards for submission," he warns as another message lands on my phone.

Have heard about the Ramada case, a weird one, Marino has texted me back.

"The FBI's database isn't the first whistle stop. We are." I carry my phone as I leave the bathroom, still talking to Clark.

I ask him to compare any unknown DNA profiles or partial ones in Cammie's and Gwen's cases. And to do it as quickly as possible, I remind him as I open my closet, wondering which suit to wear. "If it turns out both are homicides and they were killed by the same person, we have to worry that someone else may be next."

WINDSHIELD WIPERS DRAG ACROSS the glass in a light rain at half past ten, more volatile weather on the way. Traffic is slower and more snarled than usual, and that's saying a lot as congested as it normally gets in this part of Virginia.

Benton is at the wheel of his Tesla SUV, wearing amber-tinted glasses in the fog to cut down on the glare. He's changed from his earlier tactical attire into one of his impeccable suits, charcoal gray with pearl pinstripes, and over this a long black trench coat.

As usual, he's far more the fashion statement than I am in my simple Prussian blue pants suit, my sensible low-heeled ankle boots with nonslip soles. My dark brown jacket is made of a quilted waterproof fabric, nothing fancy. I might have gone to the trouble of wearing a skirt and dressier shoes were I feeling more energetic.

"What I think is that nobody bothered following up on her death. Certain parties hoped it would just go away," Benton is saying about Cammie Ramada.

"I worry they did more than hope," I reply.

"That's what it's sounding like."

"Of all days to get called to some emergency meeting in D.C., when what I really need is to go through her case," I reply. "Well, chances are I won't be getting around to that in the near future but at least I can get people started."

I try Lucy first, and most of all I want to check on her.

"How far out are you?" Her voice through the speakers, and she sounds in decent enough spirits.

"Depending on traffic," Benton says, "maybe fifteen. Not including checkpoints."

"Do you know what they want yet?" she says, and by *they* she means Benton's Secret Service colleague Tron.

The two of them are warily acquainted, and I would have predicted they wouldn't get along. Certainly not at first. They're too much alike.

"I have no idea why I'm being summoned," I reply.

Lucy hasn't been informed about the White House, only that the Secret Service needs us, that we're headed to a highly secure area in D.C. She may figure it out. But what she won't do is prod or pry.

"How's it going with Cammie Ramada?" I take a sip of water. "There certainly seem to be questions about what happened to her."

"I'm on it but nothing much out there, almost nothing in the media," she says, and I hear keys clicking. "There was some chatter on social media at the time. We're still digging," she adds, and I wonder if she's looking at Janet's avatar as we're speaking.

"I'll be off the radar for a while, possibly most of the day," I reply. "But you and Marino can conspire."

"You sure you're feeling okay?" she says, and I'll forever see her terrified eyes as I began feeling the effects of the poisoned wine.

"Almost as good as new." I'm not really. "Hopefully we can have dinner later."

I end the call as Benton follows George Washington Memorial Parkway, and Daingerfield Island is off to our right. It's not really an island but a forested swath in the northernmost part of Alexandria, between a major highway and the Potomac River.

"I have a feeling Cammie is what I call a nuisance case, a threat to local business and everything else," Benton concludes from what he's overheard so far.

"That's what I'm guessing Elvin Reddy thinks about it. Well, as my mother used to say, he's got another *think* coming," I reply, looking out my window at dense trees, most of them bare this time of year.

The park at Daingerfield Island is popular with runners, cyclists, bird-watchers, and it has a marina and a sailing club that I can't see in the overcast. Also, there's a bar and grill that Benton and I have enjoyed on occasion, looking out at the water and the boats, catching glimpses of red-tailed hawks and bald eagles.

I can see the Tidal Basin, and the Thomas Jefferson Memorial's pristine white rotunda up ahead, vague in the swirling fog, the oncoming headlights bleary. Checking my messages, I'm waiting to hear from Rex Bonetta, and I try calling him again. This time he answers, and I let him know he's on speakerphone.

"It's okay to talk. I'm in the car with Benton," I explain.

"How are you doing?" he asks.

"Much better than I was, thanks."

"I'm very glad to hear it, and my lab's in overdrive trying to find out what you got hold of last night." My chief toxicologist's quiet voice through the surround-sound speakers. "Or better put, what got hold of you."

"I'm very sorry you were visited at home in the middle of the night." I hope Marino didn't scare him to death, ringing the bell, pounding on the door. "Please apologize to your family. But as you know, the circumstances are highly unusual."

"You sound all right, what a relief."

"I have strange flashbacks occasionally. Otherwise, doing fine, headed to a meeting." I don't say where as we drive through the heart of Washington, D.C., in the dreary overcast and drizzle.

"I've got good news and bad," Rex says. "But mostly bad."

On 14th Street now, we're passing the Bureau of Engraving and Printing, colorful bunting hanging between its soaring stone columns. Concrete barricades in front of government buildings make it impossible to get close to anything in a world turned so destructive and disrespectful.

"While I had the evidence in my custody, I took it upon myself to take a look at the cork and the foil wrapper that covered it," Rex explains. "I wanted to see if I noticed anything under the microscope because the obvious mystery is how did a toxin get into the wine. And I'm assuming the tampering happened after it was bottled."

"We'd better hope so," Benton replies, and there are military vehicles, police cars at every corner. "I would hate to think there might be multiple other bottles out there, although I suspect we'd know that by now. Someone would have died, possibly many would have."

I can't get past the surreal experience. Watching my personal property packaged as evidence. Realizing how close I came to ending up in my own morgue. Imagining my biological fluids, my pieces and parts making the rounds floor to floor inside my building. What a way to return to Virginia, what a way to finish what I started.

"I found a puncture in the foil and the cork that are visible under low magnification." Rex's voice inside the car as we turn left onto H Street. "Possibly random product tampering but based on what I know, it's more likely what we're talking about is a targeted attempt."

"Are the punctures visible to the naked eye?" I remember lifting the bottle out of the refrigerator, carrying it upstairs.

But I didn't examine the foil or the cork carefully. Truth is, I scarcely looked at them, period.

"They'd be really easy to miss," Rex says. "You'd almost have to be expecting them."

It's a good thing I happened to use a nondestructive two-prong puller, he adds. Otherwise the injection site would have been obliterated by the more typical corkscrew's metal helix, the worm.

CHAPTER 18

CONCRETE BARRIERS AND IRON fencing have turned the White House grounds and its immediate surrounds into a fortress or a prison. Rising high above it all, the Washington Monument seems to give terrorists the finger.

"The poison was injected through the foil and the cork," Rex summarizes, and I should have paid closer attention to the bottle when I was getting ready to open it.

"I don't remember it looking tampered with in the least," I reply, and Benton shakes his head no as he drives.

He didn't, either. But of course the Bordeaux looked perfectly fine. That's the reason for using some type of syringe to sabotage it. No one is supposed to notice that they're about to die.

"I admit that tampering was the furthest thing from my mind. And as expertly done as it was, I might have missed it anyway," I explain without making excuses. "An injection site isn't going to jump out at anyone, I don't care who it is. But more important moving forward is the tox screen. Do we have any idea what we're dealing with, Rex?"

"That's the bad news," he says, and Lafayette Square is fenced in and empty, military trucks lining the street. "It's an unknown substance so far."

"What about carfentanil?"

The synthetic opioid is ten thousand times stronger than morphine, and I've worked many overdose fatalities where it's been added to heroin and other street drugs.

"The Russians are quite facile with carfentanil." Benton speaks up again.

He reminds us that in 2002 they pumped what's believed to be an aerosolized version of it into a Moscow theater seized by armed Chechens. The so-called sleeping gas did the trick but not without killing more than a hundred hostages.

"Based on how quickly you were overcome, Kay," Rex replies, "that's the first thing that came to mind for me as well. But like I said, the conventional screens didn't pick up anything. And specifically, I checked for carfentanil."

It was negative, he repeats, and unfortunately what that suggests is there's something new we need to be extremely concerned about. That may take a while to determine, difficult toxicology cases often dragging on endlessly, and Officer Fruge's mother comes to mind.

She may not have been my favorite person when we worked together years ago. But she's gifted. She thinks outside the box. As I'm pondering this I'm telling Rex that we'll want the bottle, the foil, the cork checked for fingerprints and DNA.

"Then everything goes to the trace evidence lab," I add to the list.

Also, samples of the wine, and I explain we'll want to focus especially on any particulate that might have settled to the bottom of the bottle.

"Thanks, and keep me updated, but I probably won't be available for the next few hours," I let him know, and as a rule it wouldn't be up to the chief toxicologist to examine evidence first the way he did.

I wouldn't be instructing him where it goes next, to whom and why, and we'd better hope chain of custody never becomes a question. Because when Marino stopped at Rex's house in the middle of the night, that was the end of anything remotely resembling proper procedures.

Driving slowly along 17th Street, we're getting close, and I dig in my briefcase for my lipstick, giving myself a quick touch-up in the visor mirror. The Hay-Adams hotel is coming up grandly on our right, one of Benton's and my favorite places to stay. I look out wistfully at its columned portico, the four flags fluttering over it in the fog.

National guardsmen and police on every corner are ready for war, armored vehicles strategically placed. The Ellipse is fenced-in like most everything else, the national Christmas tree up but not lighted yet. I know where we're going but not who we're meeting or why. Benton hasn't said anything that might give me a heads-up about what's expected of us.

But it's hopeless quizzing him further as we near the first checkpoint, the White House complex gleaming like an egg-shell in the overcast.

Across from it is the soaring gray granite Louvre-like Eisenhower Executive Office Building with its cast-iron roof sculptures and window frames.

We stop in front of barricades, the windows humming down again. National guardsmen in camouflage are no-nonsense as we show our IDs while a K-9 sniffs around. More radio calls are made, and we're allowed to move on, not getting very far before going through the same routine again.

At last, we're on the White House grounds behind thirteen-foot-high black iron fencing, the security more extreme than I remember. The guard shack ahead has pop-up steel barricades and tire shredders, plenty of ominous warning signs posted. I can see the parking places where we're going, and from here all of them look full.

"Good morning," Benton says to a Secret Service uniform division officer in ballistic gear, an MP5 on a sling across his chest.

"I need to see some identification." He says what we've heard before, and it doesn't matter if the two of them are acquainted.

They could be drinking buddies or brothers, and you'd never know. In addition to being a forensic profiler, an expert in human factors for the Secret Service, Benton works closely with cyber and counterterrorism experts. He's in thick with the intelligence community. But you'd never guess it based on the way we're being treated.

His all-access White House pass doesn't merit so much as a nod of recognition as we give our badge-wallets to an officer built like a Marvel comic book hero. He's stone-faced as he looks at our credentials, swiping our IDs on a portable scanner, never losing track of everything going on around him.

A second officer runs a long-handled inspection mirror along our high-tech electric SUV's undercarriage, making sure we're not rigged up with explosives or hauling weapons and other contraband. Then a handler with her Belgian Malinois appears, and the falcon-wing doors open up, the trunk is popped. The sleek shepherd-looking K-9 snuffles industriously, alerting on nothing beyond the pistol Benton always carries.

"Have a good day." An officer waves us through.

"You always know when something's important," Benton says. "It all comes down to parking."

The narrow road we're slowly following is lined with spaces, all of them taken.

"Usually, I'm stuck in employee parking near the Ellipse where protesters heckle you or worse if you're spotted getting in and out of your car," he says.

THE U.S. FLAG WAVES at half-mast from the White House rooftop, where Secret Service countersnipers stand sentry in the misty rain.

In tactical gear, they're armed with submachine guns and high-powered rifles, four stories up without the benefit of safety tethers, and better them than me. I can see them walking around while surveillance cameras in space and on the ground constantly stream images to tablets and other electronic devices, according to Benton.

Monitoring real-time information, they're watching every person, every vehicle in the area, and that includes the two of us inside his personal SUV on West Executive Avenue. I've not visited the White House or the Capitol since the January 6 attack almost a year ago, and it's as if our country has been occupied by the military.

"I keep thinking how much worse it could have been," I comment as we creep slowly past parked cars, and the lack of visitors isn't because of the weather.

"I think about it every time I drive to work," Benton replies, and the Secret Service's headquarters is but a few blocks from here. "Worrying about domestic terrorism, about what some fringe extremist group will come up with next."

Then Tron is stepping into the middle of the road, holding an open umbrella. She directs us to a reserved parking space between patent-leather-black Secret Service Cadillac Escalades. Removing a traffic cone, she steps out of the way. Benton backs into the space, turning off the engine, and collecting our belongings, we climb out.

"Welcome." Tron cheerfully hands us the umbrella, and one wouldn't guess she's a Secret Service counterterrorism expert permanently on loan to the CIA, among other things.

She could pass for a CEO or television news correspondent. A pretty, wholesome-looking professional in her forties, she has a contagious smile, her dark hair tucked behind her ears.

"How was the drive in this thing?" She makes a big production of giving Benton's Tesla the once-over, as if she's never seen it before. "Did you have to stop and plug it in somewhere?"

"We just barely made it," he deadpans.

"Can it do over fifty?"

"Almost." He goes along with her teasing, and she seems harmless enough.

That's until you look closely, noticing her powerful hands with their short nails, her muscularity beneath her simple black suit and open-collar white shirt. Her loafers would do fine in a foot pursuit, and I've never known her to wear jewelry or other accessories that might get in the way or be used against her.

Coatless, she likely was inside the White House until the moment we arrived, monitoring security live feeds from surveillance cameras, many of them disguised. Her gun is out of sight, only her lapel pin hinting who she is, assuming you know what you're looking at.

"I'm glad to see you in one piece. That must have been unbelievably scary," she says to me as Benton locks the doors. "And by the way"—she directs this to him—"I think your car is pretty safe here."

"I would hope that's true." He pockets the key.

We walk away from his black SUV parked in a long row of government vehicles, the rain quietly pattering our umbrella.

"Well, thankfully things weren't a whole lot worse." Tron gets down to business, saying this to me, and I sense what's coming. "I mean what kind of coward are we talking about? It could have been anybody who got killed."

Clearly, she knows about the careless thing I did. It's not my imagination. She's aware of what I've been through.

"Yes, it could have been much worse," I admit. "I was very lucky, everyone was lucky." It sounds trite as I hear myself.

"How are you feeling?" She's not asking to be nice.

What she's really doing is making sure I'm up to whatever must be expected, as if I'm about to walk onto center court or enter the boxing ring. I reply that I'm fine, maybe not completely back to normal, maybe not quite as energetic as I'd like. While Benton continues acting as if he has no idea why we're here, and I don't believe it for a second.

"The timing is never good when horrible things happen," Tron replies to my growing uneasiness. "But it would be a major problem if you weren't available, and we sure appreciate you being here to help out with this situation."

I don't know what situation she's talking about. Only that before now I've had no reason to assume I'm a major player in whatever has unfolded that demands Benton's and my presence. I glance up at him, both of us holding the umbrella as we walk, his hand warm against mine, his face unreadable.

The Secret Service knows about the poisoned wine. But that's not why I'm at the White House. I've been summoned in spite of it and any residual ill effects I might be suffering, and Benton doesn't say a word. It's not up to him to inform me about what's really happening, and it goes with the turf.

We've been together a long time, and I'm used to being in the dark. Out of necessity so is he when I can't tell him everything, the two of us having more noncommunications than any couple I know. But that doesn't mean I don't find it frustrating when he shuts me out. Especially now.

"How did you hear about the wine I carried home from Lyon?" I ask Tron since my husband's not going to tell me.

"Interpol." She leads us along in the spitting rain, the White House complex barely a block ahead.

The road is crowded with parked vehicles and big storage pods. American flags flutter from iron lampposts, uniformed guards on the prowl with their arsenals as trees drip, the grounds winter-drab and flowerless. I'm not seeing the usual mobs of tourists, mostly people in conservative business dress under their umbrellas.

"I was contacted by the secretary general's office earlier this morning," Tron says.

Of course, she would have been since she was visiting Interpol at the same time I was, both of us members of the Doomsday Commission.

"Also, of huge concern to us is that you and Benton are presidential appointees," she's saying. "So you can understand the United States having an interest."

"We can't be certain at this point of the intended target,"

Benton adds. "Although I'm willing to bet a small fortune it wasn't Kay or those of us around her."

"I suspect we're going to find it was Gabriella Honoré," Tron replies. "There are other incidents, other things going on, possibly all of it connected even if indirectly because of the Russian factor."

CHAPTER 19

IT'S ALL SHE'S GOING to divulge while noticing everyone around us, every vehicle parked in front the West Wing's entrance. She'd have you cuffed on the ground before you can think. I have no doubt of that having seen her take down metal plates on the firing range and burn rubber on the driving course.

Benton calls Tron a bona fide badass, handling business quietly, rarely reacting to much or raising her voice. We follow her to the West Wing's entrance, onto the rusty-red carpet runner under the big white awning, through the double glass-paned white doors beneath the gold presidential seal.

Just inside, she parks the umbrella in a stand, and to our left are a series of wooden cabinets that weren't here when I was last. Inside them are lockboxes for our electronic devices. I find it ironic watching Tron and Benton tuck away our phones, also fitness trackers and a smartwatch. But not their guns.

Through another set of doors, another officer checks our IDs again without cracking a smile as Tron chats with him. I'm wondering what's changed since I was here last, and I look around. Nothing seems all that different at a glance except I notice other women wearing pants and comfortable shoes like mine.

Beyond the desk, the lobby is hung with priceless oil paintings of pioneers in covered wagons, and Old Faithful going off in Yellowstone Park. I recognize George Washington crossing the Delaware in his boat, and other Americana art I've admired on previous visits.

The reception area for the public is surprisingly Spartan and bustling, the mood strictly business, not remotely ceremonial. There's little room to linger, no hosts to offer coffee or to hang your coat. The furnishings aren't nearly as lavish as one might expect when visiting the highest office in the land.

This Tuesday morning, the last day of November, there's a touch of nervous energy in the air, and Tron informs us that the prime minister of England is expected later. Meanwhile, a VIP tour of schoolteachers congregates by the door leading outside to the West Colonnade. They're from the Midwest, I gather, and they can't stop smiling and shyly asking questions.

"Also known as the forty-five-second commute," their tour guide is saying. "That's how long it takes to get from here to the executive residence, and in the process, you'll have a glimpse of the Rose Garden, the Oval Office . . ." They follow him outside.

Guides and other staffers in uniform are assigned to the White House Military Office. WHMO (pronounced *whamo*) runs all hospitality and food services. It also handles medical emergencies and transportation, whether it's the presidential limousines, Air Force One or the helicopter landing on the South Lawn.

Specially trained military personnel are the president's aide-de-camp, on hand 24/7 to take care of every need. All to say, there are plenty of brass stars and lots of camouflage to be found in here, and it's a bit like a train station this morning. People are converging from all directions, carrying paperwork, on their phones and in a hurry.

Some stop to engage in quiet conversations, casually making appointments to speak later. While important-looking guests wait on the formal blue-upholstered sofa and chairs off to the side, almost pushed against the walls to make room for traffic. There's not much other furniture, just antique brass lamps on tables and the large gilt clock that's been in the lobby forever.

As has the splendid pre–Revolutionary War breakfront with its rare books and mementos. It's awe-inspiring to imagine those who have passed through since the early days when President Theodore Roosevelt decided his office should be separate from his living quarters. Nobody is above waiting in plain view of all who come through the same front door Benton and I just did.

It could be a head of state, a princess, a biotech billionaire, a movie star or your average Joe waiting for appointments with high-level officials. That won't include the president or vice president right now. I have a feeling they're preoccupied as it's dawning on me where I'm being taken.

Along a short hallway, pale yellow walls are arranged with poster-size photographs of the president and first lady, the vice president and second gentleman. They're handing out food, getting vaccinated, meeting with refugee children, with the victims of violence and natural disasters. Down three carpeted steps, and we're on the lowest level, where I smell fried chicken.

The Mess Hall is on our left, another big gold presidential seal, this one next to the takeout window where I've grabbed to-go sandwiches on occasion. As we walk past, I glance in at the familiar sea of blue carpet and wooden paneling hung with maritime paintings, several waiters in black suits ready with water and other beverages.

The small but elegant dining facility is run by the Navy, the gold damask–covered tables set with fresh flowers, fine linens, and White House china. The military ensures the fare is excellent while safe enough for the government's highest officials. Hopefully, there's no threat of E. coli or tampering that could bring down the government, and the list of things to guard against these days is endless.

At almost eleven, there are but a handful of people seated inside. The U.S. Surgeon General is having coffee with a junior congressman from Michigan who's been all over the news. The White House chief of staff is talking to the Catholic cardinal from the Washington, D.C., diocese, and the press secretary is tucked in a corner with Lesley Stahl of *60 Minutes*.

But what snags my attention is the man sitting with his back to the door. Recognizing the narrow shoulders, the protruding ears, the Gorbachev-like port-wine stain birthmark on the back of the bald head, and I can't believe it. Fortunately, Elvin Reddy doesn't see me.

He's too engrossed in a conversation with the director of the Centers for Disease Control and Prevention (CDC), and I glance at Benton. He meets my eyes, shrugging a little.

"Do we know what Virginia's recently appointed health commissioner is doing here?" I ask Tron. "Talking to the head of the CDC?" I add, having no doubt my ambitious predecessor is angling for the next big position.

Maybe a presidential appointment, and dear God don't let him be the next Dr. Fauci. I can't imagine anything more depressing or less helpful than having the likes of Elvin Reddy deciding what's best for the health of the nation. I'm reminded of what Marino's always saying about crap floating to the top.

"No, I honestly don't have any idea," Tron replies. "Only that the two of them are on the list of visitors, and scheduled to meet later with the Secretary of Health and Human Services."

We follow another short hallway. This one ends with a red phone on the wall next to an unmarked wooden door. She scans open the lock, and we walk inside the Situation Room, the reception area an open space leading to a suite of private chambers where top secret meetings are in session.

We stop at the secretary's mahogany desk, this one L-shaped with multiple displays like a cockpit. Our gatekeeper is smartly dressed with reading glasses on, reminding me of Maggie except not the least bit imperious. She smiles at me when Tron announces our names.

KEYS CLICK AS THE secretary checks, and there's no scanner to walk through, and no one pats us down. My briefcase isn't searched again because it's not necessary.

In addition to ubiquitous cameras and microphones, I'm sure there are spectrum analyzers we can't see. No doubt they're sweeping constantly, searching for rogue electronic signals from illegal surveillance devices that might evade detection otherwise.

No food or water is allowed beyond this point, and I can see why after what happened to me last night. But the pervasive threat is espionage, and that lands my thoughts on Gwen Hainey again. Maybe I'm here because of her spying. But I can't imagine what I might have to offer that requires my physical presence before some Mount Olympian gathering.

"You're in the JFK Room." The secretary tells us where we're going as I look around at a series of shut doors with red lights indicating meetings are in session.

"We got here as fast as we could," I apologize.

"The traffic's always a nightmare, and now especially with all the barricades and everything." What she says has nothing to do with why I've been in slow motion this morning, my molecules not gathering fast enough.

Had it not been for Benton's high-fat hangover breakfast

of cheesy eggs, buttered toast and sugary espresso, I might not have shown up at all. Or everyone involved would wish I hadn't, as bleary and edgy as I was feeling, my memory spotty, and I wouldn't say I'm as good as new. But I'll manage.

"They're just getting started." The secretary couldn't be more gracious, and it must be nice working with someone like her. "Everybody's waiting for you." Maybe it's just my imagination but she looks at me as if somehow knowing what I've been through, and that I'm not quite up to speed.

Unfortunately, there's no coffee or tea, nothing but water where we're going, she tells me as if feeling my pain. Taking off our coats, we hang them on a coatrack that hasn't room to spare. There's no telling who's behind shut doors engaged in conversations impacting the welfare of all humanity, and Elvin Reddy seeps back into my thoughts.

Whatever he has up his sleeve, I'm sure I won't be happy about it, and I can't waste my energy on him now as Tron leads us along another hallway. She stops at another door with another red light glowing, and we enter a big room I've not been in before. But I've seen it plenty enough in photographs, and there must be twenty people seated in black leather chairs wherever they'll fit.

The president of the United States is at the head of a long conference table cluttered with paperwork and bottled water. Suit jacket off, he has his shirtsleeves rolled up, flipping through pages, making copious notes. The vice president is on his right, the secretary of state on his left, the room heated up by tension and closely packed bodies.

Multiple video feeds playing on the data walls show clear images of an unusual satellite circling the Earth. A Soyuz rocket launches from the Russian's Baikonur Cosmodrome, their spaceport in Central Asia, and the time stamp is mid-September. Then a few hours ago, a gumdrop-shaped crew capsule floated down beneath a candy-cane-striped parachute, landing in a tall plume of dust in the desert of Kazakhstan.

The images surrounding the Situation Room are dazzling and distracting like a mini Times Square, and I'm getting a hint what this is about at least in part. It would seem there's been a catastrophe in outer space. I can't tell what yet. But I can make an educated guess that it has to do with human health and safety. Otherwise, I don't know what I might add to the mix.

Tron directs Benton and me to the only empty chairs, side by side on the vice president's left. In her simple dark blue pants suit and ankle boots, she's not dressed all that different from the way I am.

"I'm sorry to make you wait." I feel compelled to apologize again.

"We're just getting started," she says quietly, smiling at us. "Everybody's scrambling the same way you are. We're very glad to see you. I'm aware you had a rough night that thank goodness turned out all right," she adds to my surprise.

She's aware of the poisoned wine I carried home from Interpol. But it's not what this meeting is about, and she says nothing more.

"Whatever I can do to help." I smile back at her, not feeling particularly confident.

"Doctor Scarpetta, Benton, thanks for coming on such short notice," the president begins, and I haven't met everyone in the room.

But I'm acquainted with most or at least know who I'm looking at, and surrounding me are a host of potentates including the Secretary of Defense, the administrator of NASA, directors of the Secret Service, Homeland Security, the CIA, and the Defense Advanced Research Projects Agency (DARPA). I recognize senators from Virginia, Florida, New Mexico, California, Massachusetts and Texas.

Across the table from me is the Commander of Space Force, Jake Gunner, whom I've worked with on occasion at the Pentagon. In his dress blues tunic jacket and *Star Trek*–ish Nehru collar, the four-star general brings to mind a sage Captain Kirk with wire-rim glasses and a gray buzz cut.

Our eyes meet, and he nods, his grim preoccupations obvious. Then he returns his attention to a pile of folders. I recognize from their rainbow of colorful markings that they're classified, the high-ranking officer next to him pointing out something in one of the documents.

"I'm sorry you couldn't be filled in before walking through the door," the vice president says to me. "Scarcely anybody sitting around this table has been briefed in advance because it's crucial that nothing gets out about what's happening in space right now."

"Not until we know the facts." General Gunner directs this at me and not Benton, the same way the vice president did. "Thanks for coming, Doctor Scarpetta. The way things are looking, I'm afraid it's going to require your help to figure out what we're dealing with. And no offense intended, but that's not a good sign."

"People usually don't need my help when the news is good," I agree.

"We need to get to the bottom of things quickly if we're to control the message before a pack of lies gets spread," the president adds, and if I doubted it before, I don't anymore.

Benton knows everything. His major role in this unfolding drama is making sure I'm sitting here. Of course, I understand. But that doesn't mean I don't feel handled and disadvantaged. There's only so much I can do if I'm not given data in advance and have no ability to prepare.

"What we're about to show you could incite a *War of the Worlds* panic." The vice president looks around the room. "I'm sure most of you are familiar with the nineteen thirty-eight radio broadcast of the H. G. Wells novel about Martians invading Earth?" she adds to heads nodding yes.

"I think all of us are keenly aware that misrepresented facts or fiction of any sort can result in disaster," the president reminds everyone. "And many people listening to that radio broadcast eighty years ago believed it was real."

"If that was a problem back then," the vice president adds, "just imagine what would happen today with disinformation campaigns, social media, propaganda on the Internet and all the rest."

"I think the *War of the Worlds* hoopla has been largely debunked," says the senator from California, who was around at the time. "Like Roswell," referencing the 1947 alleged crash of an extraterrestrial flying disk on a Roswell, New Mexico, ranch.

"Well, I don't necessarily place much faith in anything the government might have decided to *debunk*," says the senator from the state where the incident happened.

CHAPTER 20

Debunk is just another way of changing the message to what you want people to believe." The senator from New Mexico looks around the table. "No way it was a damn weather balloon."

"Once you start denying what else might be out there, you can't undo it," the senator from Massachusetts says in his blunted accent.

"Declassified documents show image after image of UFOs. Many of them explained. And a lot of them not," adds the Secretary of Defense.

"What about history?" says the senator from Florida. "There are paintings and stone carvings from thousands of years ago depicting spaceships and extraterrestrials."

Others continue commenting, and it seems nobody has any idea what to trust, what's true or to be counted on anymore. Including me, I can't help but think, sitting here staring up at images on the data walls, feeling lost in space, no pun intended.

"Let's talk about what we're dealing with right now some three hundred miles above the planet in what's called low-Earth orbit." The president glances through his notes. "And yes, we've got to be very careful how the news gets out."

Otherwise there may be those who believe we've been attacked in space by extraterrestrials. That we were fired upon by them early this morning, NASA adds, as I halfway wonder if I'm hearing things right.

"Earth will be invaded next," DARPA suggests with all seriousness. "When it's highly unlikely such a thing is going on." But he's not saying it's impossible, and I don't dare glance at Benton.

I don't want anyone to catch the look I might give him. It's not that I've ever been so arrogant as to think humans are the only life in the cosmos. But I never imagined that one day I would be pulled into such a discussion, most of all inside the White House.

"We can't swear yet that there's been an attack, and if so by whom or what," the president adds to my astonishment. "Just that something disastrous has occurred."

I reach for another bottle of water, unscrewing the cap, my tongue sticking to the roof of my mouth. Insatiably thirsty, I've been drinking a lot since leaving the house, and it might have been wise to visit the ladies' room before getting down to business. I tell myself not to think about it, to pretend that as usual I'm at a crime scene with no access to plumbing.

The president laces his fingers on top of the table, looking directly at me. He begins to explain what happened at 11:27

last night East Coast time. That's when Houston lost all communication with a top secret orbiting laboratory and the two crewmates still on board it, a male and a female, one American, the other Russian.

Scientists and experienced commercial astronauts, they've not been heard from since heading out on a spacewalk shortly before midnight. Their third crewmate, Jared Horton, is an American biomedical engineer who lives in Virginia. He'd been in space before but this was his first long-term mission, and the story is he escaped with his life. He's now back on the ground and out of reach in Central Asia.

"He's not talking to us directly." The story NASA tells goes from bad to worse. "What's a fact is that at around three o'clock this morning, he departed in the Soyuz spacecraft that he and his crewmates had arrived in eleven weeks ago. It's since touched down without incident in Kazakhstan."

We can see it for ourselves on the data walls, the crew capsule landing in the desert steppes rather much like a wrecking ball. Then a Russian helicopter is setting down, clouds of dirt billowing up from sagebrush and feathergrass.

"If it's top secret," says the senator from Virginia in his lilting accent, "then why are the Russians involved?"

"They've been our partners on the Space Station since nineteen ninety-eight," NASA reminds everyone. "We're still using their Soyuz spacecraft."

On the data walls, we watch the Russian search and rescue team helping Horton out of the scorched-looking crew capsule's hatch. They carry him off in a chair as he barely holds up his head, feeling the crushing effects of gravity after months without it.

"His story is that the orbiter and his two crewmates were struck by a swarm of projectiles, possibly debris too small to be picked up on radar," the president goes on to describe. "And if at the end of the day it turns out to be space trash, junk, fragments of something? Then the damage is accidental, obviously. But we don't know that yet." He looks around at the intense faces.

We can't be sure what we're dealing with wasn't an overt act of aggression, he explains. A United States spacecraft may have been fired upon deliberately. This happened after Horton had assisted his two crewmates, helping them suit up. He claims they exited the airlock at 11:46 last night, although there's no record of the hatch being opened.

As Horton's story goes, he returned to the robotic arm station to help with the installation of a new power supply on the experiment platform. His two crewmates began their spacewalk, and he described hearing the muffled clangs of their tether hooks against the hull as they began moving handrail to handrail.

Then suddenly, the cameras and radios were knocked out, accompanied by a terrible loud banging. It sounded like the hull was struck by an army of hammers hitting all at once.

"Damaging the experiment platform and robotic arm, tearing the solar arrays." NASA continues describing what Horton supposedly relayed to his Russian hosts.

"Whatever actually happened, we have no way of knowing

yet." The president picks up where NASA leaves off. "Since none of this was recorded, and we've lost all contact with the top secret laboratory. But if what we're being told is true, there were serious injuries to the crewmates out on their spacewalk."

Just how serious, we don't know, because Jared Horton bailed on them, claiming there was only so much he could do to help. Fearing for his own life, he was convinced the hull must have been penetrated, and pressurization would be lost, the air leaking out.

"Despicably, he left his two injured colleagues stranded and for dead," the president says.

"THIRTY-THREE MINUTES OUT," THE commander of Space Force, General Gunner, takes over.

Moving a remote control close, he explains that help is on the way, a rescue crew has deployed from the International Space Station (ISS), headed to the radio-silent orbiting commercial lab. Recorded videos on the data walls show the ISS shining like polished Tiffany silver against blackness.

Its four solar arrays are lit up molten orange by the sun, the Earth a blue and white marble looming large below. A Sierra Space Dream Chaser departs from one of the docking ports. Gliding away through the ether, it brings to mind a mini Space Shuttle, white with black heatshield protection and integrated wings.

The time stamp on the data walls shows the spaceplane

left an hour ago, and we're shown images of the two ISS astro-nauts inside the glass cockpit. NASA-trained Chip Ortiz from the U.S. and Anni Girard from France are on their way to the rescue with additional medical supplies, and also body bags.

Harnessed in their carbon fiber seats so they don't float out of them, they're wearing white launch-reentry suits and helmets that can be pressurized in an emergency. We watch them going through checklists on computer screens, talking to Johnson Space Center mission controllers.

But what we can't see at this point is the target destina-tion, and there's no telling what they might find once they get there. The blacked-out panels in the data walls are a re-minder that video is missing because of damaged cameras. Or so we've been told.

"In actuality, the top secret orbiter is a combination labo-ratory and habitat." General Gunner continues his briefing.

"It's simply designated on satellite maps as T-Oh-One." Benton looks at me. "Or what those in the know refer to as TO-One. T-O as in Thor Orbiter, the first of its kind." He finally tells me what he couldn't before.

"Thor Laboratories is where Gwen Hainey had been work-ing for the past six weeks." It's the director of the Secret Ser-vice speaking, and I'm stunned by the mayhem this murdered woman has caused.

We're informed that in recent hours, the phones have been ringing nonstop. Information has been coming in from people who had contact with her, and the more we learn, the more suspicious she looks.

"Benton?" the director of the Secret Service says to him. "I'll let you fill in the blanks about what it appears Gwen Hainey was up to."

"Nothing good," my husband solemnly says.

He explains that she was in and out of a number of bio-medical companies. It was her habit to skip around, to gather what she wanted. Then she'd move on to her next industrial victim. He repeats what Lucy told me about his conversation with Jinx Slater.

"The one thing every company has in common is it works on top secret projects with various governments, most of all ours," Benton explains to the Situation Room. "Other information we've gotten since her name hit the news is equally disturbing."

It would seem that Gwen already had set her sights on another high-value target. Intuitive Machines in Texas has created the next lunar lander, the first one made in America in more than half a century. It will bring small payloads down to the surface of the moon, and this could include the sorts of biomedical technology experiments that were Gwen's specialty.

"It would seem she was prepared to steal Intuitive Machines blind like everybody else," Benton says. "I'm sure you can imagine the proprietary nature of these new lunar technologies, not just to the Russians and Chinese but to any competitor."

"Well, it won't happen now, for which we can be hugely grateful," says the senator from Texas. "Not that I'm glad she was murdered." But he might be, based on his demeanor.

"Obviously, she knew what she was doing," says the CIA.

"Likely this has been going on for years," Benton replies. "But she wasn't on our radar until her former live-in partner called us yesterday morning."

Jinx Slater was voicing his concerns over what Gwen likely had gotten herself involved in. He's certain it's connected to her murder. Benton continues to offer new information. That, in combination with Jared Horton making an Internet call to her missing cell phone.

"This was just hours after his orbiting lab was disabled," Benton says. "His call to her is how we were alerted that they know each other, likely in a significant way."

"We're to assume her identification has been confirmed by now?" Homeland Security directs this at me.

"Using her toothbrush and other personal items from her residence, my labs made the comparison earlier this morning," I reply. "Rapid DNA testing verified her identity, and her next of kin have been notified."

Screwing the cap back on my water bottle, I hope we take a break in the not-too-distant future.

"And you're convinced that she was murdered on Friday, the day after Thanksgiving," General Gunner says to me.

"That's correct. Late afternoon, early evening based on her postmortem findings at the scene and other information." I give them the details as they continue taking notes.

"The question is whether what happened to her is connected to her alleged spying," says the president. "Most importantly, how involved is Jared Horton? We don't know because he's not talking to us. Maybe because he can't. Or maybe he won't."

"I'm not much for coincidences, Mister President, Madame Vice President." Benton directs this at them. "And I don't think we're dealing with one here. This disaster in space happened not even twenty-four hours after it hit the media that Gwen was the murder victim from several nights earlier."

We should expect Horton to have a meltdown, to decompensate. A violent death is the worst of tattletales, and whatever Gwen had to hide was going to be discovered.

"He knew he was going to be busted," Benton says. "And if the two of them are as dirty as it's looking, her murder would have pushed him over the edge. Simply put, he knew he was going to get caught if he didn't think fast."

"The reason he tried to call her from space was to see if she answered, if she was really dead," the FBI decides. "Certainly, he'd not risked contacting her like that before. It was the only time he'd tried her cell phone during the almost three months he'd been up there."

"He had to know we'd ping on it," Tron agrees. "But by then he didn't care. He had a plan and was out of our reach."

The vice president looks up from her notes, and I can see her quiet outrage.

"Did Jared Horton and Gwen Hainey talk prior to his being in space?" she asks. "Do we have a clue how long the spying has been going on?"

"We've found no evidence of communication between the two of them while he was in orbit, as we've mentioned," the

CIA says. "It's possible that the rest of the time he may have used burner phones like most people engaged in activities they don't want anyone to know about."

Burner phones, cell phones of any description won't work in space, Tron explains to the Situation Room. Not easily, and that wasn't going to be an option up there if Horton wanted to speak to Gwen.

"Whatever the case," Benton says, "the only record we have is that one call he made from his laptop computer at close to midnight."

But that doesn't mean he and Gwen weren't connected prior to her going to work for Thor Laboratories. A scientist and commercial astronaut employed by them, Horton may have helped her get a job there, Benton suspects.

"I'm guessing she was his boots on the ground, and likely had been for a while," Tron says. "She may have connections with others involved in espionage, as well. We don't know yet. But what I expect to emerge is she'd been helping Horton spy for the Russians, to steal any resources she could access."

"In exchange for money and other compensations that were largely untraceable," Benton says. "Explaining why she paid for everything in cash and had five thousand dollars in her wallet at the time she was abducted from the townhome she was renting."

CHAPTER 21

"As I listen to all this," says the CIA, "I'm wondering if she's a hit staged to look like something else. That could explain why her hands were cut off and are missing. It sounds like someone settling a score, sending a message."

"It could be the Russians thought she was becoming a problem, that it was time to eliminate her," DARPA contemplates.

"Or her murder may have nothing to do with any of this," Benton replies skeptically, and I have no doubt he's thinking about the flattened penny.

That one small detail seems to cry out, and what it has to say flies in the face of a murder for hire. I envision the run-over coin on the rail, an oblong coppery wafer beaded with rainwater, and it's important somehow. I don't feel it's contrived or random.

"Once we have an idea what's on her computers, hopefully

we'll know what we're dealing with," Benton says, precipitating another flurry of questions.

"What about Gwen Hainey's mobile phone?"

"It hasn't been recovered. But we're dealing with the provider," my husband answers.

"The last call she made? What do the records say?"

"Friday afternoon," he says. "She called the manager of Colonial Landing."

Apparently, Gwen was expecting a FedEx. Benton elaborates on yet more information I've not heard before this moment. According to the tracking record, it was delivered to the management office at ten-thirty Friday morning, he says as I remember the package I saw on her kitchen counter. Later in the day, she called Cliff Sallow asking where it was.

"What time was it when she finally checked on the package?" Another question.

"Close to four P.M., not long before she died." Benton looks at me. "Cliff Sallow told her no such package had been delivered. He'd not seen it."

"Was a signature required?" I ask.

"Apparently, she never requested that when she had things sent to her, the packages usually left on the management office's front porch," Benton answers as I envision the unopened package.

"What was in it?" I ask.

"Three Mophie-type chargers."

"If the package I saw on top of the kitchen counter inside Gwen's townhome is the one she called the management office about," I ask next, "then where was it after FedEx dropped it off on the porch at ten-thirty in the morning?"

"Exactly. Where was it, and who had it?" Benton says, causing more questions and comments, people talking on top of each other.

"And she didn't call looking for it until some five or six hours after it was left on the porch?"

"Who finally dropped it off to her not long before she was attacked?"

"Could be anyone who picked up the package at the office, maybe off the front porch," Benton suggests. "And the manager living there might not have been aware of it."

"What about time of death?" General Gunner directs this at me.

"Early evening," I estimate. "Possibly an hour or two after she called looking for the package."

"The DNA will be interesting, whatever might be on the outside of the box," says the FBI as if I might not have thought of it.

"The FedEx was on a countertop near the side door leading out to Gwen's patio," I explain to everyone. "And yes, of course we're testing it for DNA," I add for the benefit of the FBI director.

I'm well aware he's convinced their Quantico labs are better than mine, and am unpleasantly reminded of what nuclear biologist Clark Givens told me. DNA evidence hasn't been tested in the Cammie Ramada case, and it's not because of a backlog.

"The unopened FedEx package wasn't far from where I'd noticed a shattered mug and a puddle of chicken noodle soup on the floor," I tell the room. "Causing me to suspect she'd been startled, frightened, was trying to get away from someone."

I make the point that if residents of Colonial Landing can intercept packages left on the porch of the management office, then so could anybody.

"Including a violent offender," Benton offers, and I think of the covered cameras, the security gates opening and shutting, the creepy music playing.

Assuming Gwen's killer showed up with the package in hand, depending on who it was, she might have let her guard down. She might have turned off the alarm and opened her door.

"Especially if the person was familiar," Benton adds. "It could be nothing more than someone she's spoken to in the past or seen around the area. That could have been enough. It only takes the blink of an eye to make the wrong decision."

"Plus, she might have been distracted because this individual had something she possibly was looking for urgently," the director of the Secret Service proposes. "Something she didn't want getting into anybody else's hands."

"Our labs have the devices and the FedEx box they arrived

in," Benton tells everyone. "They'll be processed for finger-prints, DNA, and what we know already is the mobile char-gers are malware. You plug in your phone, and all of your data is downloaded."

"THE DREAM CHASER IS eight minutes from docking." Gen-eral Gunner gives us the latest update, monitoring images on the Situation Room's data walls.

Benton turns around in his chair, speaking to Tron sitting behind us. "Maybe now's a good time to play the recording."

"Absolutely," she replies, getting up.

"The message left on Gwen's cell phone early this morn-ing," Benton explains to everyone around the table as Tron finds the audio file.

"Horton probably heard all about her murder on the news last night, and ultimately couldn't resist calling her or trying," Tron explains to everyone. "But he was shrewd enough to do it when it didn't matter anymore. One reason I find his voice mail so interesting is he's speaking Russian."

"You have to wonder why unless maybe he was sending Gwen some sort of coded message. Maybe cluing her in about where he was headed," Benton guesses.

"Let's listen." Tron sets down her classified laptop computer in front of the president and plays the recording.

"Privet iz kosmosa. Kak dela?" is the extent of Horton's mes-sage to Gwen, one she never knew about or heard, and now never will.

"He's saying, 'Hello from space. How are you?'" Tron translates. "That's it. And I'm not surprised because he knew as he was leaving the message that it was going to be listened to soon enough. And picked apart, the very thing we're doing."

She informs us that Horton placed the call this morning at 2:02 Eastern Standard Time. At that moment, the top secret Thor orbiter was passing almost 300 miles (500 kilometers) over New York City, traveling at a blistering 17,500 miles per hour (approximately 28,000 kilometers per hour or Mach 22).

"As it passed over, the orbiter would have been visible from the ground for three minutes max had the stormy weather permitted," General Gunner says.

I'm reminded that spacecraft such as satellites aren't the only things cloaked by a dense overcast. Whatever, whoever passed in and out of Colonial Landing's front gates last Friday night wasn't going to be visible from above, either.

"Not everybody realizes how much can be captured on camera from up there," I add.

"That's right, Doctor Scarpetta." General Gunner nods at me. "And Horton would be well aware of details like that and much more, assuming he had anything to do with her murder. By the sounds of it, he was getting unstable."

It wasn't the first long-duration flight for his two crewmates. But it was for Horton. He was becoming increasingly isolated and paranoid the longer he was in space.

"Apparently, he would make jokes about escaping on the

Soyuz, that if they didn't treat him right, he'd leave without them," says the general.

"One of many reasons we don't want to be dependent on a foreign nation for our transportation," the senator from Florida says.

"Horton is in Russia and out of our control because it was a Soyuz, not a SpaceX Dragon, docked outside the orbiter. Had it been the latter," NASA adds, "he would have splashed down in the ocean where we would have intercepted him. He'd be in our medical clinic at Kennedy right now."

But it's only been recently that crewed U.S. rocket launches have resumed launching from Kennedy Space Center, thanks to our partnership with SpaceX, the NASA administrator continues, giving us the background. Prior to that we've had no way to reach the ISS since the Space Shuttle was mothballed a decade ago.

"But that doesn't mean the Soyuz isn't used by the U.S. and our allies, when needed," General Gunner says. "Thor and other huge commercial companies certainly avail themselves of it. Horton had been in and out of Russia for years getting all sorts of special training, and in mid-September, he and his crewmates launched from the Baikonur Cosmodrome in Kazakhstan."

These days it's mostly the commercial companies paying the sticker price, not us, NASA's administrator adds. Thor Laboratories has a steep discount compared to what the U.S. government has been shelling out at some ninety million dollars per seat every time we ferry our astronauts to and from the ISS.

"ON FINAL." GENERAL GUNNER is riveted to the data walls as the Dream Chaser's cameras show it closing in on the Thor orbiter. "Slowing the approach, twenty meters out."

We have a clear view of solar arrays unfurled like bluish-black wings edged in fiery orange, as delicate as gossamer. Bringing to mind a dragonfly, the structure glows and flares in the ever-changing light as the sun rises and sets during each ninety-minute orbit around our planet.

"Pretty strange it's just sitting there with no apparent damage," General Gunner says right away.

There are no visible tears in the two solar arrays' tightly packed cells of photovoltaic material that convert sunlight into electricity. Whatever damage there may be, it's not obvious, the unresponsive silvery spacecraft about the size of a school bus. I would think that from the perspective of a powerful telescope it could pass for your garden-variety large satellite.

But upon close inspection, one notices the attached experiment platform and small robotic arm. A normal satellite wouldn't have two docking ports, both empty, and I imagine Horton escaping by himself in the only vehicle. By all accounts he jumped ship, fled, possibly leaving two wounded colleagues to fend for themselves with no means of communicating or returning to Earth.

Such a selfish, cowardly act. His only concern was himself and the trouble that might be in store for him. But someone who steals and spies with impunity doesn't care about anybody else, can't possibly suffer from empathy, and I'm beyond disgusted.

"You can see what the cameras are picking up as the crew hand flies the Dream Chaser without the assistance of the disabled orbiting laboratory's ground control." General Gunner gives us the blow-by-blow. "We don't know what's going on with the remaining two crew members inside," he reiterates. "Or what may have become of the critically important projects they've been working on."

Billions of dollars in top secret biomedical research and development have been going on for years, unbeknownst to the public, he says.

"Thor's research and technologies include the three-D printing of human organs and skin," the vice president says, her keen eyes peering up from her notes. "I don't need to tell you the implications for the military, for space travel, for the health of world leaders, for humanity overall."

CHAPTER 22

Wᴇ ʜᴀᴠᴇ ᴄᴏɴᴛᴀᴄᴛ, ᴅᴏᴄᴋɪɴɢ latches engaged." General Gunner announces that the Dream Chaser has reached its destination.

On the live video feed, astronauts Anni Girard and Chip Ortiz are unfastening their five-point harnesses. Holding themselves in place with foot loops, they begin taking off their launch-entry suits. Stowing them in overhead netting, they go through their expedited pressure checks.

They're making sure they're safely docked, everything a challenge in weightlessness. Out the nearby porthole, sunlight flares off the orbiter's retracted robotic arm, perched over the research platform like a silver praying mantis.

"Let's get our astronauts up and talking to us." General Gunner reaches for the remote control.

As I stare at live video of the blue Earth veiled in clouds, I can't tell what the orbiter is flying over at the moment. A glimpse of white mountains, possibly the Himalayas, the topography changes constantly as the combination laboratory-habitat speeds around the planet as fast as a bullet.

"They'll be entering the disabled TO-One momentarily." The commander of Space Force keeps us updated on what's happening. "Anni, Chip, how are you reading us?"

"Loud and clear, Chief," both of them answer on the Dream Chaser's cockpit cameras, the video live-streaming as big as life on the data walls around us.

"How was your ride?"

"Couldn't be better, Chief." Chip gives the commander a thumbs-up.

"We're going to expedite the usual procedures, to go with a rapid leak check and pressurization protocol." Anni is busy on her computer display, scrolling through menus.

"We need to get in there quickly," Chip says, and no doubt they're holding on to the hope that the crewmates aren't dead.

"As you were coming in and docking did you notice any damage to the outside of the orbiter?" General Gunner then asks. "Because we didn't."

"Negative." Chip tucks his gloves into the netting.

"Nothing is off-nominal except for the Soyuz not being there." Anni's tone has grim shadings as video of the missing crew capsule landing in Kazakhstan replays nonstop on the data walls. "If the solar arrays were torn as claimed," she adds, "there's no obvious sign of it."

"And we have a good visual of the experiment platform, the robotic arm. They appear undamaged, as well," Chip confirms.

"Based on what your cameras showed us during your approach, I would agree," the president says. "Suggesting there may not be any damage at all, contrary to what we've been told."

"We know from sensor readings that TO-One hasn't lost pressurization. The oxygen levels, the life-support systems are nominal, and contrary to what Horton claimed, the solar arrays are generating power," NASA confirms. "It would seem it's only the comms, the video cameras and on-board experiment chambers that are offline."

The good news is that Chip and Anni are able to enter the orbiter without portable life-support systems, which they don't have with them. The Extravehicular Mobility Unit (EMU), the spacesuits worn during spacewalks, are far too bulky inside a confined area. All one would do is bang into things, damaging sensitive equipment.

The EMUs were left behind at the Space Station since there was no indication they'd be needed. Otherwise the harsh reality is that if the orbiting laboratory's hull had been penetrated and overtaken by the extreme temperatures and vacuum of space, there would be no point in rescuers showing up.

The orbiter, the bodies inside and the research would be abandoned. Likely, gravity eventually would drag them down into the atmosphere to incinerate like space trash, hardly anyone knowing the whole truth. But the expectation is that the life-support system is up and running fine as the sensors indicate.

Anni and Chip should find the conditions inside the same as onboard the ISS, and they're dressed accordingly. We watch as they pull on protective clothing over their typical uniforms of khaki pants, polo shirts with mission patches, and socks.

"You're going to want to double glove." I begin instructing them without being asked. "And do you have N-ninety-five face masks? Also face shields? Eye protection, masks are a must since we have no idea what might be in the air," I explain, and mostly I'm concerned about biological hazards.

"Affirmative," they answer, and it can't be easy putting on Tyvek in microgravity, the slippery coverall legs and arms floating and flailing. "We've also got chest cameras we're strapping on."

"I'm going to assume the orbiter has the same basic medical supplies the Space Station does," I inquire, looking at them on the data walls as if they're right in front of me.

One would think so, they reply. But they're bringing a soft-sided medical bag with the basics just in case. They float single file through the hatch leading into the commercial orbiter, their chest cameras showing the ghastly sight awaiting us. The two crewmates are dressed in the diapers and cooling garments worn under spacesuits, the white cotton long johns tinted a dirty dark red.

Their bodies drift facedown, arms and legs gently bent, and fans running 24/7 have created a true forensic nightmare. Flecks of dried blood have blown everywhere, dusting exposed skin a blackish red that has discolored the whites of the dead eyes blearily staring. Their longish hair floats whichever way the air moves, seeming to stand on end.

Shiny steel surfaces and fire-retardant white Nomex look

spray-painted as if a paperweight filled with gory snowflakes has been shaken up, the wet blood sticking to whatever it hits. Then much of it flaking off, drifting, never settling when drying, and I can imagine what the air filters are like. Ruined, comes to mind.

"It would appear that both crewmates are deceased." Anni states what couldn't be more obvious, and she and Chip look braver than they must feel.

"Try not to bump into them." I address the live feed on the data wall.

The inside of the orbiter lab is cramped quarters with plenty of hard objects and sharp corners.

"We don't want to send them banging into you or anything else," I explain.

The dead bodies may be weightless but they still have mass, and crashing into people and metal objects can do some real damage.

"We'll move really slowly, trying not to disturb them," Chip says, and there's no scientific procedure or instrument that can help me reconstruct what happened.

"I'm afraid we're going to have to resort to rather primitive technology," I warn the Situation Room.

No one is talking now, transfixed by the horror on the data walls.

MOST IMPORTANT IS KNOWING how and when they were injured, I tell my hushed audience around the table.

That's going to be next to impossible under the circumstances. We're able to do but so much without video or audio recordings. We have no real data to tell us where the crewmates were, and what they were doing when they were injured.

"There's no point of origin, no bloodstain patterns that make sense," I continue to explain. "Meaning I can't retrace their steps so to speak, and I don't see anything that's telling me much so far, including where they died."

Possibly it was inside the airlock they'd managed to reenter after their spacewalk, assuming it ever occurred, and there's no evidence of it. Over time their bodies may have been displaced by currents of air. Ending up in the lab section, they drifted about, bumping into bundles of cables that run along a ceiling and walls crammed with computer racks and other hardware.

On countertops are refrigerator and freezer compartments, also 3-D laser bioprinters I recognize as the type used to create human tissue. It could be skin, bone, blood vessels, organs or limbs that have been seeded with human stem cells. The three-dimensional structures can be built without scaffolds in the absence of gravity, and to date there's no way to escape it on Earth.

The best we can do is brief intervals aboard a Zero-G jet flying extreme parabolic profiles with astronauts, researchers and other scientists like me onboard. I know what it feels like to float, and what happens to fluids and other evidence in such conditions. Microgravity is disastrous for crime scenes but ideal for producing complicated organs and other soft tissue.

There could be other top secret orbiters besides Thor's, a new kind of body farm where we create life instead of studying what death does to us. I've been aware of the technologies for a while. But I didn't know the work was being done in space already, and it would seem Jared Horton didn't make his getaway without raiding the store.

Every plexiglass container we're seeing is empty, and there's no telling what he absconded with while leaving a weightless trail. As Anni and Chip move around, we get glimpses of a human-made heart drifting along the ceiling like an escaped party balloon. The 3-D printed organ looks real enough although I doubt it's fully functioning yet. The same with the kidney, the ear, and possibly a bladder wafting on loud blowing air, the fans never stopping in microgravity.

Otherwise, gases like everything else will float in place, carbon dioxide forming a deadly bubble around one's head. That's not what killed the crewmates. They didn't asphyxiate as they exsanguinated, slipping into unconsciousness. They may have aspirated their own blood as it followed skin surface tension, creeping over the neck, the mouth, the nose like ectoplasm.

"I'm going to need you to check a few things for me," I let Anni and Chip know, starting with the usual postmortem changes.

I tell them what to look for, and moving close to the female's long-johns-clad body, Anni tries an unwilling arm.

Rigor mortis is fully set, weightlessness having no effect on that. But there won't be the telltale dusky discoloration caused by livor mortis, the settling of noncirculating blood due to gravity.

That would tell you if a body was moved after death, and in this case the answer is yes. In fact, the bodies haven't stopped moving on the blowing air, and I haven't a clue what position they were in originally.

"I need one of you to turn them very slowly so I can take a good look from every angle," I explain.

"Wilco," Anni says.

"While she's doing that," I tell Chip, "I'd like you to find the spacesuits they were wearing on their spacewalk."

"They should be in the airlock." He looks around to get his bearings. "Going there now, will tell you what I find."

"I'd like to see for myself, please," I reply.

"Copy. I'll show you the suits on camera." Changing his trajectory with the gentlest touch, he follows the lights along the blood-tinged ceiling.

Floating upright through a gory haze of particulate, he's literally walking on air, passing through the galley with its Nomex bags of space food Velcroed and bungee-corded in place. He slings a left, gliding past exercise equipment that prevents muscle and bone from atrophying during long missions.

Snaking through another open hatch, he enters the airlock where two sets of disassembled white spacesuits eerily float about. It's obvious that the Thor scientists hurried out of them, the torsos, pants, helmets and boots stirred by fans blowing.

"I'm wondering how long it might have taken them to return to the airlock, repressurize and then take off their suits?" I look around the Situation Room. "Because it can't be an easy feat even under optimal conditions."

"If they went out the hatch, turned around and came right back?" NASA says. "At least thirty minutes and more like forty, and that's doing an extremely expedited suit doffing."

Grabbing a spacesuit torso size small, Chip looks it over carefully, announcing there are two holes in the upper right side of it. He maneuvers himself so his body-mounted camera shows us what he's talking about, and we can see the images on the data walls.

The holes in the heavy fire-retardant fabric are perfectly round and about the diameter of a dime. They correspond with the location of the two holes in the female's upper right side and shoulder, and she and her crewmate bled out considerably based on the amount of blood I'm seeing.

I suspect that whatever hit the female crewmate nicked a major blood vessel, and she hemorrhaged, the blood drying quickly, most of it carried away by the fan-stirred air. I'm noticing right away that the two perforations in the torso of the spacesuit seem identical, as if made by the same hole puncher.

I wouldn't expect that necessarily if we're dealing with space debris that likely varies considerably in size and shape. Rather much like shrapnel from a pipe bomb, and rarely are the entrance wounds perfectly round when caused by that.

"Chip, what about exit holes or tears?" I ask as suspicions gather. "If you look at other areas of her spacesuit, are there any defects that might be from the projectiles exiting?"

"Negative, not seeing them," he reports from inside the air-lock. "But it was just their luck that whatever hit them some-how managed to miss the integrated impact shielding," he adds as I doubt that luck had anything to do with it.

Next, he inspects the male crewmate's spacesuit, size extra-large, first the torso, then the pants. There are two similar perforations in the right shoulder and arm, and one in the right thigh. They correspond with what Anni looks at in the lab as she levitates near the bodies, and the picture I'm getting is an awful one.

CHAPTER 23

THE CREWMATES MUST HAVE taken off their suits before making their way to the lab section where the medical supplies are kept. Perhaps they lived long enough to help themselves or at least try before they couldn't anymore, and the implication is unforgivable.

"Their suits, the EMUs have holes in them, indicating they were wearing them when they were injured," I summarize to the Situation Room. "That much is a fact."

"Would they have survived long?" the president asks.

"I can say this much at this point," I answer. "They weren't disabled instantly. But I won't know until I have a better sense of their internal injuries, as much as that's possible under the circumstances."

"What did Horton do to help them?" asks the secretary of state.

"What I can tell you is the victims bled extensively, based on what we're seeing." I look around at the grim faces staring up at morbid images. "You don't continue bleeding unless you have a blood pressure. The longer they bled, the longer they were alive."

"Are there any signs that first aid was attempted?" the vice president asks me.

"Nothing I'm seeing," I reply.

"But who turned off all the cameras, the radios?" More questions and comments erupt around the table.

"Horton. Who else?"

"Why?"

"So that he could make his getaway undetected until it was too late to stop him."

"The cameras were turned off hours before he made his getaway," Benton reminds everyone.

"How is it possible his crewmates didn't realize that was happening? That suddenly they were disconnected from Houston?" the secret service asks.

"We may never know the answers to some things," Benton says.

"Horton has a lot to answer for," the FBI decides. "But good luck making much sense of the disaster up there," addressing this to me. "I'm not sure what else we can do beyond taking care of the bodies. It's not like we can bring them back down here for autopsies."

There are no good options for how to handle the Thor crewmates' bodies. They couldn't be stored or returned to Earth. We don't have morgue coolers in orbit, and forget loading the bodies onto a spaceplane and carrying them to the ISS. Then what? They can't be left at room temperature inside the trash room.

It's also out of the question leaving them inside the Thor orbiter to decompose, abandoning the laboratory-habitat. That would be a multibillion-dollar loss, not to mention the years of research and development. The only real solution at this time and under the circumstances is to litter in space, which no one is supposed to do.

The director of the FBI doesn't elaborate on the protocol for handling human remains in space, and he may not know. But I certainly do. Outlining plans for such unpleasantries, and finding shortcuts to determine what killed someone, is my responsibility on the Doomsday Commission.

"Returning to the lab," Chip says.

With a flick of a finger, he propels himself that way while I ask Anni if she can locate the emergency medical hardware locker.

"It's right here." She directs her chest camera at the large panel with the red cross symbol in the metal decking.

"Okay, very good," I reply. "We're going to want to try ultrasound, and I need you to power up the rack."

"Powering HRF One." In good astronaut fashion, she echoes back what I tell her, and NASA explains to the Situation Room what's going on.

The Human Research Facility rack feeds electricity to life-science equipment including various radiation detectors, gas analyzers and the ultrasound imaging system, NASA says as Chip gets the power going.

"And while we're at it, let's see what's going on with this." Anni floats up to the ceiling, reaching a mounted video camera. "It's been disabled manually," she reports.

In other words, switched off deliberately as opposed to a malfunction. She turns it back on just like that as the story we've been told continues changing before us. Lies and more lies.

"So much for the spacecraft being damaged," the president remarks grimly as Anni floats to other mounted cameras around the lab.

One by one she turns all of them back on, some of the lenses speckled with dried blood. Then the radios are next, and momentarily we're linked to the orbiter's camera system, more images appearing on the data walls. Another organ floats into the picture, an escaped liver that had been lurking behind a bioprinter. Stabilizing herself with a foot loop, Anni opens the medical storage locker, finding the handheld wireless ultrasound machine.

"Chip, Anni, what I'd like you to do now is to pull out medical and surgical packs." I begin shepherding them through it. "I apologize in advance that what I'm going to need you to do will be difficult."

That's putting it mildly, and I tell them that to start with we're going to need a thermometer. It would appear the only one they can find is an infrared scanner in the medical bag they brought on board. That's fine for checking fevers but not ideal for postmortem purposes.

"Go ahead and take the ambient temperature with it," I explain, not caring what the orbiter's sensors say. "We need to check everything for ourselves as much as possible."

"It's twenty-point-five degrees Celsius in here," or sixty-nine degrees Fahrenheit, Anni reports.

What we can't do is take the bodies' core temperatures. Were we able to do that, I would expect different readings than the ones we get when Anni points the infrared scanner at each victim's forehead.

"He's twenty-seven Celsius," or eighty-one degrees Fahrenheit. "And she's at twenty-five," or seventy-seven degrees Fahrenheit, and I'm not surprised the female Russian crewmate is cooling faster since she's smaller.

"What does that tell us exactly?" The vice president looks at me.

"It tells me that they've been dead in the eight- to ten-hour range at least. The best we can do is approximate," I reply.

"Since about the time they were supposed to go out on their spacewalk," Benton suggests. "Depending on when that was since there's no video to tell us."

"It was scheduled for half past eleven last night," NASA says. "A little more than twelve hours ago."

"Time of death isn't an exact science, and we won't have some of the same findings when there's no gravity," I explain. "But based on the cooling of the bodies and their extreme degree of rigor mortis, they died eight to ten hours ago."

Next, I ask if Chip or Anni see something like a backboard,

and in short order they find a folded fiberglass table inside a locker. Lifting it out, they flip down the metal feet, inserting them into the metal flooring's receptacles.

"What is it you're planning, exactly?" General Gunner meets my eyes across the table, everyone around it riveted to the sad drama playing out on the data walls.

"We need to see what they were hit with if possible," I reply. "We can't get them back home for a proper autopsy, can't possibly manage something like that up there under the circumstances. We'll have to improvise."

EACH BODY WILL NEED to be strapped facedown on the table, starting with the male, I let Chip and Anni know.

"You're going to have to be my hands up there," I say to them. "And I'm going to keep reminding you to be careful about getting cut. I expect the projectiles inside the bodies to be fragmented, possibly quite sharp," and I don't need to add the other worry.

We don't know what the two Thor scientists were hit with, and can't assume it's a material that's familiar. Bluntly put, we don't know what's true. We also have no idea what we'll find inside the bodies, and if it might be dangerous, as in radioactive or contaminated with something not indigenous to Earth.

The ripping sound of Velcro, and the rigorous dead male isn't cooperative, as if trying to get away from his rescuers. Then he's strapped facedown as securely in place as can be managed with his arms and legs bent, and I tell Anni and Chip to start by cutting through the right thigh of the long johns.

More formally known as a Liquid Cooling and Ventilation Garment, it includes three hundred feet of plastic tubing that circulates a gallon of chilled water, NASA explains to the room. But in this case, the tubing was perforated, the water long since evaporated.

"We're going to dig out some of these projectiles, bits of shrapnel, whatever they are," I continue to instruct. "You'll need a scalpel, forceps, towels. Also, sterile plastic containers or something comparable. I need you to collect whatever they were struck with so that it can be examined in labs on the ground."

Using scissors tethered to a string, Chip cuts through the cooling garment. The white cotton fabric floats away from the dead man's skin, a swarm of more dried blood flakes released into the air.

"Now before we do anything else," I continue, "let's do ultrasound, see what we find. This will give you a little guidance, so you aren't rooting around blindly. We'll do him first, then take a look at his crewmate," I explain as Anni floats over to the hardware locker.

"Which probe do you want?" she inquires.

"The linear one with a frequency of six to fifteen megahertz," I reply.

Pulling a small table closer, Chip places surgical instruments on top of it, everything Velcroed so nothing floats away inconveniently, dangerously.

"Okay, here goes." Anni has the probe in hand.

She squeezes conductive gel out of a plastic bottle, spreading it over the exposed wound on the dead man's thigh. The images are fuzzy on the laptop computer that the wireless ultrasound device is synced with, and already I have a clue. I tell them to cut through more of the cooling garment. I need them to ultrasound each wound, and as they do it I see more of the same.

Once a projectile penetrated the spacesuit and entered the body, it fragmented into a blizzard of small birdshot-like pieces that never penetrated the chest cavity or any organ. The devastating wound track in the thigh is some eight inches deep, the frag traveling downward at a sixty-degree angle.

"Based on what I'm seeing, I suspect the femoral vein was nicked," I explain to everyone. "A potentially lethal injury if untreated. But not immediately so because it's a vein and not an artery, and it isn't transected. What that means is he wouldn't have bled out as quickly, possibly not quickly at all."

That alone would have killed him eventually depending on the damage caused by the wounds to his right shoulder and arm. But it might have taken a while, and we need to ultrasound his crewmate. That's a challenge when there's one table, and the only solution I have isn't ideal. I tell Chip he needs to hold the dead woman's body steady.

Anchoring himself with a foot loop, he wraps his Tyvek-covered arms around her, holding her still long enough for Anni to cut through the cooling garment. I instruct her to ultrasound the two wounds to the upper right side, and that will be further complicated by the pugilistic position of the dead woman's body.

Cutting through the cotton fabric, Anni spreads the gel, rubbing the probe over the wounds. Fuzzy images appear on the laptop's display, and we see the same thing we did with her crewmate. The projectile began fragmenting upon penetration, in her case hitting ribs, stopping short of vital organs.

"As best I can tell, her right axillary vein was partially transected," I decide. "That's what it's looking like on ultrasound based on the location of one particular fragment I'm seeing. The injury wouldn't be survivable if left untreated."

We'll strap her body to the table later to see what we find. But first we need to finish with her comrade, and I ask Anni to pick up a scalpel while Chip floats nearby, ready with towels.

"Go more slowly than you think necessary. And let me know when you feel the blade hit something." I watch Anni's progress on the data wall.

"Not so far." She cautiously digs in and cuts, blood oozing bright red as it's exposed to the air, and without gravity it behaves bizarrely.

Pooling, creeping along the dead man's skin, it floats off in tiny orbs that splat whatever they hit. The walls, the ceiling, equipment, and the transparent plastic shield over Anni's face. She mops up with a towel, and I have a pretty good idea what it must have been like when the two Thor scientists were dying.

Wet blood from their wounds would have been in the air, spattering everywhere, and there's no way Jared Horton didn't have it all over his body, his clothing, in his hair. Not an inch of open space inside the orbiter was spared including the hygiene room where the crew takes space baths, such as they are.

The best one can do is to wash with heated water that wants to float off the same way blood and every other liquid does. No sooner would Horton wipe his skin clean then it was going to be covered again, the blood blowing as the fans dictated, drying in the cool air.

This would have gone on as long as the victims' hearts continued pumping, and the air handling filtration system could help but so much with a liquid that coagulates before finally drying. Then it fractures into particles as small as pepper flakes that get into everything.

The injured crewmates may have survived longer than we want to imagine, possibly for several hours, getting weaker. But while conscious they would have been panicking and in pain. They may still have been alive when Horton was making his plans to flee in the Soyuz, and despite it all he couldn't decontaminate himself.

Wet blood would have continued sticking to his hair, his skin, whatever he was wearing and carrying away with him. I find his predicament Shakespearean, maybe worthy of Edgar Allan Poe if not downright biblical. The Thor scientist turned spy had his dead crewmates' blood on his hands literally.

He carried their DNA back to Earth with him. That may or may not matter as one deals with the Russians, I inform the Situation Room.

"I'm guessing there was an abundance of bloody particulate

on his personal effects and inside the crew capsule," I explain, keeping my eye on our astronaut rescuers on the data walls. "How are we doing?" I ask them.

"The scalpel is in as far as it will go, halfway up the handle," Anni says, holding herself in place with the foot loop. "Maybe four inches, and I might be feeling something."

"Switch to forceps. Hopefully, there are ones long enough to go in deeper," I reply. "I don't want you or Chip digging in with a finger and being cut through your gloves."

We don't know how sharp the frag might be or its composition, I'm going to keep warning them. We wouldn't want them injured. Nor do I want them exposed to some unknown hazard in the remote chance we're dealing with space debris or material from an extraterrestrial vehicle or weapon.

CHAPTER 24

OKAY, I GOT SOMETHING." She slowly withdraws the plastic forceps, pulling out a jagged bit of copper shrapnel as bright as rose gold.

Clinging to it are fibers from the spacesuit material and cooling garment, and she digs deeper. Guided by the saved ultrasound images, she finds more copper shards and fibers, also bits of deformed lead. She places them inside sterile plastic containers, digging some more.

"Not sure what this is, something bigger," she says, pulling out the forceps.

Clamped in the tip is a deformed small bloody silver sphere. Showing it to us in her double-gloved palm, she wipes it off with a towel, and it's about the size of a pea.

"I have no idea what that is," Chip says.

Nobody inside the Situation Room does, either. But I'm pretty sure I do.

"Is it hollow and similar to plastic?" My mood sinks through the floor even as I get furious.

"Affirmative," Anni replies, and I have a good idea what must have happened last night around the time of the scheduled spacewalk.

I'm not going to say anything until I have a chance to verify what I suspect, but what a piece of garbage. I'd owe a lot of money to Janet's swear jar right about now if anyone could hear what I'm thinking about Jared Horton. Keeping my feelings to myself, I ask Chip about examining the EMUs, the spacesuits, a little while ago.

"I'm wondering if you noticed an odor they might have carried back into the airlock with them," I say to him on the data walls.

"No, ma'am," he replies, and with his face mask and shield on, he likely can't smell much of anything. "But I wasn't checking for odors. I didn't actually put my nose in the fabric."

"Maybe if you have a chance." I emphasize that I don't want him getting a lungful of the ambient air and everything in it, please.

But it's conceivable that an odor could still cling to the outside of the suits after only twelve hours.

"That's approximately how much time has passed since the spacewalk was scheduled," I explain, and they know what I'm implying. "I wouldn't ask if it wasn't important," I add, not wishing to keep them there longer, to further burden them.

But if there might be a residual telltale scent on the EMUs,

I'd like to know it for a fact while we can. If it's still there, it won't last a lot longer. Most assuredly it would be gone by the time the next crew arrives to clean up the bloody disaster Horton left.

"Wilco, doing it now," Chip says, and we follow his progress as he returns to the airlock.

Hovering close to the floating disarticulated spacesuits, he grabs a glove. Lifting his face shield, he pulls down the mask, holding the white fire-retardant fabric close to his nose. Then he covers himself just as quickly with his PPE, looking up at the cameras, shaking his head no.

He didn't smell anything, and he returns to the lab area, moving as easily through the air as an eel through water.

"What does that mean?" The vice president directs this at me.

"Most likely it means that the two victims weren't hit by debris, and their spacewalk never happened," is my answer plain and simple. "They never left the airlock, were fatally injured inside it after suiting up."

"Are we sure?" General Gunner asks.

"We'll verify when the evidence is examined in the labs," I reply.

"That can't happen immediately," NASA says.

The fragments removed from the victims' bodies can't be returned to Earth until the next crew capsule does. One is scheduled to depart from the International Space Station the end of December, and I don't want to wait that long.

"I'll see what I can find out in the meantime," I reply as Anni and Chip begin their struggle with the dead.

Spreading open a body pouch, they try to coax the female victim inside it. The job is made all the more difficult by microgravity, people alive and dead ducking, dodging, knocking into each other or the walls, the floor, the ceiling.

Such a grotesque dance, and afterward the unprecedented inevitability, one nobody inside the Situation Room would want to watch, given a choice. The experiment platform's robotic arm performs a morbid task it wasn't intended for, and it's a silent moment when the pouched bodies are jettisoned from a port into the vacuum of space.

They'll orbit the planet like other debris, maybe burning up if gravity pulls them down into the atmosphere eventually. But they could stay up there indefinitely, and as unthinkable as that may seem there's no better alternative. Not at the moment and under the circumstances because space is unforgiving.

Already I'm dreading what might hit the news. It's unnerving to think about how the public will react to the murders. I don't like to think about astronomers spotting the pouched remains orbiting like cocoons, and next they're labeled and included on satellite maps.

What's done is done, and Anni and Chip pull off their gloves. Tearing off their Tyvek, they gather up their plastic containers of evidence, their medical bag, preparing to go. Before reentering the Dream Chaser, they resort to a combination of fans, vacuum hoses and electrostatic filters to remove the bio-hazardous particulate.

All of it must be sucked up and blown off their bodies, clothing and belongings to prevent it from being carried first into the spaceplane, and next into the Space Station. We watch them decon the same way astronauts will before they reenter their habitats or board lunar landers, making sure they don't track in moon dust.

Single file, the French and American astronauts look like superheroes flying through the Dream Chaser's hatch, closing it behind them. Back inside the cockpit, they put on their launch-entry suits, strapping themselves into their seats, and I thank them again.

"I know how hard that was." I talk to them on the data wall. "I couldn't have done it without you," I add sincerely as the president gets up from the table.

"What you just did took real courage," he says to them while people collect their paperwork, getting ready to leave. "Such a tragic ordeal, and we're very grateful to you."

"Thank you, Chip, Anni, and be safe." The vice president pushes back her chair. "Godspeed."

AT FOUR P.M. THE drizzle has stopped. The overcast is clearing out as Benton and I sit inside his quiet electric SUV.

We're stuck midway across the George Mason Memorial Bridge spanning a half-mile stretch of the Potomac River. The four southbound lanes are a parking lot, the sun smoldering like molten lava, spreading electric orange and pink hues along the horizon. The waning light is reflected on the water, flickering in the lazy current.

At least we have a view. I don't know that I've ever seen a more dramatic sunset. But I'm feeling mounting pressure like an engine overheating, and am eager to get to the office. I need to change out of these clothes, to check with the labs before everyone leaves for the day. Work feels out of control, and has since I started this job.

I can't even say what cases have come in today. Nothing newsworthy, I'm assuming, or someone would have let me know, I should hope. Definitely I'd hear from Marino as he monitors his police scanner around the clock, usually finding out about most fiascos before I do.

"Television news choppers." Benton looks up at several of them hovering high in the distance, their lights bright in the gathering dusk. "Something's going on in Pentagon City."

According to the integrated navigation dash display, there's police activity ahead, and at the moment that's all we know. As we wait, busy with texts and e-mails, I send updates to Lucy, Maggie, Marino and others. I inform them that we left D.C. maybe twenty minutes ago, still not mentioning what we were doing there.

All I'm saying is we're stuck in traffic on the bridge, and they'll know which one, are well aware how slow it can be crossing the Potomac this time of day. I look out at night falling fast like a dark curtain dropping, counting four helicopters now in high hovers on the other side of the water.

The police must know what's going on, and I text Marino and Lucy again, asking if they have an idea. While waiting for them to respond, I reach out to toxicology, trace evidence, and the firearms and tool marks labs. There are examiners I need to talk to before the day is done, and not all of them answer when off the clock.

"The problem is not everybody takes calls once they leave the office." I say to Benton what I've said before, frustrated and feeling cornered. "That's assuming I have their personal cell phone numbers. And I don't yet for many of them even though crime doesn't keep banker's hours."

"People have lives," he replies.

"Of course they do, Benton. But for some of the scientists and doctors, the minute they walk out for the day, their time is their own, and it never used to be that way."

"'Used to be's don't count anymore,' to quote Neil Diamond," my secret agent husband sings badly, trying to make me lighten up.

"Well, you can thank Elvin Reddy for the attitudes I'm confronted with daily. But it doesn't do any good to complain," I reply, wishing the inside of Benton's impeccable SUV didn't smell like fried chicken.

The empty Styrofoam containers are in white plastic bags with big blue presidential seals, and I'm not keeping our take-out trash as a souvenir. It's on the floor by my feet because we had no convenient place to toss it on the White House grounds. Public trash receptacles are scarce for security reasons, and I thought it rude to ask Tron to dispose of our take-out detritus.

Especially after she was kind enough to let us stay in our privileged parking spot long enough to wolf down a late lunch, and by then we were ravenous. The Mess Hall's fried fare included biscuits and creamy coleslaw that hit the spot. I'm well fed and hydrated but feel traces of a headache again after our marathon session in the Situation Room.

Then it was alone time inside the Oval Office, the president and vice president asking all sorts of questions about the poisoned wine from Interpol. Tampering like that could happen anywhere including the White House, royal palaces, law enforcement headquarters, and government residences around the world.

Guests are always arriving with gifts that one is unwise to accept, it would seem. But we have to get food and drink from somewhere. We can't say no to absolutely everything. There's just too darn much to worry about these days, the president said as we sat on formal furniture inside the oval-shaped room, everything gold and blue.

There were follow-up questions about the double homicide, the first violent deaths in space as best we know. Benton was asked point-blank if he believed that Jared Horton also was involved in Gwen Hainey's vicious murder. In the private setting of the Oval Office, Benton countered what the FBI, Homeland Security and others had opined earlier.

He logically explained that he saw no useful purpose

Gwen's homicide might have served, especially as sensational as it was. It was the last thing Horton needed, and one can imagine his shock as he quickly calculated how to use her unexpected murder to his advantage.

One evil act deserves another, and he disabled the cameras and radios unbeknownst to his two defenseless crewmates. He did this before helping them suit up for an outing in the vacuum of space that wasn't going to happen, and the thought is enraging.

"His overriding fear was that his secret life of spying was about to be uncovered during Gwen's murder investigation," Benton told the president, the vice president and those assembled behind closed doors. "He went into a controlled free fall, panicking while keeping his wits about him."

In short order, Jared Horton eliminated his crewmates, and I'm all but certain he shot them. Believing he could pass it off as a bizarre accident or attack in low-Earth orbit, he cleaned out the lab while he was at it before fleeing to Kazakhstan. As Benton and I are talking about this now, I'm looking out at the distant lights on the shore.

The section of railroad tracks where Gwen was found is close to here, not far from the airport. I remember crouching by her crudely posed body in the rainy darkness, listening to the constant roar of jets taking off and landing. I could hear them but not see their lights in the thick clouds.

"I think Horton came prepared for the unexpected," Benton explains. "And when he feared his spying gig was up, he murdered his crewmates in cold blood. Then he tried to pass off the story that they were hit with debris, somehow managing to return to the airlock. We now know that never happened."

There was no spacewalk, explaining why Chip didn't notice the odor that lingers after being outside on one. The fleeting scent of space clings to the suits for a while, and astronauts describe it differently. Some say it's a burnt metallic odor. Others are reminded of ozone or something electrical.

CHAPTER 25

NOW WHAT?" I ASK in gridlock traffic halfway across the dark waters of the Potomac River, the slivered moon slipping in and out of clouds. "He just gets a free pass, is granted sanctuary by the Kremlin? I'm so sick and tired of bad guys winning."

"We have a partnership in space with the Russians, and while everybody has to safeguard their proprietary technologies, we still have to get along," Benton says. "My guess is that the Kremlin will deny having anything to do with what Horton's involved in, and they'll probably hand him over."

"Good. Because he shouldn't get away with it," I reply, headlights, taillights blazing in the dark, and a text from Lucy lands on my phone.

What a coincidence (not), she writes.

When I click on the file she's sent, I understand why traffic is at a standstill with news helicopters hovering. A group of anti–police brutality protesters are marching through the wealthy neighborhood of Aurora Highlands just south of Pentagon City.

"There's maybe a couple hundred people so far," I inform Benton. "And it would appear this is related to an attempted break-in at Dana Diletti's house early this morning." I continue scrolling through news feeds, and what's flashing in my mind is the timing.

Lucy's right, what a coincidence. How convenient that someone should try to break into the celebrity TV journalist's home even as she's working on a big story about the Railway Slayer. While covering Gwen Hainey's brutal murder, the reporter herself is being hunted perhaps by the very same psycho killer.

"Or I assume that's the implication," I say to Benton.

"That's what it's sounding like," he agrees, and thankfully the traffic is starting to move again. "But it doesn't mean someone didn't try to break into her home."

"Apparently, Aurora Highlands is where she lives." I'm reading on the Internet. "And her burglar alarm went off around two o'clock this morning."

"The first I've heard of it, and that was more than fourteen hours ago," Benton says. "Why all the hoopla now? What else has happened?"

"As we speak, she's holding a press conference in her front yard, the protest obviously organized to coincide with it." I continue passing on what I'm learning.

The police have responded to contain what's sounding like a manufactured situation that's creating havoc for area commuters. I have no doubt it's intentional, I say to Benton as I continue glancing through the latest accounts while we creep across the bridge.

"The gist seems to be that she's accusing the police of mistreating her," I add. "Targeting her because she dares to report the news accurately, to criticize the police and those in power."

I play a live video clip so we can hear what she's saying.

". . . The police came eventually." Dana Diletti is standing outside in the glare of television lights not far from here. "The two officers were, well, let's just say they didn't seem happy to see me, making sure I knew they don't watch my particular *brand* of reporting."

Dressed in jeans, a raincoat, she has little if any makeup on, looking more like a neighbor than a famous journalist, a strikingly tall and beautiful one. Surrounded by her crew, she tells her inflammatory story as dozens of police officers in riot gear keep a wary eye on the growing crowd, many people angrily fist-pumping, carrying flags and signs.

". . . Let me just say it required considerable effort on my part for them to take the situation seriously," Dana says earnestly, staring into the camera. "Or worse, as if it didn't matter what might have happened to me, that maybe I don't belong in this upscale neighborhood."

She accuses the police of refusing to request that an investigative unit be summoned to check for evidence. The responding officers saw no need to dust for fingerprints, swab for DNA, take photographs or do anything else, she claims. They left after searching her house, making sure no one was inside it. Or so they explained.

"But that's not what they were really doing," she dramatically declares. "Their gloved hands were rifling through my closets, drawers, cupboards and other places that had nothing to do with someone trying to pry open my bedroom window. In the process setting off the alarm, thank God. Because I was right there in the dark, sound asleep in bed."

She blatantly states that the police searched her place without a warrant, treating her like a suspect, not a victim. Their only interest was prurient details they could gossip about while hoping to find drugs or other contraband, illegal weapons, who knows what? All to discredit and destroy her, she's adamant.

"Finally, after calling the mayor to complain," she adds, "five hours after the fact, an investigative unit showed up where I live."

She looks back at her lovely antique brick house decorated for the holidays, on a generous lot thick with old hardwood and fir trees.

"And they found it necessary to remove the entire window, making it impossible for me to stay here . . ."

Why not invite some thug to break in, just send out an engraved invitation? she says, and that's rather much what she's doing on live TV. Next, we're shown images of the big plyboard-covered window at the back of her house, and I would agree that it's an unacceptable vulnerability.

She's right to feel unsafe. Were it me, I'd live elsewhere for a while or at least have someone staying with me. For sure I wouldn't draw attention to my situation by holding a press conference that not so accidentally is accompanied by protesters marching through my neighborhood.

"What she's doing is really unfortunate. Reckless, actually," I remark as the coverage plays on my phone. "And yes, that's too bad about her window. But it's a sad fact of life that if you want evidence properly tested, it's usually not going to be convenient or pretty."

As much crime as the TV journalist covers, she certainly knows that. I speak my mind to Benton even as Dana speaks hers on camera.

". . . Meaning some serial killer can come back with a hammer, pull out the nails and let himself in . . . ," she's saying.

All to intimidate her into silence or get her murdered, she goes on convincingly until I can't listen anymore.

"Talk about giving someone ideas." I end the video file. "And making everything about herself, I'm sorry to say."

"Just what nobody needs right about now," Benton agrees.

FOLLOWING THE GEORGE WASHINGTON Memorial Parkway along the river, we've avoided Dana Diletti's neighborhood and the problems that go with it.

We're just south of the airport, not far from Daingerfield Island, and I text Maggie to e-mail me the Cammie Ramada case. I also want the hard copy waiting on my desk when I get there.

Why, is there a new development? My secretary answers with an outrageous question.

Just do it, please, I text her back, adding that hopefully she'll still be there by the time I arrive, and it's more an order than a hope.

"How far out are we?" I ask Benton.

"Ten minutes, knock on wood."

I pass this along to my overreaching secretary as Rex Bonetta texts me back, and I call him. Right away my chief toxicologist lets me know that we can't yet identify the presumed opioid that could have killed a lot of people including me. They've screened for everything they can to no avail.

"In other words, I'm frustrated," he says over speakerphone. "And I'm not feeling terribly optimistic, Kay. The testing could take a very long time when there's no clue what we might be looking for. Or if it's some new drug we don't have an assay for, and that's what I suspect."

The possibilities for synthetic opioids are as endless as the number pi, as limitless as a chemist's imagination. All that's required is changing a single molecule, and fentanyl isn't fentanyl anymore. The same with carfentanil, methadone and other drugs created primarily for pain relief.

"You lose or gain a hydrogen, a carbon, a nitrogen molecule," Rex is saying. "Or add an extra bang for the user's buck like designer benzodiazepines, and the drug screen's going to miss it."

That makes continued testing extremely difficult. At times it's more like a crapshoot as toxicologists try to keep up with the latest potentially deadly spinoff.

"I'm worried that whatever we're dealing with may have hit in the U.S. and is in the Northern Virginia area," Rex says. "Possibly the greater D.C. area."

Three deaths came in today that he's pretty sure are opioid-related, and this is the first I've heard of them. But the drug screen in each was negative except for methadone in one case.

"A recovering heroin addict found dead in an alleyway near a methadone clinic in west Alexandria," he explains. "I'm wondering if what we're up against might be the same thing your wine was laced with. A new derivative of something like fentanyl that comes up negative."

"That's a disturbing thought," I reply as Benton turns us inland toward my headquarters, picking up U.S. 1.

"It sure is if your bottle of Bordeaux was tampered with in Europe"—Rex's voice over speakerphone—"and the same drug has followed you home to Virginia."

"Or if the tampering was done here to begin with," I add, a far worse thought for me personally as I wonder how that might have happened. "Some new deadly designer drug."

I think of what Officer Fruge told me about being at a scene last week, using up all her Narcan reviving multiple people who had overdosed.

"Check back with me tomorrow," Rex says.

He plans to spend time in the trace evidence lab looking at samples of residue found in the wine, seeing what might turn up on the scanning electron microscope. In the meantime, he'll let me know if there are new developments, and I end the call, the lights of my building up ahead. I look over at Benton, feeling guilty before saying it.

"It may be rather late by the time I get home." I tell him what he already knows. "Having been out the entire day with all that's going on? There's lasagna and extra sauce in the freezer, also the makings for salad."

"Don't worry about me." He reaches for my hand, lacing his fingers through mine. "I have a feeling I'll be pretty tied up with Lucy, following up on Jared Horton and everything else. Her data mining might be useful now that we're getting a better idea what he and Gwen were up to."

He'll throw together something for a late supper, have it ready when I get there, he promises, always this thoughtful.

"For sure I've got to check in with Maggie, get up to speed on what I've missed." I feel overwhelmed as I go down the list, this day a washout. "And Marino and I need to take a look at Daingerfield Island, at the areas where Gwen Hainey's and Cammie Ramada's bodies were found."

"I understand but it's already dark. I don't suppose it can wait until tomorrow?"

"Since we don't know who's killing whom, it doesn't seem anything can wait, Benton. I need to look around in the dark. It's better for what I have in mind."

"I prefer you'd get home at a decent hour tonight, that's all." He sounds like an overprotective husband, and I know when he's unsettled.

"I wish I could," I reply, my parking lot in the next block, an unbroken line of bright red taillights leading to it.

"Considering what the last twenty-four hours have been like, it would be good if you could get some rest, Kay," he says, and by now if nothing else, we know how to negotiate.

"I have a thought." I dig my keys out of my briefcase, mindful of the empty gun compartment.

Maybe my husband can pack a pistol on the White House grounds but people like me certainly can't. The Sig Sauer is tucked in my bedside drawer, the trigger lock on.

"We'll make a deal," I suggest.

Instead of meeting Marino at Daingerfield Island or having him follow me there, I'll ask him to pick me up here at the office. As I'm saying it, I'm sending him a text to that effect.

"Later he can drop me back at the house. We'll deal with my car tomorrow," I explain, and after the day I've had I wouldn't mind being chauffeured by Marino in his big truck full of weapons.

"Fine," Benton says. "That would make me much happier. With all that's going on I don't want you driving yourself around in the middle of the night."

CHAPTER 26

REACHING MY PARKING LOT, we stop at the security gate. I take off my shoulder harness, placing my briefcase in my lap.

Benton opens his window, entering my code on the keypad, and I think of Marino driving me to Colonial Landing last night. Strains of the creepy *Shock Theater* theme play in my mind, and it's ironic that the townhome development has better security than my state government headquarters.

The security gate's red-striped wooden arm lifts, a barrier you can walk around. Some employees are headed to their cars, the streetlights on their tall masts pushing back the darkness. We park next to my take-home Subaru in its assigned spot where I left it barely twenty-four hours ago.

"I'll be home as soon as possible." I grab our White House takeout trash, walking around to the back, and Benton pops open the tailgate.

I pull out the scene case I carried home last night, and his window rolls down as I walk by.

"Be careful, and I mean it," he says with a smile. "Don't forget I love you."

"And don't you forget," I reply, and he drives off quietly as I enter the bay to the strong odor of exhaust, the loud noise of a diesel engine running.

A funeral home's old white van is parked inside, its rear doors open wide. Fabian helps a smartly dressed attendant maneuver an unwieldly stretcher down the concrete ramp that leads into the intake area of the building. The rotund pouched body is covered with a blue velour quilt, the name of the funeral home, Rivers Rest, embroidered on it.

They're careful not to let their heavy payload get away from them or topple over, the attendant hanging on for dear life while Fabian mutters a few choice words under his breath. He's dressed in dark blue scrubs and rubber clogs instead of his usual investigative garb, his long jet-black hair tied back in a ponytail.

"What have we got here?" I announce myself, dropping the plastic takeout bags into the trash.

But not before Fabian notices the White House seals on them. He walks over to inspect.

"Yowzers." He picks up one of the takeout bags. "Looks like you've had quite the outing."

Ignoring his comment, I introduce myself to the attendant, an older man in a dark suit and a polka-dotted red bow tie.

"I'm the new chief," I explain to him, and his van is gushing exhaust that's filling the bay.

"Nice to meet you, I'm Howie Rivers." He nods at me, then

resumes ferrying his unwieldy cargo, one of the stretcher's wheels sticking.

I push the big green button on the epoxy-sealed cinder block wall, and the motorized door begins to retract with a loud clanking and creaking. Cold air seeps in, and through the big square opening I can see more people headed to their cars. It's getting to be the magic hour, employees egressing through the lobby, and nothing much has changed.

Most of the scientists and support staff avoid the scenic route through the morgue, the intake area and the vehicle bay. The same was true back in my Richmond days, not everybody interested in seeing the gory source of the evidence they examine. A lot of people don't want to know a story they might not forget.

DNA scientists in particular don't want to be told why there's blood on a weapon, skin cells on a ski mask, seminal fluid on a rug or where the pubic hair came from. For many, all that matters is whose DNA it is or isn't, and I have to remind myself regularly that what's routine for me is aberrant to polite society.

"We don't want to keep vehicle engines running while the door is down," I remind Fabian and Howie. "Carbon monoxide can build up in a hurry."

I shouldn't have to tell them that. They're well versed in what kills, knowing it up close and personal the same way I do, and I suppose that's part of the problem. The abnormal becomes normal, and people get complacent if not careless.

"We took a little longer than planned getting her out of the cooler," Fabian explains. "Not what I'd call a fun time."

"She weighs over three hundred pounds." Howie parks the stretcher by the van's tailgate, and I examine the toe tag attached to the heavy-duty black body bag's zipper.

The name penned on it isn't one I recognize, the location simply listed as an alleyway several miles west of here, and it's the case Rex was telling me about over the phone a few minutes ago. The death occurred late morning while I was inside the Situation Room, and Fabian responded to the scene.

"I was present for the autopsy," he lets me know as I help them collapse the stretcher's legs.

We slide the body into the back of the van, and Howie drives off in a wake of belching exhaust.

"You need some help carrying all that?" Fabian asks as I collect my belongings off the concrete floor.

"I've got it but thanks." I walk up the ramp, and he hurries ahead of me to open the door.

"I'm ready and waiting if anything good comes in," he adds, and nothing coming into this place is ever good.

He follows me inside, an empty gurney on the floor scale that he rolls past the cooler and freezer, in the direction of the autopsy suite. I head to the security office directly ahead, and Wyatt is sitting at his desk. On the ledge outside his window is the big black morgue log anchored by a thin chain, the ballpoint pen attached by a string so no one can walk off with them.

The Virginia medical examiner's system has been keeping the logs since the early 1940s, and like the notebooks I carry, the records are initial impressions. They're what first responders jotted down at the time, the entries made by those who bring the dead and carry them away.

For the most part, we're talking about funeral home and removal service attendants. But it could be one of my investigators, especially if I'm worried about preserving evidence during transport. But also, when a body has no other secure means of conveyance, we take care of it, and that became common practice during the pandemic.

Commercial transporters were overwhelmed, and my former forensic center in Cambridge, Massachusetts, had no choice but to take care of all pickups and removals in our black windowless vans. That placed the drivers solidly in the chain of evidence, and what a huge responsibility, not to mention a liability. The log is an important legal guestbook that people shouldn't want their names in for any reason.

I've always considered it my truest and most important snapshot of what I'm dealing with, and it's my habit to check the latest entries first thing when I get to work. I take a look again before leaving at day's end, and if the initial information turns out to be incorrect, a statement to that effect must be added to the decedent's record.

SETTING DOWN MY SCENE case and other belongings, I open the big hardbound ledger with its pale green lined pages.

"How are you this evening?" I ask Wyatt. "Thanks for holding down the fort while I've been gone."

"As best I can." He dabs his lips with a napkin, the crinkle of paper amplified by the window's speak-thru, and he's got his air purifier going full tilt.

I can see from the log that since Marino drove away with me about this time last night, eight cases have come in. Two motor vehicle fatalities, a suicide by hanging, two natural causes, and the three possible overdoses pending toxicology. Most of the bodies have been released, including the one I saw inside the bay a few minutes ago.

"Did you just get here?" I notice the remains of a meal from Wendy's on his desk, the overflowing trash can, and how tired and stressed he looks.

"No, ma'am. I've been here since eight o'clock and won't get off until midnight."

"Why are you doing a double shift?"

"It's not like I had a say about it." Dipping a french fry into ketchup, he lets me know that the security officer scheduled to come in this morning wasn't feeling well, supposedly.

"I'm sorry to hear that's happened again." It's not the first time, and it would have been nice for Maggie to tell me.

"Another headache that he blames on allergies." Wyatt takes a loud sip of his melted Frosty. "Huh. The only thing he's allergic to is work."

"I'm sorry you were inconvenienced," I reply, and it's just one more thing to straighten out. "I don't believe I've ever seen you eat in your office." I know full well how much he hates the morgue. "You always have your meals in the breakroom."

"Yes, ma'am, that's correct," he says, and I go on to remind him that the library and conference room also are options.

There are video monitors in most places, making it easy for the security officers and people like me to keep an eye on the surveillance cameras. In other words, it's safer and far more civilized to eat upstairs.

"You don't have to tell me." He doesn't hide his aggravation. "Especially after that funeral home just wheeled a dead body out. And they don't know what killed the person or two others that were autopsied today. How do I know what's in the air? It wasn't my idea to eat down here, and when Fabian made a Wendy's run, he dropped my food on my desk. I was told to stay put."

"He told you that?"

"Maggie passed the message along through him," Wyatt says resentfully, and my secretary acting like she's in charge seems to be an intractable problem. "She's worried about reporters showing up. Especially that woman whose crew's been hanging around because of the big story she's doing."

"Dana Diletti," I presume.

"Uh-huh, the one whose house got broken into. Well, Maggie's got it in her head that some reporter like that might sneak in when the bay door opens or who knows what." He takes another bite of chili while I turn the log's big heavy pages back eight months.

He informs me that until a little while ago, there were TV trucks pulled off the road beyond our parking lot. Journalists and their crews were filming around the complex as staff and police, the hearses and vans were coming and going. Apparently, the hope is to capture Gwen Hainey's body being driven away, and I let Wyatt know she's not going anywhere today.

"Probably not tomorrow, either. Hers is a complicated case, and she may be with us for a while yet," I say to him. "And you don't need to feel trapped inside your office. That's ridiculous."

I don't care what Maggie or anyone else says. As long as he's down here when there's a pickup or delivery, that's what matters. The rest of the time he can hang out upstairs, and turning another page, I find Cammie Ramada, her name neatly written in black ink. The address where her death occurred is the *beach at Daingerfield Island,* and I have to wonder what she was doing on the shore after dark.

Her body was delivered to the morgue at 12:50 A.M. on Sunday, April 11, and it would seem her correct identity was known from the start. Perhaps some form of identification was found at the scene, her cause of death "possible drowning." The manner of it is abbreviated as "UND" for undetermined, and I hear Fruge's voice in my head.

"But your office eventually decided it was an accident without a doubt, and without testing evidence I might add," she said, and I remember being struck by the word *eventually.*

The implication is that the death was suspicious at first, and I ask Wyatt if he happened to be working that early morning. I wonder what he might remember about the case.

"I realize it was more than seven months and a lot of bodies ago." I tell him who I'm talking about.

"Oh yeah, I remember that one all right." He takes a bite of a cheeseburger that like everything else must be cold. "After that, I wouldn't let my daughter go jogging after dark. That's when bad people come out, and it's not safe being by yourself anyway. You get hurt, there's no one around to help."

"What did you hear about how Cammie Ramada might have gotten hurt?" I close the log.

"I heard she must have fallen, hitting her head, knocking herself out and drowning. She had some medical problem, maybe got disoriented. That's all I know except it was strange," he says.

"Were you around when she was autopsied?"

"I never go in there when they've got cases."

"But were you here in your office at the time. Or was someone else on duty?" I ask, and Wyatt nods that yes, he was on duty.

The autopsy waited until Monday morning, and that's not unusual. Wyatt says he started his shift that day at seven A.M., and I ask if he might have seen police and others associated with the case coming in and out of the morgue.

"Yes, ma'am, it was busy. Mondays almost always are because of what comes in over the weekend. But that morning in particular, there were a lot of people."

"Who do you remember seeing in connection to the Cammie Ramada death?"

"Well, the FBI was involved, and a couple of their agents were hanging around." He constantly monitors security camera images on the big computer screen in front of him.

"Did Investigator Ryan from the park police show up?"

"I don't think I know who that is," he says, and I doubt August was there.

I haven't seen his name listed as a witness to the autopsy, and if the FBI had rolled in, the park police were going to be overpowered.

"What about Doctor Reddy?" I ask.

"He may have walked through once, maybe twice." Wyatt is visibly uncomfortable talking about him.

CHAPTER 27

WAS DOCTOR REDDY WITH anyone when you'd see him pass through?" I ask.

"He was with the FBI." Wyatt dips a plastic spoon into what's left of the chili, squeezing out the last few drops of hot sauce.

"Was he in scrubs?" I can bet on the answer.

"No, ma'am. I'm pretty sure he was dressed like he always is. In a suit." He confirms what I suspect, and I gather my belongings, heading toward the stairs.

I detect the familiar telltale clatter as I near the anthropology lab's observation windows. The big stockpot simmers on the portable cooktop as it has for days, and it can take quite a while to deflesh and degrease bones completely. When they're whistle clean, they'll be examined painstakingly.

We'll make sure there's no nick, cut, bullet hole or other defect suggesting violence. At least in this case we know who the man was but not what happened to him or when. We may never know what his final moments were like. But I'm grateful there won't be yet one more resident in my overcrowded skeleton closet.

I can't think of a bigger failure than never figuring out who someone was. The eighty-seven unsolved cases Elvin left go back two decades, and I envision the storage closet with its labeled archival boxes, and the distinctive paraffin-like musky odor of waxy old bones.

Reaching the autopsy suite, I don't see Fabian but his brand of pop music is booming inside the men's locker room. He's probably cleaning up, changing back into his investigative clothes, and I take the stairs, my shoes loud on the metal-edged concrete steps. I push my way through the door to the sound of Maggie Cutbush talking to someone.

". . . I thought you'd want to know." She's on her cell phone, and not always aware that her British voice carries.

There's no one else in the corridor except me, and I decide against noisily rolling my scene case along on its wheels. I keep quiet and my distance.

". . . No, no, I don't think so. Nothing new that I know of." She's maybe twenty feet in front of me talking hands-free, her wireless earpiece winking blue.

In her standard wool skirt suit and matronly shoes, her hair in a tight bun, she's carrying an armload of files that probably are destined for my desk eventually.

". . . Of course, I asked why the sudden interest. But when she gets hold of something? Well, you know this better than anyone."

I can tell that whoever she's talking to is high in her pecking order, someone she might care about deeply. There's a protective tenderness in her tone that I've not heard before, and I hope what I suspect turns out to be wrong.

"Yes, like a pit bull, not knowing when to quit, hell-bent on creating the latest drama," she agrees, walking into her office.

Then I'm walking into mine, setting down my belongings on the conference table. The first order of business is to close the shades as I watch the parking lot continue to empty. Next, I unlock the supply cabinet I obsessively keep stocked with what I consider forensic and medical necessities.

Finding the Narcan nasal spray, I try to ignore what I overheard a moment earlier, doing my best not to let it get to me. I have no doubt who Maggie was talking about, and it's not true that words don't hurt. They can hurt mightily, and if I didn't feel unwelcome and on my own before, I do now, that's for sure.

"Oh! Well, hello." She appears in our shared doorway. "I didn't realize you were here." A shadow passes behind her eyes, and it may be the first time I've seen her flustered.

I've just walked into my office, and she's worried about what I overheard in the corridor while she was talking on the phone. I play dumb, grabbing Narcan from a shelf.

"I just got here at long last." I place half a dozen doses inside my scene case, promising never to be without them again. "Between traffic jams and protests, and I appreciate your waiting for me."

"I wasn't actually, you got here just in time. I was taking

care of a few things before leaving." She watches my every move as if trying to figure me out. "You have a lot of phone messages, I just e-mailed you the list of them. And there's a stack of cases and death certificates for you to initial. I'll have them ready shortly."

"When we texted while Benton and I were stuck in gridlock, you said things are a mess, and I quote. What's going on besides the day shift security guard calling in sick again? I believe his name is Nathan." I envision him, built like a bullet, a perpetual sour expression on his face.

"Yes, he called in with a migraine late last night, said it was so bad he was in bed with the lights out. Which is exactly where he should have been anyway at almost midnight," Maggie says. "In a nutshell, today has been chaotic."

"If he continues being this undependable, we may have to let him go," I reply. "We can't have security working double shifts, and we don't force people to eat in their offices, by the way, Maggie. Not ever. Especially if it's downstairs or anywhere near bodies and other biohazards." I do my best to keep a check on my indignation.

"I've had every reason imaginable to worry about the security of our building with all that's been going on," she says presumptuously, and not a day goes by when I don't miss my former secretary Rose.

I couldn't have asked for a better aide-de-camp during my Richmond years. She was warm, trustworthy, a force to be reckoned with, and of the district offices I oversaw, she found this one the most difficult. Referring to the staff as "Northern aggressors" and "Beltway snobs," she'd shake her head if she could see me now.

"I'm sorry to hear things have been chaotic but I'm not surprised," I say to my secretary who's certainly not a Rose, more like a sharp thorn in my side.

ROOTING AROUND INSIDE THE supply closet, I can't find the premixed Bluestar reagent I know I have, and I ask Maggie about it.

"I'm not sure I know what that is." She stands nearby, watching me like a hawk.

"When sprayed on nonvisible bloodstains, it causes them to luminesce," I explain in frustration.

"Oh, yes, the sort of hocus-pocus one sees on *CSI*." She all but rolls her eyes. "That must be what Fabian borrowed the other day and promised to replace."

"I need to know things like that," I almost snap, and fortunately I have a jar of luminol powder.

It will work fine for my purposes but isn't as easy to use and has its limitations.

"People can't just help themselves to my supply closet." I shouldn't have to remind her of common courtesy.

"I'll have a word with Fabian," Maggie says, and their allegiance couldn't be more apparent.

"We need to communicate better." It's not the first time I've said this to her, and likely won't be the last. "Had I known the office was out of Bluestar or anything else, we could have reordered it ourselves, and I wouldn't be on my way to a scene without it."

"What scene?"

"There's something I need to check."

"I see. Well, it's difficult to communicate when I don't know where you are much of the time, today being a perfect example. You never mentioned you were leaving town until you were already gone."

She continues to complain as I find a spray bottle, hydrogen peroxide, a liter of distilled water.

"And now you're headed out into the night, and won't tell me where or why," she adds. "You're making it almost impossible for me to do my job."

Putting on a pair of exam gloves, a face mask, I measure fifteen grams, about a tablespoon of the luminol powder, sprinkling it into the plastic bottle.

"If I don't inform you, it's because I can't." I sound like a broken record. "Certainly, it's never my intention to make things more difficult." I screw on the spray top.

"I've never worked for anyone who marginalizes me the way you do," she says.

I feel her eyes fastened to me as I pack up my scene case, closing it with louds snaps, and I don't like her choice of words.

"I'm not marginalizing you or anyone," I reply, and that's what I call lawsuit talk. "As a rule, my government responsibilities aren't open for discussion. Sensitive investigative information isn't either." Taking off my mask and gloves, I notice the thick manila file on my desk chair.

"As you requested," she says as I walk that way. "I also e-mailed the electronic version to you. Why the sudden interest? Is this related to where you're going tonight? What scene do you need to check? Are you talking about Daingerfield Island?"

"Officer Fruge mentioned the Cammie Ramada case when I was with her last night," I reply. "And speaking of? Before you leave, I need you to track down a current phone number for her mother, Greta Fruge, the toxicologist. She's now retired from the state but works for a private lab in Richmond."

Carrying the case file to the conference table, I add that I worked with Greta years ago, and what a small world.

"Imagine my surprise when I discovered her daughter is an Alexandria police officer," I add.

"What do you need Greta for?" My secretary's face is granite. "Why would you want to stir up that hornet's nest?"

"Which hornet's nest are we talking about?"

"Exactly. There have been so many. That's what happens when your ego is as big as the great outdoors."

"The information I have for Greta probably isn't good anymore." I'm learning not to answer Maggie's impertinent observations and probes. "But I'll share what I have with you anyway." As I'm saying this I do it from my phone's contact list. "Please see if you can track her down."

I pass along the name of the biotech company Officer Fruge mentioned when we were going through Gwen Hainey's townhome.

"Why don't you ask Officer Fruge yourself how to get hold

of her mother? That would be the quickest way to get the information," Maggie suggests as if I'd never think of such a thing on my own.

"I don't want to discuss the matter with anyone else at the moment."

"Well, commonsense would dictate that Greta Fruge is best avoided."

"She's extremely good at what she does," I reply. "More to the point, in the private sector she's going to be familiar with new technologies that labs like ours might not have access to for years."

Because of our prior relationship, I'm hoping Greta might help me out, especially since we're in the midst of an ongoing opioid crisis that the public seems to have forgotten about during the pandemic. She's also not naïve about the potential for drugs being weaponized, and I remind Maggie that we're having an uptick in overdoses that come up negative in toxicology testing.

"The fear is some new designer drug might be in the area." I'm reminded unpleasantly that we don't know what was laced into the Bordeaux I tasted.

My toxicology screen would have been negative had my blood been tested after I was poisoned last night. I could have been the fourth pending overdose of the day, one of those pouched dead bodies headed to a funeral home or crematorium.

"Maybe you shouldn't be so quick to run back to things that didn't serve you well." Maggie means more than one thing.

She was by Elvin Reddy's side for twenty years, and it must

have devastated her when he resigned. I suspect she was just as upset when I took his place.

"I personally think reaching out to Doctor Fruge is reckless," she says. "Unless you're not worried about her talking all over Christendom."

"I'm far more concerned about people dying from some new potent synthetic drug making the rounds. If you get hold of her, please give her my cell phone number. Ask her to call me as soon as possible," I reply, and I open the Cammie Ramada file as Maggie returns to her office.

I begin skimming the initial report of investigation, and the medical examiner assigned to the case wasn't my predecessor. It was one of my assistant chiefs, Doug Schlaefer, a highly competent forensic pathologist I've had no complaints about since starting here. But I don't know him well enough to trust him.

In paperwork I'm reviewing, Elvin Reddy lists himself as a witness to the autopsy. But I don't believe for a moment he was looking on, much less helping as Doug spent almost five hours at the table, and that's a long haul. A straightforward external examination and dissection can be done in an hour, maybe two.

But to spend more than double that time tells me that Doug never treated the case as routine. From the start he had his share of concerns and doubts, finding the death complicated, perhaps deeply troubling. Or maybe he figured he'd end up in court for one reason or another and was careful to cover all bases.

Meanwhile his illustrious boss made himself scarce most of the time, passing through the morgue while playing host to the FBI, escorting agents in and out. Not witnessing the autopsy but fraternizing, in other words, based on what Wyatt told me a few minutes ago.

I have a pretty good idea what Elvin Reddy's agenda was that morning beyond hobnobbing with the Feds or anyone else he might find beneficial. He was protecting his political ass after dropping by Daingerfield Island the night before.

CHAPTER 28

CHIEFS USUALLY DON'T RESPOND in person or involve themselves in investigations beyond lending oversight. Our staffs are supposed to enable us to run our offices appropriately, and it's a sad fact that advancement in life can be inversely proportional to passion.

Or in the case of Elvin Reddy, some people never cared to begin with. During my Richmond years when I had the misfortune of supervising him, I recognized early on what he was. He had a heart of stone then and still does, never shedding a tear or getting his hands dirty. Yet for some reason he decided to make an appearance on the night of April 10.

Afterward, he passed along the hot potato to Doug Schlaefer, who conducted the postmortem examination. He decided Cammie Ramada's death was an accidental drowning "due to an exercise-induced seizure due to temporal lobe epilepsy," he wrote in his provisional report, dated April 12.

According to his detailed handwritten narrative, the fatal event occurred while the young Brazilian woman was jogging along the Mount Vernon Trail. This was something she did at the same time daily, a routine just like Gwen Hainey's, and there are disturbing similarities in their violent deaths.

Details that should have been followed up on weren't, and it was deliberate. If what the manager of Colonial Landing and a neighbor said are to be trusted, it was Gwen's habit to head out for a run at sunrise. She'd warm up for a few minutes, jogging around the development before exiting through the security gate.

Several blocks away, she'd pick up the popular Mount Vernon Trail. As the name implies, it begins south of here at Mount Vernon, the former home of George and Martha Washington. The paved path with its quaint footbridges and breathtaking scenery hugs the Potomac's shoreline until it reaches Daingerfield Island.

There the trail veers inland to the back of the heavily forested park, and making a right turn, it parallels the railroad tracks. For maybe half a mile the fitness path is in dense woods, and it would be easy for a predator to hide, lurking and watching. Especially in the dark when the two women jogged along this same stretch, picking times early in the morning or late at night when the fewest people would be out.

For Gwen, it was early in the morning. For Cammie it was late at night after the restaurant she managed closed because of COVID-19 and she couldn't find work. Her father lost his business in São Paulo, where he had a chain of clothing stores, all of them shuttered, Doug reports in his neat block print, and I can tell the case bothered him.

He went to a lot of trouble reviewing reports from the police and FBI, putting together a history that's unfair and tragic. No longer able to afford tuition, Cammie had to drop out of school. As months went by, her student visa expired, and she illegally stayed in the United States, living with two other Brazilian women in low-income housing.

As fate would have it, their apartment was across the parkway from Daingerfield Island, just a few minutes' jog, and someone like Cammie would have had no status with Elvin Reddy. Her case was an easy one to cover up and shelve. Those closest to her were in South America, having hit hard times like so many. They had no power, no voice, and were unable to travel.

Call sheets inside the file indicate Cammie's loved ones contacted the OCME many times, wanting to know what happened to her, talking frequently with Doug. The story they were told is the same one he wrote in his report. Their daughter was jogging along the grassy shoreline at around nine P.M. when she started convulsing, ultimately drowning.

Images of MRI scans while she was alive show cortical dysplasia of her left superior temporal gyrus. Her seizure disorder was real, and during the autopsy, a large amount of water and sand were found inside her mouth, nose, airway, stomach and lungs. She was still breathing when her face was in the water, and she didn't die quickly or easily.

I have no doubt she suffered, drowning where she was found,

fully dressed except for a shoe that was some distance from her body. But she also had broken fingernails, multiple bruises on her neck, arms, wrists and hands that just as easily could be associated with a struggle. Her face and scalp were lacerated and abraded, and she broke a tooth and bit her tongue.

When her head struck the ground, it fractured her skull, causing a contrecoup brain injury. There are scalp lacerations, temporal bone fractures with underlying epidural hemorrhages. She suffered at least three separate blows to the head, and I wouldn't expect that in a seizure. Based on what I'm seeing already, the case couldn't be more suspicious, her injuries inconsistent with a fall.

Why she left the Mount Vernon Trail to begin with, ending up acres away at the river's edge, is missing from the story. That should have been the most important question. Yet there was no attempt to answer it, and my deep-seated anger is about to overtorque. Texting Marino, I check on his whereabouts.

Be there in 20, he texts me back a little later as I'm going through the toxicology report, and it's negative for alcohol and drugs, including anticonvulsants.

Unmedicated, Cammie may have suffered a seizure right before she died but that's not why she ended up facedown in the Potomac River. She would have been better off if she'd knocked herself unconscious and drowned. It would be far more humane than what I'm envisioning, and if I'm right it won't be easy to prove depending on what's left of the evidence.

I'm not the only one who's questioned how she died and if she might have had some help. That would explain why "UND" was entered into the morgue log in the early hours of April 11. When the manner of death was amended, there should have been a note reflecting that. But I'm not seeing any such thing in the original file as I go through it.

A WEEK AFTER THE autopsy, Elvin Reddy initialed the final autopsy report and death certificate. It was ruled that Cammie was an accidental drowning, a decision that instantly unplugged the investigation, and the FBI halted testing any evidence.

If no criminal offense was committed, there's no suspect, no victim, no DNA profiles or fingerprints to run through CODIS, IAFIS or any other database. The case was closed in record time, and I'd ask Doug about it if I felt I could confide in anyone who works here. But nothing's safe when people remain loyal to their former leader.

One I predicted would run the Northern Virginia district office into the ground, and it was a bleak day twenty years ago when I heard about Elvin being hired. Then five years ago he was appointed acting chief of all four districts, and I promised at the time that he'd destroy the entire medical examiner system. Which is what he's about done.

I wasn't naïve when approached earlier this year to consider becoming the new chief. I knew I was being brought in as a forensic fixer, and in short order I've gotten a good idea of the damage he's inflicted through negligence and corruption. All the while Maggie's been his tireless first lady, a devoted office wife, and I hear her getting off the phone.

Then she's breezing through our shared doorway, her coat and pocketbook in hand. Ready to leave for the day, she places a stack of autopsy protocols and death certificates on my desk.

"Sorry but no luck," she says, and I'm where she left me earlier, standing by my conference table, going through the case file.

My shoes are off, my suit jacket draped over a chair. I'm not in a state of undress but getting there, and I pad in my stocking feet toward the bathroom.

"Doctor Fruge didn't answer but I left a message for her to call you." Maggie eyes me suspiciously. "Why are you changing your clothes? What are you planning to do during your so-called scene visit?"

"Thanks for trying Greta." I ignore my pushy secretary's questions. "And speaking of, I spent a good bit of time with her daughter last night. Apparently, Officer Fruge lives near you. She says she sees you out walking Emma." I happen to know the name of Maggie's Corgi.

"Yes, Officer Fruge indeed, driving around in her police SUV with too much time on her hands," Maggie says snidely. "One of these pointless people who can talk the paint off a wall, needing to be in everybody's business."

"It just so happened she was at Daingerfield Island when Doctor Reddy showed up at the scene." I let that sink in for a moment, flipping on the bathroom light, setting Cammie's open file on the countertop.

"Well, there you have it, showing up where she doesn't belong," Maggie answers through the partially opened door, evading the topic of her former boss. "That's precisely what I mean about her."

Inside my locker are more tactical shirts and cargo pants neatly folded, and I pick what I need. I sense I've knocked Maggie off-balance. She didn't expect me to know that Fruge was at the scene last April.

"I'm sure you're aware that Cammie Ramada may have died in Alexandria but it's not the Alexandria Police Department's jurisdiction," Maggie informs me. "Officer Fruge shouldn't have shown up at all. But she heard it over the radio, and some people just don't seem to know when to mind their own business."

I wonder how she would know what Fruge heard on the radio, and if the two of them might be better acquainted than I thought. Both of them live alone in the same neighborhood and may have gotten friendly. I could see that happening. It would be just like my charming secretary to bleed Fruge for information, to manipulate her, all the while looking down her nose at her.

"I'm well aware the park is federal property," I reply. "But if you have the shock of stumbling upon a dead body, you're going to panic. When panicky people call nine-one-one they don't care whose jurisdiction it is. And you can't expect the local cops or anyone else to wait until the FBI shows up."

"Officer Fruge is a boundary crasher. She may be something worse than that," Maggie warns.

"You and I both know that Elvin Reddy typically won't respond to anything if it doesn't involve prominent, powerful people. If there's nothing in it for him, he's not interested." I don't pull any punches. "Why did he decide to show up at this particular scene at Daingerfield Island?"

I demand answers through the cracked door, sitting on the closed toilet lid, putting on my boots. What was his motivation? What was so important that it merited interrupting him after hours?

"Well, that case was a while ago," she says as if we're talking decades instead of months.

"What do you remember?"

"Let's see, I recall they were headed back from dinner at their favorite place in Arlington. I can't think of the name of it at the moment," she says, and I don't believe her.

"Who do you mean by *they*?"

"His wife was with him," Maggie says, the story getting only weirder.

Coincidentally, they were just minutes from the scene when the medical examiner's office was notified about a dead body discovered on Daingerfield Island. Maggie claims Elvin was driving his personal Mercedes along I-395 and headed in that general direction.

But what she doesn't attempt to address is why he was contacted about the death to begin with. Especially after hours when he was headed home from dinner with his wife, and I wonder why Fruge didn't mention that detail to me. When she talked about him showing up at the scene, I assumed he was alone.

"Okay, he was notified for some reason," I say to Maggie. "Then what?"

There's no way Elvin keeps a scene case in his car. I doubt he owns one. I can't imagine he had PPE with him either when he and his wife supposedly were on their way home from a favorite restaurant that likely required a reservation. Which would have been made by Maggie, who suddenly has amnesia.

"He said he'd swing by to see what was going on," she says.

"I wouldn't expect that. Especially with his wife in the car."

"I'm quite sure she didn't get out," she says, and I don't see how she can be sure of any such thing if she wasn't there.

"Who notified him about the case to begin with and why?"

"As I've mentioned, we got the call," my secretary says, and I know the answer.

She notified Elvin Reddy, and I ask her why. She answers by putting on her coat, looping the strap of her pocketbook over her shoulder, moving closer to the door that opens onto the hallway.

"You alerted him about the body on Daingerfield Island," I outright accuse her, and she doesn't admit or deny it.

Instead she says that she advised him just as she always had, and my thoughts keep circling back to August Ryan.

"What caused you to single out this particular case?" I ask.

"I don't know what you think it is you're trying to accomplish but it won't change anything except to make your life more difficult here," she says, and now she's threatening me.

"Why did you interrupt him while he was out to dinner with his wife? I need answers, Maggie." I'm not going to give her a pass. "As long as you'd worked for him, you certainly knew what he would think is important. And you're well aware that he doesn't show up at scenes. He'll barely touch a scalpel."

"I should think it's obvious." Anger flashes in her eyes. "I wanted to be sure he was aware there was a death in a public park that might cause potential complications and problems." She explains what's probably getting close to the truth. "He agreed it was important to drop by, to see what was going on."

"To show the flag while making sure he controlled the narrative." I'm not going to sugarcoat it. "That's why he really showed up, now isn't it? To nip any potential problems in the bud. A murder in a popular national park would be most inconvenient. Thank goodness it was an *illegal*," I add with a bite. "Somebody unimportant that maybe nobody would ask questions about . . ."

"Why must you insist on poking a stick at things that are best left alone?" Maggie glares at me. "That was your reputation when you were getting started, always making a mountain out of a molehill. And here we go again when the news is bad enough as is. Why must you throw petrol on the fire?"

CHAPTER 29

SHE COMPLAINS THAT THE media has been ringing the phone off the hook about Gwen Hainey, and God only knows what will show up next in the news. Today has been a train wreck, and much of it is my fault since I was missing in action.

To hear Maggie talk, I was a no-show. I had bigger fish to fry, was too busy hobnobbing with important people, and I keep thinking about the White House takeout trash I tossed inside the bay. It wouldn't surprise me if Fabian informed her where I might have been today. Assuming Elvin Reddy didn't do it first, and it turns my stomach as I envision him sitting inside the Mess Hall.

"And now you're going to remind us of another disturbing death as if you're connecting them," Maggie is saying. "No doubt the next big serial murder case that splashes you all over the news again just like back in your Richmond days. That was a lovely historic city too until you came along and ruined it."

We don't want the public thinking it's unsafe living in Old Town, she goes on and on, sounding like a politician. How unfortunate if it's no longer recommended that people stay in Alexandria while on business in the greater Washington, D.C., area. The value of real estate would go down. Everything would, she continues painting the picture.

"Tourism isn't something this office takes into account when trying to find out what killed someone," is my response.

"You're making a big mistake," she says before walking out for the night, shutting the door behind her.

I decide to wait a few minutes, giving her a head start, and by now I've had quite enough of Maggie Cutbush. I don't know how I'm supposed to work with someone so haughty and stubborn, and I call Marino.

"Was just about to send you a text," he answers grumpily without saying hello, and I can tell he's driving. "I've got to check the air in my tires, pretty sure it's just a bad sensor. Another one, and this is getting old."

He's headed to a service station, and should be here in thirty minutes depending on traffic. I give him the upshot of what we need to do, realizing it's likely a futile scavenger hunt, apologizing upfront.

"But if I don't look, I'll have no peace of mind." I pick up my briefcase, my coat.

"Look with what? A metal detector?" His voice is skeptical. "Because it's going to ping on the iron rails and put your ears out."

"I have another idea." I explain what it is.

"Sure, it's worth a try," he says. "We should look around anyway, see what we notice after dark when there's no one around."

We end the call, and I have just enough time to have a chat with firearms examiner Faye Hanaday if I can find her. Locking up, I roll my scene case along the corridor, saying good night to people waiting for the elevator. I take the stairs, heading up instead of down, and Faye usually works late but no point in calling to check. It's not her habit to answer the phone.

On the second floor, I roll my scene case, greeting scientists I pass. Many I've yet to introduce myself to, and I don't know when I've ever hated being new on the job as much as I do right now. It's always been routine for me to make evidence rounds, stopping in at various labs, checking on my cases. But I've not been doing that much my first frenetic month as the new chief.

The corridor dead-ends at the tool marks and firearms suite of labs, and the light is green outside the firing range's thick steel door. I don't hear the muffled thud of rounds being test-fired inside a long narrow space of thick concrete. There's a steel bullet trap in back, and the floor is capable of bearing the weight of the water recovery tank.

No one's home on the range, Faye's colleagues gone for the day, and I find her alone at her workstation, staring through the binocular lenses of a comparison microscope. She has on a lab coat over her sweater and jeans, and her usual high-tops and loud socks. Her pink and purple highlighted hair is pushed back with a beaded headband, bringing to mind Cyndi Lauper.

Leaving my scene case by the door, I walk through a vast space of black countertops, and microscopes synced with video screens. Walls are crowded with poster-size photographic court displays of lands and grooves, and the marks left by firing pins. On shelves and tables are small scales for testing the pounds of pressure required to pull a trigger. Also calipers and other measuring devices for determining a bullet's weight and caliber.

There are stacks of bullet-riddled targets used in distance testing. Piled about are tire tracks and footwear impressions cast in dental stone and silicone, and the ATM parked in a corner was brazenly stolen from a kiosk. The quadcopter drone inside a cardboard box leaning against a wall is rigged with a pistol that one angry neighbor fired remotely at another, blowing a hole in the screen door.

Wherever I look I see the ingenuity of modern inventions that can be customized to destroy and kill. Spread over a tabletop are an assortment of 3-D-printed knives, guns, bullets, shotgun slugs, assault rifle parts, and suppressors. Soon enough there won't be much people can't print at home, spinning whatever they like from a range of media such as plastics, carbon fiber, resin, Kevlar, and metals like steel and titanium.

"Knock knock." I announce myself as I approach, not wishing to startle Faye, and she looks up, blinking several times. "I tried to reach you earlier." It's my diplomatic way of saying it would be nice if she'd call me back for once.

"Hi, sorry about that." She leans back in her chair, putting on her glasses. "As you can imagine, I've been tied up with that attempted break-in at Dana Diletti's house earlier today."

"I was hearing about that while stuck in bad traffic, listening to her press conference," I reply. Faye and I have worked several cases together since I took over as chief, most recently a suicide committed with an antique rifle.

Ironically, she isn't into guns even if she's a savant with them and almost any weapon you can think of. They're simply what she works with for a living. When she relentlessly visits gun shows and stores, it's not because she's an enthusiast or a collector.

Her passion is the prizewinning cakes she bakes, and around her workstation are framed photographs of her imaginatively decorated confections. A mint and chocolate jungle with dinosaurs, rocks and caves. A butterscotch moonscape with astronaut footprints, a flag, a lunar lander. Children ice-skating on a blue candy pond in a winter wonderland of marshmallow snowmen.

I don't know much about her, only that she's in her late thirties, single, no pets, just a saltwater aquarium. But I have the sneaking suspicion she and Fabian might have something going. Now and then they arrive at work together, and the other day I noticed them in the parking lot squabbling inside his vintage El Camino.

"A BIG STINK IS what we're talking about." Faye sums up the alleged break-in. "Hold on to your hat because it's coming."

"It's already a big stink. There's a protest in her neighborhood." I take a close look at the large window, the screen draped in torn brown paper propped against a countertop.

I can see black smudges left from fingerprint powder, also the tube of polyvinyl siloxane used for making dental impressions, and there are several cameras nearby. I imagine Faye's been swamped ever since the evidence was brought in, taking photographs and making casts in red orthodontic wax of any defects that need to be magnified.

"I've been making comparisons," she says. "And there's no question someone tried to pry open her window."

"Comparisons?" I puzzle. "Comparing the tool marks to what? I wasn't aware there was a suspect."

"The tools the investigators brought in for me to examine are from Dana Diletti's own house I'm sorry to say because I'm a fan," Faye explains as I look at the screen, the window still in its white-painted frame.

On a paper-covered countertop are a variety of tools including screwdrivers, a hammer and a pry bar, all tagged as evidence.

"I can tell you already that one of the screwdrivers looks like it might have been used," Faye lets me know. "In fact, I'm pretty close to calling it a match."

Opening files on the computer display synced to her comparison microscope, she shows me images of defects on the flat steel blade that were transferred to the window's bent metal latch.

"This screwdriver definitely was found inside her house?" I ask, and Dana Diletti's got real trouble on her hands.

"That's the story," Faye says. "Not that it's up to me but it's looking like she intended to give the appearance that someone was out to get her. In other words, she staged everything, and talk about fake news."

"If that's what happened, she's going to find she's created quite a problem for herself." I think of the helicopters hovering overhead while Benton and I were stuck in traffic. "Falsifying reports and evidence are criminal offenses." Then I bring up the real reason for my impromptu visit. "I've been consulted about another matter that I can address only in generalities, and I could use your help, Faye."

"What's going on?"

"The case involves two victims shot in a confined area, and the fragmented projectiles recovered from their bodies aren't something one sees very often," I begin to describe.

I apologize that I can't share most details or any images. I've just come from a confidential discussion, and don't have such things in my possession, I explain somewhat truthfully. But I'd like Faye's expert opinion about a type of ammunition the average person doesn't know about.

"I've not come across Glaser Safety Slugs in a long time, and I believe that's what we're dealing with," I let her know. "But I have to be sure before I pass that along to the parties involved." I imagine her surprise if she knew this included the president of the United States.

"It's tougher without photographs," she says with a sigh.

"I don't need them to describe what I saw on a live video feed as the scene was being worked."

"I can understand Glasers being used in tight quarters, that makes sense," she says, having no clue that we're talking about a spacecraft.

"Yes," I agree. "The sort of ammunition you'd pick for self-defense if you anticipate having to shoot someone inside an apartment, a vehicle. You want to disable or kill but not have the pellet or projectile exit the body or ricochet, hurting someone else, causing other damage."

"Correct. Which is why Glasers were created. To deal with skyjackers back in the day."

"And there's no new round out there that might be similar?"

"Not that I know of," she says, scrolling through images of fragmented ammunition. "But picking something that uncommon requires forethought. Whoever we're talking about was very deliberate about arming himself."

Astronauts aren't known to carry weapons into orbit, the exception being the Russians based on what I've learned during various Doomsday Commission briefings. Cosmonauts used to pack a particularly nasty triple-barreled "survival" pistol that includes a machete. That's not what was used in this case, not even close.

But I can't mention any of this to Faye. She may find out from the news what's happened three hundred miles above the planet but she won't hear it from me.

"Look familiar?" She shows me photographs on the video display.

The fragments of spent rounds look almost identical to what was removed from the Thor scientists' bodies.

"Yes," I reply.

"What are you thinking about the caliber?"

"Nine-millimeter."

"If it was a pistol as opposed to a revolver," she says, "it would have auto-ejected the spent cartridge cases."

"I'm going to venture a guess that the perpetrator would have collected anything like that before leaving the scene." I imagine them floating around inside the orbiter.

Jared Horton would have looked until he found them. He would have left with them and the gun. But I don't need the cartridge cases or the weapon to know what I saw.

"Number six lead shot, copper jacketed with a silver-tipped polymer nose," I tell Faye.

The ammunition's prefragmented lead projectile is designed to begin separating on impact. There's little risk of the pellets exiting the target, and perhaps hitting someone else or causing other catastrophic damage.

"The silver ball tip is the dead giveaway." Faye doesn't realize the pun. "Glasers come in blue tip and silver, and the silver has more penetrating power because it's six shot instead of twelve, exactly what you're describing."

A winter round of sorts, it's what you'd use if you needed to penetrate heavy clothing, and that could include a spacesuit. Jared Horton knew what he was doing in advance, I'm thinking. He may not have planned to murder his crewmates but he was prepared for that eventuality.

"How much longer are you going to be here?" I ask Faye, and Marino has let me know he's waiting in the parking lot.

"I don't know, for a while. This case will keep me burning the midnight oil." She's in no hurry to go home.

Not to see her fish or get back to her baking, and I might know the reason why, and it's not merely because of her case-load. Fabian is working the evening shift this week, and I'm betting that may have something to do with the long hours Faye's keeping.

I don't see him moments later as I walk through the intake area. No sign of Wyatt either, his office empty, and no one is inside the bay when I walk through. Probably they're hanging out in our comfortable, clean breakroom, watching me on the security cameras, and I can't help but smile.

Outside, Marino's truck rumbles loudly in a thick mist set-tling over the dark parking lot. There's not a breath of wind, the Virginia and U.S. flags wilted on their poles.

"I can see you're ready for anything, and frankly that's a good thing under the circumstances," I announce as I climb into the passenger seat, shutting the door.

CHAPTER 30

HE'S SUITED UP IN tactical clothes similar to mine, but under his jacket is a bulletproof vest.

A knit cap covers his bald head, his pistol where I saw it last on the console between us. When I placed my scene case in back, I noticed the extra weapons and ammunition from the night before.

"I've got nothing more than a hunch to go on, and I apologize again if it turns out to be a wild goose chase." Holding my briefcase in my lap, I'm reminded my gun is locked up at home, and this would have been a good time to have it. "Chances are we won't find anything but that's not going to change what I'm concluding."

"You and me both, and I'm surprised that when you were at the scene with August Friday night, he didn't mention the Ramada case. You were just acres away from where she died." Marino chews gum like mad. "I realize at a glance the two cases don't look similar but that's not why he's keeping his mouth shut."

August is afraid for his job, Marino says, and he's seen this before, especially when it's the Feds.

"You're trying to do the right thing, and politicians interfere," he adds.

"It's a shame when people are more territorial about a park than a human being," I reply as he stares out his side window.

"What the hell?" He scowls as my secretary's old silver Volvo backs out of its parking space, getting way too close to his truck.

"I think she's letting us know she's watching." I catch a glimpse of her staring coldly at us in the glare of headlights as she drives off in a swirl of exhaust. "She told me she was headed home, and that was forty minutes ago. Where has she been? Who's she been talking to?"

"Since I got here, she's been sitting in her car where nobody can hear what she's saying on the phone," Marino replies, and I remember the look on Maggie's face when she realized I'd overheard her conversation in the corridor.

"As if she hasn't caused enough trouble already." I put on my shoulder harness. "Mark my words, she'd like nothing better than to get me fired. I'll be lucky if I last an entire month the way things are headed."

"What does Benton think about all the crap going on?"

"That my office is close to unmanageable. The governor, the attorney general may have wanted me to fix the Virginia medical examiner system, in particular the office here. But it doesn't seem that's what anybody else wants, and I'm not sure moving back here was the best plan."

"They can screw themselves." Only Marino doesn't say *screw*. "We're not turning tail and running."

"No, but that doesn't mean I won't be invited to leave because I'm a problem." I envision Maggie threatening me. "What we're doing right now is a good example." I remember what she said about me always having to poke a stick at things.

"Does Benton know why we're headed to the park? Is he thinking the same thing we are?"

"He says what you've heard before, that when serial offenders have signatures, patterns, it's about their highly personalized fantasies," I reply. "Violent psychopaths often have rituals they repeat unless something interrupts them."

"Well, one thing I know for sure by now is to pay attention when you get one of your hunches, Doc," Marino says, and the coast is clear, Maggie gone.

He begins backing up, using his mirrors, craning his neck. Ignoring the parking assist cameras, he muscles his monster truck into a U-turn, and the more keyed up he gets, the more he tends to manhandle. He drives through my nearly empty parking lot, and I can't get the image of the flattened penny out of my thoughts.

August held it in his gloved hand, shining his light on it, and I literally couldn't make heads or tails of what I was seeing. Nothing engraved on it was legible including Lincoln's image or the date until later when the coin was magnified.

The silvery zinc was marbled with bright copper plating, the date 2020, not a hint of a brown or green patina.

"It's hard to say when something's been run over by a train," I explain as we stop at the security gate, "but it seems apparent to me the penny hadn't been out there long. Possibly hours, at the most days, because in wet conditions, the metal would have started tarnishing quickly."

"Like I said, you've always got a reason for your hunches." Marino eases forward as the security gate arm goes up. "Usually a damn ugly one." He drives out of the parking lot.

"What I think happened couldn't be uglier," I reply, and inside I'm seething. "If I'm right there will be hell to pay even if it costs me my job. The way someone dies isn't *let's make a damn deal*."

"Take a breath, Doc. We'll fix it just like we always do. Elvin Reddy's an incompetent scumbag, and I hate it when people like that get rewarded."

"We'll see how rewarded he is by the time this is over." I unpleasantly envision him drinking coffee at the White House, the back of his bald head shiny like polished stone.

"Imagine the damage he's caused over all these years," Marino says as the light turns red at the intersection up ahead, a long line of cars forming. "Like we're always saying, when you take out one person, you take out everybody. Looking the other way, lying about it means somebody else gets hurt."

"How are your neighbors holding up? They must be in an uproar. How awful not to feel safe where you live, especially if it's your dream home."

"It's bad," he says.

"Unfortunately, it seems Dana Diletti is working on a sensational story about the so-called Railway Slayer." I explain what Faye Hanaday told me in her lab, that it appears the TV journalist may have staged her break-in.

"That figures," Marino says. "But they'll run the damn Railway Slayer piece anyway."

"I don't know when it's supposed to air but one can expect it to push people over the edge."

"Well, it's looking like the title might turn out to be true if your hunch is right about the railroad tracks," he says. "And a TV news story is going to suck. My neighbors are already scared out of their minds."

Some are thinking about putting their properties on the market, and already there's a growing panic about the value going down. Dorothy doesn't want to be home alone and has been at Benton's and my place all day, I'm told.

"Meanwhile, Cliff Sallow, the manager, is trying way too hard to be helpful. I don't have a good feeling about him, Doc," Marino says.

I TELL HIM ABOUT the horror theme I heard on the security gate recording, wondering if August might have played it for him.

"We listened more than once." Marino constantly checks his mirrors as if someone might be after us. "It's probably part of some sicko's fantasy or that's what we're supposed to assume," he adds, and I know who he's thinking about.

"What does Cliff Sallow have to say about the loud *Shock Theater* music, and the gates opening and shutting?" I inquire. "What's his explanation, and was he inside the management office when all that happened? Where was he last Friday night?"

"Watching football, he claims. And he doesn't have an explanation, said he's never heard of *Shock Theater,* isn't into horror stuff," Marino says. "But he was full of suggestions such as a boat being used to get on and off the property. That's why we can't hear anybody driving through."

Possibly a rowboat or something with a small motor, Sallow proposed. Except the boat slips at Colonial Landing are covered by cameras, and all of them were working when Gwen was abducted. Only those at the front gates were obstructed for a while, making what the manager said implausible if not impossible.

"Also, the weather was terrible last Friday night," I point out while we sit at a red light. "A lot like what we're having now but windy and raining hard off and on. I can't imagine anyone was on the water, especially after dark."

"You ask me, he's trying to steer us in the wrong direction," Marino says. "Most of all, he's putting on the big innocent act. He wants to help us catch who did it, meaning he must be a good guy, right?"

"Gwen's killer had access to a vehicle of some sort." I return to the subject of how that person came and went.

He had to have a car to transport her body from her town-home to Daingerfield Island. We also don't know what we might discover when the security recordings are worked on in the labs.

"Maybe the car in question has a quiet engine, and the software can enhance it," I explain.

"Cliff Sallow has a Prius," Marino reminds me. "And hybrids are quiet."

"Have you searched it?"

"He invited us to look at anything we want. Like I said, he's too helpful."

"What about getting a swab for DNA?"

"We got that and fingerprints," he says, and traffic is moving again. "August and I told him that he's not a suspect, which isn't true because we're more suspicious of him than anyone else."

"Do you think he realizes that?"

"Nope," Marino says. "He's too busy trying to impress us. We explained that as the manager of the complex he'd been inside Gwen's place a number of times, had been handling her packages and who knows what else. We needed DNA, his prints for exclusionary purposes."

"And that was perfectly okay with him? He didn't tell you to talk to his lawyer?"

"He was more than okay. It's like he got off on it."

Marino explains that he and August went through the Prius with a fine-tooth comb, and there was no sign of anything suspicious. But Sallow is the kind of guy who would have spent a lot of time thinking about what could get him into trouble.

"And we know the killer's careful about planning in advance, covering the security gate cameras and all the rest," Marino adds.

"Someone cunning who probably gets enraged when things don't go according to plan," I reply. "I can see why the manager would make your antenna go up, and I'd like to know where he was on the night of April tenth when Cammie died not far from where Gwen's body was found. This was several months after he moved here." I repeat what Officer Fruge told me. "She doesn't trust Cliff Sallow either, has her eye on him."

"I'm aware," Marino says. "I was there last night when she was going on and on about him. Fruge's like a dog with a bone, can't let it go."

"We both know what that's like when a case haunts us."

"Yeah, it sounds like life kicked Cammie to the curb, and she didn't count." Cold air rushes inside the truck as he tosses his gum out the window.

"That was a gross miscalculation," I promise.

On King Street now, we're retracing our steps from the night before, the fog billowing as if we're driving through clouds.

"Seriously?" Marino says. "The more I hear, the worse it gets. Who drowns while they're jogging? What was she doing in that area of the park at night? Why did she leave the running path? I don't buy that something was wrong with her, and she ended up down by the water because maybe she didn't know what she was doing."

"She suffered from temporal lobe epilepsy, likely was born

with it," I inform him. "The theory is she had convulsions induced by exercise, lost consciousness on the shore and drowned. And yes, she might have gotten disoriented or confused but that's not why she's dead. I believe she had some help."

"How does her having a seizure fit with someone attacking her?"

"If someone ambushed her, the stress of that alone could have brought on a seizure," I reply as I imagine her running in terror, trying to get away. "That's what I think happened, and she started having convulsions. Her attacker was interrupted by something he didn't expect."

"Then what do you think he did?"

"I think he slammed her head against the ground at least three times and drowned her. She had a broken tooth, a fractured skull, and three discrete brain injuries accompanied by hemorrhages. Also, what look like fingertip bruises on her neck, wrists, upper arms, and broken fingernails," I recall, "and her knees were contused."

"None of it was old I don't guess," he says.

"Based on what I saw in her photographs, the bruises were bright red, probably occurring at or around the time of death."

"Crap."

"I also don't believe for a minute that her head injuries were due to a seizure. That would be most unusual."

"I didn't know the part about her having epilepsy but I assume that's the medical problem I've heard mentioned," Marino says. "I've not been able to find much about her case in the news, and Lucy hasn't, either, not even on social media. It's like there was almost no interest in the case."

"I'm afraid that was by design. Elvin Reddy wanted it to be ignored, to go away, and it might have stayed that way had Officer Fruge not continued to talk about it."

"Yeah, well, that's how I heard about it back in July, from the local town crier. Fruge's out patrolling Old Town pretty regularly, and likes to talk, as you know. We got acquainted," Marino says, and I can envision it easily.

"Let me guess, she introduced herself to you," I reply as I check my phone for messages.

Dorothy has sent one, wondering where I might have hidden the jalapeño peppers. She and Lucy are making chili, and I realize how hungry I am.

"I was gassing up my Harley at the Shell station," Marino says while I try not to think about food. "Fruge knew who I was and pulled in behind me, welcoming me to the neighborhood. She said she was glad there was a new sheriff in town."

He peels open more sticks of retro gum, Teaberry this time, and my stomach growls.

"She knew we were coming," he says.

I politely decline the pack he offers while I text my sister that as far as I know we're out of jalapeños. She used them up while making nachos last week and promised to pick up a few jars. I guess she forgot, and now isn't a good time to pester me about it.

None in the cellar pantry? Dorothy again, and what she's referring to are shelves in the basement where I keep an overflow of various canned goods and supplies.

You can check but pretty sure not, and as I'm writing this, I think about Marino and Dorothy moving into their new place at Colonial Landing last summer.

"You'd been living here in Old Town several months before the rest of us arrived," I explain. "I would expect Fruge to be well aware of people new to the area even if they haven't moved in yet."

She's a cop, and a tenacious one at that, reminding me of Marino in the old days when we first met. If sufficiently motivated, they're the type to access whatever they want by any means they deem necessary. Also, people talk, and Alexandria may be a decent-size city but its historic district has a population of fewer than ten thousand.

"It wouldn't be hard to figure out who's buying real estate in Old Town," I explain as we drive past Ivy Hill Cemetery.

It's so socked in by the fog, I can't make out the big trees and monuments uprooted by last night's storm.

"There are any number of ways Fruge could have discovered that we planned to relocate here," I remind Marino. "I'm sure she was waiting for us with bells on."

"She knows about me from my Richmond days when I was the head of homicide," he replies. "She remembers both of us, and everyone around us who matters including Lucy and Benton. She even asked about Doris and Rocky, snooping into what happened to them, asking questions."

CHAPTER 31

Doris was Marino's first wife and childhood sweetheart. I never thought he'd get over her after she ran off with the car salesman.

Their only child, Rocky, grew up to be a ruthless criminal, dying violently after trying to take out his own father. It sounds like Fruge had been busy excavating information, and it's no different from what we do when someone new enters our airspace.

"I don't blame her for checking us out," I say to Marino. "She'd be foolish not to, and I also think she's lonely, with a lot to prove."

That might be what fuels her intensity, driving her behavior, I explain. Her late father was a Presbyterian minister, and from what I recall, he wasn't easy.

"You know what her mother's like, consumed with her career and notoriety, and she lives several hours from here," I add. "I doubt they see each other much."

"I don't think Fruge's got anybody special in her life, either," Marino says. "Apparently, she hangs out alone at A League of Her Own, and I'm not talking about the movie."

He means the lesbian sports bar in D.C. where Fruge likes the baseball videos and dancing, he says. This is where she ran into Lucy and Janet a couple years ago, he continues, relaying what he's learned.

"When was she saying all this?" I ask.

"After she dropped you off last night, she came back to Gwen's place, shadowing August and me, talking nonstop," he replies. "She said Elvin Reddy is an idiot, that everybody was terrified of him while he ran the OCME, and still is now that he's the health commissioner. That's why there's such a code of silence."

"He's not an idiot," I reply. "It would be easier if he were."

"Sounds to me like he didn't want Cammie Ramada to be a homicide, end of story."

"Only the story doesn't end. Here we are after another victim has turned up in the same park," I reply. "This one with her throat slashed and hands cut off, brazenly dumped by the railroad tracks. A homicide that perhaps could have been prevented had anybody been looking for a violent offender."

"If it turns out that Cammie was attacked while jogging along that same stretch where Gwen's body was dumped eight months later?" he says. "Then we're not talking about an exboyfriend or a hit because someone's spying. We're talking a Ted Bundy, a Night Stalker, a Jeffrey Dahmer."

Marino has the same list of top serial killers that he's always had. At least those psychopaths were interesting, he'll tell you. Unlike the dirtbags who plant pipe bombs, storm the Capitol, and shoot up grocery stores, he's quick to remind everyone.

"I think you and I are worried about the same thing," I reply over the thrumming of his oversize tires, reminded of why he was delayed picking me up. "Is everything all right with your truck? Should I be concerned about having to pull over and change a tire since we're headed out in the middle of nowhere in terrible weather?"

"Squirrelly sensors again." He turns up the defrost, the lights of businesses and cars blurry as it begins to drizzle. "I'm thinking of switching to run flats, then I don't have to worry about it. But they don't make for the most comfortable ride, and the tread wears out fast."

No doubt, the pricey airless tires are in his future, maybe a stocking stuffer. Whatever he wants, my sister makes sure he gets it, and I don't know when I've seen him so bored. Except tonight he's sitting up straighter, full of vim and vigor, and there's a defiance in his voice I've not heard in a while.

"Just so you know, I dropped by today . . . ," he starts to say as my phone rings.

"Now what?" I feel a touch of dread when I see the name on the display. "I'd better take this." I answer Maggie's call as my chest gets tight.

"Doctor Scarpetta? Very sorry to interrupt, and I'll make this short." Her imperious voice sounds over speakerphone.

"Doctor Reddy needs to see you in the morning. I've cleared your calendar for the day."

"Maggie, you can't take it upon yourself to do that." I'm not nice about it as alarms sound in my head.

I'm being fired.

"Last I checked, all of us answer to the health commissioner, yourself included," she says, the George Washington Masonic Memorial ghostly up ahead, its holiday red and green lights barely visible. "He needs to see you in Richmond."

That's who she was on the phone with in the corridor earlier. I suspected as much, and it's all I can do to keep my temper in check.

"What's so urgent that it requires my showing up in person?" I ask, knowing the answer.

He wants to fire me to my face. Probably before an audience. And he'll make sure his pet journalists blast out the story everywhere. In fact, they probably already know it's coming.

"What I can tell you is it's important enough for him to rearrange his impossible schedule," she says as if she really might still work for him. "He'll expect you at ten A.M."

"It will take forever getting to Richmond that time of day," I reply. "He knows that better than anyone, and so do you."

I end the call, angrily dropping my phone in my lap.

"That's it! I've had enough." My frustration boils over.

"We'll have to leave before the sun comes up." Marino assumes he's going with me, and I won't argue.

"As if I have time for this!"

"Nobody does. We'll be in the car most of the day, and that's exactly what he wants."

"To harass, to show how powerful he is, ordering me around. All right then, if that's what he wants?" I check the weather app on my phone.

"Yeah, I think we know the drill. We'll show up with our hair on fire only to have him make us wait until hell freezes over," Marino predicts, and I wish he wouldn't rile me further. "Then he'll take maybe two minutes to say whatever it is to dress you down, make you squirm, trying to put you in your place for once."

"That's enough. You're going to make me crazy."

"Payback's a bitch, right?"

"Paying me back for what?"

"For being you, and not kowtowing to him. Most of all, he can't stand it that you can't be bought."

"Well, he's about to like me a lot less," I decide. "It's looking like tomorrow is predicted to be clear and mostly sunny with a high of forty-eight degrees. It will be nice but windy until evening when we're supposed to get light showers."

I EXPLAIN WHAT I'M considering while sending Lucy a text, wondering if her helicopter might be available early morning. If she wouldn't mind giving Marino and me a lift, especially if we can use Reagan National, as it's just minutes from home.

"Of course, that will require a TSA ride-along because of

the restricted airspace around here," I'm saying to Marino. "But she's used to that."

"I just hope she's not rusty." He slows to a stop at the railroad crossing near the metro station, the ground fog moiling like a witch's brew. "She hasn't been flying all that much since moving here. Not like she used to."

Looking both ways to make sure nothing is coming, he crosses the train tracks, slowly bumping over them. They're the same ones that several miles north of here parallel the Mount Vernon Trail where Cammie and Gwen used to jog.

"Since when have you ever doubted Lucy's piloting skills?" I ask Marino, and it's not easy for him to talk about how bad he feels.

He's known my niece since she was ten, and taught her everything she knows, to hear him talk. All of us have been through a lot together but he's never seen her this deeply hurt, and it's intolerable to him that he can't make the pain go away.

"Look, let's be honest. She's not been flying as much since the pandemic started, Doc. You know, she's not been herself." What he means is that after she lost her family, she seemed to lose her mojo.

That's the word he's used repeatedly to describe her lackluster interest in what she used to be passionate about. Like flying the helicopter that spends too much time in the hangar. And riding the motorcycle she keeps in Marino's garage. Or driving her supercars that currently are in storage. Like so many things.

Roger that, she texts me back with a thumbs-up emoji, and I'm happy about it for multiple reasons.

"I believe we have a flying horse lined up for the morning," I announce.

"Your situation probably won't be made any better if certain people find out you got there by helicopter." He can't help but smirk.

"All the more reason to do it," I reply as we stop at a red light on Prince Street.

The Hilton Garden Inn is ahead, and since leaving my office almost twenty minutes ago, we've not managed to get very far.

"Especially after you were just at the White House," Marino adds. "Talk about pissing people off. Most of all, Elvin the Chipmunk."

"How do you know where I was?" I've about decided there's no such thing as a secret anymore.

"What I was getting around to telling you a minute ago is that I stopped by your office earlier, not knowing you were out of town."

"Benton and I were called to a meeting with no advance notice." I don't need to tell Marino that I can't discuss it.

"Maybe you don't remember because you were still sort of out of it," he says. "But when I was leaving your house last night with the wine bottle and all the rest, you told me you were going to work today as usual. You were sure you'd be fine."

"That was the plan before the Secret Service called us," I reply as the light turns green.

"Figuring you were at the office, I thought I'd go ahead and get started in my new position as your trusty forensic operations specialist. It didn't go over very well."

"Who told you I was at the White House?" I ask as Maggie roosts in my thoughts. "I didn't mention it to anyone. Not even to Dorothy and Lucy."

"Your secretary, who do you think? The same person who wouldn't give me a key to your building and said there's no room for me when I'm helping out."

"We have plenty of room." I remind him of the positions my predecessor didn't bother to fill. "We have empty offices and parking places. Of course, I'll get you a key, and I'm sorry for how Maggie treated you but would have predicted it."

"She's got to control everything, that's all I've got to say."

"I imagine she's had to be that way. In many ways she was the de facto chief while Elvin did his politicking and drank his martinis after hours. Somebody had to deal with the day-to-day, take phone calls and answer questions."

"Like the house mouse who thinks she runs the police department," Marino says as we drive through the heart of the historic district, surrounded by our neighborhood haunts.

Off our nose is the Catholic church I don't attend often enough, across from it the Shell station. The colonial brick Harris Teeter is where we go for major food shopping, and Benton's and my guilty pleasure is Haute Dogs & Fries, while Marino is a big fan of the Oak Steakhouse.

"When you decided to drop by today unannounced," I ask, "who let you into the building?"

"Wyatt answered when I buzzed the gate. He was in the

bay helping with a delivery and scanned me up to your office. Turns out his brother was a Richmond cop I used to know, and by the way, the security at your building stinks."

"Obviously or you wouldn't have made it to my floor."

I ask him what time it was when he appeared at Maggie's door as I imagine the look on her face.

"High noon," he says, and by then I'd spotted Elvin inside the West Wing Mess Hall.

Likely he caught wind that I was there, and naturally he's going to contact his former secretary of twenty years who's remained steadfastly loyal to him through thick and thin. The truth is that they've never stopped working together, and it's crossed my mind she might suffer from Stockholm syndrome.

Identifying with the aggressor, she's treating me the way Elvin's treated her, and I'm not naïve. I expected Maggie to be one of many challenges facing me when I took this job. But stupidly, perhaps arrogantly I thought I'd win her over. I deluded myself into believing that if I were fair and empowering, if I were the sort of boss one ought to be, she'd come around.

She'd realize how much better off she is no longer working for a self-consumed overreacher, a misogynistic jerk, let's be honest. I suppose I hoped to re-create what I had when getting started, and that wasn't smart or completely honest. I didn't move back to Virginia for nostalgia but to serve the public and help solve problems.

The good old days weren't all that good anyway, and Maggie Cutbush will never be Rose. The past is past but never gone, and it's a sad fact that women don't always get along with each other. Some are too territorial and competitive, answering only to a man, creating the very toxic environment I've inherited.

"I'm sure Elvin would have been most unhappy finding out I was at the White House. The first thing he would have done was ask Maggie what I'm up to," I explain, and we're in Northeast Alexandria.

Following the Potomac's shoreline, our timing is just right for getting caught at every red light.

"She didn't say what either of you were doing there," Marino says.

Keeping his eyes on the road, he steers with one hand while tossing out his gum again. There's no point in reprimanding him about it.

"I asked and she wouldn't tell me," he adds.

"I doubt she knows. I doubt he does either," I reply. "I hope they don't, at any rate. Otherwise the president has serious issues with intelligence leaks."

"You were with the president today? He wanted to meet with you personally?"

"I'm saying, it's risky to national security if people can't have private conversations." That's as much as I'm going to share.

"It would be helpful if you'd tell me what was so important that you suddenly got called to a top secret meeting." Marino starts rummaging inside the ashtray for more gum, and it's a good thing it's sugarless or he'd have no teeth left. "You know, in case there's something I should worry about besides you bringing home poisoned wine from Interpol."

"I think it's pretty obvious that there's plenty for us to worry about, Marino."

"I'll take that as meaning we're back to the way things used to be, you and me swimming upstream with alligators." Peeling the wrappers off several sticks, clove again, he offers them to me.

"You know what? I could use a hit." I take the gum from him, the inside of the truck smelling like potpourri.

"Sometimes I want to smoke so bad it's killing me, Doc, and this is one of those times," Marino says.

"Believe me, I know the feeling."

"What if I told you I had a pack of Marlboros for emergencies?"

"I'd tell you that I didn't hear what you just said."

"Do you still think about it?"

"Not a day goes by."

"Exactly," he says. "One damn cigarette! What if I lit just one and we shared it?"

CHAPTER 32

IT'S NEVER JUST ONE," I reply, both of us chewing our gum.

"I thought the craving would go away but if anything, it's worse. As much as I hate to admit it." He's been saying the same thing since he and Dorothy got married.

Only Marino has been craving more than cigarettes if he's honest about it, and he's not. Easier if he's blind to what I saw when he and Dorothy started dating seriously several years ago. He was her new challenge, her next bright, shiny thing.

It wasn't for me to judge, and I was their biggest supporter despite my misgivings about my sister smothering him while sucking out his life force, emotional spider that she is. I've watched her do it to every pair of pants that's come through her door. But maybe it would be different with him, not that it was my decision, and I was careful not to interfere.

I went so far as to become an ordained minister by mail so I could marry them in Benton's and my Cambridge backyard.

I wanted their relationship to work, didn't matter the complications it would cause. Most of all, I wanted Marino to be happy. As long as I've known him, he's been trying to fill an emptiness that goes back to his earliest years in the wrong part of New Jersey.

No one quicker to fill a void, no one more exciting than Dorothy. She dotes on him, and has plenty of money, but it can't replace what he lost when he and I stopped working together.

"I'm sorry I can't talk about what Benton and I were doing in D.C. I wish I could tell you everything." I look over at Marino's strong profile in the glow of taillights ahead, chewing gum, wishing he were smoking.

I know what it is to want what you can't have. When I was a child taking care of my father as he was dying of cancer, I wanted him to get better. I wanted it more than anything. I wanted him in my life, and I've never stopped wanting it.

"Look, I wasn't born yesterday," Marino says. "I'm wondering if your being at the White House might be related to where we're headed this minute. Maybe what's going on in Alexandria is of interest because of Gwen Hainey's spying."

"As they say in quantum physics, everything's connected," I reply, and out my window is the Mount Vernon Trail, the dark void of Daingerfield Island just ahead. "Her illegal activities have caused a number of catastrophes even if indirectly, and I shouldn't tell you even that much."

"The funny thing is her killer may not have known anything about what she was doing. That's not why he targeted her," Marino says, and I agree with him, thinking about what was inside Gwen's townhome.

"If her killer knew she was a spy, and that's the motive? Then why leave her laptops and other electronic devices? Why leave thousands of dollars in her wallet?" I point out.

"Because he was more caught up in the thrill of the hunt," Marino says. "He didn't show up to steal anything, and it seems he didn't except maybe her phone."

"Cammie's phone was never found, either," I reply as we take the exit for the park.

Following the only road leading in and out, we pass the shadowy shapes of moored boats shrink-wrapped in plastic for the winter, scores of them dry-docked, with just as many in the water. Parking lots are empty, buildings dark, no sign anyone is here but us.

"Geez." He drives slowly through the billowing mist, and at least the drizzle has stopped. "You wouldn't catch me jogging out here at this hour. I can't imagine anyone doing that, especially a woman alone."

"People get lulled into a sense of false security. They leave their doors open, don't lock their windows. They let a stranger inside to use the phone, and these days post their most personal information online."

The woods are dense, and crisscrossed with narrow access roads that the park police patrol. Typically, they make their presence known when there are large crowds or if a presidential motorcade is passing by on the George Washington Memorial Parkway.

It's not possible to have a constant presence, and I wouldn't expect to see the police or anybody else out here in these conditions. Nothing is lighted except the paved fitness path that's just wide enough for cyclists and runners to pass each other. Iron lamps dimly nudge the foggy darkness, and in poor visibility like this you'd better pay attention to where you're going.

"No question you'd be a sitting duck if someone was hiding out here, waiting." Marino parks near a grassy clearing, cutting the lights and the engine.

We sit quietly in his truck for a moment, looking out at the river obscured by rolling fog, and it was right around here where Cammie lost a shoe and drowned. She didn't end up by the river on her own. If I had the slightest doubt before, I don't anymore.

"All you have to do is look around," I say to Marino. "That's the most glaring thing wrong with this case. Even if you could explain everything else? There's no logical reason why she ended up on the other side of the woods with her face in the water."

"Unless she was meeting somebody," he considers. "It's within the realm of possibility that whoever killed her was someone she knew, maybe someone she'd agreed to hook up with."

"I don't believe that for a minute." I wrap my gum in a tissue, tucking it in a jacket pocket, setting an example Marino is certain to ignore. "No way she came out here to meet anyone." I open my door.

We climb out to the roar of jets we can't see flying in and out of Reagan National less than two miles north of here. Behind us are the woods, and no one would run through them voluntarily. After dark it would be treacherous, especially if one were panicking.

There was no one to hear Cammie crashing through underbrush, weaving through trees, gasping for breath, possibly screaming. I imagine her running blindly, getting bruised and lashed by branches and other foliage before emerging into the opening where Marino and I are standing.

"It was overcast after raining most of the day, and there wasn't much of a moon the night of April tenth," I describe, checking the weather app again. "Once she left the path, she wasn't going to be able to see very well if at all."

"She freaked out and bolted." Marino opens the back of his truck, getting out my scene case. "That's the only reason I can think of for her ending up here by the water. She was trying to get away from someone."

Finding powerful flashlights for each of us, he tucks his pistol in the back of his pants, and we set out across the grass. The low tide quietly plashes, and I paint my light over the narrow lip of loose sandy dirt that no one would run along. There's really no beach, and visitors aren't invested in swimming and sunbathing.

They jog, ride bikes, go sailing, have picnics and romantic trysts or cruise by in tour boats. It's popular to take nature walks looking for bald eagles, hawks, woodpeckers, wigeons, warblers, all sorts of birds including nocturnal ones. Like the owl just now barking from somewhere in the forest, and then another one clucks and whistles its reply in a hair-raising counterpoint.

"Cammie's body was right around here." I show Marino with my light. "In photographs, the restrooms were there." I point to the building, the empty parking lot nearby, my eyes adjusting to the dark.

THE RIVER IS SHALLOW along the shore depending on the tides, and I think about what I reviewed a little while ago. She was facedown, her head turned to one side, her upper body in the water, her long dark hair floating on the current, arms and legs bent.

"She was fully clothed in running tights, a T-shirt and jacket. They were disarrayed and dirty but intact except for her right shoe." I describe what I saw in her file. "It was some twenty feet from her body, the lace tied in a double bow, her right sock grass-stained and halfway off her foot."

"How long do you think she'd been dead?" Marino looks around, his right hand ready to reach for his gun if needed.

"Not long at all based on her body temperature and other postmortem findings," I reply. "Most striking was the lack of washerwoman's changes, the wrinkling of the hands and feet when bodies are submerged. She wasn't in the water long enough for that to happen."

I explain that a couple out for a romantic interlude had the grisly misfortune of happening upon her body, and the first thing they did was pull it all the way onto the shore. Her killer may have heard these two people coming, and chances are he bolted, knowing the police would roll up soon enough.

"That in addition to her convulsions, and he was interrupted," I say in summary. "If there were other things he might have done to the body, he didn't have the chance."

"Like cutting off her hands."

"Possibly."

"Because if it's the same killer, why not remove her hands the same way he did Gwen's?"

"I suspect he was out of time."

"Let me see if I've got this straight." Marino's eyes are all over the place. "She's running along the trail at the back of the park and is confronted by some douchebag who's hiding, maybe waiting for her. She hauls ass through the woods, loses a shoe, and ends up in the water? When did she have the seizure?"

"I can only speculate." I step closer to the dark ruffled river, another plane thundering low overhead, and it wouldn't be my choice to fly in this weather. "I suspect the stress and physical exertion of fleeing an attacker triggered a seizure. Possibly this happened where she lost the shoe."

The slivered moon slips in and out of clouds as we return to Marino's truck, and I get that feeling again of being watched. I sense a presence, and someone could be hiding in the woods even as we speak. We might not see him. Or maybe what I'm feeling is the dark energy of a violent psychopath, possibly one who frequents this place.

"Maybe she was better off," Marino says. "If she was seizing all over the place? At least he didn't get to finish what he started."

"He finished, all right." Images flash as I envision what I think he did. "She knew what was happening, and what an awful way to die."

"He probably intended to kill her by the railroad tracks." Marino points his key, remotely starting his truck, the lights flaring on. "Maybe he was going to leave her body there the same way he left Gwen's, assuming they were killed by the same person," he adds, and I suspect he's thinking of Cliff Sallow again.

Back inside the truck, we follow another access road that leads deeper into the forest. We drive slowly, our windows half down, listening.

"Talk about spooky," Marino says to an owl's *hoot-hooting*. "All that's missing is that *Shock Theater* music."

"No eyes or ears. No one to hear you scream." I'll just keep saying it. "The perfect hangout for a predator."

"Yeah, this may be where he first spotted his victims." Marino follows the access road, careful not to overrun his headlights in the rolling ground fog.

"Then how did he know where Gwen lived?" I reply as we continue sorting through the information, nearing the back of the park. "It would seem that whoever abducted her would have to be familiar with Old Town, and Colonial Landing in particular."

"That's why I keep coming back to the manager," Marino says.

"Maybe," I reply.

The Mount Vernon Trail is just ahead, and its tall iron lamps don't dispel the foggy darkness but would illuminate anyone jogging by or biking. We park where I did last Friday night when arriving alone in the rain after Gwen's body was spotted by the conductor of the seven o'clock train.

I remember tucking my Subaru next to August Ryan's unmarked Dodge Charger, having no idea what awaited. All I knew was that a woman's nude dead body had been spotted by the railroad tracks running through the clearing where Marino and I are now climbing out of his truck.

We have an hour before the train comes through again, possibly the same one that shrieked to a stop four nights ago. Those aboard can't feel the same about Daingerfield Island.

"Let's do this." Marino cuts the engine. "It's getting to be Miller time," he says as if assuming we'll discover in short order that my idea is a wild goose chase.

We climb out of his truck, an owl clucking so close by that you can hear the rush of its powerful wings lifting off from a tree shrouded in fog. We shine our lights up and down the tracks, finding little evidence that runners or nature lovers spend time back here. I don't notice any trash, no sign of people having picnics or anything else.

Opening my scene case, I find the spray bottle, the hydrogen peroxide, the liter of distilled water. Resorting to basic high school chemistry, I'll mix up a solution that emits light instead of heat when it reacts to the hemoglobin in blood no longer visible.

But that's not the only thing luminol takes a shine to, glowing sapphire blue when in contact with copper, for example. While false positives like that can be problematic at crime scenes, in this instance, it's exactly what I want.

"Why are you doing it the hard way?" Marino asks as we put on gloves and face masks.

"Because Fabian decided to help himself to my supply closet," I reply. "I didn't have a choice."

Luminol is old school. Unlike more modern premixed reagents, it must be used in the dark, and is unforgiving. Once I mix it up inside the bottle, I have at most two hours. After that it's no longer effective.

"If you'll help me out with your flashlight, please," I say to Marino as I turn off mine, handing it to him. "So that I can see what I'm doing."

Pouring distilled water into the spray bottle, I dribble in a tablespoon of hydrogen peroxide, tucking extra gloves and evidence bags in my coat pocket.

"Ready," I let him know, and he turns off his flashlight.

It's very dark by the tracks as I carefully step, my boots feeling the rails, the wooden ties. I begin misting the rocky ballast where I examined Gwen's body, and don't have to go far when crevasses between the deeply piled stones give us the first hint of blue.

"Holy crap!" Only Marino doesn't say *crap* as I crouch down, moving small rocks out of the way while spraying. "Maybe it's reacting to rust?" he suggests.

"There's rust for sure. But also, something else," I reply, a flattened penny luminescing.

CHAPTER 33

SECONDS LATER, I FIND other flattened pennies glowing and dimming like fireflies to the sound of my spraying.

I place each coin in an evidence bag that I tuck in a coat pocket. After collecting several more, I stop spraying so we can see what we've got, and I'm feeling foolish.

"Somebody's been putting them out here for a long time," I decide. "Or maybe a lot of people have."

"That's what I'm wondering." Marino turns on his light, stepping close to me as I pull out the small bags so we can examine them. "I'm not sure it's a good thing to find a lot of them."

"I'm not sure, either," I reply with extreme misgivings, having found eight pennies so far. "If I've picked up that many this quickly, there's probably a lot more." I can't help but be disappointed.

Marino shines the flashlight on the misshapen, badly tarnished wafers of metal. They would be difficult to see when mixed with dirt, rocks and other debris, some of the pennies the same brown as dead leaves. Others are patinated a bluish green, and I can't tell the dates.

I start spraying again, and a few minutes later find a coin that's incompletely run over. Part of it is flattened, the rest of it untouched by the train's iron wheels.

"I need you again," I call out to Marino.

"What have you got?" He's back with his light, shining it at what I'm holding in my gloved palm.

"I can't see the entire date." I look closely, wondering why I didn't think to bring a hand magnifier. "Just the first three numbers. Nineteen seventy-something."

"That's a long time to be out here," he says as I place the penny inside another evidence baggie. "At least forty years if the penny was left back then," he adds, and I can hear it in his tone.

The penny found by Gwen's body might be significant. But it's unlikely the rest of them are, and I resume spraying like someone possessed. I find more coins, some intact, others partially run over. All appear to have been out here for months and years unlike the one minted in 2020 that August found. I'm almost out of luminol when Marino hisses at me to stop.

"Doc!" he says in an intense stage whisper, and I turn around as he pulls out his gun.

The lighted orb looks like a bleary moon floating along the dark foggy tracks, and it isn't a train headed in our direction.

There's no sound except the constant planes taking off and landing in the gloom, and what we're seeing isn't Hookerman or ball lightning, either.

"What the hell?" Marino has his gun drawn and pointed down by his side. "Who's there?" he yells as the light bobs closer. "Don't make me shoot!"

"It's Fruge!" she calls out, picking up her pace.

"You gotta be kidding me!" Marino growls as she gets closer.

In uniform with her bulletproof vest on, she lowers her big LED flashlight so she doesn't blind us, her face alive with excitement.

"You're lucky I didn't blow your head off!" Marino tucks his gun back into the waistband of his pants. "What are you doing out here? Have you lost your mind? It's not safe, start with that."

"And that's exactly the same thing I'd say to you," she replies. "I'm happy to be a backup. You know, all you've got to do is ask."

"How did you know where we were?" I ask the obvious question.

"A little bird told me you were headed this way," Fruge says. "And I have to say I sure am glad somebody's finally bothering to look into what's going on around here."

She paints her light over the train tracks, the Mount Vernon Trail, the dense woods.

"A good place for a stalker to hang out, don't you think?" she adds.

"You need to be careful about sticking your nose into everything," Marino says. "Seriously, sneaking up on us in the dark is a good way to get hurt or worse."

"What are you looking for?" She shines her light on the spray bottle, the evidence baggies I'm holding.

"Answer my question, and I'll answer yours," I reply. "What little bird?"

"Maggie," Fruge replies. "When I called her a little while ago, looking for you. And by the way, she wouldn't give me your cell phone number," directing this at me.

"Instead, she tells you where we are," I reply ruefully, and my secretary's going to be the end of me.

"Why would you be looking for us?" Marino asks before I get the chance.

Fruge proudly reports that Gwen Hainey's dismembered hands and the *Star Wars* blanket missing from her townhome may have shown up.

"I mean, I say they're *probably* hers, but it's pretty obvious. Also sweatpants, a T-shirt that look like they were cut off her." She can't keep the excitement out of her voice. "All of it was inside a plastic garbage bag that a dumpster diver found while digging for aluminum cans and other stuff."

"Oh boy," I reply. "If wet bloody items and body parts were stored in a plastic bag since Friday night, they're going to be in rough shape."

"Well, it stinks to high heaven, that's for sure," she says.

"Which dumpster?" Marino asks.

"One near the Giant Food grocery store just minutes from here."

"And where's the bag of goodies now?" he wants to know.

"Everything's at your place per Rex Bonetta's instructions," she says excitedly, looking at me. "I came straight from your office. So, tell me. What are you doing out here?"

"Checking for pennies," I reply because there's no point in being coy. "One was found near Gwen's body Friday night, and I thought it wise to make sure there weren't more."

"What's the spray bottle for?"

I explain it while using a Sharpie to date and initial the baggies of tarnished evidence I place inside my scene case.

"Maggie shouldn't have told you where we are, and you don't need to be running your mouth about this," Marino warns her. "We don't want the pennies or anything else ending up in the media. And why did she tell you? So you'd narc on us, tell her exactly what we're doing?"

"Not me," Fruge says. "I don't talk to the media, and I don't answer to her even when she thinks I'm being cooperative. And I hate to be the one to ask such a negative question. But how do you know pennies left out here have anything to do with anything?"

"We don't," I reply as doubts continue to nag. "As old as many of them seem, it's unlikely they're relevant."

"I SUSPECT IF YOU started looking you'd probably find them by railroad tracks all over the place," Fruge says. "Coins or fragments of them that nobody bothers to pick up. Or more likely they shoot out from under the wheels like bullets, ending up who knows where," she adds as if familiar with the dangerous activity.

"Do you know if that's a popular thing to do around here?" I ask her as we start walking back to Marino's truck. "Because I wouldn't think so. Leaving pennies, other coins, anything on railroad tracks is very dangerous."

"Not that I know of, and it wouldn't be encouraged, that's for sure," she says. "You'd have to ask August Ryan, the park police. It's their jurisdiction, they're quick to remind you. I personally haven't heard about kids or anyone else coming out here and doing things like that. But it doesn't mean it hasn't happened."

"Where are you parked?" Marino asks as he unlocks his truck.

"Near the sailing club. I thought it a good idea to walk, get the lay of the land, see what I felt out here," she says, and I don't buy it.

She didn't want us to hear her coming until it was too late, and I think of Maggie tipping her off. Fruge caught me red-handed as I collected what may or may not turn out to be evidence, and it's impossible knowing who to trust.

"Well, don't sneak up on us again," Marino says to her. "Hop in, I'll drop you at your car. And no comments from the peanut gallery about what I've got in back."

"No problem." She climbs in, moving his big military surplus ammo box out of her way. "I don't mind riding around with a truck full of guns. I grew up in Virginia, remember?"

"When you were talking to Maggie," I say to Fruge as we drive off, "I'm wondering if she mentioned that I'm trying to reach your mother."

"No, ma'am, she didn't. But that's an easy one. Anything special you want me to tell her?"

"I have a question when she has time to call." I give Fruge my number.

"I'm letting her know right now, texting her as we speak," she says, and then I ask about something else.

"Doctor Reddy showed up at the scene last April tenth. Supposedly he'd been out to dinner near Daingerfield Island," I explain. "He was near the scene when notified about the body."

"I remember he was looking at it with August Ryan, and it was embarrassing," Fruge says. "I don't like him in the least but it's not up to me to ruin people. That's for them to do. And you can imagine what I see around here, people getting drunk, fighting, cheating on each other."

She tells us that the former chief had been drinking, was slurring his words, and it would be bad for him if that ever came out. Maggie had to drive him, confirming what I suspect, and that wouldn't be good for him, either.

"Then he didn't have his wife, Helen, with him," I make sure.

"No. Maggie was with him but she didn't get out of the car," Fruge says.

"Whose car?"

"His Mercedes. And when I knocked on the window to say

hi, Maggie shook her head at me. It was obvious she didn't want people seeing her there, probably afraid it might look like the two of them had something going on."

"Do they?" Marino asks, and Fruge shrugs.

"If they do, it's not against the law. All I know is Doctor Reddy had been drinking, and she was driving him. This was right before August asked me to leave, saying the park police were handling things."

"I'm sure they didn't want you there, nosy as you are." Marino eyes her in the rearview mirror, and I can tell he likes her more than he lets on. "How'd you find out about the bag of clothes and body parts?" he asks as we rumble slowly along the narrow road through the woods.

"The dumpster diver who found it called nine-one-one," she says. "Dispatch called me, and off I went."

"I'm assuming the person who found the bag opened it. Or he wouldn't have called the police," I reply.

"That's right. I've gotten his DNA swab, and tomorrow he'll come into the station so we can get his fingerprints."

"Is August Ryan aware of what's happened?" I ask her.

"Besides you, the only person I've told is your DNA guy, Rex Bonetta," she replies as we stop in a parking lot by her police SUV.

"Be careful out there, Fruge," Marino says as she climbs out. "And hey, good job."

"What?" She stops in her tracks. "You talking to me?"

"Good job getting the stuff from the dumpster and being smart enough to take it straight to the labs," he says, and she couldn't look more pleased. "You know, before the Feds made off with it."

"Exactly." She unlocks her SUV. "I thought maybe we could get some real answers for once."

"What do you think?" he asks me as we watch her crank the engine, the headlights going on.

"That I'd like to check out what's in the evidence room," I reply, and most of all, I want to see the hands.

"No kidding, you and me both." He follows Fruge out of the park.

The road leading in and out crosses the railroad tracks, and the lights are flashing, the gate arm going down. It's nine o'clock on the nose, and we watch the silvery train thunder by, its passengers clearly visible in the lighted windows. Some are looking out and talking, others reading or busy with their phones, and I can imagine the killer watching the same thing we are.

"The best of both worlds," I comment, the last cars passing, the rhythmic clatter fading.

"What are you talking about?" Marino asks as the lights stop flashing, the gate arm going up.

"Dumping a body by the tracks," I answer as Fruge drives across them, and we're right behind her. "Nobody sees what the killer's doing inside the park at night. Then when it's showtime, he has a built-in audience as the commuter train goes by."

"And you're thinking that's what he had in store for Cammie, too. But his plan went off the rails, so to speak."

"Very possibly," I reply.

We're back on the parkway, traffic much lighter at this hour, and my phone starts ringing. I don't recognize the number but it's the area code for Richmond, and I answer.

"Talk about a ghost from the past." Greta Fruge's pleasantly modulated voice sounds over speakerphone. "What a lovely surprise when Blaise told me you were trying to get hold of me."

"Thanks for getting back to me. I'm with Pete Marino, and we're driving," I let her know.

"Hello, Pete. Imagine how pleased I was when I heard both of you were coming back to Virginia." She sounds like she means it.

But then she sounds like she means everything she says, and that's part of her danger and her charisma. During our early years, I trusted her too much and ended up in a few rough spots. Like her daughter, Greta is a talker, and now and then has a greater need to tell a secret than to keep it.

"I've been meaning to reach out," she adds, and I can hear the murmur of TV news playing in the background. "I heard about Lucy. That's so awful, so terribly sad, and I'm shocked and very sorry. Especially when it's people so young."

"And I'm sorry about your husband," I reply. "I know that had to be terribly hard."

"Life can deal us quite the hand, and we get reminded of our place in the grand scheme of things," she says with surprising humility, and maybe tragedy has mellowed her. "One minute, Frank and I are planning a second honeymoon to

Hawaii. The next, he's fallen off the roof, ends up with a hangman's fracture, and you know all about those."

"A devastating injury. Life-changing for everybody."

"Well, it certainly changed the trajectory of many things." Greta clears her throat several times, her voice touched by emotion. "But enough about me, what can I do for you, Kay? And by the way, I've seen you on the news trying to escape Dana Diletti and her crew. You're looking good, haven't aged a bit. What's your secret?"

"A career of being exposed to formaldehyde." I repeat my tired old joke.

CHAPTER 34

MY SECRETARY SAID SHE left you a message a few hours ago, and I'm wondering if you got it," I say to Greta.

"I don't believe so," she says over speakerphone. "But if you're talking about Maggie then I'm not surprised. We've had our differences in the past when Doctor Reddy was a little too quick to accommodate some of his constituents. You know, maybe the alcohol level wasn't really that high. Or maybe it was higher, depending on who he's trying to help or screw at the moment."

"You don't need to tell me what he's like," I reply. "I've been on the job barely a month, and let's just say I have a lot on my hands," and here I go again, confiding what I probably shouldn't.

"Blaise has been telling me about the murder and mayhem up there in Alexandria," Greta says. "It's a shame they don't make her an investigator. They may as well because she lives and breathes like one if you haven't figured that out already."

"I certainly have."

"She's always been that way, ever since she was little."

"I'm calling about a case you won't have heard about." Without giving much information, I describe the poisoned wine.

"Do we know where it was tampered with?" Greta begins her series of questions.

"Not yet, possibly in this area. Or maybe Europe. The victim survived," I reply as if talking about somebody I've never met. "But the symptoms were classic for an opioid overdose."

"How much of the wine was ingested? And how quick was the onset of symptoms?" she asks.

"From what I understand, it was just a taste before the symptoms set in. It was very fast."

"And the tox is negative for carfentanil?"

"Yes."

"Something much more potent than morphine," she considers.

"It required two doses of Narcan and that was barely enough." I text Benton that I'm stopping by my office and will be at least another hour.

"There's a new synthetic opioid out of China." Greta's voice inside Marino's truck. "As you probably know, the potent painkiller fentanyl has been banned there, and next thing you know people started creating a replacement."

She's afraid that the drug I'm dealing with might be iso-tonitazene, a synthetic version of etonitazene. Translated, iso, as it's referred to, is a potent pain reliever that isn't included on a regular forensic toxicology screen.

"Unlike heroin, cocaine and other drugs derived from plants, iso is manufactured in a lab. There's nothing organic about it, and it's sixty times more powerful than morphine," Greta says, and Marino is shaking his head, no doubt thinking the same thing I am.

"Meaning, next there will be something else we can't detect," I reply dismally. "I don't know how we're supposed to stay on top of the problem. It always seems the bad guys have all the advantages."

"That's because they do, and we're in a new wave of the opioid crisis," Greta agrees. "The white or yellow powder easily mixes with street drugs or whatever you please including food or drink. It wouldn't take much."

Iso has been showing up in Canada, Germany and Belgium, she explains, and I think of what Gabriella Honoré told me about the Bordeaux. It was a gift from the police chief of Brussels. Maybe that's where the tampering occurred. But I don't want to assume it.

Greta goes on to say that iso has made its way to America, and we're seeing variants and a surge of overdoses. Primarily in the Midwest, and also recently in Kentucky.

"God forbid it ends up everywhere," she adds.

"Possibly making its way to Virginia or maybe it already has." I explain we had three possible overdoses today that have evaded standard toxicology screens. "Given the appropriate assay, we can check for iso metabolites present in postmortem samples. But I'm wondering how we're supposed to do that for any variants."

As luck would have it, that's exactly what Greta Fruge is working on these days at her Richmond-based private laboratory. The project is a huge one that in part is funded by the National Institute of Drug Abuse (NIDA).

"We're developing assays that can be commercially available to hospitals, research and forensic labs," she explains. "Developing them quickly, trying to stay ahead of the curve in a way that government can't begin to compete with without the assistance of private companies."

"I appreciate anything you can do," I reply. "Maybe you wouldn't mind talking to my chief toxicologist Rex Bonetta."

"Happy to, since I taught him everything he knows," she fairly chortles, and there's the peacock I remember. "By the way, I'm starting a podcast, *Tox Doc,* and you'd be such a fun guest, Kay," she adds, and I can't imagine anything more boring than listening to the two of us discussing chemistry.

"*Tox Doc*? That sounds like a real snoozer. Either that or she gives ideas to the wrong people," Marino says after I end the call, and we're making good time, my office minutes out. "Imagine having her for your mother, being overshadowed like that when you were coming along. That couldn't be fun."

"I agree, and it's nagging at me that Blaise Fruge feels she has much to prove."

"No kidding."

"She doesn't always look before she leaps, that's for sure." I envision her bobbing light floating along the railroad tracks. "And she doesn't know when to quit."

"Well, she's going to get hurt if she's not careful," Marino predicts. "And I hope she's not a snitch for Maggie."

We've reached my parking lot, the only vehicles the office vans and the truck that I believe belongs to Wyatt. I hand Marino my electronic swipe so he can open the gate from his window.

"Fruge needs to be careful or she's going to piss off people like August," he says. "Maybe some of the investigators in her own department too, assuming she hasn't already."

"Sounds familiar," I reply. "Reminds me of you when we were getting started. You didn't exactly win popularity contests with your comrades, and definitely not with the brass. So, maybe there's hope for her."

MOMENTS LATER, WE'RE WALKING through the empty vehicle bay, and I'm mindful of the cameras, hoping Wyatt's doing his job and paying attention. I unlock the door leading inside as he walks off the elevator, not exactly happy to see us.

"What's going on that you're back here at this hour?" He uneasily looks at Marino and me. "I hope they haven't found more pieces and parts."

"Nothing else that we know of." I head to the morgue log, finding one new entry since Marino picked me up a few hours ago.

Human remains in dumpster, Fruge wrote and initialed, adding the address of the grocery store in question.

"Wait here for a minute," I tell Marino as I open the cooler's heavy door.

A foul-smelling condensation drifts like mist, the frigid air blowing loudly. The body parts are zipped inside a folded black vinyl pouch that I carry out, and the next stop is the autopsy suite.

"We'll take a look. Then I want to get this back into the cooler as quickly as possible," I explain. "Otherwise the decomposition will get only more advanced."

We put on masks and gloves, and I cover a stainless-steel table with a disposable sheet, placing a blue towel on it, also a plastic ruler and a camera. Turning on a surgical lamp, I open the pouch, and the severed hands are pale and wrinkled, the outer layer of skin slipping off.

"They're small enough to be hers," Marino says.

I set them down palm up and side by side on the blue towel, and he begins taking pictures.

"Like a woman's, like Gwen's would be," he adds, and each hand was raggedly amputated at the wrist joint.

The dark red wounds are dry, and adhering to them are bits of grass and other debris. The fingernails are unpainted and moderately long. Two of them are broken, one down to the quick, and it will be easy enough matching the hands to Gwen Hainey's body.

"Through a number of means," I explain, finding my magnifier glasses, putting them on.

"It looks to me like she's got good enough ridge detail left for prints," Marino observes. "And DNA should work okay."

"Yes, and also whatever cutting instrument was used will have left tool marks on bone that can be fracture-matched," I reply.

"She fought like hell."

"Does Cliff Sallow have any injuries on his arms, hands, neck or face? Scratches, bruises?" I find a pair of nail clippers.

"Nothing I could see," Marino says. "But he had on long pants, long sleeves when I talked to him."

"I'll clip what's left of her nails." I start doing it. "But I'm not hopeful about any DNA her assailant might have transferred to her body, her clothing or anything else. I doubt it would have survived five days in a dumpster. But it's not impossible."

With decomposition comes the inevitable destruction by teeming bacteria. It literally eats evidence that might identify the killer. I place the fingernail clippings into a paper envelope I mark as evidence. Holding the left hand, then the right under the light, I examine the margins of the multiple incisions and hacking injuries around the wrists.

"Some type of sharp nonserrated instrument was used." I describe what I'm seeing, and I can feel Marino's body heat as he stands close, looking on. "I'm going to take samples of muscle for toxicology. I'll make incisions into subcutaneous tissue, looking for hemorrhages associated with fresh bruising, these reddish areas we're seeing."

He watches as I do all this. I place the tissue samples, the fingernail clippings inside a locked evidence refrigerator while explaining that eventually we'll boil away the flesh so we can examine the cuts made to bone. Zipping up the black vinyl pouch, I return it to the cooler, having no doubt whose body parts we're talking about.

We stop by the evidence room on our way out. Several examination tables are covered with white paper and arranged with personal effects. Against a wall are big cabinets with glass doors, the *Star Wars* blanket opened up and hanging inside one of them. It's fouled with blackish crusty blood that's thick in areas. But other parts of the blanket have been spared.

"The blood likely will be too decomposed to help us. We're not going to get a DNA profile from it, I'm fairly certain," I tell Marino. "But we already know whose blood it is, assuming what we suspect is correct, and this is the blanket from Gwen's bed."

That shouldn't be hard to prove, I explain. Fibers can be compared to those I recovered from the body, and taking off my gloves, I send DNA analyst Clark Givens a text. I'm letting him know what awaits him in the morning. The earlier he can get started the better, and I send him a picture of the blanket.

Then I photograph the bloody sweatpants and T-shirt in a separate cabinet. The clothing believed to be Gwen's was cut off her body, and there's a pair of bloody running socks. Either she wasn't wearing undergarments or her killer disposed of them elsewhere.

"It's also possible he kept them as a souvenir," Marino says as I place the baggies of pennies inside an evidence locker.

It's almost ten-thirty when we drive out of my parking lot, and I'm getting a different impression about the killer. Despite his premeditations, he can be sloppy and impulsive. For one thing, he should have picked a more remote location to dispose of his gory evidence.

"I say *he* because it's easier." I explain to Marino we have to be careful about making assumptions. "We don't know the gender, one would assume a male but I've been surprised before. Whoever it is, this person doesn't have special skills when it comes to dismemberment. The way the hands were cut off, for example. That wasn't done by someone who's an expert. The question is why do it at all."

"I don't believe it's about getting rid of her fingerprints mafia-style," Marino says.

"We didn't need them to confirm her identity," I agree. "And I have to suspect her killer is shrewd enough to know that."

"Maybe he's sending a message," Marino supposes. "And that makes me think of the spying aspect of all this. Like maybe Gwen was messing with the wrong people, and we're barking up the wrong tree. Maybe we're way off base thinking her murder is connected to Cammie's all because of a bunch of pennies."

"That's not the only reason we're thinking it," I reply as more misgivings shake me to my core, and I text Benton I'm fifteen minutes out.

He doesn't answer but Lucy does. She's letting me know that her mother has crashed in the guestroom. It would seem

Dorothy got carried away with the margaritas and is down for the count. I tell Marino he may as well stay at my house, and it's not a problem.

He's done it before when my sister is "under the weather," as she puts it. Marino keeps an overnight bag in his truck for such contingencies, always has as long as I've known him.

"I'll throw something together for a late supper," I decide, and my White House takeout was long ago. "When's the last time you had something to eat? I'm starved."

"You know me, Doc, I can always find room," he says as Lucy texts me again.

We pull pitch at 0800 hours. She informs us that we have an early morning. Also, this is all over the Internet, she adds, and attached is a link to click on.

The Dana Diletti story aired while Marino and I were out in the foggy dark looking for pennies that probably have nothing to do with anything. "The Railway Slayer," I tell Marino as we reach Old Town, the restaurants hopping, the roadsides crowded with cars. I click on the video file, and the celebrity correspondent is live on CNN, talking about her huge story.

". . . That's right, police won't confirm it," she's saying, "but my sources tell me that Doctor Scarpetta, the chief medical examiner, is investigating this very possibility. She believes that Gwen Hainey's brutal murder may be connected to a body found on Daingerfield Island last April. The growing concern is a serial killer could be in the greater Washington, D.C., area, and just how many other victims might be out there is anybody's guess . . ."

I close the file, having heard as much as I can stand at the moment.

"Where do you suppose she heard about Cammie Ramada?" I ask rhetorically because I can guess.

"Only two suspects I can think of, and I don't think Fruge did it," Marino says.

"Maggie. So, she can blame me for creating a carnival, as she puts it, and do so on national television."

"If Elvin Reddy wasn't pissed before," Marino replies, "now he's really going to rip you a new one."

"Thanks for that. I feel much better."

"You got any bourbon in the house?" he says. "Something strong like Booker's, because I plan to get into it."

CHAPTER 35

Early the next morning, we find ourselves inside his big bad truck again as the sun begins peeking above the dark horizon. The pale crescent moon reminds me of fingernail clippings I took in the morgue last night, my mood foul and impenetrable.

The way I feel is the antithesis of the weather, and that's good at least. Skies are clear, the temperature in the low forties, and it's a fine day for flying, but the winds are picking up dramatically.

"Twenty knots and getting stronger, and we'd better hope it's blowing in our favor." I'm looking at my weather app while Marino starts on a second Egg McMuffin. "If the wind is on our nose, it will take forever to get there."

"How long is forever?" He reaches for his coffee.

"Long enough for you to be miserable." I'll just keep warning him. "Drinking a large coffee isn't the smartest plan right before boarding a helicopter. It might help your headache but soon enough you'll have a more pressing problem."

I told him the same thing when he decided to stop at McDonald's, and he didn't listen. But in all honesty, he's a little hungover. It was a long night, everybody gathering in the kitchen, including my sister after sleeping off her margaritas.

Marino got into the bourbon with a vengeance while I whipped up a parmesan frittata, and a tomato and cucumber salad tossed with olive oil and sea salt. As best I could, I explained what's going on, telling them about my unexpected trip to Richmond. I've been ordered back to my professional roots, the former capital of the Confederacy.

I'm about to be called on the carpet by the health commissioner. Possibly, he's incensed because of what's all over the media about a serial killer on the loose. But I don't talk about my fear of being fired. If that's what really happens, I'll deal with it then.

"There's no bathroom on board," I remind Marino as he takes the exit for Reagan National Airport, the traffic almost normal at this early hour. "What do you think will happen after drinking all that coffee? Nothing good."

"Lucy's landed in a field before," he says with a shrug, pretending he's not nervous about what's ahead.

In addition to being a terrible passenger whether on the ground or in the air, he's worried about me. He's also worried about himself, maybe most of all, because that's human

nature. Once Elvin Reddy hands me my walking papers, assuming that's the case, what happens to my new forensic operations specialist?

As much as Marino loves Virginia, he won't want to stay
if Benton and I are forced to relocate again. Lucy probably
won't hang around, either. I might not be working cases
anymore period, end of story, and that's about as much as I
can contemplate at the moment without getting completely
dispirited.

"The big advantage of choppers is you can set them down
anywhere." Marino goes on as if he has no fear of heights or
someone else in control. "You know how many times Lucy's
landed on farms and places like that when a pit stop was called
for and nothing else was close? Point being, you don't need a
bathroom if push comes to shove."

"There's no push coming to shove when a TSA escort is
riding shotgun," I reply. "We're not allowed to set down anywhere that's not on the flight plan. Not even at another airport along the way. Your only choice will be to hold it or have
a pee bottle handy."

"Okay, okay." He returns the coffee to the cupholder, stuffing the last of his breakfast sandwich into his mouth.

Moments later, we've parked at the airport's Marine Air
Terminal, where he makes a beeline for the men's room. Lucy
is waiting in the lounge area, and I've not seen her in a flight
suit in a while. She has on a baseball cap, sunglasses, her favorite flying boots, and there's an energy, a lightness of spirit
that's been absent for too long.

"How's he doing this morning?" She's well aware of how much bourbon he threw back last night.

She also knows that he doesn't like riding in the back of anything, getting far more anxious than he lets on.

"Other than drinking too much coffee?" I look around, seeing a lot of Transportation Security Agency (TSA) officers, and few other passengers or pilots inside the spacious old terminal.

"That wasn't very smart," she says as we watch him emerge from the bathroom, looking ominous in jeans and a tactical jacket.

"He's worried about flying with you. Thinks you're rusty," I tell Lucy.

"Good," she replies with a sly smile.

"What's good?" Marino says, reaching us.

"It's a good day for flying but we won't be able to talk much as busy as the airspace is around here," she starts in for his benefit. "I mean, one false move?" She shakes her head, whistling under her breath. "Next thing, F-sixteens are coming after you."

"You're being funny, right?" It's his first time flying in a restricted airspace.

"They'll shoot you right out of the sky."

"You're a real comedian," scowling as his face turns red.

"There's nothing funny about it." She eggs him on some more as two TSA agents approach with all seriousness.

They escort us into a private room to be searched, our carry-on bags rifled through. We're scanned with a wand up one side and down the other, and all the while a man is watching. He looks familiar at first in a gray suit that hangs shapelessly on his slight frame, his gray hair and mustache shaggy.

"I'm Bob," he introduces himself, and I realize he reminds me a bit of Captain Kangaroo. "I'll be flying with you today."

"Thanks for keeping everybody safe." I say what I always do to the TSA.

"Looks like a good one for it." He holds a tote bag that most likely has his gun in it.

We're escorted to Lucy's Bell 407 GXP, white with a blue stripe, and her copilot Clare is opening the back doors for us.

"If the winds don't flip around, we'll be there in no time," she lets us know.

A little older than Lucy, she's petite with short dark hair and smiling eyes. The two of them climb up front, Marino, Bob and I in back, and soon enough we're swooping toward the Potomac River.

"Everybody all right back there?" Clare's voice in our headsets. "Our ETA is thirty-five minutes."

WE HAVE A FEROCIOUS tailwind, our airspeed a blistering 165 knots. We fly high and fast, hugging the river until we reach Quantico. Then we cut inland, following I-95 to Richmond.

I go hollow inside as I look out at a view I've not seen in five years. That's the last time I was here, and since then the city has been ravaged by another civil war. The destruction is clearly visible as we chopper through the polished blue sky at an altitude of six hundred feet.

Some businesses have remained boarded up while others never reopened after they were vandalized, looted and burned down during protests and riots. That and the pandemic, and many places don't exist anymore, including favorite haunts of mine, landmarks to my earlier life.

"It looks like a damn third-world country." Marino's voice through our headsets, and I can sense his mood as he sits next to me, staring out at the depressing view.

"You should have seen it earlier in the year," Clare says, and we've flown with her before when she ferries Lucy's bird wherever needed.

"A miracle nobody was killed," says our TSA escort Bob, sitting in the leather seat across from me.

"It's sure as heck not the city I used to know." Marino stares down at East Broad Street where the damage is particularly bad. "I'm not sure I'd want to be a cop here anymore."

Graffiti has been spray-painted everywhere, and I can't read what it says from the air. But I don't need to, the images have been all over the news, the usual hateful vulgarities about killing police, eating the rich. For a while, people went to bed hearing gunfire and Confederate flag–waving trucks in their once-civilized downtown neighborhoods.

The capital of the commonwealth is scarcely recognizable, especially its grandest thoroughfare, Monument Avenue. We can see the marble pedestals left from statues removed, some of them forcibly pulled down by angry crowds. Only the graffiti-shamed Robert E. Lee on his horse remains, his ousting tied up in litigation.

"Apparently, some good Samaritans go out before dawn every day to scrub off the obscenities," Clare says over the intercom. "And then they just get spray-painted on again once night falls."

"It will never end," Marino says. "But you ask me, it's stupid. You can't erase history."

"You also can't rewrite it," Lucy says from the right seat where she's pilot in command, and I can see only the top of her head. "They shouldn't have built the monuments to begin with. Last I checked, Jeb Stuart, Stonewall Jackson and those other dudes lost the war."

"It would be like putting a statue of Bobby Riggs in front of the Astrodome instead of Billie Jean King," Clare agrees. "The implication is you won when you didn't."

"I hadn't thought of it like that," Bob confesses, downtown's buildings all around us. "The thing is, where does it end when you start destroying monuments, statues, artwork and other things right and left? I hear they're even going after Winston Churchill."

"Christopher Columbus. Abraham Lincoln." Marino is shaking his head, looking down on where we used to live.

"I can understand Columbus." Clare again. "He was pretty brutal to the Native Americans."

"Yeah, well, remember what they did to us at Jamestown," Marino retorts, and he'll never win awards for being politically correct. "Starving everybody to death, shooting arrows at them if they stepped foot out of the fort."

"I'm beginning to think everybody's awful to everybody," I decide, and Lucy lets us know we need to stop chatting so she can deal with the radio.

"Richmond tower." She gets on the air, announcing her tail number and how far we are from the airport. "Requesting the Alpha Corridor, inbound for HeloAir," she says.

We can't hear the tower's reply but she continues her calls, wending around the pristine Capitol grounds, and it's a beautiful morning. The temperature is mild, the sun out, and Virginia is always green even in the winter. There are multiple cranes, a lot of construction going on, but the skyline is pretty much the same as it was when I was getting started here.

It's not much more than a modest cluster of high-rises, and the tallest among them is the twenty-nine-story James Monroe Building. I know it very well. In days of old, I had many trips to the health commissioner's suite of offices, and I didn't get along with him all that well, either. But he was a prince compared to Elvin Reddy.

I imagine him looking out from his lofty perch. I wonder if he might see us flying by as Lucy does a loop around his building. Then she does another, keeping the tower informed, indicating that we're filming. I suppose we are. At least Marino is taking video with his phone.

"I thought it only polite to buzz him," my niece explains, and I can see workers looking out the windows.

If Elvin is in his office, he hears us for sure as Lucy holds the chopper in a high hover long enough to make her point. All he has to do is Google her tail number, and he'll know it's us. But I don't care. What's done is done, and I'm resigned to a fate that likely was set into motion long before I returned to Virginia. As Marino likes to say, payback's a bitch.

Or to quote my father, revenge is best served cold, and what Elvin has masterminded couldn't be colder. We curve toward the river past the gothic redbrick Main Street Station, its tower announcing the time of almost nine. Across from it is a parking deck where my headquarters used to be.

I remember watching as it was demolished. And how that felt. Empty. A sense of disbelief. Even though the old morgue was a horror. The new central district office is near the coliseum, in the heart of Virginia Commonwealth University, which has taken over most of downtown. What never changes is the James River, winding and sparkling deep blue in the sun, its unnavigable rock-choked waters a metaphor for the city's proud stubbornness.

Richmond didn't used to be all that welcoming to outsiders like me, and I'm reminded that feeling like a misfit and a nuisance is nothing new. When I moved here from Miami as the first woman chief, the person I replaced was of the same cloth as Elvin Reddy. I was called in to clean up some other person's mess, and when I did it was suggested I quit.

Now here we go again, and there will always be those in charge who hire me to find out the truth as long as it's the truth they want. I've about had enough of it. I'm trying hard to keep a lid on rage fueled by old setups and slights, and I can't promise I'm going to be on my best behavior today.

"Remember to stay seated until we shut down," Clare lets us know as we fly lower and slower over Williamsburg Road.

The blue and white air traffic control tower is in sight, and then we're settling into a hover taxi, and effortlessly landing on a wooden dolly, the touchdown as light as a feather. While our pilots run through their laminated shutdown checklist, I let Benton know we're down and secure.

I unfasten my shoulder harness, and I shouldn't have worn the simple white cotton blouse I decided on. Already it's wrinkled, and I feel frumpy in the same suit I had on at the White House yesterday. The rotor blades are braked, the battery shut off, and the doors open front and back.

CHAPTER 36

STEPPING DOWN ON ONE of the helicopter's skids, I notice the courtesy vehicle parked nearby, a pickup truck that's neither small nor green.

"I assume this is for us?" I ask Clare.

"Yes, ma'am," she says, and I tell her, Lucy and Bob that I probably won't be very long.

I don't elaborate on the reason, expecting the health commissioner to spend just enough time to threaten or outright fire me, and that's fine.

"I'll be waiting right here," Lucy says, and I've not seen her this engaged and confident in recent memory.

"I couldn't even feel the landing." I resist the impulse to hug her in front of a crowd. "You haven't lost your touch."

"I'll say she hasn't. I didn't have my hands on the controls even once," Clare brags about her, and she's one of the few people my niece talks to as far as I know.

At least Lucy confides in someone who's not an avatar, I

can't help but think as I climb into the passenger seat of our borrowed gas guzzler. Marino slides behind the wheel while I check my phone, and Benton has texted me back. He has an update I read as other messages land, two of them from DNA analyst Clark Givens. I try Benton first.

"Hi," I say when he answers. "We just landed, are driving away from the airport."

"You might want Marino to hear what I'm about to tell you."

"That sounds ominous," I reply. "You're now on speakerphone. What's going on?"

"I don't guess you've talked to your DNA lab."

"I have messages from Clark to call him," I reply as we take I-64 West, heading downtown.

"Apparently, he got started at oh-dark-hundred on the blanket, the clothing Officer Fruge brought in," Benton says. "And it's looking like I'm headed to Boston."

He and another agent are on their way to interview Jinx Slater, who doesn't know they're coming. Gwen's former boyfriend likely also isn't aware that his DNA has been recovered from an unbloodied part of the *Star Wars* blanket missing from her townhome's inflatable bed.

"The question is when his semen was deposited on it," I reply. "This past Friday night when she was attacked? Or some time earlier when she was living with him in Boston?"

"What I know is the blanket was on her bed when Lucy and I did our security walk-through for Gwen," Marino reminds us.

"But where was it before that?" I ask. "If she brought it with her when she moved to Old Town, that could be the explanation. The stain might be old."

"Do we have any idea where Jinx Slater was the past Friday night?" Marino wants to know.

"He claims he was staying with a friend over the Thanksgiving holiday, a woman he's started seeing in Cambridge." Benton's voice inside our courtesy truck. "She's confirmed that this is true, but consider the source."

"You should be able to check the airlines, tollbooths, the GPS in his car," Marino says, and he can't help himself.

He has to tell my husband how to do his job. Benton patiently assures him that the Secret Service is working closely with other law enforcement agencies. They're trying to find out if Jinx Slater left Massachusetts last week and might have headed to Northern Virginia.

"There's no indication of it so far," Benton says, and I try Clark Givens next.

He confirms the news about Jinx Slater's DNA showing up on the blanket. Clark also got an unknown profile from skin cells under Gwen's fingernails.

"I'm surprised you got anything," I reply. "But we're lucky it's wintertime."

"Otherwise forget it," he agrees. "Four or five days in a dumpster during the summer? And we'd be out of luck."

He examined the clippings I collected in the autopsy suite last night, and it's possible Gwen scratched her assailant.

"But it's not Jinx Slater's DNA," Clark explains. "As I've

mentioned, it's an unknown profile that I'll run through CODIS."

He says he hopes to have more information by the time I get back to the office, and I'm not sure that's going to happen. The way I'm feeling, I expect to arrive and find my key doesn't work, that I've lost my take-home car and parking space. Elvin Reddy will have a well-laid plan, and no doubt he's looking forward to watching it unfold.

On I-95 now, we've reached the campus of the Medical College of Virginia where I once was on the faculty. Next, we're turning onto North 14th Street, and Main Street Station is in our windshield, the site of my former life all around us.

"Now's not a good time to bring this up," Marino says. "But I don't suppose Maggie said anything about parking?"

"Of course she didn't," I reply in exasperation, and I should have thought to ask.

"Because there's nothing around here but street parking with meters, and I'm not seeing an empty space anywhere," he says, both of us looking for an empty spot or someone leaving.

I send Maggie a text, and she doesn't answer as Marino circles the building several times to no avail. By the time she gets back to me, we're in a public lot several blocks away.

"She says there's no special parking," I let Marino know as he tucks a five-dollar bill into the honor box.

"Let the games begin," he says as we follow the sidewalk, hoofing it to the Monroe Building.

It's ten o'clock on the nose when we hurry through the glass front door. Then we're waiting with a crowd of state employees gathering by the elevators, and after being early, now I'm late. The ride up twenty-nine floors takes an eternity with all the stops along the way, and when we walk into the health commissioner's lobby, I'm sweating.

I shouldn't have worn these shoes, am getting a blister, and I don't have time to touch up my makeup. Announcing myself to the young bubbly receptionist, I take off my coat as her pretty face screws into a frown.

"OH MY." SHE MAKES a big production of looking at the faux antique grandfather clock inside a spacious area recently furnished.

It would seem Elvin didn't waste any time fixing up his empire to his liking. I take in the new carpet, the overstuffed sofas and chairs, paintings and photographs of Virginia everywhere as I listen to the receptionist explain that I'm late.

"Your appointment was at ten." She looks up at Marino and me.

"It's twelve minutes after," I reply.

"I guess he thought you weren't coming. Also, you didn't call to confirm this morning."

"You're saying he didn't hear our helicopter. That he had no idea we were on our way," I reply.

"Oh, that was you?" She's a terrible actress. "I might be able to fit you in tomorrow at the same time. Is it possible you could come back?"

"What's your name?" I ask her.

"Tina."

"Is he here, Tina? Because I'm not going anywhere."

"All I know is he stepped out a few minutes ago."

"I'll wait." I find a sofa next to a silk orchid. "Let Doctor Reddy know I'm here."

I'm not going to bother Maggie about what's happened. She's clearly part of the problem, and I angrily envision us race-walking here from a public parking lot.

"But he has a booked schedule, ma'am," Tina reminds me, and she's getting unnerved.

"I'm not going anywhere." I say it again as Marino plops down next to me like a gargoyle.

"And it's *doctor*, not *ma'am*," he lets her know. "You tell the health commissioner we'll be sitting right here until we turn into skeletons if we have to."

The wait isn't that long but close enough. Two hours and twenty minutes later, Elvin Reddy looks chagrined when he walks in.

"I apologize but you weren't here at ten, and then the governor wanted to have coffee. One thing after another, you know how it goes." In his sharp double-breasted gray suit, Elvin brings to mind a wealthy businessman, a small bald one with a prominent nose and small dark eyes.

"I offered her an appointment for tomorrow," Tina, his receptionist, is quick to say.

"I'm not coming back tomorrow or any other time, Elvin." I get up from the sofa. "Say what you have to say. Or don't bother."

"I've got a few minutes." He lets Tina know that she's to hold all calls until he tells her otherwise. "Just you." He makes it clear that Marino isn't invited.

I follow Elvin through double wooden doors into his corner space overlooking his kingdom. Walls are arranged with *I love me* photographs, awards, degrees, and to look at all his trophies, you'd think he deserves the high offices he manages to reach.

You'd think he's the next celebrity health official in the making, and I imagine him hobnobbing at the White House, angling for some big appointment.

"I guess that was you flying by, making all that noise." He shuts the doors. "Please, make yourself comfortable, Kay."

He shows me to a blue satin couch that reminds me of the Oval Office while he sits behind his big desk, potentate that he is.

"As you know, my niece is a helicopter pilot," I reply. "And driving here wasn't going to be possible unless I left in the middle of the night. Traffic being what it is on I-95, especially in Northern Virginia. You've set me up for failure at every turn, and my being twelve minutes late isn't why you decided to make me wait forever. It's all about power. With you, everything is."

"How is Lucy, by the way?" He folds his hands together on top of his desk, tilting his head as if he cares. "I know she's had her struggles. Maggie's filled me in about her partner and their adopted child. I lost a few people to COVID."

He disingenuously goes on to inquire about the welfare of

everyone I care about, leaning back in his big leather chair. But he's not as smug as he was when he first came up with his little drama, of that I'm quite certain, and I tell him to throw his best punch.

"Go ahead," I invite him. "Get it over with, Elvin. I don't care but I won't take it quietly. It's too late. I know too much."

"I'm wondering if you have any concept of the fear you're inspiring in Virginians," he says, lightly touching his fingertips together. "Have you seen the piece that's all over the news? The one about the so-called Railway Slayer?"

"Yes, by the same TV journalist who may have faked her own home invasion."

"I wouldn't know, but that doesn't change what the public thinks about some serial killer terrorizing our nation's capital and its historic surrounds," he says. "It's most unfortunate you've let things get out of hand like this."

"I realize that murder is bad for local business, and serial murder is worse," I reply. "Most assuredly it could interfere with tourism, and God forbid if bodies start turning up in a popular D.C.-area national park."

"This is what I mean about you being a drama queen, Kay. That's always been your fatal flaw, turning something mundane into the next headline."

"I have many flaws but that happens not to be one of them." I look him in the eye. "Let's get this over with. What do you want?"

"Maggie says you were prowling around Daingerfield Island last night." He's not putting on the diplomatic act anymore. "And lo and behold, clothing, body parts, why, all sorts of things start turning up," he says as if accusing me of being the cause. "What is this I hear about a penny found on the railroad tracks?"

As in only one, and I think of August Ryan. He found that single penny near Gwen's body, and he doesn't know about the others. I didn't tell him what Marino and I discovered by the tracks last night, and it would seem that Fruge hasn't said a word to him or anyone else.

"Daingerfield Island is a place you're familiar with," I say to Elvin. "I have it on good authority that you responded to Cammie Ramada's scene last April tenth. You and your wife, Maggie says. Even if it's not in any paperwork I've reviewed."

Holding my stare, he doesn't say a word.

"You're not a first responder," I go on. "You're really not a responder at all, and I'd be very interested to hear why you decided to roll up on that particular scene. With your wife," I repeat. "Especially when you'd been out to dinner. You and Helen had." Pausing again. "And it would seem you'd been drinking enough that it was noticeable at the scene."

He doesn't answer, and I know the reason. Park Police Investigator Ryan gave Maggie a heads-up after the body was found because he knew trouble when he saw it.

"A woman jogger chased off the Mount Vernon Trail, beaten, then drowned in the Potomac River wasn't the story you or others wanted," I keep going. "Who did you make promises to, Elvin? A politician or two? Local businesses? If you lowered the homicide rate in the greater D.C. area, what a coup that would be. Why, even I've been impressed by the crime stats, thinking how safe things have gotten around here."

"Cammie Ramada had temporal lobe epilepsy," he starts to say, but I don't let him finish his lame excuse for a manner of death he deliberately falsified.

"I've been through her records and talked to people familiar with the case, including Officer Fruge," I let him know, and he gives me one of his condescending smiles.

"I wouldn't consider her a reliable source."

"She's not the only one who smelled alcohol on your breath." I begin filling him in on the rest of it, detailing what I believe went on the night of April 10.

August Ryan contacted Maggie, letting her know about the body in the park, wanting her to inform Elvin. What August did was bypass the medical examiner on call, and that was the main objective. Better if the chief himself showed up, and that's what he did, shutting down any potential controversy.

Likely August figured that if he didn't do this, he'd have hell to pay, and I think of what Marino said about the park police investigator. He probably means to do what's right but gets leaned on. I can imagine Elvin bullying police like August, making it difficult if they don't do his bidding.

"Supposedly you and Helen were on your way home from dinner at your favorite restaurant," I then say to him. "Only Maggie can't seem to recall the name . . ."

CHAPTER 37

THAT'S ENOUGH, KAY." HE holds up his hand as if stopping traffic.

"I'm not here to cause domestic problems," I reply quietly, after another pause. "Whatever the two of you have really isn't my concern unless it impacts the criminal justice system. Why was Maggie with you that night?"

"I don't owe you an explanation." His voice has turned cold, and he's tapping his fingers together again.

"Well, you're going to owe one to somebody, Elvin," I reply. "You swept a homicide under the rug, and now another woman has been murdered, possibly by the same killer, her body left in the same park. Aren't you even slightly worried?"

"This recent case is an obvious homicide," he replies. "Cammie Ramada wasn't. And Maggie and I were out that night, you know me, not much of a shopper. It was about finding a birthday present for my wife. She had her heart set on diamond earrings, and Maggie was kind enough to help. Afterward, we stopped for a bite to eat."

"Where?"

"The FYVE Restaurant in the Ritz-Carlton," he says, and it's an intimate place.

He and Maggie were leaving the restaurant when she got the call. August Ryan had been notified about a suspicious death on Daingerfield Island, and he didn't want to contact the medical examiner's office directly. He preferred talking to the chief first. What he says is exactly what I suspected, and it's only now that I'm realizing the full extent of Elvin's influence over those I'm supposed to work with.

"I understand you were at the White House yesterday." He gets up from his desk and begins pacing in front of the windows. "If you've not figured it out by now, Kay? All of us answer to others."

"Yes, we do." I couldn't agree more. "And we're supposed to do so truthfully. I can't work in a place where I'm supposed to lie even if only on occasion." I get up, putting on my coat.

"Not even a month on the job." He stops pacing, making a point to glance at his expensive watch.

"Yes, a new record."

"I can't get over the irony." He walks me to the double doors. "Back when I was your least appreciated forensic path in training, I never thought this day would come. That I'd be dismissing you, making you feel what I did. That you just can't measure up no matter what."

"You made yourself feel that way, and it's not because you're incapable. It's that you're unwilling," I reply, and he's heard enough of my lectures.

"You're to return to the office to clear out your belongings. I realize it might take a day or two," he says, and at least he has that much decency.

He makes sure I know that he could demand my ID badge, my credentials, my keys. But we're professionals with a long history.

"I'd rather keep this civilized," he says, and what he's really worried about is appearances. "Will you and Benton move back to Massachusetts?"

My answer is to walk out of his top-floor throne room, and soon enough Marino and I are headed back to the parking lot where we left our courtesy car.

"I can't believe this," he keeps saying, and I wish he'd stop.

"Don't make me feel any worse," I reply. "And not a word about all this during the flight home. I don't want it discussed in front of Clare and the TSA, please."

I'd prefer not advertising that I was just fired. But in typical Elvin Reddy fashion, he's made sure I don't have to worry about that. Lucy sends me a link, and already it's hit the news. Only I've not been fired. It would seem I've resigned, and how clever making it appear the job wasn't what I thought.

I've made mistakes, found the work overwhelming while managing to alienate my staff and violating protocols hand over fist, in the process creating sensational publicity. I'm guilty of nepotism, of working hand in glove with a former homicide detective who's married to my sister. The list of my failures and complaints is long, and when we reach the helicopter, I can tell everybody knows.

Clare has nothing to say, and our escort Bob is quiet during the flight back to Reagan National. Marino bites his tongue until we're alone inside his Raptor truck, driving away from the Marine Air Terminal as more bad weather rolls in. It's close to four o'clock, the sun going down as we follow I-395 South, the day ending as it began.

Benton and I talked briefly before he boarded his flight, and he won't be back tonight. Things aren't looking great for Jinx Slater, who's not entirely truthful, what a shock. He wasn't in Massachusetts last Friday night, Benton told me. And he wasn't with a new girlfriend.

On Thanksgiving Day, Jinx drove from Boston to Bethesda, Maryland. The next day, he drove back. No one knows what he was up to, possibly it's unrelated to Gwen's murder. But he was close enough to Old Town that he could have found some other means to get to her.

"He wouldn't want to use his own car if he planned to whack her," Marino says. "Maybe he rented something, paid cash, no paperwork, I don't know. Or stole something, then ditched it after he was done."

"That's assuming he killed her," I reply. "And if he did, how does that explain Cammie?"

"It wouldn't unless she was killed by someone else."

"I suppose that's possible." I'm depressed by it all, and as full of misgivings as I've ever been. "I might be wrong, Marino. I may have gotten carried away by a penny left on a rail."

"Hey, we had to look, Doc."

He calls Dorothy, leaving me to stew over what to do, and I don't know when I've been so discouraged. It's possible that I might have accused Elvin falsely. What if Cammie wasn't murdered after all, and Gwen was taken out by a spurned lover or the Russians?

". . . About to drop her off now," Marino is saying to my sister, and judging by his tone, she's none too happy with him. "Yeah, I know I promised. But we'll find time in the next day or two."

Turning onto West Braddock at the Cadillac dealership, he ends the call, reminding me that my sister can't tolerate being ignored. What he doesn't yet know is that he's seeing the first sign of her getting discontented. Next, her attention is prone to wander in a way that won't make him happy.

"That's the way she's wired," I remind him. "Which is also why she likes you retired."

"I didn't retire," he fires back defensively.

"From some things you did," I reply, and he's not naïve.

DOROTHY ISN'T THRILLED ABOUT him working with me. I've played peacemaker with them before and no doubt will again.

"Well, it gets old, Doc," he says. "At times like this it wears me thin, having to pay so much attention when there's big stuff going on. Murders, for example."

"Take her out to dinner," I suggest. "It's early. Go back to my place, clean up and the two of you do something fun. The Oak Steakhouse, you know how much you two like that place."

"With you getting freakin' fired, how is anything supposed to feel like fun right now? Judas Priest! First our neighbor gets whacked. Now you lose your job. Maybe it wasn't the best idea to move here."

"I'm sorry," I reply with surprising composure. "I never asked you to come along for the ride, and this is why. And you're going to have to explain to my sister what's going on."

"Okay, you're right," he says, and I'm glad Dorothy can't hear his reluctance.

That's part of the problem. I don't want him preferring my company to hers, and it's already happening now that we're working together again.

"It's not helpful if she resents me more than usual," I remind him.

"I'll drop you off, and take her out, but I really don't like you driving home alone," he says.

"I have to at some point," I reply, texting Rex Bonetta that I'm pulling into the parking lot.

I'm hoping he's still around, and he is. I ask if we can meet in the trace evidence lab, and he replies that he's there now. Marino stops in his usual spot, and it's not lost on me that Maggie's Volvo is nowhere to be seen.

"She picked a good day to leave early," I comment. "Not that I'd really want to run into her. You and Dorothy have a nice dinner."

Shutting the door abruptly, I turn away from him, feeling shaky inside as if I might cry. I'm hoping he didn't see the look on my face, everything catching up with me. Taking a deep breath, steadying myself, I unlock the pedestrian door. I pass through the empty bay, stepping inside the lower level where there's a better phone signal, and I call Lucy.

"I'm here at the office, safe and sound," I tell her as I walk past the empty autopsy suite. "And Marino and your mother are going out to dinner."

"The helicopter is on its way back to the hangar, and I'm headed home," Lucy says in my wireless earpiece. "How long will you be?"

"Not terribly long, and it's going to be just you and me for dinner if you don't mind waiting a bit." I walk past the anthropology lab, the bones in their big pot softly clattering.

"We've got everything for tacos," Lucy volunteers, and she's not offered to help with a meal in a while.

"That sounds wonderful." I open the fire-exit door, heading upstairs to an isolated wing that houses the scanning electron microscope.

Momentarily, I'm following the second-floor corridor, wondering who knows I'm about to be a thing of the past. Through observation windows, I glance at preoccupied scientists in the DNA clean rooms and labs with their airlocks and special ventilation, everybody covered in PPE. A few look up at me as I walk past, and it's possible they don't know the news.

Most assuredly they will by morning when I return to clear out my office. Ahead is the latent fingerprints lab, and I may as well check on one of my cases while I'm in the area. Veteran examiner Andy Patient is working under a chemical hood, gloved up and masked, trying to rehydrate the shriveled tips of fingers removed from mummified remains.

They were discovered in an abandoned barn not long after I started here, and I've yet to find evidence of violence. But the victim, an older white male, was naked when he died, his clothing strewn about as if he disrobed in a hurry. While that might look suspicious, it's not necessarily.

As irrational as it seems, often that's what people do when they're freezing to death. They have the false sense of being too warm and begin to undress. I'm suspicious he may have sought shelter in the barn during cold weather and died from exposure. But who was he, and what was he doing on a deserted farm?

"Hi, Andy." I stop in the doorway. "How are things going?"

"I'm optimistic." He turns around, a wizened fingertip gripped in the forceps he holds in one hand, a syringe in the other.

If he knows I've been fired, he doesn't let on.

"I think we'll have prints with enough characteristics to run through IAFIS." He refers to the Integrated Automated Fingerprint Identification System.

"Let's hope we get lucky since we weren't with DNA," I reply as he injects a sodium carbonate solution into what might be the tip of a thumb as best I can tell from where I'm standing.

I examined the remains days ago, noting that muscles and ligaments had decomposed but there was cutaneous tissue and visible friction ridges. Recommending we try restoring the fingertips, I cut them off at the middle phalanges. Since then Andy has been working on the desiccated digits, trying to get prints, still to no avail.

"We do have an update, a possibility of who this might be." He places the fingertip in a petri dish. "The police say an eighty-three-year-old man wandered away from a nursing home in Winchester almost two years ago."

A widower suffering from dementia, he has kids who don't live here or care, it seems. Delusional and paranoid, he believed the government was after him, and had tried to escape multiple times in the past.

"Well, I think you may have figured it out," I say to Andy. "And that would explain why his DNA's not in CODIS."

"What's really bad is the barn where he was found isn't even two miles from the nursing home." Taking off his gloves and mask, he walks over to me, his blue eyes tired behind his glasses, the stubble on his chin salty white. "I'm getting the impression nobody looked all that hard. What it sounds like is he wandered off in his confused state and sought shelter."

"What time of year was it?"

"February during a cold snap," he says, and how terribly

sad. "Do you think you'll sign him out as an accident?" he asks, and I don't answer.

I won't be around to do that. The next chief will have to but I act as if business will go on as usual.

"We'll see what else we find out," I reply.

"I have a feeling this is going to end up in a lawsuit." He takes off his lab coat.

"Yes, I'm sure the kids who had no use for him will go after the nursing home," I reply, walking off.

CHAPTER 38

WHERE I'M HEADED IS in a wing of its own for good reason.

The lab is windowless, its walls, floor and ceiling thick concrete reinforced with steel to minimize vibrations or anything else that might interfere with highly sensitive instruments. When I walk in, Rex is seated at the scanning electron microscope (SEM) with trace evidence examiner Lee Fishburne.

"She's never been known for her modesty," Rex says instantly, and I don't know what he's talking about. "Greta Fruge," he explains. "I was on the phone with her a little while ago."

"She can be a showboat but is one hell of a toxicologist," Lee volunteers, and I remember him from my early years when I was in Richmond.

His thick black hair is now a white crescent around the back of his head, and he's thinner, a little stooped.

"She's going to work with us, supplying assays," Rex says, his attention lingering on me, and he knows.

I can see it in his eyes.

"Hopefully, we can find better ways to identify what's hitting the streets, bad stuff like iso," he says. "And that might be what was used to poison the wine you carried home from France."

"What we're looking at right now is microscopic evidence that was in samples we took from the bottle." Lee indicates the images on flat screens above a console as complicated as any cockpit.

At a magnification of 2000X, he's identified trace evidence that includes multicolored paint pigments, copper, lead, silica, bat hair and periwinkle pollen grains that look like pinkish-yellow coral.

"Periwinkle?" I inquire, and while it's not indigenous to Virginia, the creeper vines had overtaken the garden when we moved into our new home.

The perennial is native to Europe, and was brought to America in the 1700s, the very time our house was built. Without a doubt there's an abundance of periwinkle pollen on the property inside and out. There would be paint pigments and everything else I'm seeing. Even bat hair, I suppose.

How distressing if it turns out the wine was tampered with inside our own basement. Could I get more things wrong? I'm plagued by doubts that are growing by leaps and bounds.

"What can you tell me about the paint pigments?" I look at them on the video displays.

"They're old, real old," Lee lets me know. "The green pigment has arsenic in it, and that's not been used for centuries. The white paint you're seeing is made of lead. The blue is lapis lazuli, one of the most expensive pigments long ago, usually reserved for important works of art like painting the Madonna, for example."

"I'm wondering if what we're finding means anything to you," Rex says to me.

I think of the trace evidence that we'd discover if we started analyzing microscopic samples from my own place. The house was hung with valuable old art while the former ambassador to the U.K. lived there. From what I gather, he collected rare paintings, sculptures and tapestries during his travels, and had them throughout the house.

I don't let on that what Lee is finding on SEM and X-ray diffraction might have anything to do with me personally. Even Rex doesn't know the whole truth about the poisoned wine, only that it was given to me overseas, and I made the mistake of tasting it. At least I can be grateful that Elvin is none the wiser about that, not yet at any rate, and it's time to go home. I've done enough damage for one day.

"Carry on no matter what." I figure Rex knows what I mean, and he walks me into the corridor. "I'll be around in the morning," I say to him. "Let me know when you get a confirmation with the drug screen."

"I know you didn't really resign," he says. "Screw Elvin Reddy. Don't let him run you off. The way people are acting is because of his influence, Kay. You're the most hopeful thing that's happened around here, the only chance of getting rid of that influence."

"For now, it seems he's gotten his way," I reply. "But thanks, Rex." I can feel him watch as I head back to the stairwell.

Maybe Lucy hasn't lost her touch but I'm worried I may have lost mine. Second thoughts and misgivings are seizing my thoughts, and it plagues me that Cammie's death will be left unsolved. Once I'm out of the picture, the labs will stop the analysis I told them to restart. Her case will be ignored again, and her family will never get the satisfaction they deserve.

Wyatt is opening the bay door as I walk through, letting in a hearse, and I tell him good night.

"I heard about you quitting," he says. "I wish you wouldn't."

"Thank you, Wyatt," I reply. "I'll see you tomorrow."

Climbing into my Subaru, I start it up. I listen to music on the radio all the way home, in no mood to chat with anyone else, dreading what my sister will have to say when she hears the news. Probably she already has, and I imagine Marino getting her lubricated with cosmopolitans, maybe the apple martinis she's fond of, and lowering the boom.

He'll let her know I didn't resign, if he hasn't already. I was fired, and they aren't staying here if Benton, Lucy and I don't. If we return to Massachusetts, so will Dorothy and Marino, and from there it's simple to script what will happen. She'll feign shock and upset, and I'll hear about it forever.

How terrible for me. How unfair, and she'll hound me with endless advice and questions, all the while secretly pleased by my failure. It's time to clear out the negativity, I tell myself as I reach the house. I don't need Lucy worrying about me, and she must have seen me on her many cameras.

In a sweat suit, sneakers and her bomber jacket, she's waiting by the carriage house when I pull up. She lifts one of the wooden rolling doors, her flat-eared cat pacing nearby, his tail twitching. I wait until she picks him up, making sure he's safely out of the way as I tuck my take-home car inside. Climbing out, we pull down the door together, and I give her the hug I wanted to give her earlier.

"Lucy, you were amazing today," I say as we walk to the house. "And it seems your aunt can't stay out of trouble."

THE NEWS IS PLAYING as I unlock the front door, and Merlin follows us to the kitchen where spicy ground beef is simmering on the stove, a cookie sheet lined with taco shells, and my stomach growls. An aged añejo tequila is on the countertop next to a shaker filled with ice, and two glasses.

Lucy pulls her pistol from the back of her sweatpants, placing it on a countertop. Her pump action shotgun is parked in a corner, and I ask her about it.

"I don't walk back and forth to my place without protection," she explains. "Not anymore with all that's going on. Plus, Mom's nervous, and nothing better for home protection than a shotgun."

"That's a scary thought." I'm not eager to think what might happen if Dorothy decided to defend the fort. "I guess she's planning on staying here for a while." Opening a drawer, I get out napkins and silverware.

"Things are tough at Colonial Landing." Lucy takes off her

jacket, hanging it on the back of a chair. "The media's all over the place, and people are showing up, gawking. Dana Diletti is still at it if you can believe that. I guess being a suspect in her own attempted home break-in doesn't matter. If anything, she's more popular, trending all over the Internet."

"I'm sure she'll say the police planted the evidence or something to that effect."

"She's already saying it. You ready for a drink?"

I couldn't be readier, I tell her. But there's one order of business I need to take care of first.

"The wine downstairs," I explain as I think about what I just saw in the trace evidence lab. "I want to check just in case there's any chance that bottle wasn't the only one tampered with."

"I think you're worrying too much," she says, wearing the bracelet I gave her.

"It looks nice on you." I touch it while walking past to a cabinet, getting out plates. "And it's not about my worrying. It's about the evidence."

Setting the breakfast table by the curtained window, I pass on what I discovered before coming home. It's possible the microscopic debris inside the bottle of Bordeaux could have come from here.

"What if the wine was injected with poison inside our own basement?" I say to her. "There have been people in and out since I got back from France."

"That's true," Lucy says. "But I found nothing on the security videos that would indicate someone was on the property who shouldn't be."

"I'm going to check, no way I wouldn't after what happened." Opening my briefcase, I pull out my magnifier glasses and a pair of nitrile gloves. "It shouldn't be hard to tell if the other bottles have been tampered with now that I know we're looking for an injection site."

"You want some help?" She stirs the ground beef on the stove.

"No. I'll be back in a few minutes."

"Maybe bring up another bottle of tequila while you're at it."

"You got it." I head for the basement, and Merlin is on my heels, keeping me company.

Down the wooden stairs, I flip on lights as I go from one room to the next, feeling the same strange icy draft. Then I hear a faint noise from outside the door with its locked acrylic flap that clicks open when Merlin slinks past. The wind is starting up again, branches *tap-tapping* a window.

Lucy's cat follows me like a shadow as I reach the refrigerator, putting on the exam gloves and magnifier glasses. I count fourteen bottles, beautiful Burgundies and Bordeaux. Robust Italian reds, and delicate whites, and I begin examining them one at a time. The foil-wrapped corks I'm looking at haven't been perforated by a syringe or anything else.

"So far, so good," I let Merlin know as he rubs my legs. "Maybe I won't have to lose all these wonderful wines I've carried home for years," I add as the cat door lock clicks free again, and he's not close enough for that to happen.

Taking off the magnifier glasses, I freeze in shocked disbelief. A muscular male hand covered with angry red scratches pushes through the flap, followed by a black sleeve–covered arm as Merlin hisses, arching his back. The man reaches up toward the inside door handle, and my response is automatic.

I kick his elbow with all my might in the opposite direction that it's supposed to bend. The sound of the joint breaking is as loud as a stick snapping, and he howls and shrieks in furious pain. Hurrying through the basement, I'm yelling for Lucy as I thunder up the stairs, and there's no sign of her anywhere.

I grab her pistol off the countertop, flying through the house, and out the front door, my heart hammering through my chest. Running through the near dark, I can hear the thudding before I see the source of it. My niece is caving in the man's head with the butt of her shotgun. Lifting it and slamming it down again and again.

While our intruder lies motionless, his right arm bent at an unnatural angle. Nearby is a can of spray paint. Also, Merlin's missing collar, and I get the impression of someone stocky dressed in dark clothing and boots.

"Lucy, it's okay." I'm careful not to startle her as she continues maniacally, and each time the sound is sickening. "Lucy, you can stop. It's okay."

Breathing hard, she turns around, her eyes wide and staring. I put my arms around her, smelling blood, her face wet with it.

"That's enough," I tell her, getting a closer look, and the man isn't moving.

He never will again, and I take the shotgun from Lucy, the stock of it slippery. It vaguely occurs to me I'm still wearing exam gloves as I crouch by the body.

"I couldn't shoot. I didn't want it going through the door and hitting you or Merlin," she says, as if that explains the overkill I witnessed.

Pressing my fingers into the side of the man's neck, I don't feel a pulse, not that I'm expecting one as I look at the carnage. Digging my phone out of a pocket, I turn on its flashlight, shining it over bright red blood and bits of bone and brain tissue. I roll him over, and as bad as he looks, it takes a moment before we realize who it is.

"Oh my God," Lucy says. "Oh my God."

EPILOGUE

THE SAUCE IS BETTER than I expected, and I set the wooden spoon on top of a neatly folded paper towel.

"You can never have enough garlic," I tell Marino. "And the same with wine." I show him, adding more. "An inexpensive table wine works best, something not too terribly complicated."

Inside the kitchen, he has an apron on, and we're cooking Lucy's birthday dinner. Belatedly, after all that's gone on. It's been hectic since she killed Boone Cotton, the fifty-two-year-old construction worker who started helping with my garden back in the fall.

More recently, he was buttoning up Gwen's townhome when she insisted on taking the place as is, never really moving in. Cotton's Honda minivan has a quiet engine, explaining why the sound of it was almost undetectable when he drove in and out of the townhome complex while playing creepy music, the volume turned up loud.

This was after stealing Gwen's FedEx package earlier in the day, and it's no wonder she was eager to know what had happened to it. She didn't want someone else getting hold of malware disguised as mobile chargers. She called Cliff Sallow at the management office, demanding to know where her FedEx package was.

Since Cotton had done work at Colonial Landing, he easily could have shown up after dark and covered the entrance gate cameras with plastic bags or something similar. He might have been clever enough to appear at her patio door with the missing FedEx package in hand, perhaps claiming it had been delivered to the wrong townhome.

He may have been familiar to her, and she turned off the alarm, opening her door. Cotton did a lot of work in the Alexandria area, and was intimately familiar with Old Town. He knew how to get in and out of places, and somehow must have figured out Gwen's passcode for the gate.

We don't know the answer to that and many questions, and possibly never will, as is true in so many atrocities. The only two people who could tell us are dead, and I doubt Cotton would admit anything if he weren't. Most psychopaths don't. They deny and lie until breathing their final breath, still convinced they can outsmart everyone.

"What I can't get over is Dorothy was in the townhome with Gwen when the guy was upstairs in the bonus room, wrapping things in tarps." Marino slices open loaves of focaccia bread on a big cutting board.

"We don't know for sure that he was in the house when she was." I tear up fresh basil, stirring it into my special Bolognese. "We just know that she heard male voices in the bonus room."

"It was probably him. His DNA and fingerprints were up there."

Boone's DNA was on the ten-pound kettlebell. It was under Gwen's fingernails after she scratched him, and that's likely the reason he amputated her hands. He didn't mean to lose control of her. Just as he didn't mean to lose control of Cammie. Just as his uncle Ace didn't mean to lose control when he would take young Boone to the railroad tracks cutting through the park on Daingerfield Island.

This was back in the late 1970s, and Uncle Ace would give him a penny to put on a rail. Waiting in excited anticipation, they'd listen to the *Shock Theater* theme on the cassette player inside the truck, waiting for the train while Uncle Ace molested him. According to family members Benton has interviewed, this went on until the boy was twelve, and Uncle Ace went to jail for beating someone nearly to death in a bar.

Boone Cotton's story isn't so different from those of other criminals who do unto others what was done to them. He was abused and humiliated, and each time he raped and later on murdered, he was reliving his own victimization. That's what my husband has to say, and he believes Cotton didn't start killing until his encounter with Cammie.

It's possible the stress of the pandemic may have escalated

his violent fantasies and behavior. He stepped up his predatory game, committing his first murder, Benton feels sure. Before that, Cotton committed a string of fetish burglaries that escalated to rape in the 1990s. He was never a suspect, just a nice guy who always had a friendly word or a joke.

Women found him attractive, even charming, and he fancied himself a lady's man. That was part of his autoerotic delusion, Benton summarized. Cotton believed the women he stalked wanted him just as much as he wanted them. It didn't matter if they were perfect strangers, and when they resisted, it set him off like a bomb.

Infuriated, he chased Gwen through her townhome with a ten-pound kettlebell. He slammed Cammie's head into the ground and drowned her. It would seem the only thing he stole from them were their phones, which were recovered from his home not far from Reagan National Airport.

"Well, we don't have to worry about him coming back for more," I say to Marino as the doorbell rings. "I just wish it hadn't been up to Lucy."

Then she's walking in with her birthday guests. She got to ask whomever she liked, and Benton, Dorothy, Tron, Lucy's copilot Clare, and Blaise Fruge have invaded. They're talking a mile a minute, getting on with the business of tequila. Everybody is dressed casually, and having fun, my niece included, at least superficially.

Lucy has killed before, and if need be would kill again, and that's not what's eating at her right now. She's having a hard time coming to grips with Janet's avatar dropping the ball.

The algorithm didn't include that someone might use spray paint on the camera lenses, and Boone Cotton had the lay of the land.

He'd talked to all of us at one time or other, and I remember he had lively eyes, a flirtatious smile. He was attractive and funny, and I'm pretty sure that on one particularly humid hot day, I brought him an iced tea while he was pulling up periwinkle and other creepers. He'd been on our property multiple times, most recently five days ago to paint the new trellis.

There are images of his Honda minivan parked on our driveway, and later on he must have coaxed Merlin close enough to take his collar. Cotton knew exactly where the cameras were located and planned accordingly. When he returned and entered the property with the collar and his can of spray paint, Lucy was busy making tacos.

She wasn't looking at security live feeds, and Janet didn't alert her there was a problem until Cotton opened the cat door with the stolen collar. The serial number isn't the same one that's on Merlin's RFID-implanted replacement, and the algorithm caught it. Lucy got an alert on her phone, and realizing what that meant, she was out the door with the shotgun.

LATER, MY NIECE WOULD tell us that Cotton was clutching his broken arm when she raced up in the dark, crashing the butt of her shotgun into the back of his head. Rather much like he did to Gwen with the kettlebell.

"If you'll get the secret sauce out of the microwave, please," I instruct Lucy as Benton sets a margarita next to where I'm working at the butcher block.

"Just the way you like it," he says. "Just the barest breath of agave nectar, fresh lime juice, shaken, never stirred."

"Thank you, Secret Agent Man." Opening a drawer, I find the pastry brush as Lucy sets the glass bowl of melted butter, cheese, garlic and other ingredients I won't discuss.

"It's to die for," Lucy tells Tron, and they seem to be getting along. "You won't believe how good her garlic bread is," my niece says to her, no one else, and it would be good if she could care about someone again.

"What's in it? Come on," Clare badgers me. "No fair, you got to tell us."

"It will never happen." Dorothy fills the margarita shaker with ice. "I've eaten enough of her garlic bread to be the size of Mount Rushmore. Thankfully, Pete and I are faithful about working out or neither of us would look like this. Anyhow, Kay won't tell anyone how she makes it."

"Not even me," Lucy says.

"She won't give it up," Marino concurs. "I've gotten her drunk, and she won't spill the beans."

"I'm good at getting things out of people," Fruge taunts.

"You can cut out the busybody act," Marino says to her. "It won't work. Not with the doc."

"You can forget it," everyone says in chorus.

I paint my secret sauce over the split focaccia loaves, and into the oven they go, as Benton's phone rings. Glancing at the display to see who it is, he walks away from us, answering, and he does nothing but listen at first.

"That's good news, at least," he finally says, turning around, locking eyes with me and smiling a little. "She's right here." He hands me the phone. "The Russians have turned over Jared Horton to us. And someone wants to say hello."

"He's now claiming that the two Thor scientists killed each other," Gabriella Honoré informs me over the phone. "And he escaped, not knowing what else to do."

"What about the space debris story?" I ask.

"Yes, indeed. What about it?"

"Of course, we know what really happened," I reply.

"We've been flooded with information about their activities over the years," Gabriella says. "No question what they were up to, and it will take a long time to undo the damage. Well, some of it will never be undone. His plan was for Gwen Hainey to join him in Argentina, where he has a getaway. She'd already moved a lot of her things there."

"Explaining why she had so little in the way of belongings here," I reply.

"They had an apartment ready and waiting in Buenos Aires. It's quite apparent they were more than just comrades in their espionage. But enough of that for now. How are you, Kay? It's good to hear you alive and well after what happened. I want to thank you for tasting the wine instead of me," she quips.

"Anytime," I quip right back at her, and now Merlin has appeared, rubbing against my ankles again.

"As it turns out, it was tampered with by a very rich disgruntled winemaker who wanted to destroy his competitor's business," she informs me.

I ask a few questions about this disgruntled winemaker, and he lives in a sixteenth-century château in France that's filled with rare art, and landscaped with sumptuous gardens. That makes sense when I recall the trace evidence we found in the bottle of Bordeaux.

"This individual injected iso into several other bottles that the French police have seized," she says. "We're confident there aren't any others."

"Well, I'm glad all of us lived to tell the tale," I reply.

"I was very pleased to hear you'd changed your mind, deciding not to *quit*." She says the word ironically, and it wasn't me who decided anything.

Elvin Reddy had a change of heart, refusing to accept my bogus resignation, and rumor has it he may be up for another appointment. What I have to say about that is good riddance. Whatever it is, Maggie won't go with him, and I'll figure out later how I'm going to deal with her day to day.

"I'm looking forward to seeing you back at Interpol, soon I hope," Gabriella says, and we end the call as I pick up my drink.

"A toast," I announce. "To Lucy, a happy belated birthday." We clink our glasses together.

"And to you," Fruge says with a nod. "Welcome back, Chief."